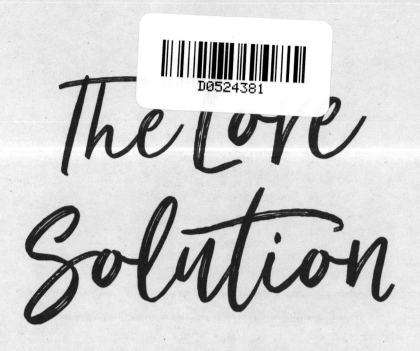

The Love Solution

ASHLEY CROFT

avon.
A division of HarperCollins*Publishers*
www.harpercollins.co.uk

Published by AVON
A division of HarperCollins*Publishers* Ltd
1 London Bridge Street
London SE1 9GF

www.harpercollins.co.uk

A Paperback Original 2019

Copyright © Phillipa Ashley 2019

Phillipa Ashley asserts the moral right to be identified as the author of this work.

A catalogue copy of this book is available from the British Library.

ISBN: 978-0-00-829488-5

This novel is entirely a work of fiction. The names, characters and incidents portrayed in it are the work of the author's imagination. Any resemblance to actual persons, living or dead, events or localities is entirely coincidental.

Typeset in Birka by Palimpsest Book Production Limited, Falkirk, Stirlingshire
Printed and bound in UK by CPI Group (UK) Ltd, Croydon CR0 4YY

All rights reserved. No part of this text may be reproduced, transmitted, down-loaded, decompiled, reverse engineered, or stored in or introduced into any information storage and retrieval system, in any form or by any means, whether electronic or mechanical, without the express written permission of the publishers.

MIX
Paper from
responsible sources
FSC
www.fsc.org   FSC™ C007454

This book is produced from independently certified FSC™ paper to ensure responsible forest management.

For more information visit: www.harpercollins.co.uk/green

For my dear friend, Janice Hume,
and in memory of her sister, Alison

For there is no friend like a sister
In calm or stormy weather;
To cheer one on the tedious way,
To fetch one if one goes astray,
To lift one if one totters down,
To strengthen whilst one stands.

Christina Rossetti

Prologue

'Sarah. I'm sure you'll think this is a very stupid question, but have you any idea what your sister is doing crawling under the rhododendrons?'

Sarah Havers sighed and put down the earring she'd been trying to finish for the past hour. One was already complete and lay on the felt mat on the kitchen table. The earrings were delicate drops fitted with three tiny shells in summery blues and seaweedy greens. Sarah was making them for her sister Molly's birthday, although Molly – currently stuck under a bush in the garden – didn't know it.

Their mother, Naomi, was standing in the open doorway that led from the kitchen to the rear garden of their house. It was early April but her mum was wearing a silky shift dress and a thin cropped jacket and the chilly evening breeze – which blew straight from the Urals to Cambridge, according to an urban myth – was making Sarah's fingers too cold to work.

Her mum peered into the lengthening shadows of the garden. 'Oh no, she's disappeared now. We're going to be late.' She stepped down onto the patio. 'Molly Jane Havers! Come out of there this minute.'

Trying to block out the noise, Sarah picked up the earring

and focused on teasing shut the wire loop with her pliers. Even though she'd made countless pairs, the job still required concentration and all the distractions were doing her head in. On the other hand, it *was* fun to hear her younger sister treated like a toddler.

Their mother groaned in frustration. 'What on earth is she doing out there?'

'Trying to catch a frog, probably,' Sarah muttered, sticking out her tongue in concentration as she focused on the earring. The loop was almost closed. One. More. Tiny ... *tweak* would do it.

'A frog? God, no. What does she want a frog for?'

'Dunno. I think she wants to cut it up at school.'

'What? You're joking?'

Sarah cursed as her pliers crushed the delicate wire into a pretzel. 'Oh, shit!'

'Sarah, stop swearing,' her mother called but she was already on her way onto the lawn. Her voice rose higher. 'Molly! Stop that. Leave that poor creature alone.'

With a sigh, Sarah laid down her pliers next to the wire and beads. She should really be revising for her upcoming A levels, but creating jewellery from shimmering shells and beads was far more fascinating than poring over Business Studies papers. She got up and stood in the doorway, peering out into the shadows.

Her mum's new heels sank into the turf as she tottered over to the bush, which Molly was crawling out of backwards like a demented crab. Sarah rolled her eyes as her sister scrambled to her feet, brushing blossom and leaves from a sweatshirt with a graphic photo of a giant tarantula on the chest.

Sarah despaired. Her younger sister was a fully paid-up

2

member of the Geek Club. Seeing that horrific sweatshirt and her dirty jeans, Sarah wondered if Molly would even wear the earrings that she'd been making for her upcoming fifteenth birthday. Judging by Molly's taste for things that crawled and skittered, the earrings ought to have featured snails and tarantulas, but shells and starfish were as far as Sarah was prepared to go. She went inside as Molly trudged to the house, their mum tottering after her.

Molly leaned against the kitchen worktop and Naomi folded her arms. 'Molly. Is it true you want a frog to dissect? Please tell me now,' she said.

Molly laughed. 'Shit, no. Not to dissect, anyway. To study.'

'You can't take a live frog to school and please stop swearing.'

Molly slid a sly glance at Sarah. 'Maybe I could take Sarah's hamster instead?'

Sarah shrieked. 'You dare!'

Their mum groaned. 'Girls. For God's sake, will you please hurry up and get ready? Dad and I have to leave very soon or we'll be late for our *very special anniversary dinner.*'

'I was only joking about Roger,' said Molly, as their mother locked the back door.

Sarah snorted. 'I wouldn't put anything past you.'

Molly gave a smug grin and pointed at Sarah. 'Ah. Got you. Actually, I wasn't after a frog, I was looking for my cuddly Ebola germ.' She turned to her mother who was brushing pollen off her new dress. 'Sarah's been winding you up, Mum.'

'Maybe but I'm not the one with fox poo on her jeans,' Sarah shot back, angry for letting herself fall for Molly's teasing.

Molly glanced down at her muddy jeans. 'What? Shit!'

Their father stuck his head around the kitchen door. 'Molly. Can you not use that word *quite* so often, and can everyone get a move on, *please?*'

'I am trying, Will,' said their mum, then caught sight of her feet. 'Oh shit, look at my new heels. They're covered in mud and grass. I'll have to clean them before we set off for Carol's.'

'Can you not use that word quite so often, Mum?' said Molly, picking a biscuit out of the barrel. Sarah tried not to giggle. She could strangle Molly sometimes but her one-liners were very funny.

'Molly, don't try to be *too* smart,' said their dad and tapped his watch. 'The traffic will be murder if we don't get a move on. It is *our anniversary*, after all. The first time we get a weekend away from the girls in years and we might be late.'

'Yes, it is our *twentieth* wedding anniversary,' said their mother, emphasising the words in a dramatic way. 'And we're off to a *very posh hotel* for the weekend *if* we can ever get our daughters to leave the house.'

'OK, OK. Enough with the guilt trip. I get the message,' said Sarah, rolling the pliers and other tools up into their felt case.

'Thank you,' said her father. 'Now, I'm going to pack the car and I expect everyone to be ready by the time I'm finished.'

Ignoring her father, Molly's bottom lip jutted. 'I do *not* have fox shit on my jeans,' she said mutinously.

'Ha. Got you,' Sarah said with a triumphant grin that she knew would drive Molly mad.

'Molly, wash your hands and change your jeans,' her mum said.

'It's not fox poo. It's only mud.'

'I don't care. You can't go to Auntie Carol's in filthy clothes. Go upstairs, get changed and hurry up.'

Sarah snorted.

'And you, Sarah, can tidy all your junk away and make sure you have your overnight stuff. I don't want to have to come back because you've forgotten your phone or your pyjamas or something.'

'It is *not* junk!' Sarah protested.

'You know what I mean,' said her mum, adding an indulgent smile that did nothing to soothe Sarah's ruffled feathers.

'My bag has been ready *for hours*, Mum,' said Sarah. 'Unlike Mol, who hasn't even started packing. And I don't see why I have to stay at Auntie Carol's tonight. I'm eighteen. I could stay here on my own and I'd be fine. I could have mates over for the evening or I could have gone with Tilly to Ibiza. It's Molly who needs the babysitter.'

Molly gasped. 'No, I do *not*. You're the one who'd end up in A&E or a police cell if you were left on her own. I'm the responsible one. Everyone knows I'd have my head in a book the *whole* time Mum and Dad were away.'

'More like blow up the whole house and experiment on Roger,' said Sarah.

'I love Roger. He's my hamster too.'

'This is pointless because I'm not letting either of you stay here on your own,' said their mother, rubbing at the heel of her shoe with a piece of kitchen paper.

'I can manage without you and Dad, you know. I'm not a little girl,' Sarah muttered, knowing she was pushing her luck.

Their mother stuck her hands on her hips. 'No, but I'm turning into a very old lady waiting here. Get your stuff, both of you, and get into the car!'

5

Twenty minutes later, Will Havers drummed his fingers on the steering wheel as he waited for the girls to finally climb into the car. The engine was running as Sarah shoved her overnight case into the boot and Molly climbed in behind their mother, clutching her rucksack to her chest. Sarah shut the car door, fastened her seat belt and stared pointedly out of the window. Maybe, she thought, watching raindrops gently spatter the window, she wouldn't give Molly the earrings after all.

As they drove the short distance to Auntie Carol's, their parents turned on Radio Five. Sarah risked a sideways glance at Molly who had her nose stuck in a thick paperback entitled *Guns, Germs and Steel.*

Sarah shook her head. *Guns, Germs and Steel?* What was that all about, for God's sake? Molly was barely fifteen. Why wasn't she into *Sweet Valley High* or *Twilight* like Sarah had been? Her sister really was weird, sometimes. Not the gifted genius everyone said, just a freak.

Unexpectedly, Molly glanced up and their gazes met. Molly's light blue eyes were innocent and amused. Her light brown hair, which reminded Sarah of runny honey, was secured in a messy ponytail with a pink elastic band. She'd changed into ripped but clean jeans and was still wearing the disgusting spider sweatshirt. Somehow, she still managed to look terrifyingly pretty. In fact, Molly could have worn a sack and still been stunning. Sarah knew that most of the boys in the sixth form, let alone those in Molly's year, would have given their right arms to date her.

Sarah returned her gaze to the scenery outside the window but the reflection showed Molly's slim wrists as she turned the page of the book. A bracelet would look beautiful on her, especially if Molly wore the new blue dress she'd chosen for her birthday from Oasis. Maybe Sarah would make her a bracelet to match the earrings … because no matter how annoying and weird Molly could be, Sarah couldn't help but love her. And no matter how much she longed to leave school and start her jewellery design course, she was secretly dreading the idea of leaving home and being so far away from her family.

Her parents had promised to support her in doing an arty course in Falmouth, so far away from Cambridge. She knew that they were keen to be even-handed with both daughters and they'd let her know that they took her hopes and ambitions as seriously as Molly's, who was a shoo-in for Oxbridge with her precocious talent for science. She'd make new friends, obviously, but the thought of not having Molly to tease and to guide – Molly needed a lot of guidance – and to share a joke, was scary.

Ever since she could remember, Molly had been a part of her life, like a limb or a vital organ. Her mother had told her that when she first saw Molly in the incubator at the hospital, Sarah had stroked her tiny finger and asked if she would die after a couple of years like their latest hamster. Sarah had apparently cried real tears when her mum had said that Molly was here to stay, as long as Sarah herself – and almost as long as them.

At the traffic lights, Mr Havers twisted round, a grin on his face. 'Everyone OK? No one feeling sick?'

'Molly, is it a great idea to read in the back of the car? You know what these roads on the way to Carol's do to you,' their mother added.

'If we weren't going to Carol's, Molly wouldn't feel sick,'

Sarah muttered, her mind still on the impending change in her life.

Molly calmly turned a page. 'I don't feel sick.'

'And are *you* OK?' her mother asked Sarah.

Sarah let out an exaggerated sigh. 'Of course I am, Mum.'

Their mother exchanged a knowing glance with their father. 'Good. I'm glad everybody's happy so your father and I can leave you with Auntie Carol and not worry. You *will* have a lovely time, you know, and Dad and I can enjoy ourselves knowing you're safe and happy. OK, girls?'

'Yes, Mum,' they chorused from the back seat.

'Great. Now all's right in the world, we can all relax.'

The girls exchanged their own knowing smiles. There was a roll of the eyes from Sarah and an answering tut from Molly that said far more than words. Their gestures were acknowledgement of a bond that no sisterly spat could break. If she could find one at the bead shop, she might even put a little silver frog on the necklace.

Mol wasn't all bad and her sharp tongue *was* very funny. Plus, Auntie Carol was a laugh when she was in a good mood and let the girls have a glass or two of Chardonnay and watch *Skins* as long as they didn't tell their parents. And her course in Falmouth *would* be cool, once she got used to it, and she might meet a surfer and have sex on the beach and start her own boutique jewellery business after uni ... and they'd soon be at Auntie Carol's. She pulled out her new phone and scrolled through her texts. There was a lot to look forward to. An *awful* lot.

*

Later, much much later, Sarah couldn't remember if Molly had screamed before Sarah had looked up from her phone or the other way around. Snatches of their journey came back to her, like jumbled-up pieces of a jigsaw that had tumbled onto the carpet. In the days and weeks that followed, Sarah kept finding new pieces at random, trying to put them together in a picture but never having all the bits at one time.

She remembered something about a surfer and a frog and the shops blurring into one another outside the car window. She recalled hearing the traffic report about chaos on the A14, then a roar and a shout from Molly. And then lights: blinding bright lights. Purply white and violet pulses that made her skull ache and her brain throb. In the snatches of consciousness after the accident, she remembered Auntie Carol sitting next to her bed, holding her hand, with mascara running down her face. And she remembered asking where Molly and her parents were but all Auntie Carol would say was: 'I'm sorry, love. Oh God, I'm sorry.'

Chapter One

Almost thirteen years later

New Year's Eve

Department of Behavioural Ecology, Fenland University

Dr Molly Havers slid off her stool and sashayed over to the fridge. She'd gone to town this evening and made a special effort with her outfit. White plastic onesie, safety glasses and sky-blue accessories. Well, it was a special occasion. How could he possibly resist?

She pulled out a small plastic pot and minced across the lab to her boss's workstation. 'Here you are, Professor Baxter. One pot of gorilla semen, as you requested.'

Ewan Baxter didn't so much as lift his eyes from his keyboard. 'Is it fresh?' he growled, sounding not unlike a gorilla himself.

'Of course it's fresh, I made it myself,' said Molly, aiming for an ironically sexy purr.

Ewan swivelled round on his stool and peered at her through his safety glasses as if Molly was one of his samples. 'I hope you're not developing a throat infection, Dr Havers, because if so, you know the rules. You shouldn't be in the lab putting your co-workers at risk, not to mention jeopardising this project.'

Molly resisted the urge to throw the semen over Ewan. 'I don't have a throat infection.'

Ewan frowned. 'Are you sure? You look a bit flushed and you sound pretty rough too.'

'There's nothing wrong with me. Actually, I was only trying to be sarcastic.'

'That's a relief, but I'd appreciate it if you tried not to be so sarcastic in future. You had me worried for a moment.' His expression was deadpan.

'In case I was ill?' asked Molly.

'No. In case you ruined our work. You know we can't afford to let any rogue bacteria in here. Can I have the semen, now, please?'

Molly slapped the pot onto his nitrile glove, knowing the gleam of desire in his eyes wasn't for her, but the pot of gorilla jizz that had been flown in a week ago at vast expense from an animal conservation project in Rwanda. 'And I promise to try not to be so sarcastic in future,' she said, even more sarcastically.

Ewan's eyebrows lifted, the way they did when he'd read a scientific paper he'd been asked to peer-review and was about to rip to shreds. 'That would be helpful,' he said. 'Or I might have to think about getting a research assistant who's more respectful. Thank you for passing the semen.'

Molly detected a nano-smile before he returned his attention to his work. He *was* joking about getting a new assistant, of course, because Molly knew he had a sense of humour. Unfortunately, it was often so well hidden you needed an electron microscope to find it. Then again, maybe it was a good thing that Ewan was so dour he made a high court judge look frivolous. It would be excruciating to be working on the "Love Bug" project with a boss who pumped out innuendos to rival a *Carry On* film.

Molly went back to her own desk and her work on the Love Bug, a name that had stuck after one of the lab technicians had seen an old film on the TV and joked about it to Ewan and Molly. The top-secret project was a revolutionary hormone designed to help humans bond. Theoretically, it could make two individuals fall in love with each other. *Theoretically*.

Ewan wasn't amused – as always – about his complex work being reduced to a "sound bite". Molly thought he was right about one thing: the Love Bug wasn't accurate because the bonding agent was actually a synthetic hormone, not a "bug" or bacteria and definitely not a "love potion".

Ewan would have hit the roof if anyone described their precious project in such romantic terms. Well, thought Molly as she looked down her microscope, it had certainly been proven scientifically that Ewan didn't have a romantic gene in his body. She'd lost count of the times that Sarah had told her Ewan was a lost cause and that there "were plenty more fish in the sea". Sarah had taken on the role of surrogate mother since their parents had been killed in the accident on the way to Auntie Carol's, even after Molly had ceased to need parental guidance where men were concerned. However, Molly thought – glancing over at him, oblivious to anything except the semen – maybe she *did* have a point about Ewan.

She tried to focus on her own samples but then caught

sight of the time on the laptop. It was half past six on the party night of the year and what was she doing? Smearing gorilla jizz onto a sliver of glass. That wasn't normal behaviour by anyone's standards, not even a dedicated research scientist such as herself.

'Did you know the solitary confinement cells at Alcatraz were designed to face the mainland so the prisoners could actually hear the sounds of revelry in San Francisco?' she muttered.

'Sorry?' said Ewan, hunched over his microscope.

'I said I was thinking of ripping off all my clothes and running down the corridor shouting, "I'm a badass babe."'

'Mm. Of course.'

'Ewan?'

He swivelled round again. 'Yes, Molly?'

His eyes met hers through their safety glasses. Perhaps a ghost of a smile tugged at the corners of his mouth but it disappeared so fast, she must have imagined it and the Baxter lab, of course, was no place for imagination.

'It's getting late. Do you mind if I call it a day and get ready for the party?' Molly said.

He frowned. 'The *party*?'

She pulled off her glasses. 'Yes, Ewan, the party. It's New Year's Eve if you hadn't noticed.'

He took off his own glasses and blinked. Molly's determination to hate him from now on, melted like butter in a pan. Despite his name, wherever Ewan's genes had originated from, it wasn't Scotland or anywhere within a thousand miles. He had dark brown hair, not red or blond, and his eyes were the colour of strong espresso, rather than the blue or green a geneticist would have expected. Somewhere along the way,

Ewan's ancestors had coupled up with a tribe from the Mediterranean – and a pretty hot one at that.

'Surely, you hadn't forgotten?' she asked.

'No. No, of course I hadn't.'

'Are you going? It starts at eight, you know.'

'Um. I don't know yet.'

Molly bit back a gasp of exasperation. The party, and the potential for getting pissed, was her one hope of persuading Ewan to let his hair down.

'Well, it's up to you, of course, but everyone will be expecting you,' she said, turning her back on him and unzipping her onesie. 'Especially after this morning ...'

Ewan pulled a face.

'Well, when you get awarded the MBE in the New Year's Honours List, people want to celebrate.'

He grimaced again. Ewan might not have a sexual response but he also didn't have an ego and had refused to accept that he was responsible for the lab's pioneering work into parent and baby bonding among primates.

'I suppose I'd better put in an appearance, if only to thank everyone who helped us win the gong. I can always come back to the lab when I've shown my face and it will be quiet as everyone will be at the party.'

'The Love Bug will still be here tomorrow ...' said Molly, in despair.

Ewan clicked his tongue against his teeth disapprovingly. In fact, he was the only man Molly knew who tutted in a non-ironic fashion. 'Please don't call it the Love Bug. It trivialises a very important project and it's also completely inaccurate. You and I know it's not a bug, it's a genetically synthesised bonding hormone but if that ... descriptor ...

slipped out to the press, they'd jump on it like a ... like a ... dog on a bone.'

Molly resisted the urge to snigger. Ewan might be a genius, and gorgeous, but he was shit at similes.

'You know what will happen, if some clever dick from the papers gets a whiff of our work before we're ready to announce it publicly, it will end up splashed on the pages of some rag as a "sex bullet" next to a picture of Brian Cox showing his ...'

'Calm down. Our work is under wraps for now and the Love Bug will still be here tomorrow,' she said, deliberately using the despised descriptor again and dumping her gloves in the waste bin. 'But the party and your adoring fans won't.'

'I do *not* have adoring fans.'

'Oh, I don't know,' said Molly mischievously. 'What about Mrs Choudhry from admin and that guy from the equipment supplier with the hooked nose who smells like chloroform?'

'I've no idea what you're talking about.'

'Really? Well, I'm going and if I don't see you at the party, I'll see you next year.'

Molly made a meal of taking off her onesie, in the hope Ewan might change his mind and leave the lab with her but he pulled up his hood again and started tapping away at his laptop.

'Maybe I can just fit in one more run of tests ...'

One day you will be found dead in this lab, Ewan Baxter, and eaten by fruit flies. In fact, it may be that someone – probably me – kills you out of sheer sexual frustration.

'Up to you,' said Molly through gritted teeth, 'but I have to get down to the fancy-dress shop and find a costume before it closes.'

At first she thought he hadn't heard her but then, slowly

16

and very deliberately, he swivelled round again. There was genuine terror in his eyes and she thought his face had definitely turned a shade paler.

'The fancy-dress shop? Why would I need a *costume*?'

Power surged through Molly's veins. 'Didn't you realise?' she said, picking up her backpack. 'It's a fancy-dress party. The theme is movie heroes and heroines. Good luck with what you can find in the next half hour.'

Chapter Two

Five miles northwest of Molly's lab, in the village of Fenham, Sarah Havers inched open the drawer of the dressing table in the cottage bedroom. The white test stick still lay on top of her frilly red thong – the same one that had got her into trouble in the first place.

The face of her partner appeared in the mirror behind her. 'Is that feckin' fireworks going off already?' he said, fastening the top button of his uniform shirt.

Sarah nudged the drawer shut. 'It's only six o'clock – surely they aren't setting them off this early?' Her heart thudded. She hadn't heard Niall come out of the en suite.

'Believe me, it's *never* too early to set fire to your dad's shed or blow your fingers off.'

'Eww. Spare me the image, Mr McCafferty.'

Niall ran his fingers through his quiff. Sarah thought he'd overdone the gel for work, but Niall's "thing" about his hair was a small price to pay for living with a real-life hero, not that she'd ever tell him that of course. 'Hey, I'll be delighted if all we get tonight is a few lost fingers and some burns,' he said, teasing his hair into an impressive ski slope. 'It's more likely that we'll have someone die of alcohol poisoning or a juicy stabbing but as long as it's not me, I can cope.'

Sarah twisted the stool around to face him. 'I wish you didn't have to work on New Year's Eve. You've already done the Christmas Day shift.'

Niall frowned as he dabbed at a tiny shaving cut on his chin. 'Most of the other crew have kids. It doesn't seem right not to give them time with their families and you know we need all the overtime I can get these days.'

'I'll still miss you like mad. It means the world to me that you've been behind me giving up my job to start the business, especially a tiara-making business.'

'You won't miss me. You'll have a fantastic time with Molly at the scientists' ball.'

Sarah laughed. 'I'm not sure what it'll be like with eighty geeks bopping away.'

Niall flicked one of the crystals on her tiara and they shimmered in the lamplight. 'And I'm sure you'll liven it up, darlin', though I'm not happy about letting my sexy fairy out of my sight.'

'Actually, I'm a princess. The party theme is "movie heroes and heroines" and I decided that Anastasia counts as a heroine. Some people say she survived when the rest of the Russian royal family were murdered.'

'You can be a sexy princess, then, I don't really mind.'

She traced a nail down the open V of his shirt, enjoying the softness of his chest hair under her fingertip. 'And I love a sexy paramedic.'

'Now, now, it wouldn't do for Cambridgeshire County ambulance service to send a staff member out with a massive hard-on, would it?'

'Oh, I don't know. It would add a little frisson for the patients.'

'Not with the kind of patients I'm likely to encounter on New Year's Eve. You'll get me into trouble ... Now, I *really* have to go. Be careful out there and enjoy yourself. What time do you want picking up from Molly's place tomorrow morning?'

'Oh, erm ... whenever you like.' Sarah felt guilty about lying but she didn't want to drop a momentous bombshell on him just before he headed out on his shift. New Year's Eve was his busiest night of the year and he'd need every ounce of concentration as he hurtled along the roads of Cambridgeshire on his way to a shout. OK, she might be paranoid and sound like an old fogey, but surely anyone would be after what happened to her and Molly's parents? You never lost the anxiety after a tragedy like that: part of you always knew that the worst could happen no matter how unlikely.

'I know you worry but we're trained professionals, remember? And if anything does happen, well, at least we'd have the paramedics on site.'

'Don't joke, Ni!' said Sarah, then softened her tone. She was being silly and she knew Niall's black humour was designed to jolly her out of her fears about him hurtling round the roads at top speed. The banter was the only way he and his colleagues could deal with their jobs most of the time.

He kissed her again. 'Sorry, babe ... bad taste but honestly, my love, nothing is going to happen to me tonight, I promise you. I'll text you if I can but it's going to be a manic night. I'll be back around four a.m. but it could be lunchtime before I surface properly.'

'I suppose I can hang on until then to give you your New Year's present,' she said, growing excited again at the prospect of sharing her news and focusing on new life, not the past.

'My *present*?' He raised an eyebrow. 'Oh, I can't wait.'

Sarah was still staring at her reflection when the front door shut and she heard Niall whistling "Happy" by Pharrell Williams on the drive. Only after she heard the engine of his motorbike dying in the distance, and when the pop and fizzle of the fireworks sounded loud against the newly silent house, did she dare to open the drawer again.

She picked up the test stick and butterflies stirred in her stomach. Would Niall actually *like* his present? Getting pregnant now was hardly ideal timing. She'd given up her job to start her new business only a few months before and on top of the mortgage on the cottage, and the bills, they had to find the payments on Niall's new motorbike.

She spread her palm over her stomach. It felt exactly the same as it had for the past year. Not flat, of course – she hadn't had a flat tummy since she was about ten – but it certainly wasn't any rounder. She didn't feel sick, either, unless you counted the butterflies of excitement and apprehension that had been fluttering away for the past half hour. Her body gave no clue whatsoever that it had another person inside it yet someone was there right now, its heart beating because hers did, breathing when she did, and relying on her for its survival.

Niall loved kids and he adored his huge extended family. Sarah would never forget the first time he'd introduced her to them two years before. It had been at a party for his Nana McCafferty's ninetieth birthday and a bit like being thrown into a pit of friendly lions and their cubs. And now she and Niall were starting their own tiny clan.

Emotion bubbled up in her throat. She picked up her mobile and dialled the second most used number on her phone.

'Hello, this is Molly, I can't get to the phone right now ...'

Damn. Was Molly *still* at work at this time of night? It was New Year's Eve – but then, her little sister had always been the biggest geek on the planet, next to her workaholic boss, of course. To be fair, Molly's latest crush on Ewan Baxter had lasted well over a year now – far longer than any of the others. Sarah wasn't terribly hopeful; Ewan had failed to respond to any of Molly's hints so far. Sarah thought he was mad; Molly was gorgeous and fun and bright – when she wasn't infuriating and impulsive, of course.

'Hi, Molly, it's me,' Sarah spoke into the answerphone. 'Are you *still* at work? If you are, don't let Professor McDreamy make you miss the party. I'm still coming but I can't stay over at yours after all so I'll drive us home and before you ask, I don't mind staying sober and no, I'm not ill ...'

Even hinting about the baby to Molly made Sarah want to laugh out loud and burst into tears at the same time. What would she be like when she told Niall? She imagined breaking her news in front of the embers of the cottage's log fire. She imagined his gasp of amazement and his gobsmacked face. She wanted to hold the moment forever in her mind.

'I'll tell you more when I see you,' she said when it was obvious Molly wasn't going to pick up. 'Now, get the hell out of that lab and put your glad rags on.'

Chapter Three

Brushing past a Wookiee who smelled of mould and a rugby player dressed as Hermione Granger, Molly hurried away from the bar with a pint of cider for herself and a Coke for Sarah. It was slightly surreal to see the Biology Faculty staff restaurant decked out in streamers with a large glitter ball suspended from the ceiling above the salad servery. The faculty Entz Committee had obviously spent ages on the superhero-themed decorations, trying to cover the yellowing walls with posters of Marvel heroes but Molly still thought the place looked like exactly like a 1960s canteen. And a Wookiee wasn't exactly a typical movie hero.

Then again, quite a few people were pushing the boundaries of what qualified as a hero or heroine. Take Pete Garrick, the parasitic worm expert from the next lab to Molly's, who was also acting as DJ for the evening, fiddling with the knobs on the decks. He was wearing what looked like an Iron Man T-shirt with fake muscles stencilled on the front. He cut the Mid and the vocals dropped out, so you could hear everyone screaming along to "Livin' on a Prayer".

Wincing, Molly put the Coke on the table that she and Sarah had bagged in a relatively quiet corner. 'Are you sure you don't mind driving tonight?' she said, leaning in closer so Sarah could hear above the "music". 'You can still stay over at mine if you want and we can get a taxi home, if I book one now.'

'I don't mind driving,' said Sarah. 'Anyway, I want to go home afterwards and give Niall my news.'

'Ooo. News! Does this news have anything to do with the "tell you more when I see you" message?'

'Might have.' Sarah sipped her Coke and her eyes twinkled, reflecting the lights from the disco.

'Oh my God, you're pregnant, aren't you?'

Sarah gasped. 'Is it that obvious already? I'm only seven weeks at the most.'

Molly grinned in delight. 'No, but you said you had a secret to tell Niall and you're obviously desperate to stay sober on the party night of the year. I don't have to be a rocket scientist, or even a behavioural ecologist to work out what it is.'

Sarah nodded excitedly. 'Oh, Mol, I know Niall ought to be the first to know but I only found out for sure tonight and he was just about to go out on shift. I didn't want him driving round the streets of Cambridge at sixty miles an hour with that on his mind.'

Molly hugged her. 'I'm so happy for you, and for Niall. I know you're going to make an amazing mum and dad. You deserve it so much.' She meant every word; she could never wish enough good things to happen to Sarah, after what she'd done for Molly. After their parents had died, it was Sarah who'd kept her on the rails and made sure she went to uni. Sarah who'd encouraged her and supported her through some of the darkest days of her life; of both their lives.

'We were both there for each other,' said Sarah but then her smile faded. 'But it's not the best timing, with me just starting up the business. Niall only took tonight's shift for the overtime. I hope he's not too shocked.'

'Only in a good way, I'm sure. You two are the most loved-up pair I've ever seen. You were made for each other.'

'"Made for each other" ... and you know that's possible, do you, Dr Havers?'

'Shh. You really will get me into trouble.' Molly tapped the side of her nose. 'And I ...' The words stuck in her throat as she caught sight of what Mrs Choudhry would call a "kerfuffle" happening by the double doors leading into the canteen.

'On my God, it's Ewan and he's wearing a sodding *kilt*. What the hell am I supposed to do about that?'

Molly sat open-mouthed as Sarah followed her gaze. 'I don't know. Ask him what he's wearing under it?'

'Arghh. Don't. It doesn't even bear thinking about.'

'And yet, you often have.'

'Please, no, I think I'm going to self-combust.'

Sarah's eyes had a glint to rival the rhinestones on her "Princess Anastasia" tiara. 'I thought you told me spontaneous combustion was an urban myth and that only people on *Jeremy Kyle* believe it actually happens?'

'It is – I mean, I thought it was a myth but I think that tonight might be the first documented case. I mean, *look* at him.'

What Molly really meant was for Sarah to wait patiently while she stared at Professor Ewan Baxter for the umpteenth time that evening. Her earlier annoyance at his rudeness/ignoring her in the lab had disappeared in a haze of wine/kilt-induced amnesia. The kilt showed off legs that Molly had only ever seen clad in denim, or occasionally, a pair of suit trousers if Ewan had to visit someone important. His calves were firm and well developed with exactly the optimum amount of soft, dark hair.

'OK. I admit, he's very sexy for a biochemistry academic, although that's not saying much when you look at the competition,' said Sarah, giving the room a withering appraisal.

'You do know these are some of the finest scientific minds on the planet? Some of these people are going to save the world one day.'

'God help the world,' said Sarah. 'More wine?'

Half an hour later, whoops and screeches cut through the disco beat. Ewan had joined a group of people at the bar. Molly wasn't the only one in the faculty who had a crush on Ewan. In fact, there was so much drool – of the real and intellectual variety – she could have gathered a lab full of samples. She watched his guns as he lifted the pint; his mouth tilting upwards at the corners as he laughed with his PhD students, the slight stiffening of his body when one of the younger female professors touched him "playfully" on the arm. The academic was brilliant, single and gorgeous but Ewan seemed oblivious even to her.

'It must be heartbreaking to be in love with your tutor,' Sarah teased.

'Firstly, he isn't my tutor, he's my boss. Secondly, I'm not his student, I'm a research associate; and thirdly, I'm not in love.'

'Mum used to sing that song when she was ironing,' said Sarah.

'Did she? I don't remember,' said Molly, trying to picture their mother holding up her school blouse and asking her if she'd been using it to help their dad clean the car again. She knew the event had happened, but she could no longer see their faces distinctly in her mind. Her memories were fading after thirteen years. She wondered if Sarah had the same problem but had never dared to ask her and certainly wasn't going to tonight.

'Mum said "I'm Not in Love" was the ultimate song about being in denial,' said Sarah.

'But I'm *definitely* not in love with Ewan,' said Molly, wishing Sarah hadn't referred to their mother so casually. Oh God, her parents would have been grandparents. Molly gulped down her wine, desperately trying not to cry. Sarah did not need that kind of reminder tonight. She tried to drown the reminder of her loss with another large glug of wine. It had struck suddenly, as if she'd sat on a sharp thorn that was working its way into her flesh again. It seemed cruel that the pain took longer to fade than her memories.

'Romantic love is just the brain pumping out a cocktail of chemicals: pheromones, dopamine, serotonin ... plus a few others,' she said, babbling away to try and erase the memories.

'Okayyy ...' Sarah's eyes were glazing over; and Molly couldn't put it down to the booze because Sarah was stone-cold sober. Molly had always driven her sister mad with her obsession with science, zoology and anthropology. Any *ology* in fact. Sarah, in contrast, had ended up joining a bank's training scheme straight after her A levels so she could stay at home and look after Molly, rather than going to university to study jewellery design. Molly owed her sister a lot and she was delighted that Sarah had finally been able to leave her job and fulfil her dream, with Niall's help and support.

'I'm not denying I'm in lust,' Molly said.

'Is it so different?'

'Totally. Love requires mutual dependence while lust is a transitory condition, involving an overload of oestrogen and testosterone.'

'And?'

Molly grinned. 'I'm completely powerless to do anything about my hormones.'

'Have you actually let him know what he does to your levels of oestrogen yet?'

Molly snorted. 'Of course not! He'd run a mile!'

'Why?'

'Because ... because ... he's a workaholic who lives for his research. A relationship would only distract him from that purpose. Sometimes, he actually sleeps in the lab.'

Sarah laughed. 'I thought you said there were lots of geeks who slept in the lab.'

'Yes, but Ewan has a sleeping bag and a packet of Coco Pops in his filing cabinet.'

'I thought even you'd spent all night in there sometimes.'

'Occasionally, yes, when I've got an experiment running and I can't let the samples die. It would ruin the project and it is important.'

'Ah, the Love Bug project.'

Molly put her finger on her lips. 'Shh ... You can't get infected by it, it's a hormone and it has to be specially tailored to your DNA and delivered in a very specific way. I could get the sack for telling you about it but it isn't a "bug". Look, can we talk about something else? *Please?*'

'Like Ewan?'

Molly nodded, relieved and happier than was probably

healthy. Or normal. Or smart. Sarah was right, she was probably a tiny bit obsessed, or worse, maybe she *was* a teeny bit in love with him.

'Look, he is single right? And straight from what you've told me?'

'Divorced. His wife lives with a barrister in Dulwich according to one of the lab assistants. His workaholism was why they split up. Apparently.'

'Single, then, with a bit of baggage, but you can work through that. Also, straight, in that case, unless that's why he split up with her?'

'Oh, he's straight.' Molly surprised herself with her own vehemence. She did know Ewan was straight, even though all the recent evidence was against it. 'Though it's feasible that he could be asexual, I suppose ...'

Sarah laughed. 'I doubt it. Look, it's New Year's Eve and even though I hate to swell your ego, you're the most gorgeous girl in the room. Why don't you just go and ask Professor McDreamy if he wants to dance?'

'Dance? Are you mad?'

'Only as crazy as you are if you don't take your chance while he a: doesn't have his face glued to a microscope and b: is probably a bit pissed. Go on, ask him. Otherwise, shut up and come and dance with me. It's New Year's Eve and as you know, I don't get out much so I'm bloody well going to make the most of tonight.'

'Oh God, Sarah, I'm a selfish bitch, going on about Ewan. What a shame Niall couldn't make the party. It must be shit having to work on New Year's Eve but Niall's a hero, and hunky; he loves you to bits. I could hate you, if I didn't love you to bits as well, hon. I really envy you though.'

'Gorgeous brilliant "gonna save the world" Dr Molly envies her sister?'

'I'm not gorgeous – especially not dressed like an extra from Television X – and I doubt I'll ever save the world but you know what I mean. You have a lovely bloke who's crazy about you and would do anything for you.'

'I don't know what I'd have done without him; he's stuck with me through thick and thin, mostly thin for the past year.'

'You don't regret leaving the bank to start up the business, do you? You're so creative. It was time you did something for yourself. By the way, I love the outfit.'

Sarah touched her tiara. 'I hoped it met the definition of movie hero. I thought coming as Princess Anastasia might be a bit fluffy for this event but then I thought, it might attract some customers.'

Eight assorted biologists were throwing shapes on the dance floor.

'Even geeks fall in love and get married. Eventually,' Sarah said, watching them.

Molly wasn't convinced.

'But I don't think they go in for tiaras much. Another?' said Sarah, pointing to Molly's empty glass.

'I think I'd better if I'm going to ask Ewan to dance.'

A few hours later, Molly fished a party popper out of her glass and finished up a large vodka while Sarah went outside to phone Niall during his break. Molly could tell her sister was anxious about him and she didn't really blame her; Sarah must be desperate to tell Niall about the baby. Sarah looked tired too, and Molly wasn't pissed enough to ignore the fact that her sister and niece/nephew-to-be really ought to be in bed.

It was well past midnight and there were just a few party people jigging around on the dance floor. She tried to spot Ewan at the bar. The shutters were already down on one side of it and only a couple of people queuing at the other. Ewan had probably gone home; or more likely, back to the lab. The party was over, and so was her opportunity.

Just when she'd given up all hope and was shouldering her handbag ready to join Sarah outside and leave, she swivelled round.

Ewan was right next to her. He looked down at her with a sheepish expression, rubbed his chin and said: 'So, Dr Havers, would you like to dance?'

Chapter Four

'Ewan. I didn't notice you creep up on me.'

'Creep up on you? Is it that bad?' He folded his arms. A knot of lust twisted low in Molly's stomach. She stared at him as he swam in and out of focus.

'No, of course not but, did you just ask if I'd *dance* with you?'

'Yes.' He nodded in the direction of the space between the serving counters that served as a dance floor. 'That thing where two – or more – people try to move their bodies in time with music. Which in this case, I'm afraid, is George Michael.'

Ewan's face changed from orange to green to red and back to orange as the disco lights pulsed. He was a human traffic light.

'But ... are you *sure*?'

'Do you mean am I statistically certain that I want to dance or merely sure in a slightly pissed, relatively normal kind of bloke sense?'

Molly giggled and then regretted it. Ewan never giggled, he was allergic to the concept and so was she under normal circumstances but these weren't normal circumstances; they were slightly drunken circumstances. She stood up and almost had to hold on to the table for support. Make that very drunken circumstances because it could only be alcohol making her legs this wobbly.

'Oh, go on, then.'

She tugged her nurse's hem down, which had the effect of also lowering the neckline to pornographic level, just as Ewan moved closer to her.

'It was all they had left in the shop, apart from a comedy Boris Johnson outfit,' she said, feeling the need to explain, as the dress pinged up her thighs again.

His eyebrows shot up his face. 'Interesting choice and um … call me a bit dim but what movie hero are you meant to be?'

'Um. Nurse Ratched from *One Flew Over the Cuckoo's Nest*?'

Ewan winced. 'Great film. Terrible nurse.'

'Kate Beckinsale from *Pearl Harbor*, then?'

Ewan tutted. 'Terrible film. Very sexy nurse.'

Molly's face heated up like someone had taken a Bunsen burner to it. 'You're William Wallace from *Braveheart*, of course.'

'Well … not really. I borrowed this from my brother. He stayed over Christmas and said I could borrow it. He's Scottish, you see.'

'And you're not?'

'Technically, yes. I was born in Edinburgh Royal Infirmary but our parents moved down here when I was six weeks old.' He narrowed his eyes at her. 'Why? Do you have a problem with me being Scottish?'

Molly smiled, suddenly floating on a cushion of air. 'Not if you don't, Professor Baxter.'

'I'm glad to hear it Nurse Beckinsale. So – shall we before they put on something even worse than George?'

He didn't take her hand and lead her to the dance floor, as George had in "Careless Whisper", and the soles of her stilettos stuck to the tiles as she followed him. Silly string trailed from his backside and there was also a strand stuck to his calf, curling through the dark hair and over the contours of his muscles.

Molly shuffled closer, not knowing what she should do with her hands, but Ewan seemed to have at least a rough idea and there they were, pressing his around her waist, not too lightly but not too firm either. Perfect, in fact, the way she'd always imagined them. Her fingers rested on his back, beneath his shoulder blades. The laces of his Highland shirt were loose, revealing the hairs sprinkled across his broad chest. Ewan's fingers brushed her cheek, and Molly's hormones pinged so loudly she thought everyone must hear. Not that hormones could make any kind of noise, obviously, but if they did a ping would be appropriate ...

She homed in on a hot pink strand dangling in front of her nose and the fingers that lifted it out of her line of vision.

'You have silly string in your hair,' said Ewan.

'Thanks for letting me know. You ... um ... have some on your bum ... I mean, the back of your kilt.'

He twisted round. 'Oh God. Do I?'

''Fraid so. It gets everywhere, doesn't it?' she said, instantly regretting her words in case he thought she was referring to something *under* his kilt.

'Apparently so.'

Molly glanced down at the party popper nestled between her cleavage. What else was she going to find on her person?

'Shall I um ... help you retrieve that? I'll be careful,' said Ewan, as if the popper was a seal pup that needed rescuing.

'Oh, go on then.'

His fingers fumbled inside her plunge bra, fished out the popper and dropped it on the floor. Goose bumps popped out all over her skin. Just another totally normal reaction to external stimuli, thought Molly, nothing to do with Ewan per se ...

'Mol, I really think I may be a bit pissed ...' he whispered into her hair.

'I *know* I'm a lot pissed.'

'Then by the laws of the universe,' he murmured as George warbled on, 'we must cancel each other out so that's acceptable.'

Ewan was smiling happily, in the way she'd occasionally seen him do before. Like when one of the retiring admin ladies had given him a fruit cake for his birthday because he "needed feeding up". Was that how he saw her? Kind and hardworking but harmless? No way. The way he'd retrieved that party popper had nothing to do with pity, she decided as they swayed in time and George crooned about getting away from the crowd. The hem of Ewan's kilt tickled Molly's knees and as his hands slipped lower to her bottom and he pressed against her, Molly realised he wasn't *that* pissed and that he obviously didn't think she was harmless.

There was hope, more hope than there had ever been, that this year would be a new start for her. Maybe a new start for Sarah too ... They both deserved it and at this moment, in the first hour of the New Year, anything and everything was possible.

Ewan pulled her a little tighter and Molly made no attempt to resist. She rested her cheek on his highland shirt, and the laces tickled her nose. George started wailing about giving his heart to someone nameless and non-gender-specific. Molly knew how George felt. Ewan was now in possession of her heart too, in the metaphorical sense, of course, but it was also trying to escape from her chest.

His arms tightened around her back.

She took her chance. 'You know, Ewan, when I first joined the lab, I thought you were a bit – you know stiff?'

He waggled his eyebrows. 'Stiff?'

'Whoops.' Molly laughed, although actually, what she'd just said was probably anatomically accurate. 'I meant uptight.'

Ewan frowned down at her. 'Uptight? Me? Never.'

'What did you think of me then?'

'You? That you were probably one of the most promising young research associates who'd applied for the job.'

'Oh,' said Molly.

'And that some genetic quirk had given you the most kissable mouth I'd ever seen.'

'Ah.' Just as George was moaning that his cold-hearted ex didn't recognise him, Ewan lowered his face to hers and went for a full-on snog. His eyes were closed so she did the same. His stubbly chin rasped against her skin, his lips tasted of Greene King's finest. The synthesised bells of the song sounded like fireworks and a full-on symphony orchestra.

She wasn't sure who broke the kiss but when it ended, she whispered softly in his ear. 'Wow.'

'Ditto.'

'I never expected that.'

'Nor me.' He sounded throaty and she was sure it wasn't the start of a bacterial infection.

'You know, Professor Baxter, there's something I've been dying to ask you all evening.'

'And?'

'Just what have you got on under the kilt?'

Ewan whispered in her ear. 'That's for me to know and you to find out. What have you got on under the nurse's outfit?'

'Ditto,' said Molly, feeling like she could take off and fly out of the canteen if Ewan wasn't kissing her again, anchoring to him while their tongues danced a reel in each other's mouths. Not even the tinny bells at the end of George's song could spoil the moment. *Happy New Year to me*, thought Molly with a blissful sigh, as Ewan's hands rested contentedly on her bottom.

'And-dd, sadly that is all, folks. Happy New Year, have a safe journey home and gooooood-nighty.'

Molly opened her eyes and blinked as the DJ cut the music. The fluorescent lights were on and from the edge of the room there was a round of applause and some ear-splitting whistles.

'Always said you'd benefit from medical attention, mate!'

Gleeful hoots and a couple of "phwoarrs" echoed across the canteen. Molly's face heated up and she rolled her eyes. 'What are they like, eh?'

'Quite.'

Molly wanted to kill Ewan's rugby mates and a few of her colleagues but decided to laugh off their banter. She could handle a few pissed geeks, and anyway, she was about to get her hands on the biggest prize of all. An image flashed through her mind that made her stomach clench with lust so tightly it hurt. Ewan's shirt and kilt cast aside on her bedroom floor, along with his uptight façade. Ewan, stark naked, standing by her bed shouting 'Freedommmm!' She giggled and rested her hand on his kilt, loving the feel of scratchy wool under her fingers.

Catcalls rang out from the side of the room. Sod them. Sod

them all. Let the boozy gang say all they liked. With one hand still on his arse, she reached up and touched his hair. 'Did you know that you now have silly string in your hair?' she said, shaking with lust.

'Do I? Oh, fuck.' Ewan dropped his hands from her waist and reached up to pull out the strand himself. He rolled it between his fingers and lowered his voice. 'I think the party's over, Molly.'

'Yes, but it doesn't have to end here, does it?'

'Erm. Well it *is* late.'

'Not that late. It's not even one o'clock yet.'

He frowned. 'Well, that is still *quite* late.'

'But not *very* late. The night's young.'

Ewan's Adam's apple bobbed as he swallowed. He did look tired, he'd been working very hard and they'd both had a lot to drink but surely, he wasn't too tired for *that*.

'Thanks for retrieving my party popper,' she said, going for humour and hoping to refocus his mind on the task in hand.

'Yes, I ... um hope you won't hold it against me. I mean, it is New Year's Eve.' He looked sheepish, and sexy. Sheepishly sexy. The perfect combination. Wow. How great was it going to feel when she finally unwrapped that uptight, stiff exterior ...?

'I had noticed. Tends to happen on December thirty-first every year,' said Molly, plucking a stray piece of string off his shoulder. 'And I won't hold anything against you that you don't want me to.'

'Hey. Are you gonna pop your stirring rod into Molly's beaker, Ewan?'

'Ewan! The minibus is here, mate, but I guess you've found a better ride?'

'Oy, Boss. Molly looks so hot in that nurse costume, she'll denature your proteins!'

The shouts from the sidelines grew louder. Molly wanted to strangle them with silly string.

'I'd call them Neanderthals, but we both know that would be an insult to Neanderthals.' She forced a smile to her face while wishing she could vaporise their lairy co-workers.

'You can say that again,' he muttered.

'Phwoar, I sense some DNA sampling is going to happen in the Baxter lab tonight!'

Ewan grimaced – not in a good way. Suddenly, he looked like someone had stuck a ruler up his bottom. 'Molly, I'm sorry ...'

'That's OK. I guess we can both handle them.'

'No, I meant ... I'm really sorry but I don't think this is such a good idea. I guess I'd better go. I was offered a lift in the minibus and I think I should be on it. Team bonding eh? You know I have to be in the lab first thing tomorrow.'

What? He was bailing out? Just because of a few crass comments from a bunch of drunken knobheads?

'You are joking?' Molly refused to let him off the hook.

'No. I mean, I have the press to deal with – they want interviews about the ... er ... MBE thing. Look, do you have a lift home? I can call you a cab if you like?'

A chilly wave of nausea washed over her, mixed with growing anger. Had he got cold feet because of a bit of banter from a bunch of drunken nerds? 'I'm fine,' she said tightly. 'I'm getting a lift with my sister.'

'Good. Um. Well, thank you for the dance ... I um, think you'd better let go of me now.'

Molly snatched her hands from his bum as if it was a red-hot potato.

Ewan reddened. 'Goodnight. Um, see you tomorrow?'

She simmered with shame and anger. 'Actually, Ewan, no, you won't because tomorrow – technically today – is New Year's Day and I'm going to spend it throwing up, enjoying a splitting headache and crying at *Ghost* like normal people, so Happy New Year and congratulations, *Boss*.'

Ewan's lips parted, closed, then he threw her one last guilty glance and walked off the dance floor, trailing silly string.

She closed her eyes but she couldn't shut her ears to the cries of 'What? Changed your mind, mate?'

When she opened her eyes, Ewan and his stupid sodding kilt and brain-dead groupies were gone. At least, she told herself, she could get the walk of shame over with now, rather than in the morning. But if she had gone home with Ewan, her walk of shame would at least have been from his bed – or hers – to the bathroom, not across the canteen, in the full glare of the remaining staff who'd all seen her get blown off by their boss. She glanced at her shoes, covered in sticky string and shiny confetti and at the ladder in her black seamed stockings and the six-inch tear in the hem of the nurse's outfit.

Well, Happy Sodding New Year to her.

Sarah met her at the edge of the dance floor, holding Molly's coat. 'Oh God, please tell me that wasn't what it looked like.'

'I'm afraid it was. I should have known it was all too good to be true! Ewan Baxter is only interested in one thing and that's the bottom of a bloody petri dish!'

Sarah draped her coat around her shoulders and squeezed them slightly. 'Come on, hon, the sooner we get out of here the better.'

'You're absolutely right,' said Molly, as a fresh wave of nausea swept over her. Once outside, the raw cold of a

Cambridge winter night took her breath away. The wind gusted up her skirt and sleet blew in their faces as they walked across the faculty car park, Molly's heels sliding dangerously in the wet slush.

Sarah put her arm around her. 'It's for the best you know. Sleeping with your boss is never a great idea. He's obviously a sociopath. Wouldn't you rather it had ended now before you woke up in his flat and had to do the walk of shame?'

Molly thought of Ewan, naked except for the kilt, frying bacon at her cooker.

'No.'

'OK. Well, it could have been worse. I suppose. If I hadn't waited to make sure whether you'd pulled Ewan, you might have been going home on the minibus with a bunch of pissed geeks.'

Molly bit her lip and told herself to lighten up. Sarah didn't need her moaning on a night when she'd had such good news to share. 'Yeah ... thanks, Sarah. I'm sorry if I've spent half the evening mooning over Ewan bloody Baxter but it won't happen again. I've learned my lesson ... Did you get hold of Niall by the way? I bet you can't wait to share your news.' She forced a smile to her face, reminding herself that she was going to be an auntie and how amazing that would be.

Sarah grimaced. 'No. His phone was off but it is his busiest night of the year and he probably didn't take a break at all. I just wanted to know he's OK, with all the drunks – the extra drunks – around tonight. Since one of his colleagues was stabbed in that pub on Christmas Eve, I guess I'm paranoid.'

'No, you're just worried but he'll be OK. Niall knows how to handle himself.'

'Yeah, you're right and you never know, when he's sobered

up, Ewan might realise what he's just missed. He could be on the phone to you in the morning.'

'Yeah, and I've probably won the Nobel Prize.'

Sarah flicked the remote at the car and the sidelights winked. 'It's not as if that was your only chance. You'll be back at work soon and you can be together every day of your life.'

As she was about to climb into Sarah's Fiesta, an icy blast blew straight down Molly's cleavage. 'It's the scar, isn't it? It's the elephant in the room.'

'Molly,' Sarah said wearily, the way that Molly remembered their mother doing. 'You have a teeny tiny scar that is barely noticeable and with the amount of booze Ewan has got down his neck tonight, I doubt he can even find his own balls let alone notice a scar on your face. He's a tosser who doesn't deserve another minute's thought. Now, let's get you home and into bed.'

'I know. I know. I wish Ewan could be like Niall.'

'Ni's not perfect, not by a long shot.' Sarah smiled.

'But he is about to be a daddy.' Molly reached over and hugged Sarah, desperately trying to fight back the post-party, post-Ewan tears. 'Phone me in the morning. I'm *dying* to hear what he says.'

Chapter Five

After dropping off Molly at her flat, Sarah drove out of the city towards Fenham. It was bitterly cold, a typical Fenland night. Frost glittered like a trillion rhinestones on the pavements and as her headlights swept over the roadside, the fields glowed blue-white under the moon.

As she negotiated the icy roads, Sarah thought the fens had never looked more beautiful but she also felt guilty for feeling so happy when Molly was so miserable. They'd been like two balloons on the way home: Sarah about to go pop with excitement and Molly shrivelled up with misery and the start of a killer hangover.

Despite how long it had lasted, Sarah hadn't really taken Molly's crush on Ewan Baxter *too* seriously until that evening. Molly had had a lot of crushes over the years, usually short-lived and never very heavy. She'd ignored all the boys at school but had a few flings while she was at university, including one with an English Literature student and another with the captain of the university cricket team. Then there'd been the Australian who'd lasted a year on and off while Molly was studying for her PhD.

Sarah had thought he'd be The One for Molly and they'd shared a house together for a while but he'd gone back to

Sydney. Molly had cried for a week but then thrown herself back into her research, landing a post-doc place in the prestigious Baxter lab.

Since then, there had been nothing very serious, although Molly had plenty of offers, Ewan Baxter seemed to have totally captured her imagination and heart. Sarah blew out a breath of frustration as she turned into the road that led through Fenham. She wanted to shake Ewan Baxter and tell him what a total prat he was for upsetting her sister.

She just hoped that Molly would get over her disappointment quickly and realise what an idiot he was and refocus her attention on someone deserving. There was nothing she could do about the situation and besides, Sarah couldn't be too unhappy for long, not tonight.

She remembered Niall's final words as he'd called up the stairs. 'Drive carefully, there's bound to be all kinds of drunks and dickheads on the roads.' She didn't need him to remind her of that, after what had happened to her parents and, besides, she was far more worried about him than herself. She also remembered the sharp tang of his aftershave and the fresh clean smell of his uniform. He always showered before he went out and the moment he got back. No wonder – after New Year's Eve, he'd probably seen, touched, heard and smelled more bodily fluids than she cared to imagine.

Poor bloke; what a shitty job, literally, he had.

She was glad – and slightly guilty – that her own job couldn't have been more different. She ran her jewellery-making business from a small cabin at the end of the garden. She and Niall had built it together and while it was modest, it was exactly right for her. When she wasn't making up commissions for weddings, she ran workshops there where brides and teenagers going to proms could make tiaras and headdresses, and jewellery.

It had been a big risk to give up her safe but boring job at the bank and finally realise her cherished dream to start her own business, but Molly had been spot on. After so many years of acting as surrogate mother as well as big sister to Molly, Sarah had been ready to take a risk. So what if they hadn't planned things this way, working for herself would fit in better with starting a family.

She parked on the pavement outside and pushed open the little wicket gate in the hedge. The path was icy and she almost slipped on one of the flagstones, which brought a smile to her face. 'Don't go arse over tit tonight; I don't want to be called out to save my gorgeous girlfriend – I may be a bit busy,' Niall had joked as he'd kissed her goodbye.

The lamp was on in the sitting room, exactly as she'd left it, knowing she'd be back before Niall. She wondered whether to watch a late-night film on TV and curl up on the sofa to wait for him. She certainly didn't feel sleepy, not after a night on Coke and mineral water, and Niall would be home in a few hours.

She felt a twinge of guilt as she pushed her key in the front door, picturing Molly in bed alone, then told herself that with any luck Mol would be out cold after all the wine. Sarah would call her in the morning and maybe pop round later for a New Year's Day coffee, with Niall. They could celebrate their news together properly. Molly was going to be an auntie. Comforted by this thought, Sarah pushed open the door and stepped into the hall.

Light spilled down the stairs from the landing. Sarah

stopped and the hairs on her arms stood on end. She was sure she hadn't left the light on. Or had she? She'd gone out in a rush and her mind had hardly been on such things.

She put her bag down on the hall table.

'Arghhh ...'

Sarah froze. Her stomach clenched sharply. The floorboards creaked above her and there was a soft thud and another groan.

'Oooo ... ahhhh ...'

There was someone upstairs.

She held her breath. Only in TV thrillers did women walk upstairs to confront a burglar. Sarah was not in a TV thriller; she was much more scared than that. Her hands were clammy as she twisted the Yale knob and backed out of the door.

It was as she ran down the step to the garden that two things happened at once. She realised she'd left her handbag, and therefore her phone inside the hall, and she heard a man say, 'Oh fuck, it's Sarah.'

Sarah stood on the flagstones, staring at the open door of the cottage. Surely, she hadn't heard Niall? He couldn't be home yet.

And yet, she knew the sound of her own partner's voice.

She walked slowly back into the hall. From upstairs she heard the sound of thuds and whispers; a giggle then a plea: 'For God's sake, Vanessa, she'll hear you.'

Hardly daring to breathe, she slowly climbed the narrow staircase. There were no more voices but she could hear telltale creaks from the floorboards, the soft click of a door closing, perhaps a desperate "shh". She reached the turn of the stairs and stepped over a pair of dark blue work trousers, a thick-soled boot and a white shirt. Another shirt and three more safety boots were scattered along the landing like a trail of crumbs leading to the Gingerbread Cottage – or in this case, her and Niall's bedroom.

Light sneaked out from the foot of the door.

'Christ, she's coming upstairs!'

It was unmistakable this time: Niall's soft Irish brogue, the one she'd fallen for at the club two years before.

Sarah didn't feel afraid anymore; she felt as if she was sleepwalking around the cottage, in the midst of a bizarre dream. She stood outside the door to her bedroom and lifted the latch on the braced door. It swung inwards with a familiar creak but what she saw in front of her was so unfamiliar, so bloody plain unbelievable that her legs almost gave way.

'*Niall?*'

Niall was lying in bed, his wrists tied to the bedposts with two of Sarah's silk scarves. He was naked except for a tiara.

'Um, hello, babe.'

She stared at him, trying to compute the scene before her. 'What are you doing home, Ni?'

'I thought you were staying at Molly's tonight,' he said.

'No. I'm not.'

'You said you were.' He said it accusingly as if Sarah was the one who was naked in bed wearing a tiara.

'I said I probably wouldn't.'

'When?'

'While you were getting ready to go out. Maybe you didn't hear me?'

'No, I didn't.'

She gawped at his naked body, at his waxed chest and his scar from a run-in with a drunken motorcyclist and his willy, now deflating like a party balloon that had been left behind the sofa.

'Right. Well, forgive me for asking, but why are you tied to the bed, Niall?'

He peered down at his tackle as if he was surprised to see it at all. 'I ... um ... this is not what it looks like, Sarah. I promise you.'

'What is it, then, Ni?'

'It's um ... ah, just a game, Sarah. I came home early and I'm ... um ... so embarrassed.'

'Tied yourself up, did you, after putting on the tiara?'

'Well, er ...' His wrists strained against the scarves. She realised that one of them, the silk one with the camellia print, had been her mum's.

The door to the en suite opened and a tall, spiky woman with inky, poker-straight hair stood in the doorway. She was wearing Sarah's purple bathrobe and stared at her pityingly. 'Give it a rest, Niall. I think we've been rumbled.'

Niall cut across her. 'Oh, fuck ... Look, Sarah. I can explain. I mean it looks bad. It is bad but I never meant to hurt you.'

The woman swore and folded her arms.

'That's my bathrobe,' Sarah murmured, still half in a trance.

The woman shrugged. 'It swamps me, anyway,' she said untying the belt and slipping it off her bony shoulders. She was stark naked underneath apart from two sparkly nipple clamps that tinkled when she moved. Sarah had the bizarre thought that they were actually really pretty and that she should add a new line to her business.

Niall groaned. 'Jesus, Vanessa!'

'She may as well know everything – you can't talk your

48

way out of this one,' said Vanessa, casually plucking a leopard-print thong from the bedside table. 'It can't get any worse for you.'

Niall met Sarah's eyes. His Adam's apple bobbed. 'Oh, it can, believe me.'

Sarah stepped out of her trance. 'Get out,' she said, quietly.

'Don't you think I'd better get dressed first?' Vanessa stepped into the leg of her thong, a smirk on her face.

'No, actually, I don't. Get out of my house.'

A great wave of rage hung over her head, on the brink of breaking. She took a step towards the other side of the bed, shaking with anger and shock.

Vanessa's cocky expression changed to dismay. She held up her hands. 'All right, love. I can see you and Ni need some time to talk. I'll just get me uniform first.'

Sarah flashed her teeth at Vanessa. 'Why don't you let me help you get dressed?'

Vanessa shook her head and struggled to pull up her thong. 'No, it's OK ...'

Sarah grabbed the nearest thing to hand: a purple glass tea light holder.

'Christ, no, Sarah!' Niall screamed a fraction before the tea light sailed through the air. Vanessa shrieked as the tea light hit the wall, bounced off and knocked the bedside lamp onto the floorboards. The lamp flickered and went off.

'Jesus, Sarah!'

Ignoring his shout, Sarah dashed around the bottom of the bed. Vanessa leapt onto the duvet.

'Arghhh!' Niall screamed as she kneeled on his genitals in her haste to get away from Sarah. She scrambled off the bed with the nipple clamps tinkling madly.

'Go on, get out of my house!' Sarah shouted as Vanessa fled out of the door.

'You're mad!' she screeched, scuttling onto the landing like a giant hairless spider.

Sarah followed her onto the landing, picking up the uniform shirt and trousers. She threw them down the stairs on top of Vanessa.

Vanessa clutched her clothes to her body. 'I can't go out like this. I need me boots!'

'Oh, I am soooo sorry, how rude of me. Here you are.' One after the other, Sarah hurled the boots down the stairs. They thumped against the wall and Vanessa swore as one whizzed past her head and knocked a picture of Niall on his Triumph clean off the wall. Clouds of plaster dust flew into the air.

'Your girlfriend is fucking mental!' Vanessa attempted to step into the boots but toppled against the wall.

'Yeah, I am. Hasn't Niall told you? I must be to have trusted him!' Sarah stood at the top of the stairs, not trusting herself to run down them in her condition.

Vanessa's hair and face were coated in dust. 'Keep away from me!' she screeched, hobbling through the front door.

As Vanessa fled, Sarah made her way downstairs, still trembling with shock.

Wearing one boot, with her clothes clutched to her boobs, Vanessa tinkled off down the icy path.

Sarah's shout echoed into the night after her. 'And don't come back!'

Wailing like a banshee, Vanessa scuttled up the pavement, still trying to put her clothes on. A light flicked on in the bedroom of their elderly neighbour who occupied the cottage next door. Sarah didn't care who heard the row. She slammed the door shut behind her and leaned against it, tears running down her face. She sank down with her back to the door when a bellow cut through her sobs.

'Sarah! Sarah? What's happened? Will someone untie me and take this feckin' tiara off?'

Chapter Six

Department of Behavioural Ecology

Fenland University

January 2nd

(Scientifically proven to be the most depressing day of the year)

Research Proposal

Objectives *To determine why, when a human male asks you to dance at a party, calls you a "sexy nurse" and snogs you in full view of your colleagues, he then proceeds to drop you like you had Ebola.*

To discover why male subject #2 allowed (half-witch/half-she-devil) female subject #1 to tie him to a bed and dress him up like a fairy. To discover whether there is a specific reason for this behaviour or whether man in question is just a shit, like 99% of the rest of his sex.

Design *Longitudinal cohort study.*

Setting *Male #1 Research institute.*

Male #2 County ambulance service.

Subjects Male #1. Fit and healthy, technically Scottish, demonstrably a genius and a fuckwit. Observed almost daily over six months and two weeks.

Male #2. Not quite so fit. Physically sound but clearly suffering from (temporary) insanity. Demonstrably a total shit with pervy tendencies. Observed daily over two years, five months.

Main outcome measures Determine male subject #1's behaviour and reasons thereof. Create method to alter male subject's pattern of behaviour to achieve desired outcome of date/sex/commitment, ideally all three.

Determine male subject #2's behaviour and reasons thereof. Create method to spontaneously make his tiny dick shrivel up and his balls drop off and/or realise what he has done and crawl back on his belly to lovely, amazing sister who will then walk all over him in her stilettos and tell him to fuck fuckity fuck off.

Results To be advised but not hopeful.

Conclusions To be determined.

Molly stopped typing and stared out of the window of the lab. The sky was the colour of an old dishcloth and big wet snowflakes were settling on the statue of Isaac Newton outside her window. It was a grey, soggy January the second and even Isaac looked pissed off. It also seemed wholly appropriate considering what had happened over the past thirty-six hours.

She'd been woken at nine a.m. by Sarah sobbing down the phone. Apparently, she'd got home to find Niall having kinky sex with a naked woman who drove his ambulance. Sarah had been almost hysterical – not that Molly blamed her – and

Molly had spent the rest of the day dispensing tissues, chocolate and vodka – for herself – at Sarah's cottage.

Molly had listened to the whole sorry story, almost in tears herself. Niall had apparently begged Sarah to forgive him for three hours, until Sarah had finally untied him from the bed and kicked him out. He'd fled to his mother's, blaming Sarah for causing Vanessa "mild hypothermia" and himself severe emotional distress. Sarah had then had to go around to her neighbour, Mrs Sugden, and apologise and explain that Vanessa wasn't a prostitute, but a friend of Niall's who'd been to a nearby fancy-dress party, got very drunk and sought refuge in the cottage before becoming violently deranged. Sarah couldn't bear to tell her neighbour the truth yet.

Molly had to admit that next to Sarah's woes, being publicly rejected by Ewan paled into insignificance. However, it was still humiliating and hurtful, especially as she had to work with him.

She returned to her paper, trying to concentrate until her desk phone rang. When she saw the extension number, she swore and braced herself.

'Good morning, Professor Baxter.'

'Um. Molly. Would you mind popping into my private office for a few minutes? If it's convenient, of course. I'd like to discuss our next grant application for the Love Bug.'

Molly inspected her nails before replying. 'Surely, you're referring to Hormone XTB229, Professor Baxter?'

'There's no need for sarcasm.'

'Of course not, Professor Baxter. I'll be up in five minutes, Professor Baxter.'

'Molly, can you please stop calling me Prof—'

Click. Burr. Molly winced. She'd dropped the receiver a

nanosecond sooner than she'd really intended. Or maybe not. Ewan didn't deserve an ounce of her guilt. She took a deep breath and attempted to get things into perspective. They'd both had too much to drink; it had been New Year's Eve. Surely, you were allowed to make a pass at your boss, photocopy your arse, dress as a naughty nurse, ask him what was under his kilt? It was the Season of Misrule and anyway, it was only a kiss ... followed by a moment of public humiliation that was excruciating but would pass. Eventually.

Not like Sarah had endured. Catching the bloke she adored and trusted shagging another woman; having her world turned upside down when she was at her most vulnerable. Molly should probably man up, although if "manning up" seemed to mean behaving like a cowardly louse, she'd rather stick pins in her eyes.

The blind rattled in the draught and the snow, now sleety, skittered against the pane. Molly held her finger on the file delete button and then changed her mind. Instead she pressed save and salted away the study in a file marked: "Reminder to reorder glove supplies" in a folder marked "Missellaneos", which was deliberately spelled wrongly to remind her not to attach it to a real email.

Gathering up her notepad, she trudged down the corridor towards Ewan's "private" office. So he wanted to discuss the abstract, did he? Well, she could tell him a few places where he could shove his "abstract". That was one of the advantages of having a PhD in behavioural ecology.

For half an hour, they discussed the abstract while Molly simmered silently. Judging by the way he kept fiddling with his pen, Ewan was squirming as much as her. Finally, the discussion was over.

'OK. I think that will do it,' he said, sounding relieved, like he'd been let off a life sentence.

Molly got to her feet, clutching her notebook to her chest. 'Right, I'll get back to work. I'm *so* busy in the lab.'

Ewan stared at her from his deep espresso eyes. Molly suddenly decided a stain on the tiles was intensely interesting.

'Before you go, I think it would be a good idea if we discussed the elephant in the room.'

Molly couldn't help herself. 'What elephant's that, then, Ewan? Are we moving on from primate research to pachyderms?'

'There's no need for sarcasm. I'm trying to be mature about this.'

'Really? And it was mature to snog me and pull a party popper out of my top and then get cold feet?'

'First, that party popper could have gone off at any moment and second, I didn't get cold feet.'

Molly snorted.

'I *didn't* get cold feet,' Ewan said. 'Believe me I *wanted* to ...' His voice tailed off.

'Wanted to what?'

'You know ...'

Molly put her notebook back on the desk and raised an eyebrow. 'Not really. Could you be more precise, please, Professor Baxter.'

'I wanted to take you to bed!' Ewan burst out then threw up his hands and groaned. He lowered his voice. 'Please don't make this any harder for me.'

'I wouldn't dream of making anything hard for you. Not after the other night.'

Ewan covered his face with his hand. Molly hated him and

herself for the shivery tingle in her limbs when he'd said, "take you to bed". It was pathetic.

'If you wanted to do it, why didn't you?' she said. 'Are you that worried about what those idiots in the lab think?'

'No, of course not!' He tapped his pen on the table. 'No, that's a lie. Yes. Yes I *am* but not because I'm put off by a few stupid comments. It's what those comments have made me realise.'

'And that is?'

'I don't have to spell it out, do I? It would be unprofessional of me. If I sleep with you, start seeing you, how can I supervise you and work with you after that? What if I need to promote you or interview you for a job? What if I have to ...'

'Discipline me?' she cut in.

'For God's sake. Can you please not say things like that?'

'Why not?'

His pen clattered onto the desk top. 'You know perfectly well why not and there'll be no need for discipline, because you – and I – are going to behave with utmost discretion and professionalism. We are going to focus one hundred and ten per cent on our work.'

'I don't think that's actually possible, Professor Baxter, or did you fail statistics?'

He glared at her. Molly fancied him more than ever, if it was possible. 'We are going to focus totally on our research, making this project a success and publishing our results. There will be gossip and speculation, naturally, for a few days but it will pass. People will soon realise that there is nothing between us beyond a professional relationship.'

'Of course not, Professor,' Molly said coolly.

'Please stop calling me Professor. You'll thank me for this

one day. One day very soon. There is nothing worse, believe me, than a relationship failing, and that's when the two people have to see each other every day at work. If you want to know what it's like to hate the sight of someone you once cared for, then let's go ahead and shag each other's brains out for a few weeks but then it will all go wrong. Office romances are a recipe for disaster. Trust me.'

She was momentarily stunned into silence by this outburst.

'So you care about your career more than being happy?' she said, eventually.

'No, I care about *yours*.'

His phone rang. He mouthed "fuck" before snatching up the handset. 'What is it? I'm in a bloody meeting ... Oh, yes, Dame Eleanor. I'm so sorry. Yes, I was working late last night and went to the party on New Year's Eve. You're right, I should probably get more sleep but you know how busy we are ... Come to your office now? No ... no ... I'm almost done here. I'll be up in five minutes ... Yes, coffee would be a great idea.'

She sat, arms folded, enjoying him squirming as he spoke to their eminent head of faculty.

Eventually, he put the phone down. 'And, that,' he said quietly, 'is *exactly* what I meant about bringing relationships into the workplace. Now, as you heard, I have a meeting with Dame Eleanor. I expect you to go back to the lab and get on with the abstract for that paper. I want to get into a decent journal with the two of us as co-authors, which can only be good for your career. And the next time we meet, I also expect things to be back on civil, professional terms. Am I making myself clear?' he said coldly.

There was something in his tone that told Molly not to argue. He was, after all, her boss and she'd pushed him further than she ever thought she'd dare. It was all hideously unfair of course, but possibly, maybe, he had a point and she *really* wanted her name as co-author on the paper. It would be a big thing to be associated with Ewan Baxter, in scientific terms if not in other ways.

She picked up her notebook again. 'Perfectly clear,' she said and walked to the door, hoping that the clogging in her throat wasn't the start of an infection.

'I'm sorry, Molly. It just wouldn't work between us,' said Ewan. 'No matter how much I like and respect you. Let's not spoil what is, after all, a great working relationship.'

Molly's favoured replies included an expletive but she stopped short. 'You're probably right,' she muttered and shut the door.

Chapter Seven

In the Tiara Kabin, Sarah fixed on a smile as her first wedding client of the year unfurled a list of demands that would rival a hip-hop diva. She just hoped her customer wouldn't notice her puffy eyes, but luckily Cassandra Burling rarely noticed anything that didn't stare back from her own mirror.

'I'd want the pearls dyed to *exactly* match my shoes. I've brought one of them so you can see what I want,' said Cassandra Burling, 'and there will be six matching hair slides for the bridesmaids and two smaller ones for the flower girls.'

'I'm sure I can help ...' said Sarah with a smile, while silently screaming.

'*And* I want a Swarovski crystals dove with a pearl in his beak to symbolise our union. And I want the bridesmaids' hair clips all done to match but not as nice as mine, obvs. *Then* there's the necklaces for my mum and his mum, not that the evil cow deserves anything but we can't leave her out or she'll probably cut us out of her will ...'

Finally Cassandra drew breath. She picked at the plastic on the edge of the coffee table with a Barbie-pink nail.

'You can do that by the end of the month, can't you?' she added, flicking a piece of plastic onto the floor of the workshop.

Sarah swallowed down a gasp of dismay. 'The end of this *month*? As in the end of January?'

'Yeah. Why?'

'I thought you told me your wedding was in May?'

'Oh, it *was* but we've got a cancellation at a theme park. It's on Valentine's Day and there's a cable telly contest for Valentine's Day brides. I want to have the ceremony on the Termination ride at Adrenalin Park. We'll be upside down while the celebrant marries us but I still want to look ahmazing. If you win, the telly company give you all your money back for the wedding and honeymoon.' Cassandra folded her arms. 'No one will be able to beat *that* idea.'

Sarah wanted to vom at the very *thought* of being upside down. 'No. I doubt if they will, but won't the headdresses fall off on the ride?'

'Oh, you'll come up with something and if I win, your tiaras and stuff will be all over *Brekkie*.'

'Wow,' said Sarah.

'Anyway, we've brought everything forward and I need the headdresses for a trial run at the salon at the end of January. You can do it, can't you?' Cassandra's voice took on a vaguely menacing tone.

'Well, there's a lot of work, especially if I have to adapt them to being worn upside down, at high speed with all that G force.'

'Well, I'd have thought you'd have been gagging for the work, and maybe offering me a discount if I'm going to advertise your work on *Brekkie* ... but if you don't need the business, I could try someone else.'

'Yes, I do. Of course, I want the business and of course, I'll do it.' Sarah forced a smile to her face. She needed the business more than ever now that Niall had moved out. 'Don't worry, everything will be ready for your big day,' she said soothingly.

'Good, because I want it all to be totally one hundred and ten per cent perfect.'

'Of course, it's once in a lifetime.'

Cassandra examined her nail. 'Well, yeah, I suppose so. If it lasts. But that's marriage, innit – a lottery?' she added cheerfully.

Cassandra didn't sound the slightest bit bothered by the prospect of her relationship not lasting and Sarah couldn't say she was shocked or even surprised. Cassandra wasn't the first bride she'd had who looked on the wedding mainly as an excuse to have a party and be a princess for the day. And after all, wasn't that what *she* was selling? Be a princess. Wear a tiara. Pretend you're Kate or Meghan or Princess Aurora? Sarah *was* in the fairy-tale business after all, but she'd liked to think she had a slightly less cynical approach than some of the suppliers – a more personal touch, a genuine sincerity that most customers recognised even if they didn't all appreciate it.

'The headdresses will all be ready,' she said, hardening her heart and opening her appointments book. 'Shall we say you come round for a fitting four weeks from today?'

'Fab.' Cassandra studied the Kabin, sighing wistfully. 'What a cute little hut this is. It reminds me of a fairy grotto. I wish I could give up my job and play around with crystals and beads.'

Sarah restrained herself only by a great effort of will. 'So do I.'

Digging her Swarovski-encrusted pearlescent pink iPhone

out of her Mulberry bag, Cassandra left the Kabin with a tiny finger wave.

After she'd left, Sarah made herself a ginger tea and sat down. She couldn't really criticise Cassandra. Who was the deluded one? Cassandra who was determined to make a statement on this one day – and stuff the lifetime afterwards, which was optional anyway? Or Molly who was, despite her protests, patently in love with her ambitious, frigid boss.

Or Sarah herself? Deluding herself that she and Niall were different. Special.

Until now Sarah had been happy that she'd given up a decent job with a bank to pursue the creative hobby she loved. She'd spent enough time helping other people get their businesses up and running in the decade or so that she'd worked at the bank. Although she didn't begrudge a nanosecond of the time she'd devoted to making sure Molly had a good start in life, she'd been so excited at finally being able to do something for herself that was a bit risky, a bit crazy and a lot wonderful.

So what if some people at the bank had thought and told her she was selling brides a cheesy, sparkly pipe dream? She was doing what she loved best, while trying to make a future for herself and her baby.

Closing her appointments book, she took a few deep breaths and told herself to snap out of her gloom and get on with her work. Cassandra was her only appointment for the day, although she had several workshops to prepare for later in the week.

In fact, she ought to get started on Cassandra's commission right now, but she simply couldn't face it. It was far more tempting to curl up in bed and bawl her eyes out again –

although even that would mean sleeping in the bed where Niall had been shagging Vanessa.

She locked the garden gate as Cassandra roared off in her BMW and a lump formed in her throat. The early morning drizzle had cleared and the sky was now an unblemished blue. Birds cawed from the cottage chimney, the sun gave the creamy stone a mellow hue and the whole place looked impossibly cute and picturesque. She and Niall had worked their butts off to afford it. She swallowed down her tears as she heard the "beep beep" of the bin lorry reversing up the lane. It wouldn't do to blub in front of the bin men and anyway, she would *never* have Niall back again, even if he begged her on his knees in front of the bin men.

She hurried back to the workshop. Anger had replaced the initial shock of finding Niall in bed with Vanessa, combined with worries about what their split meant for her future and that of the baby. She needed to make her business work more than ever if she was going to be a single mum.

Another wave of nausea washed over her but she took a few deep breaths. She had to think of the baby now though it was hard to imagine a life beyond the cottage and the Tiara Kabin. She remembered the days they'd toiled on it in rain, hail and shine the previous autumn. It had a space where she could run her small workshops and entertain clients, with a tiny kitchenette for preparing drinks and snacks. Niall had got a mate to plumb in the sink and Sarah's electrician cousin had wired it up to the mains. It was hardly the Grand Arcade but she loved it and the investment had finally been starting to pay off.

Closing the door behind her, she took some long, slow breaths. If she had to move out of the cottage, she'd have to find somewhere with room for the Kabin. But where and how could she possibly afford another place near Cambridge with outdoor space on her own?

On the desk, a light flashed on the phone. A message had come in while she'd shown Cassandra to the gate.

It could be Niall again ... saying he'd made a massive mistake and begging her to let him back. She wouldn't, of course ... absolutely no way.

Sarah listened then rolled her eyes as she heard heavy breathing then a clatter and a groan and someone muttering, 'Oh bugger.' Her finger hovered over the delete key. The last thing she needed was a pervert asking the colour of her knickers.

'Erm. Really sorry about that. I dropped the phone.'

Sarah listened. It was a man's voice. Neutral accent, older than her, maybe, but not much? There was more heavy breathing. Sarah's finger touched the button then he spoke.

'I was wondering if you er ... had any places left on your tiara-making workshop?'

Sarah removed her finger from the button. OK. Probably not a pervert and it wasn't unheard of for guys to attend a workshop but ... She'd had a couple, once, who wanted to make matching Swarovski crystal cravat pins for their civil partnership but, without stereotyping people – actually she *was* stereotyping people – she was ninety-nine per cent sure this guy must be gay. Or he could be a cross dresser, of course, which was fine, or at a push, the director of a local am dram group.

'The tiara's not for me, of course,' he said.

'Of course not,' Sarah muttered to herself.

'It's for my daughter who's getting married ...'

Sarah arched an eyebrow. 'Really?'

'I know it must sound strange …'

'Just a little.'

'But it's something I want to do.'

Sarah sighed. She really didn't need to know all this in an answerphone message but this poor guy clearly needed to get it off his chest.

'So if you can phone me back, I'd appreciate it.' Brisker now, faster and more confident. He'd obviously got through the worst part and felt on safer ground. 'And if you could call me back as soon as possible, I'd be grateful. I'm in a bit of a rush, you see.'

'A rush? Hey, you should meet Cassandra.'

'Thanks.'

The phone went dead.

Sarah sighed and tidied up the bundle of bridal magazines that Cassandra had flicked through while Sarah had made her a coffee. Behind her the phone started buzzing again. Sarah's heart beat a little faster. This time it really might be Niall but she was frozen to the spot, not knowing what to say to him if he called.

The answerphone pinged again and the same voice echoed around the workshop.

'Erm. Sorry for this but it's Liam Cipriani again. I don't think I left my number in the last message. Or my name for that matter. But as I said, it's Liam. Cipriani. Here it is. 0787 …'

'No shit, Sherlock?' Sarah's shoulders slumped as with another apology and a further request to "phone him back as soon as she possibly could", Liam rang off.

She hovered by the phone a few moments longer, just in case he felt the need to tell her his life story or provide his inside leg measurement, before stacking the magazines in the middle of the table. As she rubbed the lipstick off Cassandra's mug in the sink, she wondered why Liam had booked when he sounded as if he'd rather have his chest hairs plucked out one by one than attend a tiara-making workshop. Why was he coming at all, rather than his daughter?

And she really should phone him back right now.

'Hello!'

Startled, Sarah saw a face at the window. A bald red-faced guy in a hi-vis vest grinned back at her. She opened the door and the cold hit her.

'Erm, excuse me, love, this dropped out of the bin and I'm not sure you want to throw it out or if you dropped it on your way to your shed?'

The bin man held up the tiara, slightly deformed but still recognisable. It had a string of spaghetti dangling from it.

'Oh, I see. I ...' Sarah couldn't think of a way to say why she'd thrown the tiara in the bin, but worse than that, she couldn't let the tiara go. Not even after its last wearer had been Niall, and Vanessa had possibly worn it too, for all she knew.

'You want it then or shall I chuck it on the wagon?' he asked.

'No. I'll have it.'

She took the tiara from him, shivering. 'Thanks.'

He grinned. 'Pleasure. Happy New Year.'

Sarah looked at the tiara. It was slightly bent but it had always been a reject. It was one from the early days when she was still learning her craft. Not good enough to sell but one of the first she'd actually been pleased with. The first one worth keeping.

The bin man jogged back up the path, steam rising from his head in the chilly air. Sarah stood by the door, the tiara between her frozen fingertips. The string of spaghetti slithered to the paving stones. Why hadn't she let him take the bloody thing to the tip, which was what it deserved – just like Niall.

Chapter Eight

A couple of days later, Sarah sat nervously opposite the GP in her surgery. The doctor was new and probably even younger than Sarah. She beamed in delight. 'So, Mrs Havers, you're almost eight weeks pregnant. Congratulations.'

Sarah didn't know what to say. Of course, she already knew she was pregnant, but hearing it confirmed officially was surreal.

The GP smiled encouragingly. 'Pregnancy and motherhood is a huge change for any woman and it can come as a bit of a shock. Are you OK?'

'Yes ... yes, like you say, it's a bit of a shock.'

'Does your partner know?'

'Not yet.' Sarah thought of the six missed calls on her phone. Niall had been trying to reach her over the past few days but she hadn't trusted herself to answer him. Her focus had been on the baby and today's doctor's appointment. 'It's Ms Havers by the way.'

Sarah didn't think the GP had heard her reply because she just carried on. 'Going by the date of your LMP, your due date should be the thirtieth of August. I'll send you for a scan as soon as possible and the midwifery team will take over from there. You'll also need ...' The GP went on, listing all the places Sarah needed to be and people she had to see and things she couldn't eat, drink or touch. That was one thing then: she now had a great excuse for never going near goat's cheese.

'Now, I need to ask a few questions about your family health history. Is there any history of ...?' The GP reeled off a list of diseases and genetic conditions.

Sarah knew the answer to a few of the questions but most were answered with: 'I'm not sure.'

'I'm sorry to be so vague but my parents died when I was a teenager so I can't ask them. I'll have to phone my auntie and uncle and see if they know.'

'And I'm sorry to hear about your parents,' said the GP, looking genuinely sympathetic. 'And all these questions and information must seem like an awful lot to take in when you're still coming to terms with being pregnant. Maybe you can ask your partner about his own family history when you give him the news?'

Oh hell, she *had* to tell Niall at some point, if only in case there was some terrible genetic problem in his family that she didn't know about. It wasn't likely as he'd never mentioned any problems but then, they'd never discussed having children. She felt rather than heard the buzzing of her phone in her bag at her feet.

'Yes. Yes, I will,' she said and hurried out of the surgery.

There were two more calls from Niall. Knowing she couldn't ignore him forever, Sarah found a parking space on a side street near one of the university departments and walked through the Backs into the centre of the city where she was due to meet Molly. She listened to one of Niall's messages.

'Sarah. Where the hell are you? I've been trying to call you.

You must let me explain about the other night ... me and Ness. It's not what you think. It was ... a huge mistake.'

'Gah!'

Sarah's snort of disgust sent a flock of ducks scattering onto the river, quacking loudly. Even though it was winter, there were still plenty of tourists taking selfies, loitering in the middle of the road and almost getting run over by bikes. Students whizzed around the narrow streets by the market square, ringing their bells when a hapless pedestrian dared to cross. Sarah wandered in and out of JoJo Maman Bébé and John Lewis, looking at the cribs and baby baths, the tiny pairs of jeans and miniature Ugg boots.

Her eyes watered at the price tags but her baby would need all of these things from somewhere. She definitely wanted it to have them, except it would be summer when she or he made an appearance and she – or he – would need pretty dresses or cute shorts and mini jelly sandals. She would have to provide it all, with Niall's help, of course. The responsibility was overwhelming ... and apart from Molly, there was no family to share the news with, no mum or dad ... Her parents would have loved a grandchild, if they'd been here. God, she'd give anything to share her news with them, even if she and Ni had split up.

She'd give anything to turn back the clock. She stopped on the edge of the pavement, her legs suddenly weak and her head light. It was only the shock of the past few weeks and the baby making her feel faint. It was understandable, normal ... Her legs almost gave way and she stumbled into the road.

'Whoa!'

She stepped back onto the pavement just as a cyclist

whizzed by, so close she felt the rush of air against her face. Sarah hadn't even noticed him approach. Had she got baby brain already? She glanced around, expecting people to stare or roll their eyes at her doziness but everyone hurried past, oblivious to her presence. That's what it would be like from now on, she thought. She was on her own.

Feeling hot despite the bitter air, she hurried along the narrow lane that snaked between the market and the street where the café was situated. A cool drink and a sit-down would help but the stone walls of the colleges seemed to press in on her and she had to dodge round tourists taking photos outside porters' lodges.

Although it had started to sleet, she pulled her scarf out of her coat to let the sharp air cool her chest, but she still felt hot and light-headed. If she could make the café and sit down, gulp down a glass of iced water, she'd be OK ... She spotted the railings outside the café, with student notices and playbills fluttering in the wind, and put her hand over her mouth.

Oh no, she was going to be sick! But far better to throw up in the café toilets than vom over a tourist.

She hurried down the pavement and stepped onto the wet cobbles.

'Look out!'

A bell jangled loudly and she felt a sharp tug on the back of her coat.

'Hey!' The curse from the cyclist was already just a streak of noise.

'Are you OK?' A tall man in a black padded jacket held her by the elbow.

Sarah caught her breath 'Yes. I ... yes, of course.'

'You do know you almost stepped right in front of that idiot?'

'I know. I wasn't looking where I was going. I think I might be the idiot.'

'He was on his mobile, the twat, but you did seem to be in a world of your own.'

If Sarah hadn't felt so crap, she might have been offended but she didn't have the energy. 'I'm not feeling that great, but thanks.'

'No problem.'

'You can let go of my elbow now,' she said. 'You're Ewan, aren't you?'

Ewan's bushy eyebrows met in a frown that weirdly did nothing to spoil his ruggedly handsome looks. 'Do I know you?'

'I'm Moll's sister.' Sarah hoped she wouldn't throw up on his Timberland boots.

'Mol?'

'Dr Molly Havers. Your colleague from the lab? I was at the – um ... New Year party with her.' Sarah could have kicked herself for mentioning the scene of Molly's humiliation but it was too late now.

'Oh yes. *That* Molly, of course. Sorry.' He glanced down at Sarah. 'You do look pale. Are you ill?'

Wow, he *is* blunt, thought Sarah. No wonder Molly's having a hard time with him and judging by the way he hadn't instantly recognised her sister's name, it didn't bode well.

'I just felt a bit light-headed and nauseated for a second.'

'Do you want to sit down? I can get you a glass of water from the café?' His dark brown eyes held genuine concern and boy, was he gorgeous. Poor Molly, thought Sarah, he might be a bit of a prat but close up he was a real heartbreaker.

'I think I was just too hot but I'm feeling a bit better now and I don't want to put you to any trouble. You must be busy. In the lab ...' she added, remembering Molly's comments about her boss being a workaholic.

'It's no trouble. I came out for some fresh air, and to be honest I could do with a break. I've been in the lab since four o'clock this morning.'

Ewan smiled, the way Sarah had seen him smile when he'd asked Molly to dance, only this time he was sober, she was sure, unless he had a secret daytime drinking habit. Sarah hesitated a moment longer then decided. Surely this was the perfect opportunity to bring Molly and Ewan together on neutral territory?

She threw him a smile. 'Then for your sake, I'll say yes. Thanks.'

'Good. Is the Old Church Café OK? It's right opposite.'

'Perfect.'

By the time they'd found a table in the café, Sarah's sickness had subsided although she still felt what her and Molly's mum had liked to call "peculiar". However, seated in a cool corner of the café next to a window that Ewan had insisted on opening, she was beginning to feel more normal. While Ewan queued at the counter, she glanced at the text she'd just had from Molly and felt slightly guilty.

Running 10 min late. Just setting off from lab. See you asap. x J

Would Molly thank her or be furious? Would Ewan be embarrassed? Sarah didn't think so; he seemed quite kind and considerate under the blunt exterior and he must fancy

Molly or he wouldn't have come onto her at the party, even if he was pissed. Perhaps he was being kind to Sarah specifically because she was Molly's sister: maybe he wanted to show Molly he did have a softer side. Then again, Sarah thought, she might be making the situation far worse than it already was, but it was too late now.

Carrying a tray, Ewan weaved his way between the tables, drawing admiring glances from several of the other customers. When Molly arrived, how would Sarah explain that she'd arranged to meet her and hadn't mentioned the fact to Ewan? Oh shh ... sugar.

With a smile, he put the tray in front of her. 'OK. I got a glass of iced tap water and a ginger tea and some ginger biscuits. It's meant to be good for nausea although of course it's purely the hydration and rise in blood sugar that helps.'

'Um. Thank you,' said Sarah, wondering if this could really be the cold and mercurial man who'd dumped Molly at the party. 'How much do I owe you?' she asked.

'Nothing.'

'Oh, I can't let you pay.'

Ewan looked at her sternly but not unkindly. 'Shut up and drink your tea.'

Right, thought Sarah, I will do. Bloody hell, Molly had definitely bitten off more than she could chew with this one. She was mightily glad he wasn't her boss and that she didn't have a boss at all because if she was going to feel sick, faint and burst into tears at random moments, she didn't know how she would have held down a conventional job as she once did. But then again, a job would have come with its salary and rights and maternity leave ...

'Better?' Ewan cut into her thoughts.

'Yes, thanks.'

Sarah sipped the water and tried the ginger tea while Ewan tackled a large cappuccino. Molly had told her he was an Iberian Celt. Sarah wasn't entirely sure what that meant genetically but it had produced a very alpha human being and Sarah could understand exactly why Molly had fallen for him. It must be excruciating to work together on a project like the Love Bug ...

'Are you very busy at work? Molly says so,' she said, hoping Molly would put in an appearance soon.

'Does she?' said Ewan, his interest piqued. Sarah wondered if she'd said the right thing.

'Well, she obviously never tells me anything about what you're working on,' said Sarah hastily. 'That would be unprofessional. She loved Science at school and always had her head in a textbook. I preferred English and Art.'

Ewan smiled. 'I enjoyed Art but I had to drop it. My teachers thought I had too much on my plate with my Science GSCEs and A levels and they were probably right. What do you do now?'

'I run my own business.'

'Really? What do you do?'

'I used to work in a bank. I managed the SME liaison team but now I um ... have my own small craft business.'

'Craft? What sort? Sculpture? Woodwork?'

'Jewellery, actually.' Sarah knew she should be proud of her business and hated herself for feeling embarrassed about it but Molly had banged on so often about Ewan's fearsome intellectual reputation.

'Silversmith? Or another material?'

'I do use silver wire. I make tiaras ...'

'That sounds high-powered. For royalty?' He smiled – briefly – probably to show he was joking and wasn't used to it, Sarah decided. Whatever, she wasn't offended at his joke.

'In my dreams. No, for brides, mainly, though some of them do behave like princesses. Most, in fact,' she said, thinking of Cassandra Burling's demands. 'I sometimes do commissions and I run workshops for brides and people who want to create their own jewellery.' Like Liam Cipriani, she thought, making a mental note to call him back.

'I must admit that bridal tiaras are out of my sphere of expertise,' said Ewan.

But he *was* married once, Molly had said. Sarah wondered if the ex-Mrs Baxter had worn a tiara. Somehow, she couldn't picture it.

'How are you feeling? Do you think you should see your GP about the faintness?'

'I already have. In fact, I saw her this morning. I'm pregnant.'

Ewan looked taken aback but then nodded. 'Aha. Congratulations.'

'Thanks.' Sarah managed to squeeze the muscles of her mouth into a very fleeting smile. Even though Niall was a shit, she still desperately wanted this baby, but Ewan was too sharp not to notice her reluctance.

'Did I say the wrong thing?'

'No. You didn't. It's just ... well, my partner and I have split up.' Christ, it hurt her heart to even say it out loud. 'The night of the party actually.'

'Bummer. I'm sorry.'

'Yeah.'

Ewan fiddled with the wrapper off the biscuits. 'It's never easy, when a relationship goes wrong. Spectacularly wrong in 'my case.' He glanced up at her. 'I'd like to say it gets easier and I suppose it does but it takes a long time.'

'How long?' asked Sarah, wishing he hadn't said anything that made her heart hurt. But now like a child drawn to a flame, she had to feel the pain, know the worst from someone who'd been through it.

'Everyone's different, obviously, but for me? Six months before I even accepted she'd gone.'

'And now? How long has it been since she left you?'

Ewan blew out a breath. 'Two years, eleven months and ten days.'

Sarah's jaw dropped. 'Please tell me I can't feel this bad for the next three years.'

'Oh no, I hope not. You won't, I'm sure.'

Sarah's disbelief must have been obvious because Ewan's voice took on a slightly more soothing tone. 'Sorry. I shouldn't have said anything. I'm making things worse, aren't I? I do that: make things worse for people whenever I open my mouth. I think I'm trying to help but I end up making people feel like shit. Anna – my ex – said I was the most tactless man on the planet. It was one of the reasons she ran off with a colleague, along with me being a workaholic and possibly a little bit obsessive.'

Even though she wasn't reassured, Sarah managed a smile for him. 'You're not making things worse. I don't feel they could be any worse at the moment and I know that getting over Niall will be awful, even though I would never take him back of course, which is exactly why I can't face it.'

'Well, at least you don't work with this guy. Do you?'

'No. He's a paramedic.' Hot anger surged through her veins again as she relived the scene in the cottage bedroom. 'I came home after the party to find him having sex in our bed with the bloody woman who drives the ambulance. He was wearing one of my tiaras.'

'Bloody hell ...' Ewan had hissed the words through his teeth but a nearby customer glared at him. He lowered his voice. 'That's terrible.'

All Sarah could do was nod.

'Anna left me for one of the post-docs in my lab at my old uni. She was his boss and I was her colleague. It was crap having to work together every day. I left in the end and got the job here in Cambridge but the last three months were a hell on earth, seeing her and him together every day.'

'I'll bet it was,' said Sarah innocently, knowing that Molly had told her about Ewan's lecture on the perils of people working – and shagging – together.

'However, I've learned my lesson. I will never get involved with anyone I work with again as much for their sake as well as mine,' said Ewan firmly.

'It sounds awful.'

'Everyone in the lab knew what had happened between the three of us and I know most were waiting for me to have a meltdown or us all to have a bloody duel or something. People ended up taking sides and the atmosphere in the lab was a nightmare. You know, refusing to share offices or go to the pub together, sitting separately at lunch; acting like school-kids. It was impossible to behave professionally or focus on our work and excruciating to have everyone at work knowing about our private lives.' Ewan went on gloomily. 'I took my eye off the ball and we missed out on a major grant that was vital to our work.'

Sarah felt sorry for him but she was way more worried for

her sister's chances with Ewan. They were looking worse by the minute and she had a suspicion that Ewan might be telling her his sorry tale precisely because he knew Sarah would be bound to pass on the conversation to Molly and warn her off. Oh shit.

Molly breezed up to the table in her hi-vis jacket carrying a cycle helmet. 'Sarah! I am *so* sorry I'm late ...' She stared at Ewan like he was a zombie. 'Ewan? What are you doing here?'

'I was just going actually.' He scraped back his chair and got to his feet with indecent haste.

Sarah cringed on Molly's behalf. 'I wasn't feeling well and Ewan saw me. He bought me a drink,' she said hastily.

'I can see that. Why didn't you text me?'

'I ... um ...' Sarah floundered. Ewan didn't have to be a professor to realise that Sarah had expected Molly all along.

'I must go. I'd hate to interrupt your lunch,' he said coolly.

'Wait, Ewan. I was going to mention that Molly was meeting me here but when we got talking, I um ... forgot. Thanks for the tea and helping me.'

Ewan shrugged. 'No problem. Take care. Bye, Molly.'

'You don't have to go.' Sarah cringed as she and Molly both spoke at once and both sounded desperate.

'I've been away long enough. Molly, see you later. I presume you were planning to come in later to finish the sequencing?'

'Yes, but ...'

But Ewan was out of there, leaving Molly glaring at Sarah.

'Right. I'm going to get some more tea and when I come back,' she said in an ominous tone, 'I want you to tell me what Ewan said and I mean *everything*. Don't spare me. I want you to be *brutally* honest.'

Sarah wasn't in the mood for being brutal. She wasn't even

in the mood for being a teeny bit harsh. She would, eventually and tactfully, drop hints about Ewan's private life but she wasn't sure Molly could cope with the whole truth in one go.

Molly put a cup of ginger tea in front of Sarah and a hot chocolate topped with cream and marshmallows for her. The sight of the cream made Sarah feel woozy so she sipped her tea.

'OK?' Molly asked.

'Yes, thanks.'

'Good. Now, spill.'

'We, um ... just talked about the weather, mainly.'

'The weather? Ewan doesn't register if it's arctic or tropical, he spends so long in the lab. You *must* have talked about other stuff.'

'Honestly, I wasn't feeling very well and I almost walked in front of a cyclist and he brought me in here and then, you came.'

'Just what I suspected. He fancies you.' Molly scooped some of the cream, and it oozed over the rim into her saucer.

Sarah tried to avert her eyes. 'He doesn't fancy me. He was just being kind because he's a nice guy but I can see what you mean about him being blunt ... Molly, don't do that thing with your lips, like you're pissed off because I swear on my life that Ewan likes *you*, because he pulled silly string out of your boobs and he snogged you with tongues and told you he wanted to take you to bed. He feels sorry for me and he wanted a break and a chat to someone who is nothing to do with the lab ... Men don't get much opportunity to talk about their feelings so I guess he just took a chance.'

'Ewan looking for the chance to talk about his feelings?'

Molly snorted chocolate on the table. 'But he must have known that whatever he "shared" would get straight back to me. So come on, share.'

Sarah tried, as tactfully as she could, to relay what Ewan had told her. Molly munched a pain au chocolat gloomily while Sarah relayed the conversation.

'Jesus, you've found out more about his private life in ten minutes than I have in ten months. He hinted to me that his split with his wife had caused a lot of trouble at work but you got all the details. He must have *known* you'd pass it on. It's a message to me: back off, there's no hope.'

'I'm not sure he did tell me so I could warn you. I think he genuinely wanted someone to talk to from outside of work.'

'But he knows you're my sister. He must have had an ulterior motive.'

'Mol, have you ever thought that you might be overthinking this?'

'Overthinking is my job.' Molly paused. 'He *must* fancy you.'

'You're wrong and even if he did like me in *that* way – which I'm absolutely sure he doesn't – it wouldn't matter. He is gorgeous and he's nice but I don't want Ewan. I don't want anyone. I just want things back the way they were.'

'Oh, hon, I wish I could do something to help you ... Are you absolutely sure Ewan didn't say anything else about me?'

By the time Molly had drunk the chocolate and eaten her pastry, Sarah had almost managed to convince her that Ewan hadn't said anything momentous. Eventually, just as Sarah had despaired of ever being let off the hook, Molly gave her a sympathetic look.

'You do look knackered. Here's me, obsessing over bloody

Ewan again and you have real problems. How did you get on at the doctor's? Have they given you a due date?'

'Uh-huh. Towards the end of August.'

'Wow. That's a long time away.'

'It seems horrendously close to me.'

'I suppose so, if you're the one with the baby. Oh, ignore me, Sarah, I'm hopeless. I may know a lot about reproduction in theory, but in practice, I'm worse than clueless.'

'Join the club.'

'God, I hope not. Not yet anyway!'

They both laughed. 'Even though I really wanted a baby one day, I hadn't planned for it to happen like this. It's like one of those bad dreams where you think you've got to do your exams again and you haven't done any revision. Only worse. Much worse.'

Molly laughed. 'I'm sorry but that does sound horrifying. I'll do everything I can to help, in my useless way. I'll never forget the way you helped me through A levels and uni. Even when I was an arsey little cow, you were there for me.'

'I'm glad you remember being arsey,' said Sarah, smiling. 'But you don't owe me anything. I did it because I wanted to and Mum and Dad would have wanted me to. This is totally different. You can't wave your magic wand over me or magic up a solution this time. Neither of us can.'

Sarah shoved a clump of croissant in her mouth to distract herself then thought, almonds? Was she allowed those?

'Have you told Niall yet?' Molly asked. 'Even though you hate him right now, and I don't blame you, hon, he needs to know. After all he was responsible for fifty per cent of it. Although that's not quite true – Niall's will be more like forty-nine-point nine per cent because you'll pass on the

83

mitochondrial DNA, of course … that's Mum's DNA too, and Gran's and our great-grandma's …'

Molly's voice tailed off. Sarah knew what she was thinking; she didn't have to ask. How much their parents would have loved to share this moment; how proud and thrilled and angry and hurt they would have been, all at once. Molly stared into her mug, avoiding Sarah's eyes, probably, not wanting to see her own grief reflected. Neither of them dared share what they were thinking about their parents. The news about Niall and the baby had brought the loss so near the surface for both of them all over again. It wouldn't take much, Sarah knew, for them to start bawling the café down.

'Is the cheating little toe rag still staying at his mum's?' Molly asked eventually. Her voice was tight and fierce.

Even with a mouthful of tears and croissant, Sarah managed a brief smile at Molly's sisterly loyalty. She didn't fancy Ni's chances if he walked into the café at this particular moment. She could well imagine him pinned on a specimen board like some helpless insect. Sarah found that idea quite comforting.

'He's tried to call me. At least ten times in fact and um, he left me a message … He wants me to meet him. He says he's "eaten up with guilt" and wants to know if I could ever forgive him.'

'What? No way!' Molly burst out.

Sarah cringed as diners at the nearby tables stared at them. Molly glared back and they quickly looked away.

'Sorry, Sarah, but how dare he ask you that. You're not going to see him, are you? Or get back with him?'

'Of course not. What do you think I am? I haven't even answered his calls yet. I don't trust myself, but I will have to speak to him sometime, even if I'd rather never see the slime-ball again.'

'I know, I know ...' said Molly glumly. 'I suppose you're right. You will have to tell him about the baby. He is the father and you can't do this alone.'

You can't do this alone. Sarah was stung by the statement, even though Molly was right. 'Why not?' she said slowly. 'In fact, why does he have to be involved at all? He's forfeited the right and thousands of women bring up families on their own.'

'I – well, I guess there's no reason ...' Molly said warily. Sarah realised her sister was trying desperately not to upset her. 'You're independent and I know you'll cope brilliantly, but *surely*, he ought to take the rap for his part in it? He definitely ought to give you financial support.'

Sarah knew that Molly was right but doing what was right wasn't high on her list of priorities. She was drowning in a morass of confusing emotions. Anger and grief, excitement over the baby despite everything. The whole thing was completely overwhelming and even though she knew she wasn't thinking logically, she didn't care. 'I suppose so,' she said. 'But I can't face it yet. Before I tell *him*, I need to get used to the fact I'm going to be a mother first.'

Molly left her with a huge hug and they went their separate ways. By the time Sarah got back to the cottage, the answer-phone was beeping with four messages. Sod it, she *had* to phone Liam Cipriani back. She pushed the button and scrolled through a message from Cassandra, a PPI company and a friend from her yoga class.

She braced herself for the second message from Liam, doubtless accusing her of ignoring him.

'Sarah, it's me. We need to talk.'

Niall's voice, low and annoyed, rasped through the phone line.

'Too late for that,' she shouted, drowning out the rest of the message so that she had to suffer the agony of replaying it.

'I know you won't answer your mobile but I have to see you. Can I come over tonight for a chat?'

'A chat? What do you think this is? The *Graham Norton Show*?' Sarah glared at the phone but her fingers twitched nonetheless.

'Are you there, darlin'? I'm worried about you. I've been a mess since the other night. I almost had to go off sick. I can't stand not hearing your voice. Just a word from you to let me know you're OK would be enough ...'

Sarah's hand hovered over the phone to pick it up and immediately call him back. Niall sounded weary and beaten down. She had no sympathy, obviously, but she did believe he was genuinely worried about her.

'I'll be round at half past seven whether you reply to this or not. It can't be any earlier because I'm on shift tonight. Please just hear me out for five minutes. That's all I ask. I ...' His voice broke and he seemed to be fighting back tears. 'Sare. I'm not sure I can handle life without you ... How many times can I say I'm sorry?'

The line went dead.

Sarah stabbed the button to end the messages and collapsed onto the sofa, hugging a cushion. She didn't want to talk to Niall or see him but she had to sooner or later. He did sound desperate. He was a happy-go-lucky sort, the joker in the pack, the life and soul of any party. To hear the edge of panic in his voice disturbed her. He'd said he couldn't handle life without her ...

Her stomach turned over.

What if he did do something drastic? No matter how much she hated him right now, she didn't want that.

Chapter Nine

It was a Friday lunchtime and Molly was glad to have managed to bag a table in the back bar of the Eagle. The end of January heralded the start of the spring term for students, which was a joke considering it was almost freezing outside and blowing a hoolie. Ewan had decided it was the ideal place to celebrate the fact that his and Molly's research paper had finally been accepted by a prestigious science journal and the rest of the lab had jumped at the chance of escaping their caves for free beer and crisps.

The past few weeks had been ... *weird.* An uneasy peace had broken out between her and Ewan and finally getting their paper published had relieved some of the tension between them. Ewan had tried to be scrupulously polite to her, but nothing more, even though they'd spent more time together than ever while they worked on the Love Bug. Molly had tried to damp down her lust by reminding herself that every response to him was purely down to biochemical and/ or neurological reactions. If she recognised the symptoms and analysed them, she reasoned, they'd cease to affect her.

Ewan put a tray of drinks in front of Molly. 'Half a cider OK? Wasn't sure what you asked for but that's your usual.'

'Thanks,' she said.

Pete Garrick, the party DJ/parasitic worm expert from the next lab to theirs, added another tray and the rest of the lab guys fell on the beers like a pack of wolf cubs.

'Here you go. Congratulations to Ewan and Molly.' Pete lifted his pint just as a massive bloke bumped into him. 'Whoops!'

Beer sloshed onto Molly's lap, making her swear.

'Shit, sorry,' Pete started to dab at her mini skirt with a dirty hanky.

'It's OK,' said Molly, grimacing as the sticky Guinness soaked through the denim and her woolly tights.

'Here.' Ewan handed her a paper serviette from the cutlery jug and took the bench seat next to her.

'Thanks.'

'You'll smell like a brewery this afternoon,' said Ewan helpfully. 'Here, have another napkin.'

'Sorry,' said Pete with a grin, adding, 'Squash up, then, there's room for one more.'

Even though she could cheerfully have strangled Pete, Molly had no choice but to move even closer to Ewan as Pete squeezed in next to him. There definitely hadn't been room for "one more" before and even though Pete was skinny, you now couldn't get another molecule between them all.

On one side of her was Pete, who reeked of Deep Heat muscle rub. On the other was Ewan, who smelled of antibacterial handwash. The heating in the pub was up full and with so many bodies, it was very stuffy. Ewan took off his sweater and rolled up the cuffs of his shirtsleeves. Every time he lifted his pint or delved into the communal packs of crisps, the hairs on his forearms skimmed her skin. His thigh muscles flexed against hers when he shifted in his seat and he kept accidentally brushing against her thighs where her mini had ridden up. It was too embarrassing trying to keep tugging it down so she tried to keep her hands in her lap.

In the end, she daren't even reach for her drink, for fear of touching him or him touching her. Surely, he could tell how turned on she was? She didn't believe in telepathy, of course, but she did believe in body language and hers was screaming at her to jump him in the middle of the pub.

Pete's voice grew louder and more excited as he started to tell everyone about the charity tandem ride he was taking part in later in the spring. 'Tandems look difficult to ride,' he was saying, 'but as long as you have a competent pilot, they're relatively simple to master ...'

Ewan shifted his muscular thigh even closer to hers.

'Of course, with a stringent programme of training and fitness, even a novice like Molly could complete the challenge ...'

Molly was trying hard to listen politely but her mind had wandered on to other forms of exercise. She imagined her and Ewan rolling around on the floor of the pub, having mad, passionate sex. Ewan's buttons were pinging against the bottom of the bar as she ripped his shirt off. Her bra and knickers flew into the air as he tossed them onto a bar stool.

Oh, the pub would be empty of course; Molly wasn't into exhibitionism. In fact, it would be after closing time when a freak one-hundred-year snowstorm (unlikely in Cambridge but, hey) had forced them both to seek shelter inside. Come to think of it, the rest of the city would have been evacuated but she and Ewan would have bravely stayed behind, working on an antidote to a new virus – and then got caught out by the blizzard while trying to get the cure to the outside world.

They would have had to light a fire from the bar stools (using booze as an accelerant). And then, Ewan would have suggested that the best way to keep warm was to have sex. Lots of sex, until help arrived, which it probably wouldn't until the following morning. So they'd have ripped off each other's clothes and gone at it all night long, over and over and over again ...

'Ready for another one, Molly?'

'Eh?'

'It's my round again. Would you like anything stronger this time?' Ewan said.

'Stronger?'

He pointed to her glass. 'Than half a cider? As we're celebrating.'

'Oh, I see what you mean. Um ... no thanks, I have to drive later. Better have a Coke.'

'OK.' He peered at her closely. 'You seem a little flushed. Not running a temperature, are you?'

'It's hot in here, that's all,' she said, annoyed he'd noticed the tinge on her cleavage and neck. Only she knew it was her blood vessels dilating due to arousal but he didn't have to draw attention to the fact.

'OK. I didn't mean to be personal. It is very hot in here ...' His voice was husky, and edged with the tang of Greene King bitter.

His arm brushed hers again and her pulse rate spiked. 'It is *very* hot. I don't think they need the fire and the heating on.'

'I agree. It's too much. Especially when it's so packed in

here on such a mild day. It seems madness to have the fire and heating together.' Was it her imagination or had he leaned even closer to her? And had his Scottish accent taken on an even huskier tone?

'Mm.'

'Ewan, how long do we have to wait for this bloody drink?' one of the post-docs called.

Everyone laughed and Ewan rolled his eyes. 'OK. OK. I'm coming.'

'About time, mate!'

Pete the Parasite had to move so Ewan could exit the booth and Pete immediately filled the space, much to Molly's despair. He started to tell her about his latest project on tapeworms, growing more excited by the second.

'And then they turn them into a sort of soup and it's supposed to be very good for eczema ...'

Molly tried to listen politely and make sensible comments, while making a mental note not to have tagliatelle for dinner. Or soup. She suppressed a shudder as Ewan returned and glanced over at the seat. Obviously deciding it wasn't worth butting up to Pete, he started holding forth about the upcoming Six Nations series. Once or twice he slid a quick glance in her direction, when he obviously thought she wasn't looking.

Molly was completely confused.

'So, how's your top-secret project going?' Pete asked, dragging her attention away from Ewan.

She tapped her nose. 'It wouldn't be top secret if I told you that, would it?'

'No. Of course not although half the lab has a pretty good idea of what you and Ewan are up to in the lab till all hours.'

'Do they?'

'In a strictly professional sense, of course. I know it's a genetically engineered hormone.'

She hid her annoyance with what she hoped was an enigmatic smile. 'Really? I couldn't possibly say.'

Pete tapped the side of his own extensive nose. With his long black hair, pale complexion and imperious air, he reminded her of a seventeenth-century portrait in the college hall. Some women might fancy his brand of the Cavalier-meets-mosh-pit look but Molly wasn't one of them.

'I shan't probe you any further,' he said, giving Molly an image that wouldn't be easy to erase from her mind. 'Now, what about this tandem race?' he went on. 'Why don't you give it some thought? It's a very good cause – a charity that looks after children with genetic disorders.'

Feeling guilty, she mumbled that she'd seriously consider it and to her relief, Pete's attention was finally claimed by a mate from the bioengineering lab. Molly was relieved when Ewan tapped his watch and suggested they return to the lab. It was only half past two but the sun was already sliding towards the horizon and their breath made misty clouds in the air as they walked.

'What did Pete Garrick want?' Ewan asked as they walked side by side past King's College chapel on their way back to the department.

'Oh, nothing much. He was mostly going on about the charity tandem race.'

Ewan frowned. 'Did he want anything else? You and he seemed thick as thieves together.'

'He was also asking about tapeworms and a bit about the Love Bug,' Molly replied, knowing it would rile Ewan.

'Well, I sincerely hope you didn't tell him anything. This project must remain confidential until we're ready to publish.'

'Of course I didn't, but he reckons that half the Biology faculty already has an idea of what we might be working on.'

He snorted. 'Bollocks.'

'Calm down, I didn't say anything,' she said, satisfied she'd succeeded in winding Ewan up. 'And Pete's not interested in people anyway, he's only interested in his worms.'

'Maybe,' said Ewan, giving her another suspicious glance as they cut through a narrow alley into the small courtyard that gave access to a back entrance to their lab. Everyone else had already gone in ahead. Her pleasure in annoying Ewan had been tempered by the fact he might genuinely believe she'd tell Pete any details about their project. Of course, she'd joked about it to Sarah but that was different; Sarah wasn't a biologist and had no interest in her work.

She swiped her card through the door reader. 'Pete's not that bad. He's just very tenacious when he gets his teeth into something.'

'And full of crap, a bit like one of his worms,' said Ewan. 'Be careful, Molly. Some people aren't what they seem.'

She picked up her lab coat from the peg. Tell me about it, she thought, settling down for another session with her microscope.

Chapter Ten

Sarah had to take a few calming breaths when she heard Niall's motorbike pull up on the driveway. After his desperate phone message, she'd finally sent him a text saying he could pop round for five minutes that evening.

Now here he was, perched awkwardly on the edge of the sofa while she stood with her back to fireplace. He looked haggard, with grey smudges under his eyes and a couple of days of stubble on his chin. She'd been shocked when she'd opened the door and the tirade she'd been ready to unleash at him had died on her lips.

'You said you had something important to tell me.' She folded her arms defensively, determined to be calm and assertive.

'Don't worry, I'm not here to grovel.'

'That's a comfort.'

'You look tired, Sarah.'

'I haven't exactly been getting my beauty sleep and I could say the same for you.'

'I've hardly had a wink for days.'

'I bet. Vanessa's nipple clamps been keeping you awake, have they?' Sarah couldn't help her sarcasm.

'That's not fair. I'm not with Nessa. She wanted me to move in – still wants me to – but I've held off.'

'Oh, how noble of you.'

'Please hear me out. I don't want to move in with Nessa while there's still hope for us. If you'd just think for a moment about what we're chucking away. I've been a useless bastard. I've made the mother of all mistakes and I'm sorry. We were a great team.' His voice wobbled. 'We still *could* be a great team and we were happy, you have to admit that.'

Sarah's throat clogged with emotion. He was right. She'd never been happier than the moment she'd seen the test kit result, and she could still feel the excitement of New Year's Eve, knowing the news she had to tell Niall when he returned from his shift.

'If it hadn't been for my one moment of madness, we still would be happy, darlin'.'

Sarah snapped out of her sentimental daze. Niall gazed up at her pathetically. He was full of regret that was for sure, but was it only because he'd been caught out? '*One* moment? Do you expect me to believe that's all there was to it? That the other night was the only time you had sex with her?' She snorted in disgust.

Niall toed the rug with his biker boot. He couldn't even meet her eye. She fought down bile in her throat. To think she'd even allowed herself to contemplate letting him come back home at some point.

'God, Niall, how long had it been going on? How long have I been a fool for?'

'Not that long.' She could barely hear him.

She swore loudly.

'Not more than a month or two ...'

'A month or two! You've been shagging her for *two months*?'

96

'And I regret every moment. The pressure was getting to me, darlin'.' He glared at her.

'Don't you darlin' me, you lying toe rag. I knew I was wrong to even let you back into this house!'

Niall glared at her. 'Well, it is my house too. I pay half the mortgage. Don't forget that.'

'How could I?' Icy fingers clutched at her skin and a wave of sickness swept over her. She didn't want to throw up in front of him.

'I can't stay with my mum and dad forever. I need somewhere to live and if you're not even willing to give me another chance to come back and sort things out, then what can I do? If you're going to be totally unreasonable, then I've no choice. We're going to have to sell the cottage.'

Sarah clutched at the mantelpiece for support. Niall hadn't been in the house for five minutes and he'd started. 'Sell it? Already?'

'You chucked me out. You won't even think about having me back. What else can I do?'

'You can't want to get rid of this place after only four weeks of us being apart.' Sarah's voice rose.

'I know you love the place,' he said in what he obviously thought was a commanding tone, 'but I can't afford the mortgage on it on my salary, not as well as the rent on a flat.'

'A flat? I thought you were staying with your mum.'

'Yes but I've got to clear out as soon as I can. You know that my brother is back home and my youngest sister can't afford the rent on her student place so she's moving back too.'

Sarah rolled her eyes. 'My heart bleeds for you.'

'I can see you're still full of anger,' Niall said, his wheedling tone turning colder. 'It's understandable but you've given me no choice. I'm sorry you had to find me and Nessa like you did. I wish I'd had the courage to walk away from the affair before it got to the stage it did but now it's happened, it's been a wake-up call.' Niall's tone hardened. 'Maybe it's for the best for both of us. I hadn't realised how the pressure was getting to me.'

'The pressure? What pressure?'

'The pressure of trying to earn enough to pay for this place ...' Niall said slowly as if Sarah was stupid. 'I thought I could handle supporting you and the mortgage. I thought I could do it all but I was wrong. I should have been more honest. Vanessa always said that I'm the type of man who takes on too much and I can't say no to people who need me. It's why I kept getting those rashes.'

'But ... you said it was the washing powder I was using on your shirts. You said you were OK when I switched to non-bio ...' Sarah's voice tailed off as the full impact of Niall's words began to sink in. She could still hardly believe the injustice of what he was saying.

'Wait a minute. You told me you were fine with me giving up my job to start the business. I know it's been tough but orders have been taking off recently and it's prime wedding-prep season. It'll get better, I promise. I'll work night and day.'

'It's not only the financial stuff, it's me too. My psyche will be strangled if I stay here.'

'Your psyche? What the bloody hell does that mean?'

'Keep your voice down! Mrs Sugden will hear.'

'I don't care if she thinks I'm killing you!' Sarah's disbelief had morphed into anger. 'What the hell has Vanessa been doing to you?'

'Leave Vanessa out of this. It's my decision. I thought I was happy settling down here, but I was stagnating.'

'Stagnating? Well, yeah, that figures, you're definitely pond scum.'

'I know you're bound to be upset and hurt but this isn't like you. You used to be such a ... such a nice laid-back girl.'

'Well what do you expect, when I get home to find my partner having pervy sex with Miss Whiplash?'

'Bondage isn't pervy. Everyone does it nowadays as you'd know if you had a bit of imagination.'

Sarah gasped. She would have to tell him about the baby. Surely he'd come to his senses and see what a dick he was being about the house if he found out she was having his child?

'We've been together for a few years,' said Niall, hardly able to look her in the eye. 'It's been great, babe, but lately ... I've felt stifled and I don't want to end up like my bloody family. I don't want a brood of kids by the time I'm thirty-five and drowning in school uniforms and a caravan. I'm still young, I can't do it.'

Bile rose to her throat. 'I thought you wanted family. You love yours.'

'I do like them. I just don't want a bloody great big one myself yet. If ever. I want something different. Travel, adventure, spontaneity, you know.'

Sarah almost choked. Niall didn't want a family? 'And you'll get that with Vanessa, will you?' she said, trying to come to terms with his comments. 'She's going to take you round the world?'

'I don't know but she knows the score. She doesn't expect anything and right now, I don't want to be with anyone who does.'

'Just someone who'll tie to you to the bedposts and dress

you like a fairy! How very exciting and spontaneous and edgy, Niall.' All Sarah's resolve to be cool and sophisticated and to show him she didn't care had gone up in smoke.

'Babe. Don't do this. It doesn't suit you. You're a nice person. Lovely and kind and – one day you'll find the right man to settle down and be a great husband and give you a brood of kids.'

Her lips felt as if they were glued together. She was afraid that if she spoke she might throw up. She'd been about to play her trump card, telling him about the baby, but what was the point now? Hearing she was having his baby would probably drive him out of the house for good.

Niall went on. 'I've arranged for an estate agent to come round. Vanessa's brother-in-law manages the branch and he can do us a favour and fit a valuation in at short notice. If all goes well, he can get the cottage into the paper this week and online even sooner. This is tough on both of us but it's the only way. I always say, a clean break heals faster.'

'A clean break? Niall, I have no idea how you ever passed your paramedic exams.'

Sarah jumped up and knocked over something cool and smooth, which tumbled onto the rug with a soft bump. It was Niall's favourite Toby jug. It rolled onto the carpet and came to rest, its sinister face staring upwards. Sarah picked it up and its lurid mouth seemed to laugh at her. She'd always hated the thing but hadn't wanted to hurt Niall or his mother's feelings.

'Can you please be careful with Toby?' Niall sounded worried, far more worried than he had about leaving Sarah and selling the cottage. 'In fact, I think I'd better take him back to Mum's with me.'

Toby grinned back at Sarah but she smiled benignly at him. *You had this coming, Toby, you asked for it ...*

'I think you'd better take him, Ni. In fact you can have him right now.'

She raised her hand high, gripping Toby so hard her knuckles ached.

Niall held up his hands in surrender. 'Look, I don't think this is a good time. I'll come back when you feel less emotional or perhaps we should meet on neutral territory in future.'

He backed towards the door to the hall. 'Now, don't do anything silly, Sarah. Why don't I call you when you've had chance to calm down? But we do have to sell this place – that's non-negotiable.'

Sarah took a step towards him. Toby was still smooth and cool in her hand, and she felt powerful as Niall backed through the doorway and into the hall. 'Ni. I want you to know something. I will never let go of this cottage until hell freezes over.'

She wasn't really sure how Toby left her hand or came to be flying through the air but seconds later, Niall was crouching down in the doorframe. Toby hit the frame with a crack and shattered into a hail of coloured shards. There was a shout of pain and a string of groans from the direction of the doorway.

'Jesus! What have you done?'

Expecting to see blood spurting from his face, Sarah gawped at Niall but he seemed unharmed apart from a few slivers of china on his jacket. The moans of pain continued but they weren't Niall's.

'Feck it, Sarah!' he shouted. 'I think you've killed someone!'

Pushing past him, Sarah ran into the hallway. Icy air hit her face. The front door was wide open and a man was leaning against the radiator, holding the side of his head. Blood trickled between his fingertips and there were shards of pottery all over the floorboards. The jug must have bounced off the frame and hit him.

Sarah ran towards him. 'Oh, God. I'm sorry. That was meant for Niall.'

Niall appeared. 'What the hell are you doing in my house, pal?'

The man groped his way along the wall, obviously dazed. 'I ... The front door was open and I heard shouting and screaming. I was worried someone was going to get hurt so I decided to see if I could help.'

Hearing his voice, Sarah's heart sank. 'Oh God, I'm sorry, we were just having a few words. Are you OK? It is Liam, isn't it? Liam Cipriani? Niall, take a look at Liam's head.'

Sarah put her arm around his back but he gently pushed her off. 'I'm fine, really.'

'You're cut and my partner's a paramedic – I mean Niall, here, is a paramedic. Come and sit down and let him check you over.'

'Really I'd rather just leave you to it if you're OK? It sounded like things were kicking off big time in here.' He directed this at Sarah alone.

'I'm all right, no thanks to Sarah,' Niall cut in.

Liam glared at him. 'I'm sure it takes two to tango.'

'We're fine, mate, so you can be on your way.'

'He's not fit to drive with that head injury, is he, Niall?'

'I don't know, Sarah, I'm a shit paramedic, remember?'

More concerned about Liam than scoring points off Niall, Sarah moderated her tone. 'Look, can you just check Liam over while I make him a cup of tea?'

'Do you mind telling me who he is first and why he's in my house?'

'He's Liam Cipriani. He is – was – coming to my tiara-making workshop.'

Niall raised an eyebrow but Sarah shot him a look that would wither roses.

Liam dabbed at his hair with a handkerchief. 'I am still here, you know, and actually, I think it would be better if I did go.'

Sarah dashed forward. 'No, please don't. Stay for a few minutes until you feel better. I'm really really sorry about this whole thing. I'll get the first aid kit.'

Niall folded his arms. 'She's right,' he said grudgingly. 'You'd better sit down, pal, and I hope you don't need stitches 'cos there's a fecking long wait in A&E today.'

*

'How's your head?' Sarah hovered anxiously over the sofa after Niall had finally left. Her anger with Niall had been replaced with regret that Liam had ended up in the thick of their slanging match.

'I'll live.' Liam gingerly touched the crusted blood in his hairline. Niall had checked him out, cleaned and disinfected the small cut and declared it was worse than it looked.

'I really am so sorry that you walked in on that row. Niall and me, we've recently split up and he'd just told me I had to sell the cottage. Things are ... a bit volatile between us at the moment.'

'I gathered that.' Liam winced and Sarah didn't blame him. 'I'm sorry you're having a difficult time. Maybe I should go.'

103

'No, please. Stay until you've finished your tea. Shall I make you a fresh one?' Sarah was desperate to make sure Liam really was OK and at least try to prove to him that she wasn't a raving madwoman before he left. She took the chair opposite him.

'This one is fine, thanks.'

'I – um – expect this means you want to cancel the tiara workshop?'

Liam's cool blue gaze was the kind that missed nothing. Oh God, he could sue her for assault, if he wanted to. 'Why would you think that?' he asked.

'Because I threw a Toby jug at you and caused Actual Bodily Harm?'

'It wasn't the greatest piece of customer service, I must admit, but I realised you were aiming for your partner.'

She covered her eyes and spoke through her fingers. 'Oh God, I really *am* sorry.'

'Sarah. Can you please stop apologising?'

When Sarah met his eyes, she saw that they had the slight glimmer of amusement in them. She was lucky he hadn't called the police, let alone seemed to have a sense of humour. He also didn't look like she'd expected him to. She'd imagined a fey, delicate man, going bald on top with a long thin nose. While he was a decade older than her, he had the physique of a much younger man, thick black hair going grey at the sides and his nose was just ... normal. In fact, she could barely believe he had a daughter old enough to be getting married.

Her shoulders slumped in relief. 'I just wanted you to know I don't try to brain all my customers ... but you *do* want to do the workshop?'

'Yes. I said I did on the phone. It may sound weird but my daughter's in the Army and she's getting married in the summer. My wife, Kerren – Hayley's mother – died twelve years ago and she always wanted to make something for Hayley on her wedding day. Hayley's been serving in the medical corps in West Africa so I want to surprise her.'

'That's a lovely idea,' said Sarah, grateful to move the subject on from her jug throwing. 'And in the circumstances, the least I can do is let you do the workshop for free.'

Liam smiled properly for the first time since he'd entered the house, and his blue eyes crinkled at the corners. 'Well, that's a kind offer but in view of the fact that you've split up with your partner and he's forcing you to sell the cottage, and that you're self-employed, I think you need all the paying customers you can get, don't you?'

'Yes, but ...'

'No more "buts". I run my own business too and I know there's no room for sentiment,' he said kindly but firmly, a completely different man from the hesitant speaker on Sarah's answerphone. 'Now, can you tell me more about the workshop? How long will it take and do I need to bring a crash helmet?'

Chapter Eleven

Molly peeled the lid off the "luxury" Oriental Noodle Pot she'd microwaved in the staff kitchen before taking it outside into the small garden at the rear of the lab. Steam curled into the air along with an aroma about as exotic as a damp sock. Molly didn't care: she'd have eaten anything hot at this moment. It was the very start of February and not really warm enough to sit outside for lunch, but wrapped in her coat, with the sun full on her, she was OK. She blew on the noodles and waited for them to cool when glimmers of white in the dark soil caught her eye.

'Oh, look, the snowdrops are out.'

Ewan, sitting next to her, stopped unwrapping his plough-man's baguette and followed her gaze. 'Looks like it,' he said.

It was rare for him to have a lunch break and even rarer for him to take it in the small garden area at the back of the lab but Molly wasn't complaining. He returned to his sandwich, munching away while gazing out across the grass towards the other science and engineering buildings.

'Mum and Dad always loved seeing the snowdrops come up at home. Mum would point them out every year; but I never took much notice then. I guess she was desperate for some sign of spring.'

Molly stopped. She wasn't sure if Ewan was aware that she and Sarah had lost their parents when they were young and, unless the subject arose, she didn't tell people and certainly didn't elaborate on the circumstances. It generally caused embarrassment and awkward silences, not to mention an outpouring of well-meaning pity that she couldn't take too much of.

Not that Ewan was given to outpourings of well-meaning pity. Tough love was more his style.

Ewan didn't reply for a while but eventually said, 'They won't be out in Scotland for a while.'

A large grey cloud covered the sun. Molly shivered and clutched her noodle pot tighter. 'Chilly isn't it?'

'Do you want my jacket over you?' said Ewan.

Molly was amazed. 'No, thanks for the offer but I'll manage.' Maybe he wasn't wholly an insensitive prat, after all. She smiled as he broke off a small piece of his baguette and tossed it onto the grass. A robin immediately swooped down from a tree and snaffled it.

'Or you could always go back inside,' he added.

She avoided the urge to swear. 'I'd rather be cold,' she declared. 'I'm desperate to get some sunlight and fresh air after so many months living under artificial lights and filtered air.'

'Humph,' grunted Ewan and returned to his baguette.

A few minutes of silence later, she'd almost given up trying to make conversation. If Ewan didn't want to speak to her, there was nothing she could do about it. She'd concluded that he had definitely told Sarah about his wife to warn her off.

Ewan tossed some more bread the hungry robin's way. The

sky had clouded over and Molly was shivering. She decided it was more than time to go back inside.

'What's this about you doing that charity tandem ride with Pete Garrick?' Ewan said as Molly was about to get up.

She almost dropped her noodles.

'Who told you that?' she said.

'Pete did.'

'What? When?'

'This morning,' said Ewan, abandoning the remains of his lunch. 'He came up to me while I was getting a coffee from the machine and told me you'd agreed to it in the pub.'

'No, I didn't. He asked me to do it and I said I'd think about it but there's no way I'm going to. Me on a tandem with Pete?' She snorted. 'You have to be kidding.'

Ewan smirked. 'You do realise that telling a guy like Pete that you'll think about something is as good as saying you'll do it?'

'No, I hadn't realised that and I'd have thought that Parasitic Pete, the most pedantic man on the planet, would know the difference.'

'Clearly not. He told me you were going training with him at the weekend.'

'I never said that.'

'Well, Pete said that *you'd* said "mm, yes" when he asked you about doing the training when we were in the Eagle.'

'I don't remember saying "mmm, yes" to anything ...' Her toes curled. She might have muttered something like "Mm, yes" but only in relation to her fantasies about Ewan. And anyway ... 'So, would you have a problem if I did share Pete's tandem?' she asked, testing Ewan out.

He hesitated. 'No, of course not but ... I didn't think it was your kind of thing. The tandem, that is.'

'It's not. In fact, I had no idea about the ride until he mentioned it at the pub. Only you seem concerned about it.'

He shrugged. 'I'm not concerned. It's really none of my business what you do and who you do it with.'

Molly wouldn't let him off the hook. 'Because if you think I can't do it because it's too far or I'd never make it. Is it *so* obviously amusing that I might be able to ride a tandem? I do cycle to work every day, you know, and I once did a mini marathon when I was an undergraduate.' She left out the part about it being a pub mini-marathon.

'Of course, I think you can do it. But Pete, you know, he can get a bit enthusiastic about things. Besides, you and Pete, it doesn't strike me as a match made in heaven.'

'It's not a match made anywhere.'

'OK. OK.'

'And anyway, what's wrong with Pete?' she said sulkily.

'Nothing. He's a nice enough bloke. If you're into parasitic worms, that is.'

She almost snorted her noodles because *no one* was more into their subject than Ewan but before she could think of a witty reply, Pete emerged from the sliding doors on the opposite side of the courtyard.

'Oh God, talk of the devil ...' Molly dug furiously into the remains of her lunch pot.

Ewan smiled and waved enthusiastically at Pete.

'Can you please *not* do that,' she whispered.

It was too late. Pete's face lit up and he bounded across the courtyard. 'Aha, Molly. I've tracked you down! I was beginning to think you'd turned into that very rare species, *Mollissius elusiva* ...'

She mumbled, 'Ha ha.'

'Anyone would think you'd been avoiding me. You haven't replied to my texts or emails.'

'Noooo. I've had my head down in the lab all morning, slaving over a hot Western blot, haven't I, Ewan?'

'Allegedly,' said Ewan. Molly was sure his shoulders were shaking. The git was obviously enjoying watching her suffer.

'Well, whatever, I do need to speak to you in case there's been some kind of misunderstanding because when I saw Ewan on my way into work, he seemed surprised when I told him you'd agreed to the tandem ride.'

'Did he?' She shot Ewan a death look.

'Yes, so I'm here to confirm that I haven't got the wrong end of the stick. If you can't do it, can you let me know ASAP because Devi Kumar from epidemiology is very keen although of course, I'd far rather have you behind me, if that doesn't sound like an innuendo.'

Ewan appeared to have trouble swallowing his sandwich.

'I ... well ... I don't think ...'

'Just in case, I've devised and printed off a novice's training regime. It's tough, I'll admit, but I know you can do it if you're prepared to put in the time and effort. It means training together before work most days and at the weekends. I'll need you to commit to the programme one hundred per cent, if you're going to do it.'

'I don't think I can ...'

'Of course you can. Banish those negative thoughts. I'll send you some links to a sports psychologist's site.'

She squirmed. 'Thanks, but I don't think even a psychologist could work that kind of miracle. I like cycling but I'm really not up to your standard, Pete.'

'What Molly's trying to say, very badly, is that she would have loved to have joined you if she hadn't already agreed to do the ride with me,' said Ewan.

Molly's mouth fell open like a trapdoor.

'*You?*' she and Pete said in unison.

'Yes, I asked her a while ago and in fact, she'd agreed when we were in the pub,' Ewan said firmly. 'I know she probably doesn't want to do it and feels she has to because I'm her boss and she's squirming now because I'm here and she doesn't know how to wriggle out of it ...' He laughed at his own joke. 'And I'm sure she'd much rather do it with you ...'

'No!'

Pete glared at her.

'Over to you, Molly,' said Ewan.

'Well, this is awkward, Pete, but Ewan's right. He did ask me first and I hate to let anyone down. And he's as rubbish at me at tandem riding so it's far better if the two of us are crap together, isn't it, Ewan?'

Pete smirked. It was obvious he was enjoying the idea that Ewan was crap at something.

'And I know how desperate he is to do the ride. It is in aid of the new children's genetic screening unit, after all.'

Ewan, to give him credit, managed a cool smile. 'I wouldn't say desperate, exactly ...'

She batted him playfully on the arm. 'Oh, come on, Ewan, you know how keen you are and it's for such a worthy cause.'

'Yes, that's true.'

'Guess what, Pete?' she chirped up. 'He's even managed to

get hold of a top-of-the-range tandem especially for the event, haven't you, Ewan?'

Pete blew out a breath. 'Awesome. What make is it?'

'Um. I'm not sure. It's been custom made by a friend of mine,' said Ewan. 'So you don't mind, Pete?'

'If you have first dibs on Molly, so to speak ... But I'd no idea you were interested. In the tandem ride, that is.'

Ewan did a Scout salute. 'First dibs. Yes.'

'Sorry about that,' said Molly, still trying to process Ewan offering to do the tandem challenge with her. Was he jealous of Pete Garrick? Was he being kind in "rescuing" her – or just *very* cruel?

'Well,' said Pete, a little huffily. 'It's probably for the best. I *was* willing to train Molly up but Devi has a lot of tandem experience. Are you an experienced tandem pilot, Ewan?'

'I wouldn't say experienced but I'm sure we can rub along well enough, can't we, Molly? After all, it is in a very good cause.'

Molly smiled, homing in on all that "rubbing along". 'Very ... um, *how* far did you say it was again?'

Pete grinned. 'Only seventy-five miles.'

'*Seventy-five miles?*' She felt faint.

'Yes. Just a little jaunt *if* you know what you're doing.' Pete rubbed his hands together in delight. 'I expect the charity thought they'd have to make it an easy challenge to attract more entries from amateurs. I could email you the training schedule and some tips.'

'Thanks. You do that,' said Ewan.

'I'll do it tonight after my gym session. Meanwhile I'd better leave you two to it,' Pete said, smirking at her Pot Noodle and the baguette crumbs on the ground. 'I can see you're

112

already doing some serious carb loading. I'll send a detailed training and nutrition schedule and doubtless, I'll see you both out on the roads in the next couple of days.'

After Pete had oozed off, she dumped the remains of her noodle pot in the bin at the end of the bench. She turned to Ewan in horror. 'Ewan. *Please* tell me that I haven't just had a nightmare in which you committed us to a seventy-five-mile tandem race?'

His expression was grim. 'No, *you* had a dream in which I *saved* you from a seventy-five-mile tandem race with Pete Garrick. And by the way, where are we going to get this top-of-the-range tandem from?'

'Why, from your specialist friend who custom-makes them. Oh God, have you ever actually *been* on a tandem?'

'Of course,' he said, clearly affronted. 'Actually, my uncle and auntie had one, so me and my brother tried it once.'

'Why only once?'

'Because we rode it straight into a ditch full of nettles. We were rubbing cream onto our bruises and rashes for days.'

Molly watched the sparrows pecking at the breadcrumbs while Ewan took solace in his chocolate muffin. She tried to analyse the pros and cons of doing a tandem cycle challenge with him. It would mean training together, relying on each other, trusting each other ... It could end up with them both pedalling off into the sunset ... or crashing into a ditch full of nettles ... but that would mean they'd have to rub cream on each other. *For days.* So, on the whole, this was a very good thing, wasn't it?

If only it didn't involve a bloody tandem.

Chapter Twelve

Sarah ramped up the heating in the workshop. It was barely above freezing outside and the sky was so grey and heavy, she was sure it would snow by the end of the day. She hoped it wouldn't put off Liam or any of the other six students attending the Basic Tiara class.

After laying out a mat, a set of pliers and clippers, and a selection of wires for each student, she prised off the tops of the Tupperware boxes that contained the beads and gems. The beads made a soothing whoosh as she ran her hands through them and the colours never failed to give her a lift, especially on a grey day like this. She'd sorted each box into basic colours: orange, red, purple, and so on, yet each box shimmered with a myriad of hues. That was the hardest part of the class, usually, prising away the students from the boxes. They cooed and swooned over the beads like kids in a sweetie shop. Although she had a feeling Liam wouldn't be in the mood for cooing and swooning, the familiar act of preparing for the workshop soothed her.

If only she could afford to keep the cottage and the workshop on her own – or Niall would change his mind about selling. That fantasy was blown away when her mobile rang as she laid out the mugs ready for the workshop coffee break.

It was the estate agent, asking her to show a 'very keen' buyer round at short notice.

'So soon? I didn't think it had even been in the local paper yet? Your valuer only came round at the weekend. I haven't even seen the details.'

'Mr McCafferty approved them,' said the agent breezily. 'And we have buyers already on our books who are desperate for properties like yours. It's on our website and I don't think we'll have any problem securing a quick sale. I wouldn't be surprised if Mr and Mrs Pratt make an offer as soon as they've seen it. It's exactly what they're looking for.'

'Well, they'll have to be gone by ten at the latest, because I've got a workshop to run.'

'They won't be late!' trilled the agent. 'They're super keen to see inside.'

Biting back the urge to scream, Sarah locked up the workshop and went back to the house. She gathered up the soggy tissues from the floor, shoved her dirty breakfast dishes in the dishwasher, wondered if she had time to tidy up her bedroom then thought, *Sod it*. She already felt knackered from preparing the materials. She really hoped the fatigue would diminish and the "blooming" stage would start, because all the emotional energy and workload were knackering her.

The one good thing was that Cassandra's order was well underway. It had already taken her more time than she'd allotted for it, which annoyed her because she knew she was allowing herself to be intimidated by Cassandra. Then again, she often spent more time on commissions than she charged for. She'd tried to make the tiaras look as classy as possible but it was Cassandra's wedding and Sarah had to look upon it as business. Liam was right in that there was no room for sentiment when it came to making a future for herself and the baby. Besides, while she was intent on her bead-making or teaching, she wasn't dwelling on Niall's cruel comments or losing the house.

She sat down in the lounge, so she could hear the doorbell ring. Mrs and Mrs Pratt were sure to arrive at any moment and the faster she showed them round, the sooner she could get rid of them and finish her prep.

She woke to the sound of the doorbell ringing continuously.

'Shit ...'

Still groggy from sleep, she dragged herself off the sofa and opened the door. A young couple who both looked about twelve stood on the doorstep.

'This Lilac Cottage?' the man, grunted. He had streaks of what looked like fake tan on his collar – it was either that or wood stain. The woman was chewing gum furiously.

'Yes, it is. You must be the Pratts?'

'Jez is the Pratt, I'm a Death, and it's pronounced *De'ath* before you ask. It's French,' said the woman. 'And this place looks a lot smaller than on the Internet, doesn't it, Jez?' She popped a huge gum bubble.

Jez stroked her arm soothingly like she was a pet chinchilla. 'Well, we may as well take a look at it, Gales, now we've come all this way.'

She popped a bubble. 'S'pose so.'

Gritting her teeth, Sarah let them in and led the way half-heartedly round the cottage.

Jez kept saying everything about the cottage was "awesome" while Gales continued popping away. Sarah led the way into the garden.

'What d'you call that?' he said, smirking at the workshop. 'Fancy garden shed?'

'It's my Tiara Kabin,' said Sarah icily.

'Right. A kiddies' play hut.' Gales blew a huge bubble. 'We don't have kids.'

Thank God for the world, thought Sarah.

'When I've pulled that down, the garden will look a lot bigger or I s'pose I could use it for the jet ski once I've gutted it,' Jez muttered.

Sarah had been about to swear and correct him but something pinged in her mind.

'Well, I might take it with me,' she said. 'And it would be no good for kids or a jet ski because it's going rotten and it would need new felt on the roof.' She lowered her voice. 'I shouldn't really tell you this, but I think we have a rat infestation.'

Jez screwed up his nose and the fluff on his top lip bristled. 'Rats? I hate rats. I'm phobic about them. I go all ... sweaty.'

'He sweats like a pig if he sees a rat or a mouse,' said Gales, before popping another piece of gum in her mouth.

'They come from the chicken farm down over the fields and tunnel under the side of the shed. I'm amazed you haven't seen any yet. Some of them are as big as dogs.'

'Dogs? You're joking.' Jez's forehead was beaded perspiration while Gales's bubble was so big, Sarah couldn't see her nose anymore. 'I think we'd better go inside,' he muttered.

'It might be best, you never know what diseases rats carry but you won't let them put you off, will you? It is a nice cottage and you could get the pest control officer in, although I must admit, we've had them three times and those pesky rodents just keep coming back ... They seem to love it here.'

'Jesus.'

'Oh look, is that a tail I can see twitching behind the shed?'

Gales's bubble burst, covering her face in sticky pink goo. Jez was already gone, shooting up the path and through the back door.

Five minutes later, they left, muttering that they'd 'let the agents know'.

Whatever they were going to let the agents know, Sarah suspected it wouldn't be an offer. She closed the door behind them, a smile on her face at the memory of Gales's bubble and Jez's sprint for the back door. It was funny … *but* if word got back to Niall, he'd soon put the agents straight about the imaginary rats. Not everyone would be as gullible as Jez and Gales, and Sarah couldn't prevent people putting in an offer at all.

Maybe, just maybe by putting people off – or reducing the offers they made – she could delay things and give Niall time to change his mind.

Surely, he'd come to his senses? Maybe she should tell him about the baby? He would have to take responsibility for it, she needed the support and the baby needed a father … and despite everything, she still loved him, no matter how often she told herself she shouldn't and he wasn't worth it. Love just didn't work like that.

Knowing Liam and the other students would be there very soon, she told herself to get a grip, slicked on some lipstick and brushed her hair. She was just arranging biscuits on a plate for the tea break when Liam poked his head around the door.

'Oh, hello …' He paused in the doorway of the Kabin. 'Bugger. I'm not too early, am I?'

Sarah threw him her best reassuring smile, in case he decided to bolt out of the door. 'Only twenty minutes or so.'

He winced. 'Sorry. I'm usually late for meetings and appointments but I didn't want to rush this one. As it's pleasure not business. By the way, you're not going to throw that mug at me, are you?'

He was wearing jeans and a dark blue polo shirt that showed off his broad shoulders. He pushed a lock of black hair, tinged with grey, out of his eyes.

Sarah put the mug down on the worktop. 'That depends if you're going to behave in my class.'

'I'll try, though I warn you I was a bit of a rebel at school.'

Sarah handed him the worksheets, explaining to Liam that tiara making wasn't really for beginners so he might have to come back to further classes to complete the project.

'You said the tiara was for your daughter's wedding?'

'Yes. Hayley's getting married in a few months' time. She loved dressing up when she was a little girl and Kerren – my wife – always promised her she could have a princess's tiara on her wedding day. Obviously Kerren won't be here to arrange that so I thought I'd do it for her. Not that I could or would ever try to take Kerren's place, but this is one thing I can do.'

'Hayley's a lucky girl. She can't be very old,' said Sarah.

'She's twenty-four. Kerren and I married when we were barely nineteen and Kerren was already expecting her,' said Liam, seeming not to have noticed that Sarah was fishing for info. 'And she may not think she's lucky when she sees my tiara ...' Liam's eyes twinkled.

'She'll be impressed, I promise. I'll make sure you do a professional job. I won't go easy on you.'

Liam laughed. 'No, I've already experienced your brand of tough love.'

Sarah covered her face with her hand in embarrassment. 'Oh, please don't remind me!'

Just then two of Sarah's older regulars bustled in to the Kabin, followed by a teenage girl who almost walked into the closing door because she was scrolling through her mobile. Sarah asked people to turn their phones off during the workshop but it didn't always work.

The older women did a double take when they spotted Liam.

'This *is* the tiara workshop?' one asked with a sly grin.

'Thought we'd got the wrong date ...' said her friend, flicking back her own hair girlishly. Sarah could see she was going to have trouble here but couldn't hide her amusement. Liam was younger than either of the ladies by at least a decade.

'No. This is the right date. I'm here for the Basic Tiara class,' Liam cut in before Sarah could rescue him.

The women exchanged glances as if a strange but very welcome alien had landed in the middle of the class.

'Hi, I'm Liam,' he said warmly.

'Pleased to meet, you, Liam. I'm Helen. Do a lot of jewellery workshops, do you?'

He smiled. 'Actually, this is my first time so I hope Sarah will be gentle with me.'

The presence of Liam caused great amusement and intrigue, not to mention a lot of suggestive comments and jokes about George Clooney looking good in a tiara. Sarah thought Liam wasn't as much of a smoothie as George, and fifteen years younger, but she wasn't going to make things worse for him, though he seemed to take everything in good part.

They chatted as they worked, quizzing Liam on his job and whether he was married. Sarah cringed a little at the interrogation he was subject to, but she was also interested to hear his replies. It turned out he lived in a thatched cottage in a village just outside the city. She found out he loved Italian food – no surprise there – had been trying to make his own pasta and went to the gym when he could find time away from running his business, which was something to do with commercial property.

The chatter died a little as the students got to the trickier bits of the tiara-making process. Sarah was kept busy herself, helping each person with their individual problems, suggesting solutions and offering encouragement. It was a part of her job she loved, and she realised that she hadn't thought about Niall or the cottage for almost an hour. By the end of the workshop, everyone was high on astonishment at their own creativity and congratulating each other. Liam seemed quietly pleased with his first effort but it wasn't finished and Sarah, if she was honest, thought it needed more work, or even better, he needed to make a fresh start on a more elaborate project.

Sarah "oohed" and "aahed" over the tiaras – all of which were decent first-time attempts – and answered an endless stream of questions about her craft. She signed up four of the six, including the mobile-glued teenager – to other classes and sold take-away kits to the other two students.

By the time she'd waved them off with a smile, all she wanted to do was lay her head on the worktop and fall asleep. Even though she'd enjoyed the distraction of the group, how was she going to get through the next six months if she felt this shattered by lunchtime?

She started to tidy away the bits of wire and broken seed beads. Even though she was knackered, she loved teaching and would have hated to be working at the bank. She tried not to dwell again on the bank's maternity leave, and maternity pay, and the job to come back to at the end of it.

'Shall I help you clear up?' Liam's voice came from the doorway.

'Oh, I thought you'd gone.'

'I left my car keys on the table.'

Sarah glanced at the keys. A Range Rover key ring ... though he might not actually be driving one. 'Yes, I can see them. But you don't have to help. It's all included in the fee.'

She handed him the keys.

Liam jingled them from hand to hand, hesitating. 'Mind if I offer you a piece of advice from someone who hasn't actually been pregnant but has started up a business? You're trying to do both and if I were you, I'd take every offer of help I could get, particularly when it's free.' He said the words jokily enough but Sarah guessed he meant them.

'In that case, would you like to collect up all the tools and put them in the top drawer of the unit, please?'

He put his keys in his jeans pocket. 'Yes, Miss.'

Sarah had to laugh. It was funny to be called "miss" by an older guy and it was possibly a bit cheesy but she didn't mind. Liam made her smile, although she was also worried she was going to cry – for no reason whatsoever other than he'd been nice to her. She'd felt the same when Molly's boss, Ewan, had offered her a cup of tea after the Bike Incident. Was this her fate, now, to be cared for and pitied by kind men? They obviously didn't feel in danger from her sexually – that was for sure – and she didn't even look pregnant yet. God, when she started showing, she'd probably have old guys in mobility scooters offering her a lift.

'Everything OK?' Liam asked, popping the lid on a box of azure beads.

'Yes. Why?'

'You looked worried for a moment and then you started grinning.'

'Hormones,' said Sarah. 'Pain in the bum. Actually, a literal pain in the bum. Sorry was that Too Much Information?'

'I've heard a lot worse.' Liam grinned. 'I've brought up a teenage daughter on my own, remember?'

'That must have been hard.'

'At first after Kerren died, I was completely lost. There were so many things she did that I had no insight into: boys, clothes, crushes, emotional stuff in general. I had to learn how to be Hayley's mum and dad, though I could never replace her mum. I had a lot of help from my in-laws and parents too, with babysitting and school runs but, in the evening, when it was just the two of us, we both really felt Kerren's loss.'

'You must have done a good job. Any dad who feels able to make a tiara for his daughter's wedding can't be all bad.'

'I muddled through somehow and like I say, I had a lot of support.'

'Did you ever think of getting married again?' Sarah asked then wished the words back. 'I'm sorry, that was nosy of me.'

'Not at all. My own parents asked the same. Friends tried to fix me up numerous times and even Hayley attempted it with one of her mate's divorced mums. I dated a couple of women but there was no one I really clicked with. Now the business takes up a lot of my time.'

'I can't imagine being with anyone else but Niall either,' said Sarah, thinking that judging by the reaction from the ladies at her workshop, Liam wasn't short of offers. 'Not that I want him back,' she added sharply.

'No. I can see that. It's early days for you and it's raw since Niall's still around. It's different when you know someone's never coming back.'

'I'm sorry to moan. What happened to you with Kerren is far worse than Niall and I splitting up.'

'Maybe ... but it's still hard for you. Be kind to yourself, Sarah, you need time to grieve. It hasn't been that long since you lost your parents either. Believe me, you never really get over these things.'

Grieve? Sarah shivered at the word. She didn't want to grieve or have the word associated with losing Niall. Although she didn't want to admit it, she *had* imagined what it would be like if he came grovelling back then dismissed it angrily. She swiftly changed the subject to work and Liam took the hint, telling her a little more about the property management business he ran.

'This may not be what you want to hear right now and please don't think I'm touting for business, but if you are looking for a new place to work, I may have a solution,' he said.

'A solution?'

He smiled. 'It's just an idea. My company has developed some craft units not too far away from the centre of the city. There's a small one still available so if you'd like to take a look at it, I'd be happy to show you around it.'

'Oh ... I ...' Sarah didn't know what to say. Even though she knew she might have to find a new home and place of work, she hadn't wanted to face up to taking any practical steps to do it. Now here was Liam presenting her with a decision to make.

'Don't worry about offending me. You've got my number so please let me know if you're interested in seeing it.'

'Thank you. I will think about it. I just need to get my head around moving out of here full stop,' she said, aware that he'd opened up another uncomfortable topic that she didn't want to face yet.

To give herself breathing space, she made him another cup of tea and they chatted about his daughter and her role as a medic in Sierra Leone and how proud he was of her work, when he wasn't terrified of something terrible happening to her. But she was due home in a few months and after her wedding to another officer, he hoped she and her husband would get a posting in the UK. He mentioned his late wife sometimes but in a matter-of-fact way that didn't make Sarah feel sad or uncomfortable.

He put down his empty mug. 'So, what do you really think of my tiara?' he asked with a piercing look. 'I want you to be honest.'

She took a deep breath, knowing that Liam wasn't a man who'd want to be flattered and flannelled. 'It's not bad – really – for a first attempt, but it could be even more ... glamorous,' she said. 'I could offer some design tips if you like and loan you some proper tools so you can work on it some more at home or even try a new one.'

'Hmm. Or alternatively I could book into a couple of your advanced workshops.'

She smiled. 'You could, but it will turn into a very expensive tiara.'

He raised an eyebrow. 'You mean, by the time I've got a result that I'm happy with, I could have commissioned you to design it?'

She smiled. 'Possibly but that's not the point, is it? The important thing for you and your daughter is that *you* made it.'

'True.'

'Look, I promised you'd have a piece you were proud of and that your daughter will love, and I keep my promises. What about if I offer you a ten per cent discount on the advanced workshop?'

'You drive a hard bargain, Sarah.' With a glint in his eye, Liam held out his hand and shook her hand firmly. 'It's a deal. Done.'

Chapter Thirteen

'Oh, my God. Is that *it*?' she blurted out.

Molly couldn't help her dismay when she saw the Thing Ewan had just wheeled out of his garage. She'd hoped that he wouldn't have managed to get hold of a tandem at such short notice. Besides, it had snowed for a short while overnight and the roads were slushy and wet. She'd rather have sat on the sofa, carb loading on toast and jam, hoping Ewan would call to say it was too dangerous to go out. No chance. He pushed the bike over, obviously pissed off at her lack of enthusiasm. 'This is a vintage Peugeot tandem. It would have been state of the art when it was new.'

She curled her lip. She'd expected the tandem to be like two bikes stuck together but that wasn't the case. The frame was short which made the saddles very close together, meaning the rear rider would have his or her head alarmingly close to the pilot's bum.

'Where did you get it? The *Antiques Roadshow*?' she said, wondering if it would even take both their weights.

'My friend from the rugby club bought it off eBay a few years ago but apparently, his girlfriend hated it. He let me have it for a pint,' Ewan said.

'You should have made him buy you a pint for taking it off his hands. It looks very ... *industrial*.'

'It's pretty hefty, I'll admit. These vintage models don't have the lightweight frames of a modern bike but luckily the roads are flat around here so we won't be pedalling it up any hills.'

Shivering in her Lycra leggings and jersey, Molly clapped her gloved hands together to try to keep warm. 'I don't think we should be pedalling it at all and especially not on these roads.' She gestured to the slushy streaks in the tarmac outside Ewan's Victorian semi. 'It's bound to be icy out of the city. What if we came off and ended up in Addenbrooke's with broken bones? You might have to take weeks off work and that would delay the project.'

'Nice try,' said Ewan, 'but the main roads and cycle ways will all be clear by now. Besides, it's a lovely morning and don't forget, you could be riding behind Pete.'

'What makes you think I'd be riding *behind* him?'

Ewan shrugged. 'I'd assumed you'd want to be the stoker.'

'The stoker?'

'The rider on the back who puts down the power, but you can be the pilot if you want to. I really don't mind,' he said huffily.

Molly checked out the saddles again, realising that Ewan would have his face almost in her arse if she took the front seat. Whereas she'd have a close-up of his Lycra-clad glutes if she opted for the rear. 'Are you sure it's safe to ride?'

'I am,' said Ewan firmly. 'Now, don't be a wuss. Why don't you put your helmet on and we'll give it a whirl?'

A *whirl*? Whirl conjured up images of Waltzers, Highland flings and possibly chocolate cones with whipped-cream toppings. Getting on the back of the tandem conjured up feelings of terror, exhaustion and nausea, and having her face inches from Ewan's bum wasn't compensating.

After several abortive attempts to get moving at all, they'd wobbled the length of Ewan's street and onto a cycle way that led past the laboratories and out into the country lanes to the west of the city. Initially, several toddlers in trail bikes and a hundred-year-old man on a tricycle easily outstripped them, and Molly had lost count of the number of smart-arsed blokes who'd shouted, 'She's not pedalling, mate,' or some other crap.

As they left the city behind, they managed to get into some kind of rhythm. Molly's curse was snatched away by the wind when Ewan's muscular bum cheeks and thighs set a punishing pace and the novelty of having an excuse to analyse them close up rapidly wore off. They were also now going *much* faster than she ever did on her road bike. Hedges whizzed by and she had started to puff.

'Can you please try to keep up?' Ewan shouted.

'No, you should slow down!'

'OK, but whatever we do, we need to move in synch, as one. That's the key to mastering this thing.'

She tried to match his rhythm and speed and not to lean the wrong way or tense up at every bend in the road, but she hated being out of control, and having to trust Ewan's frankly suicidal approach to cornering. She also couldn't see ahead and had begun, bizarrely, to feel travel sick.

Outside in the country, snow covered the fields and lay in drifts in the ditches. A cutting wind howled across the fens, and tiny icy shards blew from the tops of the hedges and battered Molly's face. In spite of her cycling gloves, her fingers were numb from gripping the handlebars too tightly.

'This is much better. I'm actually enjoying it now,' Ewan shouted, his glutes working even more enthusiastically.

Molly gritted her teeth and tucked her head behind his back, pedalling harder, determined to keep up with him.

'This is a lot more fun that I thought and you can go really fast!' he shouted.

Molly glanced up. A "Z" sign loomed ahead and a hedge raced towards them.

'Oh, shit!'

Ewan's shout was cut short by the screeching of brakes.

'Arghh!'

'Christ!'

One moment Molly was gripping the handlebars for grim death, the next she was screaming as she fell off the bike and landed with a soft thump in a snowdrift. There was a loud crash next to her and a series of 'fucks' and a low groan.

Molly lay on her back, the cold wet snow seeping through her cycle tights. For a few seconds, she couldn't breathe but then she lifted up her head. Ewan was a few feet away, sprawled in the slush in the lay-by they'd ended up in. He wasn't moving but he was swearing.

The tandem lay in the middle of the road, the rear wheel spinning.

Molly scrabbled to her feet and limped over to retrieve the tandem before a car ran over it. She was breathing heavily and feeling shaky but she managed to lug it into the lay-by while Ewan sat up groggily.

Molly crouched down beside him. 'Are you OK?'

Grimacing, he rolled his shoulders. Molly heard bones crack but Ewan managed a grim smile. 'Seems like it. Are you?'

'A bit shaken up but fortunately the snow broke my fall.'

'Sorry. I think I took the bend slightly too fast and we skidded on some ice.'

Now Molly knew he was going to be OK, the anger and shock hit her. 'Slightly too fast? I did tell you. This isn't a race, it's a ride. We don't have to try to be Bradley bloody Wiggins!'

'I'm not trying to be Bradley Wiggins.'

'You could have fooled me! Jesus, look at your leg.'

Ewan glanced at the ripped Lycra over his left knee and at the raw skin underneath. It looked very sore and there was blood oozing down his shin.

'It's only a graze. I'll live. Are you sure you're OK?'

'I'm *fine*,' said Molly, torn between concern for Ewan and annoyance at his reckless riding. This was definitely turning into a disaster. It was as far from romantic as it was possible to get and also, if she and Ewan couldn't get along on a tandem ride, how would they ever manage a relationship? Having the hots for him was all very well but she wasn't sure she could cope with his moods.

She waited as he got to his feet, shivering in her wet kit. The seat of his tights was also shredded where he'd scraped along the ground and his boxer shorts were soaked through.

'What's up?' Ewan asked, catching her staring at him.

'You have a very wet bum.'

Even though she was cold, wet and pissed off, Molly had to try not to laugh as Ewan inspected his impressive rear.

He raised his eyebrows. 'That makes two of us.'

Molly suppressed any urge to smile or be turned on. 'Look, how are we going to get home? I don't fancy getting back on the bike after that crash.'

'It's either ride or walk and as the bike looks in one piece, I suggest we give it a try.'

'How far have we come?'

Ewan checked the GPS on his wrist. 'About eight miles.'

'Shit. OK, let's give the bike another go but I'm going to be pilot this time. I hate being on the back. I can't see ahead of me and I feel a bit sick. You can be the stoker.'

'Fine by me.'

Molly knew Ewan would be inches from her bottom all the way and she didn't relish handling the tandem but there was no choice. Gingerly, she eased her herself onto the front saddle while Ewan climbed onto the rear.

Somehow, they made it back to Ewan's house. Steering was trickier than she'd expected but being able to see the road ahead was much better than relying on someone else, especially a speed merchant like Ewan. Despite her wet clothes and her bumps and bruises from the fall, she preferred being in control of the speed and direction of the tandem and was almost enjoying herself by the end of the ride.

'There, we made it,' said Molly, relieved to have made it onto Ewan's driveway without further mishap.

Gingerly, he slid off the bike. 'Eventually.'

'And in one piece,' she darted back. 'Well, one of us is.'

She winced at the sight of his knee, which was swollen and crusted in blood.

'You'd better get your knee cleaned up before it gets infected. I hope it isn't dislocated.'

'I've had a lot worse at rugby,' he said. 'I'll lock the bike up first. It doesn't seem to have suffered too much but I think I'll take it to the service centre and get them to check it over anyway.' He tutted at Molly, shivering on the driveway. 'Have you got any dry clothes?'

'Yeah. I bought some in my rucksack.'

'OK, why don't you use the bathroom while I sort my leg out and then I'll make us both a drink?'

Limping slightly, Ewan showed Molly into the downstairs shower room of his house. It was a modest Victorian semi in a pleasant part of town, which in Cambridge meant it was probably worth upwards of half a million. She reckoned he must have bought it after he'd moved to the lab following his split with his wife.

She realised that she'd never been in the place before in all the time she'd worked with him. He certainly never held lab social events at the house although she didn't blame him for that. The potential for total wreckage was too great but also, she knew he would never invite work into so intimate a space. She was surprised that he'd asked her in now, although he may have felt obliged to after their "accident".

After she'd changed into warm clothes she waited in the sitting room for him to reappear. She wasn't sure what she'd expected the place to be like: perhaps coldly minimalist and devoid of clutter. While the house was tidier than her flat, which wouldn't have been difficult, there were plenty of personal touches. Interesting prints of landscapes and botany hung on the walls while stripy rugs covered the oak boards and scatter cushions adorned two squashy, well-worn sofas. The cupboards and dresser were home to a variety of interesting objects: bottles of weird booze, ethnic statues, oriental vases and photographs of Ewan in exotic places.

Molly picked one up. It showed a younger Ewan with his arm around a guy and two young women, but she couldn't tell from the pose if either of them was a girlfriend – or his ex-wife.

'Didn't know which you'd prefer so I made coffee and hot chocolate ...'

Guiltily, Molly turned round, still clutching the photo.

Ewan stood a few feet away with a steaming mug in each hand. He was wearing a Cambridge blue sweatshirt and dark shorts that showed off his rugby-honed and hairy thighs. His knee was patched with a white absorbent dressing, which only seemed to add to his appeal. He looked hotter than July and Molly's hormones started bubbling away like a cauldron.

'Sorry. I shouldn't be nosy,' she said, replacing the photo on the dresser.

Ewan walked over and picked up the photo, his expression frustratingly neutral. 'That's Nepal. We were on an expedition during the third year of my PhD. Although it was more of an excuse for a piss-up than an expedition.'

'Are these your lab colleagues?'

'Two of them are. The other is my ex, Anna.'

'Oh, I see ... I didn't like to ask.'

'But you wanted to know?'

'I wondered.'

'We met during our second year but we weren't seeing each other when this was taken. Soon after though.'

He edged the photo back into the exact same position. Molly wondered why he hadn't thrown it out.

'Do you want something to eat?' he asked, as they moved back to the sofa. 'I don't know about you but I'm starving and we should replenish the calories we've used.'

'I was hoping to lose some,' joked Molly.

'Rubbish. Trying to diet while you're doing such a lot of intense work is stupid,' he said gruffly. 'And anyway, you don't need to lose any weight. I'll get some food.'

He returned a few minutes later with a plate laden with brownies and flapjacks.

Molly sniffed the air. 'Mm. They look good.'

'I hope so. I made them.'

'*You* did?'

'Don't sound so surprised.' The smile he tried so hard to suppress during the week appeared. It changed his whole face.

Molly's mouth watered and it had nothing to do with Ewan's brownies. She took one from the plate and crammed it in her mouth. Crumbly chocolate fell onto her tights and the seat of the sofa. Ewan watched her as he demolished a flapjack. Molly shifted around in her seat. Was he into watching women devour cake or something? Was he one of those guys who posted photos on the Internet of women eating?

'Sorry, making a mess,' she said, brushing the crumbs off her lap and onto the floorboards. 'Oh, that's worse.'

'It's OK,' he said. He picked up the plate. 'Another?'

'I shouldn't.'

Molly couldn't take her eyes off his thighs. He kept talking in his deep voice. When he leaned over to reach for another brownie, his T-shirt rode up and she caught a glimpse of his stomach. It was toned, taut, not a six-pack but probably four. She'd love to make a closer examination.

She wanted to bite her fist in frustration. The lust hormones had her in their grip, pulsing through her and making bits of her hum like power lines in the rain. She curled her toes into the soft pile of the rug then stopped when she noticed Ewan watching her. She tried not to tense up her body and nodded and smiled and hemmed in all the right places while barely taking in a word he'd said.

'Maybe I will have another,' she said, reaching for the plate on the coffee table.

He held it out but Molly knocked it from his hand. It fell onto the floorboards with a sharp clatter. China exploded over the boards and rug.

'Oh shit, sorry!'

She knelt on the boards.

'Don't worry, it's fine,' said Ewan, crouching next to her and helping to clear up the broken crockery. Molly cursed herself for her clumsiness.

'It looked like an expensive plate.'

'It was.'

'Oh dear. I'm really sorry.'

'But Anna chose it so it doesn't matter and for God's sake, stop saying sorry.'

His hand brushed hers as they reached for the same shard of china. The hairs on his wrist tickled her fingers. She couldn't see his face but his skin was warm. His hand rested over hers. Flattened it against the boards.

'Ow!'

'What?'

Ewan pulled his hand away. Molly held up her open palm, a tiny globule of crimson glistened on the fleshy pad at the base of her thumb.

'Wait.'

Ewan plucked a shard of china, so thin it was almost invisible, from her hand.

'Got it.' His voice was husky.

Still kneeling on the rug, he held the shard between his fingers. Molly sucked her palm, where the sliver of china had pierced it. Ewan stared at her sucking her hand, seemingly fascinated. What was this? *Twilight?* Molly felt her cheeks warming. His lips parted and he swallowed. She felt shivery with lust. Were they going to do it here on the rug?

'Ewan?'

He frowned, and stood up abruptly.

Molly got to her feet too but the spell was broken.

'I'm sorry about the plate.'

'Like I said, I didn't like it anyway. In fact, I'm glad it's gone.' He turned away with the pieces of plate in his hand. 'Um, if you're OK, I'll get rid of this mess and then I have work to do if you don't mind.'

What? One moment he could barely take his eyes off her and the next, he couldn't wait to be rid of her?

'I'm busy too,' said Molly coolly. 'There's no need to see me out if you're busy.'

'It's no trouble.' He strode ahead of her into the hallway.

'You could have fooled me,' she muttered, picking up her cycle helmet from the bottom step of the stairs.

'What?'

'I said, I'll see you at work tomorrow.'

'I'll email you some suggested times for our next training session,' he said, still holding the plate.

'You mean, there's going to be *another* one?'

He frowned. 'Of course. Why wouldn't there be?'

'No idea.' Molly walked out of the house without looking behind, unlocked her road bike and cycled off. Annoyance and frustration with Ewan had given her fresh energy. Bloody, bloody Ewan: if the DNA of Brian Cox, Aidan Turner and

Doc Martin had been blended together, you'd have something close to him.

If he was so hell bent on keeping her at arm's length, why invite her into his house? Why engage her in conversation and say she looked OK as she was and touch her hand and act like he wanted to swallow her hole then bundle her out? She'd thought the tandem was a cry for help but he was driving her insane with his mixed messages. She would make a renewed effort to be as grumpy and cool as he was. She wasn't going to waste any more time on him.

Chapter Fourteen

Sarah was working on some new tiara designs for a wedding fair while also trying to boost her jewellery stock for a Valentine's craft event the following weekend. She'd been working flat out and showing a string of prospective buyers round the cottage. Some – OK, most of them – hadn't been as hideous as the Pratt-Deaths, but she'd still found it almost impossible to show any enthusiasm for selling the cottage. Despite this, it was clear that several couples were very taken with the property's pretty exterior and its garden. One or two had even mentioned her Kabin and their plans for it. Although no one had put in a serious offer yet, she knew it could only be a matter of time.

After a busy morning, she made a mug of ginger tea before preparing to face Cassandra Burling who was coming for a final fitting for her tiara.

Sarah slapped on a happy smile as she saw Cassandra hold the finished tiara up. The crystals and pearls shimmered in the workshop lights. Although it wasn't her favourite creation, she was quietly satisfied with the job she'd done. She'd worked extra hard on it, way beyond what she was charging for, and hoped her client would be satisfied. Cassandra's eyes narrowed and she wrinkled her nose, as she turned the tiara to and fro before letting out a dramatic sigh. Sarah's hopes nosedived.

'Hmm. It's OKayyyish ...' Cassandra drawled. 'But not exactly what I'd imagined. I wanted a dove with pearl in its beak and that thing looks more like a pigeon.'

'It is a dove,' said Sarah patiently. 'It's the one you saw and loved in the online catalogue.'

'Well, it looks like a pigeon now it's here. Can you find another dove? A cuter dove?'

'That's the only dove I've seen. The only other birds I've ever come across are owls and you don't want an owl on a bridal tiara, do you?'

'No ... but what about another animal? Something cute and classy, and tasteful.'

Sarah stopped a second before she suggested a hippo and gritted her teeth instead. She'd already spent hours over the time she'd allow for a normal bridal tiara, and she thought the finished result *was* tasteful and pretty instead of tacky. Even the dove with a pearl in its beak, which had been tricky to work into the design, looked quite quirky and cool ... 'Well, I'll scour the web now and send you some links but you need to make a quick decision because I need time to order it – and if it's a new supplier to me, I can't guarantee it will arrive – and I need time to rework the commission.'

'Thanks. I knew you'd work a miracle. Now, I like the bridesmaids' headdresses. They're gorgeous but I did wonder about one more teensy little thing ...'

As Cassandra spoke, a wave of nausea sprang out of nowhere and rolled over Sarah. 'One teensy thing?' she said, holding on to a chair back for support.

'Yes. I know the peachy pink is lovely but you don't think

they'd have been better in a pinky peach, do you? Sarah? Are you OK?'

'Sozcassandraamgonnabesick.'

In a brief hiatus between bouts of throwing up, Sarah found time to apologise to Cassandra and promised to search to the ends of the known universe for a replacement bird, while convincing her that the tone of the bridesmaids' headwear was just right.

No sooner had Cassandra tottered off down the path than Sarah had to race to the cottage again. Finally, she finished retching and lifted her head out of the toilet. The flush died away and she'd started brushing her teeth when someone knocked on the door.

Damn, it must be Cassandra with more demands. Cursing, Sarah splashed her face and hastily wiped it before trying to fix on a smile and opening the door.

It was Niall. Her heart sank and her smile slipped. That was all she needed.

He stared at her and pulled a face. 'God, Sarah. You look terrible.'

'Thanks a lot. I um ... I'm um ... feeling a bit peaky.' It was on the tip of her tongue to tell him about the baby but she held back. She wasn't sure of his reaction and if he started ranting and raving she couldn't handle it. She might see how the conversation went.

'Sorry to hear it. Well, I won't get too close to you but I do need to talk to you.' His voice softened. 'It's important, Sarah, which is why I wanted to see you face to face.'

All trace of his cocky demeanour had vanished. He did seem serious. Maybe he was regretting what he'd done and wanted to ask her to let him move back in. Sarah was torn.

If he wanted to move back that would mean Sarah wouldn't lose the home she loved. But if that was the case, she had to stand firm. There was no way she could forgive him, even if it meant that she could stay at the cottage.

He stamped his feet. 'Can I come in? I'm freezing my nuts off out here.' He tried a small smile and reluctantly, Sarah let him in, steeling herself for what was to come.

He sat down on the sofa and peered at her. 'There's toothpaste on your jumper.'

'I've just brushed my teeth. Busy day.'

'Oh.' He glanced around him, taking in what must have been the familiar sights of the cottage sitting room. He seemed very subdued. She braced herself for another plea to let him back.

'Well, I may as well come right out with it. The agent called me this morning. She said you've been telling buyers that we have rats and subsidence and that Mrs Sugden runs a bondage den.'

'That was a joke, Ni,' said Sarah.

'They obviously took it seriously. Now I know why some of the buyers didn't even come round for a second viewing.'

Sarah shrugged. 'Obviously some people have no sense of humour. And I've been so bloody busy keeping the place tidy and showing people round. It's a lot of work.'

'I did offer to do some of the viewings myself.'

'No! I mean, it's more convenient for me to do them when I can fit them into my schedule,' Sarah said hastily. She hadn't wanted Niall in control of the situation or in the house at all, but it looked like she was losing the battle to avoid selling. Pretty cottages in nice villages around Cambridge weren't going to hang around for long.

'Anyway,' he said. 'Luckily you haven't managed to scare everyone off. I had a call this morning. We've actually had a sensible offer from one of the viewings. It's a cash buyer and is only five hundred short of the asking price. I've told the agents yes, but I need your say-so too. There won't be a problem, will there?'

Sarah swallowed down her shock and disappointment. 'No, no problem. No bloody problem at all ...'

'Jesus. I knew you'd react like this ...' Niall slammed his mug down on the table but his next words were softer. 'Look, darlin', things are hard for all of us but this is a great offer and it gives both of us the chance to make a fresh start. That's what you want, isn't it?'

Niall's voice cracked with a wobble of emotion and Sarah thought she glimpsed regret in his eyes. He looked tired but still handsome. Her stomach flipped with a familiar feeling of lust. No matter what he'd done, she still loved the glint in his eye, that cheeky smile, even his bloody quiff. She remembered the night she'd first met him, how she'd thought he was a bit of a chancer and then how he'd told her risqué jokes and insisted on calling her a taxi and told her how he'd wanted to be a paramedic since he was four and his mum had caught him dismembering his sister's Barbie dolls.

'Look, Sare. I'm sorry it's come to this. Really I am. Sorry I caused it.' He covered her hand with his. She let it rest there a second and her heart softened a degree. She'd loved him once, and despite everything she still did *and* she was carrying his child. How would he react if he knew? Would it make him change his mind about selling the cottage? Although he was happy for Sarah to move, he surely wouldn't want to see his own child kicked out of their home? They could start again … though it could never be the same, not even with a baby on the way. *Especially* with a baby on the way … but she at least owed it to him to tell him, even if he'd said he was dead against a family. The words were on her lips, waiting to be said. Any moment.

He took his hand away from hers and got to his feet, with a sigh. 'I didn't only come round to tell you about the offer. There's something else and I wanted you to hear it from me before you find out on the grapevine …' His tone hardened. 'I may as well tell you. I've decided to give things a go with Vanessa. We've had a good talk and she's asked me to move in with her and I've said yes.'

Chapter Fifteen

Molly rang the bell at the cottage and stamped her feet to keep warm while she waited for Sarah to answer. When no one came she rapped the knocker, waited another couple of minutes and then peered through the window. Sarah's car was on the drive and a lamp glowed behind the curtains but there was no sound of the TV on in the sitting room.

The letterbox almost took her fingers off as she called through it. 'Sarah, it's Molly!'

Getting no answer, she fished her phone from her bag. Her fingers were numb with cold as she prodded the buttons. Sarah's mobile and house phone went straight to answerphone. Anxiety tugged at her: what if Sarah had had an accident? What if she was losing the baby and lying in a pool of blood on the floor?

No, she was probably in the shower or having a nap or something or in her workshop; that was far more likely than any disaster. Molly dragged an empty stone flower tub to the garden gate and stood on it to unlock the latch. Relief flooded her when she saw the lights of the workshop casting pools of yellow on the frosty path. Sarah was working and must be distracted by her work. She pushed open the gate, calling cheerfully, 'Hi, hon. Nice to see you're doing some—'

She didn't get any further. The workshop looked as if a bomb had gone off in it. Beads, wire and tiny gemstones covered the worktops, the chairs and floor like glittering colourful snow. In the centre of it all sat Sarah. Mascara streaked her face, her hair shimmered with tiny beads and she held a broken tiara in her hands.

Molly dashed forward and fell to her knees, taking Sarah in her arms. 'Oh God, hon, are you OK?'

Sarah let out a huge juddering sob. 'I'm f-f-fine.'

'What the hell happened? Have you been burgled?'

'N-n-no. It's N-n-niall.'

Molly gasped. 'What? He hasn't smashed up your workshop!'

'No. Ni didn't smash it up. I did.'

Molly hugged Sarah, feeling as if her own heart would break. '*Why, hon?*'

'I'd had a string of bloody loved-up brides all week long, rattling on about their gorgeous fiancés, and their wonderful bloody boyfriends and weren't they lucky and blah di blah until I wanted to stick my fingers down my throat, not that I need any help to throw up these days. And then Cassandra Burling said her dove looked like a pigeon – a fucking pigeon! – and wanted me to find her an owl or a hippo or something and I can't – and then *he* called, the bastard, going on about me dragging my feet over the sale of the cottage ...'

Sarah dabbed at her eyes with a soggy piece of toilet paper.

'And – and – then Niall told me he was moving in with Vanessa.'

'Oh my God, no! He can't do. I thought he said that shagging her was a mistake.'

'He did but now he's changed his mind. He said he needs a place to live and he wants to give things a chance with her.'

'But she's a health nut, isn't she? She's not up his street at all ... apart from the kinky sex I guess.'

Sarah let out a cry.

'Sorry, Sarah but I can't believe it.'

'Neither can I. I thought he'd come round to grovel and to be honest I wasn't sure how I was going to react. I almost told him about the baby I even – oh God – I even considered letting him have another chance for a nanosecond. Then he told me that we'd had an offer on the house and then he dropped the bombshell about Vanessa.'

'Now, I understand why you had a meltdown, hon. Damn, I've run out of tissues. Here, have this.' Molly shoved a piece of blue lab roll from her bag into Sarah's hands. 'It's clean. No gorilla jizz.'

'I never want to be within fifty miles of any kind of jizz, ever again, human or animal. I'm sorry f-for whingeing again. It's my hormones. I can't seem to control them. One minute I'm together and stable and the next I want to hide in a corner and howl or puke. I meant to be cool and calm with Niall but I just flipped. I threw him out – again – and then I came into the workshop and I did this.' She waved her hand at the carnage. 'I don't know why.'

Molly sighed, her heart breaking for her sister's distress. 'I'll help you clear up when you're feeling a bit better but, Sarah, you're going to have to tell Niall about the baby at some point. He's going to notice sooner or later, isn't he?'

'Yes, but he's so dead against having a family, I don't know how he'll react. I could just about handle things when I thought he'd only wanted Vanessa for the sex. He swore she didn't mean anything and that he still loved me. Even though I didn't really want him back, God help me, I actually thought about having him back for a moment... it's hard to let someone go when you've been together that long, Molly. I can't expect you to understand that.'

Molly held her tongue, even though Sarah's last comment had stung her.

'No, I can't,' she said, forcing herself to remember that Sarah was going through hell.

Sarah leaned against the worktop. 'Now I can't bear the thought of him with her. The idea of them having a relationship makes me feel sick. It's completely irrational because I loathe him but I do still love him too. Sometimes I think anything would be better than feeling like this ... You know I didn't want him to still love me but now he's gone off with Vanessa, I really do. Does that sound crazy?'

Molly thought Sarah's hormones were screwing up her judgement. There was no way on the planet she would ever have forgiven Niall or wanted him back but she kept her thoughts to herself. Sarah was in no state for tough love at the moment.

'Not really. Not at all, in fact.' Molly thought of her own "irrational" feelings towards Ewan with his own wild mood swings and tried to empathise with her sister.

'Oh hon. I'm so sorry. The hormones can't help and I don't blame you for being upset but you can't possibly want Niall back ...'

'He's a shit but a shit who I still love. And despite everything, I wish he loved me.' Her voice trailed off and she stared at her surroundings, finally seeming to register the thousands of beads, flowers and findings littering the workshop floor.

'Oh shit,' she said quietly. 'What have I done?'

Molly put her arm around Sarah, hoping that she'd feel better when she'd had some sleep and time away from the workshop mess. 'Look, hon, you know I'd do anything I could to help you feel better. For now, let's go into the cottage. I'll make you a cup of tea and then I'll clear up this mess while you get some rest.'

A couple of hours later, Molly had cancelled her spin class and was returning the final few beads to their plastic tubs. Scrabbling around on the floor for the tiny objects had given her sore knees and eye strain and she was sure Sarah would be finding bits and pieces for months to come.

Sarah had tried to put her feet up but soon joined her and seemed to have calmed down a little. Maybe the action of being busy had helped more than sitting around dwelling on her situation.

Sarah closed the lid on the plastic box she'd refilled with seed beads and sighed loudly. 'Molly ...'

Molly got up and felt her spine click. She was still sore from a mammoth training session with Ewan. 'Yup.'

'You know that thing I said – how if only there was a way of making Niall fall in love with me again so he'd come grovelling back and I could keep the cottage?'

Molly paused, midway to screwing the lid on a jar. The tiny hairs on the back of her neck seemed to stand on end. 'Ye-es ...'

'And how you said you'd do anything to help me if you could?'

Sarah's eyes were strangely bright and there was a smile on her face. She looked almost feverish.

Molly's blood seemed to run cold, even though she knew

that wasn't actually possible. 'Yes, I did, but I can't do *that*.'

'I haven't said what "that" is yet ...' Sarah said.

'You don't have to and I'd crawl on my hands and knees to Australia if I thought it would make you happy, Sare, but I can't possibly do what you're thinking.'

'Why not?'

'Because we don't know if it will work. Because we haven't tried it on people yet. Because it's still theoretical. Sort of.'

'But you said it does work ...'

'Yes. We know it works in some specific applications but it's only been trialled so far in the military and for soldiers with trauma ... and psychiatric disorders where people have difficulty empathising fully. There's a long process to go through before it could be certified for manufacture and the Research Ethics Committee would only approve it for one use at a time.'

'You also told me that it could be used as a next-generation aphrodisiac,' said Sarah.

Molly wished she'd never even joked – or mentioned – the Bug with Sarah.

'Eventually. A few years down the line ...' she said.

'You said it was already more powerful than anything on the market and that Ewan was a genius for coming up with it. You said he was the Stephen Hawking of the sexual behavioural ecology world.'

'Hawking? Ewan? I never said that! Hell, *when* did I say that?'

'At the New Year's Party when you were really pissed.'

Molly took a deep breath, regretting ever going to the party in the first place.

'OK, the Love Bug *could* in theory be used for that purpose but it hasn't had any clinical trials yet. And using it is at the very least serious research misconduct and unethical, and giving it to Niall could be – *is* – technically assault or administering a noxious substance or something even worse. I could go to jail for it and you'd be in serious trouble too and you don't want your baby born in jail, do you? You don't want to be one of those women in a Channel 4 documentary. You know *Knocked Up and Banged Up* ...' Molly tried, hoping humour would make Sarah realise the craziness of what she was asking her to consider.

'Of course not. I was only wondering ...'

'And even if I *did* design a Love Bug that worked, both for you and Niall, and I don't know if I *can*, ask yourself this: would you really want to live with Niall, knowing that his feelings weren't genuine? Could you spend the rest of your life with him, knowing that it was only the Love Bug that made him stay with you? Not that I could guarantee the effects would last, either, and then you'd be back in the same boat, only worse because you'd feel guilty about conning him.'

'When you put it like that, the idea sounds bonkers but ... I just want the chance to remind him what he's missing. Once he got used to the idea of the baby coming, or being here, he'd be over Vanessa and realise what true love is.'

Molly lost patience. 'Oh, Sarah! Don't let that bastard make you desperate.'

'I don't care if I am desperate ... and be honest, Mol, aren't *you* just a tiny bit desperate to know if the Love Bug works? Imagine if you had actual proof? How useful that could be to your work? You could make giant strides forward. Even the Great Ewan Baxter couldn't possibly match that.'

Molly paused, letting her mind dwell on the idea of knowing that the Bug worked; the secret knowledge, how it might advance the project ... In the past great scientists had taken risks for the greater good. They'd experimented on themselves, risked everything ... and although she wouldn't dream of telling Sarah, in some of the more maverick parts of the scientific world, it was *exactly* the sort of thing that went on.

But not in her world.

With a shudder, she snapped back to reality. 'I can't. In fact, as I said before, I shouldn't have even told you I was working on it. *Because the Love Bug doesn't exist, right, Sarah?*'

Sarah sighed. 'OK, I respect your decision. I wouldn't want to ruin your career. It was probably a mad idea anyway, so let's just forget about it.'

Driving home, Molly felt bad about being so harsh with Sarah but she needed to nip any idea of using the Love Bug on Niall in the bud. Sarah wasn't thinking straight and she was desperate: she had to be to want Niall back for any reason.

She turned in to the parking area at the back of the flats where she lived behind the pub. Some idiot had thought it was fun to kick over a wheelie bin and the rubbish was scattered all over her parking place. Molly cleared away the worst of it with her boots but there was no way she was touching the rubbish.

After locking the car, she went into the flat and sat on the sofa.

She wished she'd never mentioned the Bug to Sarah.

Then she wouldn't have had to lie to her sister. Because while the Bug *was* experimental it had undergone more clinical trials than she'd let on. A very similar hormone had been tested in a North American lab recently and it had been proven that it *did* work. In fact, it had worked a bit too well as it had made individuals *very* friendly to their "in" group and more aggressive to outsiders.

But her – and Ewan's – version of the Bug was slightly different. Different because it was designed to be even more powerful and its effects even more long-lasting. In fact, that was the problem: she and Ewan weren't really sure, yet, how long-lasting it was or if there was a way of reversing it. So there was absolutely no way she was going to help Sarah. Her sister was just going have to get real and accept that Niall had chosen to be with Vanessa.

Chapter Sixteen

What a way to spend a Sunday, thought Molly, hunched over the handlebars of the tandem. She could barely see because the wind was making her eyes water continuously. Her nose was running too but she didn't want to stop to wipe either of them. She had a goal: a pub on the edge of a Fenland village where she intended to stop before they turned around, whether Ewan moaned or not.

She'd spent most of the day before helping Sarah at a wedding fair at a local hotel. The event had gone well, with Sarah taking tiara commissions and selling heaps of jewellery sets as Valentine gifts. She'd seemed more stable, seemed to be enjoying focusing on her business and hadn't mentioned using the Love Bug on Niall again, to Molly's huge relief. As for Ewan, he'd either been out of the office or back to his usual morose self.

But there was no escaping each other now. Ewan shouted something that Molly assumed to be "go faster" or "don't stop". She pushed down harder on the pedals, motivated by the thought of a hot meal and a cosy fire in the pub. It *had* to be just around the next bend in the road.

'Molly! Stop!'

Molly squeezed the brakes harder than she'd meant to and they both almost fell off.

'Arggh.'

She slowed down. 'What's the matter? I almost crashed!' she called behind.

'Something's wrong,' said Ewan. 'Stop!'

He was right. The bike did feel strange. In fact, it seemed the wheels had almost stopped turning. It stuttered and came to a halt.

'Careful!'

'What's up with it?'

They climbed off the bike. 'I don't know. I heard a bang as we came around the last corner and then the bike just didn't feel normal.' He crouched down, examining the rear wheel while Molly held the bike upright.

'Shit, we've broken a spoke.'

'You're joking?'

Ewan poked at the broken spoke. 'Sadly, no.' He stood up, hands on hips. 'That's it, then. We can't ride it home or anywhere until it's been repaired.'

'Maybe we should get a new bike,' Molly said. 'We could ask Pete if he could help ...' she added mischievously.

'Over my dead body. I don't want to ask anyone in the lab for help or Pete's bound to hear about it. We'll have to get it repaired. The layoff will eat into our training time but we've got no choice.'

Ewan held the tandem while Molly stretched her arms. God, her shoulders were so stiff she could hardly lift them over her head. 'How are we going to get back?' she asked.

'I don't know,' said Ewan. 'We're almost thirty miles from home. Christ, we're in a different county ...'

'We're going to have to call someone to come and get us

though God knows who, unless you know anyone with a van or a bike trailer.'

'No, I don't. This is what comes of not having a support crew,' muttered Ewan, staring at the spoke as if it had bitten him on the bum.

'We could always ask Mrs Choudhry and that bloke from the supplier who fancies you ...'

Ewan laid the bike on the verge. 'It's not funny. The spoke will have to be replaced and the wheel will have to be re-trued and that's *if* the bike shop has the right length spoke and the nipple to fix it in stock.' He aimed a kick at the bike and winced as his toe made contact with the frame.

Molly started giggling. She was freezing, her nose was running, they were stranded in the middle of the most godforsaken part of the Fens and Ewan was talking about nipples. She couldn't help herself.

'What's so funny?' he asked.

'N-nothing,' she said, wiping her eyes with a tissue.

'Then why are you having hysterics?'

'It's you, going on about s-spokes and n-nipples.'

'I'll have you know that nipple is a technical term,' he said.

'I know but ... kicking a bike?' Molly laughed so hard, her stomach hurt and she suddenly realised how much she wanted a wee. She had to get a grip.

Ewan stared at her and then, suddenly, a smile spread over his face. 'Well, it deserved it, bloody thing. And we will need a *nipple*,' he said, stressing the word and setting Molly off into gales of laughter again.

'Remind me ... why the ... hell we're doing this?' she squeezed out between hysterics.

'Because neither of us wanted you to be doing it with Pete Garrick?'

Had Ewan just said what she thought he had?

Ewan picked up the tandem again and wheeled it over to her.

'I could have just said no to Pete. I am capable of telling him to piss off without you rescuing me.'

'I know that. But you could also have told me to piss off too.'

'I still might.'

'Not before you've worked out a way of getting us and the bike home, I hope.' The moment had passed. Ewan retreated into his normal brisk and morose mood, while he tried to find a signal on his mobile. They'd both realised they were going to have to fork out for a van to fetch them and if they couldn't use their phones, they were going to have to drag the bike to the village until they could get a signal or use a landline.

It was hopeless so Molly took out her phone. After walking a few hundred yards up the lane, and a few dropped calls, she managed to reach Sarah.

'Oh, thank God for that. Sarah, it's me and I have to make this quick because it's a lousy signal. This is a long shot, but do you know anyone who could rescue us and the bike from the middle of Suffolk?'

Molly could almost hear Sarah's cogs whirring. 'I don't know ... um ...'

Even while Sarah hesitated, Molly had a sudden rethink. It might be better if she didn't risk bringing Sarah into Ewan's presence at all. Despite the fact Sarah hadn't mentioned it again, she didn't entirely trust her not to mention the Love

Bug in front of him. Under normal circumstances, Sarah could be relied upon but nothing was normal about the circumstances they were in at the moment.

'Don't worry. It was just an idea in case you knew someone. We'll try to get a people carrier taxi or a van or something. But you might have to call one for us because the signal is well dodgy here. The GPS says we're half a mile on the B4542 south of Ditchfield ...' she rattled on.

'Hang on, wait ... Give me a little while and I'll get back to you.'

'OK. We're not going any—' The phone went dead. Well, it was too late now, thought Molly as her teeth had started to chatter. Now she wasn't working hard on the bike, her damp clothes felt clammy and cold. If Sarah did find someone to help, Molly would have to manage the situation and she would be very grateful to be warm and dry and in a mode of transport that didn't require thigh-burning effort and a massive masochistic streak.

Ewan carried the bike towards her. It was heavy for one person and as he walked, his arm and thigh muscles flexed. He was a little out of breath and dumped the bike down when they met.

'Any luck?'

Molly held up crossed fingers. 'Possibly, but shall we walk towards the village anyway? I'll help you with the bike.'

'It's fine,' he said. 'And why don't you put my jacket on? I'm warm enough carrying this bloody thing.'

Molly opened her mouth to protest.

'Don't be predictable,' said Ewan. 'Just put it on.'

An hour later, a large silver van with the logo of LC Holdings pulled into the car park of the pub where Molly and Ewan waited with the bike. Sarah had managed to text them the very welcome news that one of her students was coming to collect them in one of his company's vans.

It didn't take a rocket scientist, or even a molecular biochemist, to work out that the tall man with dark hair climbing down from the drivers' seat was Liam Cipriani. He looked remarkably chilled and friendly for a man whom Sarah had almost brained with a Toby jug.

Sarah's car arrived while Liam walked over to them.

'Hello. Taxi for the Tandem Two,' he said.

Ewan blew out a breath. 'Thanks, mate. Sorry we had to drag you out here.'

Mate? Molly bit her lip. Ewan rarely called anyone mate. A social anthropologist would have a field day analysing this situation.

'You must be Liam,' she said. 'Thanks for coming.'

'Not a problem. I don't mind helping out.'

Ewan showed Liam the bike while Sarah hopped out of the car and hugged Molly.

'Thanks so much for this. Do you think Liam minds?' Molly asked.

'He wouldn't have come if he did. I've had to follow behind because there's not enough room for us all in the front of the van.'

'I'll pay for your fuel. I feel so stupid, dragging you both out here.'

'Forget it. You couldn't help it and I wasn't doing much. Well, I was fixing a kingfisher into a tiara for a client, actually, but don't let that worry you. I dropped it round to her house on the way here and you gave me an excuse not to stay any longer or have to change the design again.'

159

While Sarah watched, Molly and Ewan loaded the tandem into the back of the van. Molly thanked Liam again. 'Hope I haven't ruined your Sunday.'

'It's fine, I was only working on my tiara when Sarah called me and asked if I knew anyone who could help. I nipped over to the office and picked up the van.'

'Your tiara?' Ewan's face was deadpan.

'It's for my daughter's wedding.'

'Ah, I see.' Ewan nodded sagely.

'I'm one of Sarah's students. Now, as we're out at a pub on a Sunday, we may as well all have lunch. You two look like you could do with a hot meal.'

'You're not wrong, but I'll pay,' said Ewan. 'I don't know what we'd have done without you.'

'We'll go halves,' said Molly firmly.

'Is it OK with you if we stay for lunch?' Liam asked Sarah.

Molly was glad to see Sarah smile. 'Why not? It'll keep me out of the way of Cassandra and I seem to be getting my appetite back these days.'

Shortly afterwards, they were all sat in the bar, shovelling down roast dinner. Sarah did seem to have a decent appetite and over the meal, Liam asked them more about their training and the charity race. Molly started to thaw out and Ewan perked up considerably now he had a pint in his hand and someone to talk to about the tandem.

'We'll have to get the bike fixed before we can resume the training,' he said as they tucked into bowls of apple crumble and custard.

Molly waited for mention of nipples but none came. 'It'll have to go the repair centre,' she said.

'I can drop you and it off there on the way home if you

like,' Liam offered. 'We should just make it before they shut. Your bike looks vintage. I used to ride quite a bit when I was younger but I'm too busy now. How's your sponsorship target going?'

'OK,' said Molly. 'But there's another team from our lab who have entered the same event, so we can't ask the same people for cash. Most of the students and post-docs are broke anyway after they've paid their rent.'

'I could help you out there.'

'You've already done more than enough by coming out to rescue us. I wasn't fishing for money.'

'Well you should be.' Liam laughed. 'I'll tell you what, how about if I provide you with the van as a support vehicle on the day. After all, you're going to need a lift back from the finish line, unless you plan on riding home.'

'No way,' said Molly.

'Thanks,' said Ewan. The offer of the sponsorship had perked him up.

The conversation moved on to Ewan's and Molly's research. Liam nodded and asked questions in all the right places but it was obvious Sarah was his only true focus. He couldn't take his eyes off her. He's mad on her, the poor guy, thought Molly and pitied him. Falling for Sarah while she was still obviously in love/loathing with Niall was even more hopeless than her falling for Ewan. Her skin prickled. Was *she* in love with Ewan? Or only in lust? Despite what she'd told Sarah, Molly couldn't deny her feelings for him had changed, deepened even … Oh, shit.

Ewan was chatting and smiling with Liam and Sarah, and Molly realised that he wasn't moody all the time, just with her. Therefore, her logical mind debated, there had to be a reason for that. Could he be trying to deny his feelings for her or was that only her wishful thinking. He caught her eye and held her gaze until Molly joked about putting on weight like Sarah because of all the food she'd eaten. It was a very lame joke but Ewan smiled. Molly was more confused than ever, and also felt a creeping sense of gloom, which wasn't like her at all. Fancying Ewan had been fun at first; just a lark and a challenge but lately, her feelings had definitely changed, almost without her realising it.

Was this her fate, to work alongside her gorgeous brooding boss and spend her life in a state of permanent sexual frustration and emotional turmoil?

Maybe it would be better if she left and found a new job.

After the waiter had cleared away their dishes, Molly and Sarah went to the ladies' together. Molly came out of the loo to find Sarah splashing her face with cold water.

'Are you OK?' she asked.

Sarah dabbed her face with a paper towel. 'I'm fine. I just felt a bit hot in the pub by the fire. I haven't felt sick for a while now though, so I'm hoping that phase is on its way out. I should start to bloom soon.' She laughed.

'You already are.' Molly turned off the taps, watching Sarah's face in the mirror next to hers. She giggled. 'Can you imagine Mum and Dad's faces if they knew I was out on a tandem?'

'No,' Sarah said, laughing. 'They'd never have believed it.'

'You do look well, Sare,' Molly said, turning to her sister. 'Is it anything to do with Liam? He seems a really nice guy.'

'He is.' Sarah's voice was neutral.

'And he *really* likes you.'

Sarah laughed again. 'He's just being kind.'

Molly pulled a handful of paper towels from the dispenser. 'No, he *really* likes you, Sarah.'

'Do you think so?'

She dried her hands. 'How do you feel about him?'

'How do I feel? I like him ... a lot. He's a good friend.'

'And he's hot.'

'You think so? He's twelve years older than me.'

Molly threw the paper towels in the bin. 'And miles younger than Brad Pitt, and Keanu Reeves. He has some great genes – with a name like Cipriani, I guess he's Italian?'

Sarah laughed. 'His dad's from Sardinia and his mum's from London. They met while they were both backpacking in the seventies.'

'This may be a coincidence but Sardinia has one of the highest concentrations of centenarians in the world. So I was right about the genes.'

'He often talks about the village where his father grew up. It's in the hills above the south-east coast. It sounds idyllic.'

'Do you fancy him?' Molly lowered her voice as she followed Sarah out of the toilets and into the pub corridor.

Sarah stopped by a fruit machine. 'Fancy him? Yes. No. I *can't*.'

'What do you mean, you can't?'

'Because of Niall. I couldn't possibly think of getting involved with another guy so soon after Niall.'

'No, I see what you mean. But one day ...'

'Even if I *did* fancy Liam and yes, I admit he's hot – for an older guy – but I couldn't hook up with someone so soon.'

'Does Liam know that?'

'He's aware of my situation,' said Sarah firmly, 'and that I'm not ready for anyone else. I know you think I'm crazy but I still have strong feelings for Niall – especially since he moved in with Vile Vanessa – and however wrong and mad that may seem to you, that's the way it is.'

Molly hugged Sarah and decided to shut up. Her hopes that Molly might have come to her senses had taken a dent. She only hoped her sister had abandoned any ideas about using the Love Bug on her ex, whether to actually get him back or for revenge – or both. She walked back into the pub lounge where Ewan was showing Liam something on his phone. Probably a particularly fascinating bacterial infection.

Liam glanced up and smiled when Sarah came back. His eyes filled with pure pleasure but he made a gentle joke about the girls going to the loo in pairs to hide how he felt. Ewan glanced up at Molly and their eyes met briefly before he said something neutral about the tandems. If only he was as easy to read as Liam.

Who was she to criticise Sarah's feelings, when her own for Ewan were all over the place – and his were a complete mystery? They were four people sitting round a pub table, laughing and having a good time yet none of them seemed to know how they felt towards the other person or how to reach out to him or her. She had a horrible feeling that the four of them were the right people in the wrong time and place but who was she to judge the way people felt and the stupid things they did for love?

Chapter Seventeen

Molly was so shattered after the wedding fair and tandem training that she slept through her Monday morning alarm and had to drive to the lab, munching on a piece of toast as she queued in the traffic. At least, with the bike in for repair, she had a few days off from bike-based torment.

After a tense morning in the lab, she was grateful to escape with her lunchtime sandwich into the lab garden while the Love Bug had gone off to the mass spectrometry team to test its purity. She and Ewan had also been preparing for the QA team to come in and audit the lab so it was a relief to feel the stray shafts of early spring sunlight on her face and see snowdrops nodding in the breeze next to a few brave purple crocuses that had burst through the soggy grass. Soon there would be bright narcissi and pale primroses too. Winter had seemed long this year.

Molly bit into her chicken wrap, just as Ewan walked out of the lab doors sneezing into a large white hanky. After waiting for him to finish she clucked her tongue in mock sympathy. 'Oh dear. I hope you haven't got a cold, Professor Baxter, or I can't allow you into the lab.'

'It's all those bloody flowers in reception and stuck in buckets in the canteen.' Ewan sneezed again.

'Well, it *is* Valentine's Day.'

'Really? I dought it mubt be something like dat.'

She waited while he put away his hanky and sniffed loudly. 'So, you haven't noticed the shops full of big pink hearts and cards and chocolate on your way around town lately?' she said when he'd sat down on the bench next to her, obviously with no qualms about spreading his germs around. Not that she'd have minded *too* much.

'Funny you should mention it but yes, I have. Now, I realise what all that shit is for.'

She rolled her eyes. She knew he was joking but *still*.

'I expect you'll be sharing an intimate dinner with someone special this evening,' he said sarcastically.

'Funny you should mention it but yes, I will.'

He frowned at her. 'I was joking.'

'Is it really so amazing that I've been asked to dinner?'

'No. I suppose not, but the restaurants will be packed and the prices will be sky high. People will be doing stupid things like proposing and giving each other roses and teddies.'

'How awful and deluded of them but I can assure you that I won't be doing any of that stuff,' she said.

'Right, well I hope you have a lovely time.'

'I'm sure I will. Oh, look, it's Pete!' Molly gave Pete a little finger wave, enjoying the gloomy befuddlement on Ewan's face. Jesus, if he *was* jealous – of Pete and her mystery Valentine's date – then that was his problem. If he *was* interested, why didn't he just do something about it? All he had to do was book a table at Cote, or invite her to the Picture House or skip the dinner altogether and just take her to bed. Because if the tandem ride was his way of pursuing her – an excuse so he could spend time with her without actually doing it – it was *weird*. Maybe the cycling was a substitute for having sex with her. Now that really *was* weird.

'Hi, guys.'

'Hi, Pete.'

Pete grinned. 'I'm surprised to find you here, Molly. I thought you might be busy collecting all the Valentine's cards and flowers that must have arrived for you.'

He beamed at his own joke while Ewan took refuge in his baguette. 'Yeah, well, you know I had my personal assistant collect them and take them home for me. Flat's going to look like an Interflora branch,' said Molly, squirming. 'I expect you know what it feels like, Pete?'

Pete's smile evaporated. He pushed his specs back up his nose. 'Just the one card, actually.'

'Oh, who was it from?'

'It was anonymous, in the time-honoured way. What about you, Ewan? Has Cupid fired his arrow your way?'

Ewan seemed to be choking on a baguette before muttering, 'I didn't even know it was Valentine's Day.'

Pete sat down next to them. 'Hmm. I can understand that kind of trivial, commercial shit would pass you by.'

But clearly it wouldn't pass by a girly girl like her, thought Molly, quietly simmering.

'Moving on to the important stuff,' said Pete, about as sensitive as a lump of wood, 'how's the training going? I saw you out on your vintage bike the other day. What happened to the top-of-the-range custom-made model?'

'My friend from the rugby was going to loan us one but his mum and dad needed it for a cycling tour,' said Ewan.

Molly marvelled inwardly at his ability to tell such porkies. Not that Pete believed a word of it judging by his smug smile.

'Bummer, eh? So where did you get the er ... vintage Peugeot from? She must be pretty heavy to handle.'

'*It* is perfectly fine to handle,' said Molly.

'Really? I must say I was surprised to see that Ewan had let you pilot it.'

'Why?' Molly and Ewan spoke in unison.

Pete eyed them with suspicion. 'Because I thought Ewan would have wanted to be in the driving seat.'

'Actually, Pete, Molly's doing a great job as pilot.'

'And Ewan's the natural choice for stoker,' added Molly, chalking up a rare Brownie point to Ewan.

Pete smirked. 'I suppose so. So, how far have you got with the training schedule?'

'Far enough,' said Ewan.

'Good. Because the race is only a few weeks away. You should comfortably be able to do almost the full distance by now.'

Molly almost choked on her sandwich.

'Thanks for your concern, Pete, but we're on track,' said Ewan politely. 'Now, what's happening with that paper you're trying to get in *Parasitic Science*? How many rounds of revision have you had to make to it so far?'

'Remind me how far we rode on Sunday?' Molly asked Ewan when Pete had shuffled off, muttering about "bloody peer reviews".

'Forty-eight point nine miles.'

Molly groaned. Her nether regions were still sore and she was stiff even after sitting down to eat her lunch. She might have to get a gel saddle cover but she wasn't going to tell Ewan that. 'Only twenty-six point one to go then.'

Ewan stepped into his onesie. 'We'll have to up the training and go out twice a week.'

Molly pulled her hood up. 'In the dark?'

'No choice I'm afraid. It's either after work or before. I'd prefer it to be before work because I've got meetings most evenings.'

Molly suppressed a groan. 'Do you really think we need even more training?'

'I do, otherwise we'll never make the distance and it's going to be tough as it is. What about starting tomorrow morning? There's no ice forecast and after our training session, we could cycle straight to the lab and get changed here.'

'Well I suppose if there's no choice.'

Ewan adjusted his safety glasses. 'Good. I'll come round at six a.m. sharp, so it looks like you'll have to restrain yourself on your date tonight.'

She grinned. 'Oh, don't worry. I'll try not to enjoy myself too much.'

By the end of the working day, she was in no fit state to enjoy anything. She was knackered and ready to collapse on the sofa with a ready meal and a glass of wine but she didn't want to leave Sarah alone on Valentine's evening. She was definitely going to stay sober and drive rather than bike to Sarah's, what with Ewan calling round at six o'clock the next morning. Eww, even the idea of such a small hour made her feel queasy.

She unlocked the door, shoving her way past free newspapers and pizza leaflets. She scooped them up and was about to deposit them in the recycling basket when a padded envelope slid onto the kitchen tiles.

She picked it up, frowning at the black felt-tip scrawl on the front of it. Just one word: "Molly". The package had obviously been crammed through the letterbox, judging by its mangled state and it was a second-hand envelope because you could see where the sender had torn off the previous address and resealed it with parcel tape. It was obvious there was a card inside and also something round and squishy and soft.

Dumping her bag, she grabbed the scissors from the drawer and carefully slit the top of the packet open.

The card was tasteful enough, she supposed. It was plain matt silver with a red heart in the middle. The message was typed on a computer and stuck onto the card with Pritt, a bit like a ransom demand, she decided.

HOT BRUNETTE IN THE BEHAVIOURAL ECOLOGY LAB
WANNA BE THE ANTIGEN TO MY ANTIBODY?

Molly groaned. It was the kind of message she'd read in the lonely-hearts column in the free papers they gave away on trains. The soft parcel was wrapped – very badly – in white tissue paper that was obviously recycled, probably from round a wine bottle. She pulled off the tissue, pulled out a purple furry lump and burst out laughing.

'Nice. A cuddly microbe. What every woman wants.' She read the label. 'And how romantic. It's an Epstein-Barr Virus. The kissing disease.'

Molly put the furry toy on the coffee table and it smiled at her from its fringed eyelashes. 'Suppose it could be worse. Could have been Ebola.'

She looked at the card. It *had* to be Pete. She shuddered. Well, if he thought he was going to have the chance to pass on his EBV to her, he had another thing coming. Unless she had another admirer in the lab. Briefly, it crossed her mind that Ewan might have sent it but then she dismissed the idea. There was no way Ewan would send anyone a cuddly microbe and a line obviously stolen from the personal ads in the free newspaper.

She changed into fresh jeans and a jumper and drove round to Sarah's, racking her brain to think of other candidates all the way. There was an older technician who was always making jokey but innocent remarks to her, but he was ready for retirement and as far as she knew, married. He didn't seem like a cuddly microbe kind of guy and the message was a bit young to have come from him.

She longed to tell Sarah about the package and, in the past, she'd have giggled and groaned over her mystery Valentine's admirer but it seemed tactless since Niall had walked out, so she kept schtum. Sarah was tired after the wedding fair anyway, and had spent the day working commissions she'd taken on. Alcohol was off the menu for both of them so they consoled themselves with pizza and elderflower fizz.

'It was really nice of you and Liam to rescue us last weekend,' Molly said, tucking into a large slice of pepperoni.

'Yes, he's a nice guy.'

Sarah swallowed the last morsel of ham and pineapple. Molly thought her sister had a soft bloom to her cheeks and her hair was thick and bouncy. The baby was suiting her.

'Does Niall know about Liam?' she asked.

'Why should he? Liam's just a friend. He knows Liam exists, because he had to do first aid on him after I hit him with the Toby jug, but other than that, it's none of his business. Why should Niall care?'

'I don't know. I wondered maybe if he was jealous or something.'

'Why would he be jealous? He's got bloody Vanessa now.' Sarah spat the name out and pushed her plate onto the coffee table. She sighed. 'Ewan seems nice though.'

'Oh, he can convince strangers he's almost normal for a short time,' said Molly tartly. 'It's me he's rude and grumpy with.'

'Have you thought that's because he's constantly trying to hide the way he really feels? Maybe he's in a state of perpetual sexual frustration.'

'Well, I hope he's suffering because I know I am.'

'You would tell me if there was anything more between you, wouldn't you, hon? I won't burst into tears. Just because I've had a crap time lately doesn't mean you shouldn't have a good one.'

'Thanks, that means a lot to me, but to be honest I don't know where I am with Ewan. He can't seem to make up his mind whether he's interested or not and I don't want to risk another humiliation like at the New Year's party. If he wants me, he's going to have to come and get me.'

'Way to go,' said Sarah, yawning.

'I shan't hold my breath.'

'Nooooo ...'

Sarah had fallen asleep so Molly flicked between three different romcoms on the TV while her sister snored gently on the sofa. She smiled to herself, wondering if Ewan was picturing her enjoying a cosy dinner for two. Well, she hadn't exactly *lied*, had she?

Chapter Eighteen

Niall stood in the lounge, his face bright red after the dash straight from work on his motorbike. He'd called to discuss the progress of the sale and insisted on calling in person. Knowing she had to face up to him sometime, Sarah had agreed although the thought that he'd be going home to Vanessa's kinky charms was literally nauseating.

He peered at her. 'Jesus, Sare. Would you like me to make you a cup of tea? You look really pale and knackered.'

'I'm fine. Just been busy with work. Valentine's Day and wedding fairs. You know how it is.'

'I suppose so. It's that time of year.' He tried to flash her a smile, but it rapidly vanished, presumably when he saw Sarah's frosty expression.

She resisted the urge to ask him what he and Vanessa had done for Valentine's Day. He'd probably spent it chained to the bed, being flogged with a fluffy whip while Vanessa trod on him with her work boots.

'Are you really OK?' Niall's face was full of concern.

'Like I said, I've been busy.'

'It's a stressful time for both of us. Look, why don't I make the tea and we can deal with some of the paperwork for the sale. I must admit it's looking very smart,' he said soothingly, probably hoping to win her over.

'I decluttered a few things,' said Sarah, hoping he wouldn't go upstairs and discover she'd taken his science fantasy novels and jazz vinyl collection to the tip, along with some of the downstairs junk.

'The flowers are a nice touch.'

Sarah glanced at the bunch of daffodils and tulips in the hearth. Liam had bought the daffs and one of her brides had given her the tulips as a thank you.

'Yes,' she said neutrally before flashing him a smile and heading for the kitchen. 'But I'll make the tea.'

She made the drinks and steeled herself for the discussion. She read through some paperwork and agreed to deal with some of the admin with the solicitors and agents alongside Niall. It at least gave her some sense of control over the situation. After finishing his tea, Niall got up to leave. Sarah's resolve and energy levels were flagging. It was exhausting trying to put on a front of control and calmness when you felt like screaming.

At the door, Niall put his leather jacket on and hugged her briefly, although Sarah remained stiff under his embrace. The scent of the leather made her want to cry but she toughened up.

'Sarah. Thanks for being so good about this. I know it must be hard. Shit ... I never ever thought it would end like this ...'

And that, thought Sarah, was where they were different. She never thought it would end at all.

*

On the following Sunday morning, Sarah felt some proper warmth to the sun as she unlocked the door to the workshop. Daffodils nodded in the tubs on the patio and there were already some yellow flowers on the forsythia. The cottage garden was so gorgeous in spring and it would break her heart to leave it. Molly had offered her a temporary home in her flat while she found somewhere suitable for the business and the baby, but Sarah couldn't bear to think about moving. She switched on the heater and laid out the materials. Liam was a little late and she found herself worrying that he might not turn up at all. In the end, he arrived a few minutes after they'd started. He'd been Skyping Hayley, he said, to ask her opinion on the suggested menus for the wedding.

He stayed behind after the others had left, raising a few eyebrows from Sarah's regulars.

'Well, what do you think?' he said, as Sarah modelled the new tiara in front of the workshop mirror. Sarah looked at the silver and seed pearl confection resting on her auburn waves. Liam's face appeared behind her and she had a flashback to New Year's Eve when she'd first found out she was expecting the baby and hidden it from Niall.

He frowned. 'Hmm. I'm not sure it's quite turned out how I envisaged,' he said. He blew out a breath and his brown eyes were clouded with doubt. 'I think it's almost there ...'

'But that doesn't mean it isn't beautiful or even better than you'd expected,' said Sarah.

'No ...'

She smiled at his thoughtful face. 'Then what's wrong?'

'Nothing. I suppose.'

'I was just thinking it would be nice if Hayley had a

175

matching necklace, earrings and bracelet. How long would they take to make?'

'A morning at most.'

'I see.'

'And won't your daughter's husband want to give her a special gift to wear on her wedding day? Or something of her mum's? I think it might be better if you made something completely different for her birthday or Christmas.'

'You're right, of course. Christmas is a long way off but her birthday's in June so that's a good idea.'

'I can sell you a kit or you can do another workshop.'

'Or both,' he said. 'I'd like you to meet her one day.'

'I'd like that too,' said Sarah. She might have baby brain and be grieving for Niall but she wasn't totally brain dead. She knew Liam wanted an excuse to keep seeing her and she knew she'd miss him a lot if he disappeared out of her life.

'What I'm really asking is if we can stay friends,' he said.

'I know and the answer's yes. Lots of my clients become friends.'

'I expect they do but I probably didn't quite mean it like that ... but I also don't want to put you under any pressure. I know how you feel about Niall and the baby's on its way. The last thing you need is someone like me hanging around, complicating things so tell me to bugger off, if you need to.'

'You're not complicating things ... and thanks for understanding how I feel. It's just, I don't want you to think I'm using you.'

'Using me? What for?'

'For support. To help me fix dripping cisterns and tidy up the mess here and find me a new workshop. I'd hate it if you thought that.'

'You mean you'd hate it if you thought I was doing the things a friend does?'

'No. I like having you as a friend. I just don't want to exploit you.'

He smiled, his eyes crinkling at the corners. He was every bit as fit as Niall and probably, if she was honest, much better-looking – for an older guy – and he had a quiet inner confidence that was as appealing as Niall's larky charm.

'Sarah. No one has ever managed to exploit me yet. I'm happy to do anything I can to help you move forward from what's happened. I like being with you, even when you're telling me my wire work isn't right and my choice of colours doesn't gel.'

'Do I do that?'

'You do and it's what I need but please don't think I'm helping you to put you under any obligation or pressure. You know I enjoy being with you but I also know what it's like when you've lost someone.'

His blunt words made her heart ache, for a few seconds. Literally ache but she wasn't angry with Liam. Under other circumstances, in another life, another time, she could imagine herself falling for him, falling in love with him. The moment she let the thought into her head, she felt sick. She couldn't fall in love again after Niall. Not with anyone but the Niall she'd first known.

'I haven't lost Niall,' she said. 'Not in the way you lost your wife. I won't compare it.'

'No, but some of the feelings must be similar and just as devastating but worse in one way because he's still here, coming round, confusing you. It must be very difficult to let go of him.'

'It is.' Sarah fixed on a smile. 'But I am trying.' Not very hard, she thought. *Not hard enough.* 'Liam, I like being with you too. You make me laugh and you're extremely useful round the house and you don't have to sign up for another class to have an excuse to visit.'

His dark eyes sparkled. 'No, but I *do* feel as if I need an excuse.'

She laughed. 'If you really feel that, you'll just have to make one up.'

'I guess I'll have to be more creative.' As she handed him the tiara, his fingers brushed hers and lingered for a nanosecond longer than they needed to. Sarah didn't rush to move her hand either. She felt a tingling low in her stomach that felt remarkably like lust. Her face heated up. It must have been the baby stirring, but surely it was too soon for that? She put the tiara back on the countertop. She mustn't, couldn't flirt with Liam. It was cruel to him when she still loved Niall.

'Have you thought any more about checking out the craft unit?' he said, cutting through her confusion.

'I have and I'm still not sure. It's very kind of you but don't wait for me to make up my mind, please.' The feeling in the pit of her stomach was back and it wasn't the baby or lust but guilt. 'Liam, I'm sorry but I'm still all over the place, in every way.'

'I can see that. I understand. I couldn't make a decision for months after losing Kerren. I went around on autopilot and it was only thanks to the managers and staff at the business that we didn't go under. For what it's worth I think you're doing a great job keeping things going, if that doesn't sound patronising.'

'No. Some days I've just felt like chucking it all in.' Literally, thought Sarah, cringing at the memory of trashing the workshop.

'You'll get through this,' he said softly. 'I promise you will because you're strong and determined. I tell you what, why don't you come and at least take a quick look at the unit? Are you still planning on moving in with Molly for a while?'

'I ... don't know yet. We still haven't found a buyer for the cottage. We had an offer but it was withdrawn because they found another property they liked even more.'

'I'm sure you will soon. Come and see if the unit would suit your needs. It might help make your decision easier. You'll need a workshop whatever happens, and even if this one isn't right for you, it will give you an idea of what you do and don't want.'

Sarah smiled weakly. Liam was absolutely right, of course. Taking the craft unit and living with Molly while she looked for something more suitable for her and the baby was the sensible thing to do. The logical and practical thing to do, but love wasn't any of those things.

'OK,' she said, forcing brightness into her voice.

He smiled warmly. 'Let me know a time that suits and I'll meet you there.'

*

A few days later, Liam parked his car outside a row of business units. After meeting outside his office, he'd driven her to the site on the edge of the city. Sarah got out, pleasantly surprised at her first impressions. The word "unit" had conjured up images of metal-roofed factory buildings but the centre was far more rustic than she'd expected. The site backed onto open meadowland with a pond and trees and the land-scaped areas in front were neatly kept and planted with pansies and spring flowers.

Liam clicked the car shut and joined her in the courtyard at the front of the development.

The wind gusted and Sarah pulled her hair out of her eyes. 'Are these units really brand new?'

'Yes and no. There were some farm buildings on the site that had been used as motor workshops and body repair. We've tried to redevelop them in a sympathetic style. There's the empty unit, between the wood turner and the bakery.'

'That's the Kingfisher Bakery. They make amazing wedding and celebration cakes.'

'Could you use the connection to help increase your business?'

'Definitely. I could pop in and have a word with them. If I took the unit, of course,' she added hastily.

'Well, you don't have to decide now. Would you like to take a look inside?'

Once in the unit, he explained about the site's facilities and amenities. The unit had a good-sized space that would be ideal for the workshop and its own separate cloakroom and kitchen area for making refreshments, plus a useful storeroom. He talked about the security available and the car park spaces allocated for her and customers. The scent of baking wafted into the unit occasionally but Sarah knew she and her customers could definitely live with that. It was actually rather comforting ... and she could pick up cakes for the refreshment breaks. Maybe even run cake and beading evenings ... hook up with the bakery for the promotional events.

Liam's voice cut into her thoughts. 'It can get busy outside, but there's always some space so people can park off the road.'

'Who owns the unit? Is the developer OK to deal with? I've heard of nightmares with dodgy landlords hiking rents and not doing maintenance et cetera.'

He laughed. 'There's no need to worry. I think the developer can be relied on.'

'Even so, I'd like to know who they are.'

'They're us, LC Holdings. It was my company who developed and let the units.'

'Oh, I see.'

'Is that a problem?'

'Not really but I don't want you to do me any special favours.'

'I know you want to be independent and not beholden to anyone. The rent is a commercial one less a small discount because I know you'd be a good tenant and pay the rent and not burn the place down or turn it into a crystal meth factory.'

Sarah had to smile. 'I don't know, those beading fanatics can really kick off if they want to.'

'I'll bet. You can check out the rents for the other units on our website but I won't force you into a decision although I could do with knowing at some point soon.'

'I know. I don't mean to be ungrateful; and the unit is perfect. It's just a big decision to make.'

'Yes, I can imagine that. Have a look around while I make a few calls.'

She had another look round while Liam finished his call. No matter how hard she tried to find fault with the building and location, she couldn't. No decision, big or small, seemed easy to make these days, not even one about how she felt.

She kept trying to blame it on her hormones and the upheaval in her life but the constant readjustment to her hopes and dreams, combined with her body's physical changes, was exhausting.

Liam finished his call and got out of the car. 'Are you ready to go back to the office?'

'I think so. It's impressive.'

'Thanks. Maybe we could have a quick cuppa before you drive home and I can answer any more of your questions?'

Liam's office was a small but modern block at an enterprise park. She'd been there before, visiting clients, when she worked in the business section of the bank. She smiled when she saw the Director sign on the wall.

The guy on reception made her a herbal tea and showed her into a small meeting room while Liam vanished into the office to take an urgent call, saying he'd only be a few minutes. Through the glass, she checked out the reception area, which was immaculately tidy and freshly decorated. She flicked through a glossy brochure detailing some of the properties that LC Holdings had for sale and rent, and read a profile in a business magazine about the company. She had enough experience of business to see that the staff, professional but relaxed and smiling, seemed happy with their lot as they came and went through the reception area.

As she'd half expected, the "few minutes" stretched into twenty but she didn't mind. It felt strange to be sitting in a business setting, in her casual tunic and leggings and boots rather than a suit with a corporate logo. Part of her felt a flutter of regret that she no longer had the security blanket of a full-time job, but the other, larger part was relieved that she could match her working hours to the demands of a new baby. As a single parent, it would have been even harder, perhaps, to keep up with the demands of a high-powered job and once her maternity leave was over, she'd have had to fund childcare costs.

If only Niall was still in her life; happy and excited about the baby. If only he wasn't so dead against having a family. She thought again about how things might change if she told him ... Surely, when he heard the news – which he had to sometime – he might want to leave Vanessa and come back to the cottage. She'd have no need of a new unit then, and she wouldn't be sitting here. She knew it was wrong to even want him back; that jealousy of Vanessa was probably influencing her feelings; that in every way, she really should be moving on and not wanting to turn back the clock.

Yet in trying to move on by checking out a new location for her business, she'd reminded herself of just how much her life was going to change.

She looked around her at the brightly lit reception, the smart walls and heard Giles the receptionist, purring into his phone. 'LC Holdings, Giles speaking, can I help you?'

It was totally surreal.

Liam opened the door, smiling apologetically. 'Sarah. I am so sorry – that call ran on. Has Giles been looking after you?'

'Of course I have,' Giles called from behind the desk.

Sarah forced down her qualms and smiled at Liam. 'Giles has been great. He rustled up my favourite tea and biscuits, chocolate ones too.'

'I won't have to sack him then,' said Liam.

Giles rolled his eyes.

'You can see I rule this place with a rod of iron,' said Liam.

'We're all quaking,' said Giles, before purring down the phone again.

After a brief conversation, Sarah said she had to get off, and left cheerfully, with a promise to let him know about the unit as soon as possible. Her smile faded once she'd left the car park, and the moment she saw her garden again she knew her decision in her heart. The unit was perfect but it wasn't the Kabin. It wasn't the quirky not-quite-straight walls or the leaky roof or the dodgy plumbing. The Kabin was a symbol of her old life – with Niall – and letting it go also meant letting go of all her once-cherished dreams forever. Liam seemed to understand how she felt. He understood a lot and never pushed her but he was practical and Sarah wasn't ready for practical. She closed the door of the cottage behind her, threw her keys on the carpet and sobbed her heart out.

Chapter Nineteen

Molly hauled herself off the bike after their latest training session. She felt sore in places she hadn't known existed, even though she was a biologist.

'How far have we done this morning?' she asked, trying not to wince too loudly.

Ewan checked his GPS. 'Forty-three point six miles.'

She resisted the urge to rub her aching glutes in front of him. 'Oh, goody. Only thirty-one point four extra to do on the race day.'

Ewan unclipped the drinks bottle and offered it to her. 'Not much left I'm afraid.'

'Thanks, but I've got some Powerade and energy bars in the house. Do you want to come in for a drink?' she asked, fully expecting him to say he had to get back to the lab.

He hesitated then said, 'Why not?'

Surprised and a little thrown, she let him into the flat, immediately regretting her invitation when she saw her washing festooned on every inch of space. Ewan knocked a black push-up bra off the radiator as he squeezed between it and the hall table.

'Um, sorry about the mess. My tumble dryer's packed in and I'm afraid my cleaner's off sick,' she joked.

Ewan held up a bra. 'Long-term illness, is it?'

She snatched the bra from him. 'It's not that bad!' She caught the twitch of amusement on his lips and groaned. 'I suppose that was meant to be a joke?' she said.

'Yes. Hadn't you noticed?'

'Sometimes it's difficult to tell.'

Blushing as she spotted a peach thong and push-up bra draped over one of the dining chairs, she went to her room and pulled on a dry sweatshirt and leggings. She also took the opportunity to scoop up some of the scantier items of her washing from the drying rack in the bathroom. If Ewan wanted a pee, she didn't want him making intimate acquaintance with her lingerie. Then again, if she was wearing the shorts and bra, she wouldn't have minded at all.

'Here you go,' she said, carrying two bottles of Powerade into the sitting room.

Ewan perched on the sofa. In his hand he held up the furry microbe.

She groaned inwardly. 'Oh God. I wish you hadn't seen that.'

'Why?'

'Because it was a Valentine's Day present.'

He raised his eyebrows. 'Really? Who from?'

'I don't know. It was anonymous.'

'Was it from the friend you had dinner with?' he said, his eyes glinting.

She knew she was being wound up. 'Ha ha. We both know that was Sarah,' she said neutrally.

'Was it? I didn't know.'

'You might have guessed I wouldn't leave her alone on Valentine's Night.'

Ewan picked up the microbe and passed it from hand to hand. 'You said there was a card with this?'

She rolled her eyes. 'Yes.'

'Didn't it give you any clues?'

'It had a corny verse. I thought it was Pete Garrick to be honest.'

'Pete Garrick!' He snorted. 'Do you really think Pete would send something like that?'

'Why not? The message was cheesy enough.'

'How cheesy?' he said quietly.

'Cheesier than a whole wheel of Brie with a side of Parmesan.'

'Right. OK. That bad, eh?'

'It's burned on my memory. 'Hot brunette in the Behavioural Ecology Lab. Want to be the antigen to my antibody?'

Ewan grimaced. 'Ouch. That *is* cheesy but it could have been worse.'

'I don't see how. The message was stuck on with a print-out like it was a ransom note and it came with a Kissing Disease furry microbe wrapped in old tissue paper. He even used a second-hand Jiffy bag and you know how hot Pete is on the recycling. It has to be him.'

'You're probably right. No one else could possibly be that corny.' Carefully, Ewan put down his bottle on the table.

Molly's heart sank. A horrible idea slid into her mind. Oh, *fuck*.

'Well, I've no proof it was Pete, of course,' she said hastily. 'It could have been anyone and the microbe's cute and I haven't got the heart to throw it out and I admit I did have a giggle at the message ...'

Ewan was silent and then smiled again but his eyes gave him away. 'It's certainly laughable.'

'For a second or two, I thought you might have sent it,' Molly blurted out.

He snorted. 'Me? Don't be ridiculous. Like you say, it probably was Pete Garrick.'

'Well, I only wondered and I did think it wasn't your style but you know, people do out-of-character things; mad and crazy stupid, cheesy things when they're in love.'

'Hmm. They probably do.' He jumped up, making a show of checking his watch. 'Like I said, I'll get off home. I've got a paper to review. See you in the lab bright and early. This training has put back my preparation for the genome conference in Bern. It'll be a good thing when that bloody race is over.'

After closing the door, she immediately let out an "arghh" of frustration. She grabbed the microbe and lobbed it at the bin. It missed and lay on the carpet, its long lashes fluttering and grinning at her. She was ninety-nine per cent certain that Ewan had sent the card but after her sarcastic comments, he'd never admit it now. 'I've got some news,' Molly told Sarah later that evening at the cottage.

'Oh, are you and Ewan finally together?'

Molly pulled a face. 'No, and not likely to after this morning's disaster.' She told Sarah about the microbe incident.

Sarah pulled a face. 'Ouch and if he denied sending it, there's not much you can do. He seems nice too, apart from the reluctance to admit his feelings.'

'He's driving me mad. I've decided to give up and resign myself to staying celibate.'

'That sounds boring. Can't you try Tinder? There must be tons of geeks all logging in, desperate to meet someone like you.'

'That's what worries me and anyway, much as I can't stand Ewan's messing about, he's the one I want. Everyone else seems second best ... I don't fancy them ...'

'I have news too,' said Sarah. 'We've had a fresh offer on the cottage from a cash buyer so maybe I'd better tell Liam that I want the unit and—' she took a deep breath '—temporarily at least, you might have a lodger.'

'God, I'm sorry. You're more than welcome, of course, both of you,' Molly said. 'You and the baby can have the double and I'll move into the single room.'

'Well, it's only a contingency. I'll start looking for something for me and the baby to rent straightaway ... And there's something else. You know I went out to lunch with some of the girls from my beading course. Well, I heard from a friend of Vanessa's that Niall's asked her to marry him.'

'Oh no! That can't be true. It's way too fast!'

'She must have her hooks in him. Vanessa's sister-in-law works for the council with one of the girls. That's what she told me.'

'Has Niall said anything to you about it?'

'No and I haven't asked him.'

'I'm sorry. He's a bastard. If it's true – because Vanessa could have made it up or just be hoping he'll ask her. God, I hope you realise now that he's not worth wasting another second on.'

Molly could have bitten out her tongue, because she could tell straightaway that her comment had hurt Sarah. 'I know that but I can't help how I feel. If it really is serious ... well the closer those two get the worse I feel to be honest.'

'It must be a nightmare. He's not worth it.'

'I can't forget him. It's not that easy. If it was, I would. I still

189

love him and it hurts. I can't help it. I know it's not sensible or practical or what "sensible Sarah" should do.'

'You have to move on for your sake and the baby's,' Molly said firmly.

Sarah gawped at her. Oh no ... Molly had seen that look before. Sarah looked hurt, like a wounded animal. She'd gone too far ...

'If you can't understand why I still love Niall and wish we'd never split up then it's because you've never really loved anyone.'

'What? I don't have to have loved anyone to know a lost cause when I see one,' Molly snapped, stung into a retort.

Sarah recoiled as if she'd been slapped. 'You have *no* idea. You've never been in a proper long-term relationship. You just lurch from one hopeless crush to the next ...'

'That's not fair. Ewan is not a hopeless crush.'

'It looks like it to me.' Sarah folded her arms defensively. 'He isn't worth it either, leading you on and then dropping you like a ton of bricks. That man has serious commitment issues.'

'And Niall doesn't? Maybe Ewan is just a crush or maybe you can't accept that I've fallen in love. Properly. With someone worth loving, not a cheating rat.' Molly felt ready to burst. 'And maybe you don't want to see what I see: how "real" love has turned my sister from a strong woman to a wreck who smashes up her own workshop and behaves like a lunatic. This isn't like you, Sarah. What would Mum and Dad have said?'

Sarah glared at her. 'I don't know, Molly, what *would* Mum and Dad have said?'

Her voice was tight and dangerous. Molly felt almost faint

with remorse, even seconds after she'd made the remark about their parents, but it was too late. Oh God, no, why why why had she brought them into it?

'I don't know ...' she said, desperately back-pedalling but not wanting to cave in completely.

Sarah snorted. 'Really? You seem to have a supernatural line to Mum and Dad.'

'Don't be horrible. I just think that they wouldn't want you to do something stupid to keep a louse like Niall. It's not like the savvy, sensible sister who gave up everything to bring me up.'

'Isn't it? Oh dearie me. How *terrible*,' Sarah said in a sarcastic whiny voice that wasn't like her at all. In fact, Sarah had become a stranger. Molly felt physically ill knowing that there was no stopping the whole agonising rollercoaster now.

'Well, maybe I don't want to be *sensible* anymore,' Sarah went on. 'Maybe I'm sick and tired of it. God knows, I had enough of doing the sensible thing when we lost Mum and Dad. Why shouldn't I be stupid and crazy and madly in love now? You did what *you* wanted. If I want Niall back now, then I can be fucking stupid and mad. I've a baby on the way, this should be happiest time of my life and instead it's the worst and if you don't like it then tough!'

Abandoning any attempt to soothe Sarah, she went on the offensive. 'If that's what you want, I'll leave you to wallow in misery.'

Sarah curled her lip and folded her arms. 'Great. You could try helping me get him back. You know you could if you really wanted to!'

Horrified, Molly shook her head. 'Oh no. No way. Don't

throw that at me. You're just desperate and not thinking straight.'

'Have you quite finished with the counselling?' Sarah said tartly, winding up Molly again.

'Yeah 'cos it seems hopeless trying to help you. You obviously know everything. You did when we were little and you think you bloody do now, even when you're completely wrong and totally deluded.'

Sarah's mouth dropped open. Molly's clamped shut. Sarah's arms were wrapped around her chest. Molly's were in the same position. They mirrored each other.

It was weird. Molly knew she was throwing fuel on the fire but she couldn't stop herself. It was too late to avert disaster so why not say what she really meant, how she really felt. It was too late to change anything, bring anyone back, so why not just leap headlong off the bloody cliff and crash and burn.

'Is Niall really worth all this pain?' Molly began, her voice high and tight.

'I'd like you to leave now,' Sarah cut across her words.

'What?'

Sarah lifted her chin but refused to meet her eye. 'I want to be on my own,' she said quietly.

Molly took a step towards her. 'Sarah, please, I didn't ...'

Sarah walked to the door and opened it. 'Leave me alone.'

Molly thought about hugging her, begging her, bursting into tears, and then anger bubbled up again. She'd been trying to help; considered doing something outrageous and stupid to help Sarah and all she'd got was thrown out of the house. Her heart was a tight ball of black hurt. She grabbed her coat and marched out of the front door.

192

She heard it close gently behind her as she walked down the path, shaking with shock. She knew she shouldn't turn around and give Sarah the satisfaction of showing she'd wobbled, but she couldn't help herself. She stopped at the gate and looked back, expecting her big sister to run to meet her, consoling, soothing, calling her back and trying to make peace. That's what Sarah did. Sarah poured oil on troubled waters. Sarah made things right. Sarah had all the answers.

But Molly had miscalculated massively; she realised that now. Sarah had reached the very end of her tether, had stretched it to the limit and it had snapped. Sarah was not Sarah anymore and Molly couldn't handle it. It upset her and scared her. This row wasn't about her. It was about Sarah and *her* choices. It was about the sacrifices she'd made to make sure Molly could have her dream job and lurch from one crush to the next, blithely stepping over the wreckage around her. With tears streaming down her face, she leaned her head on the steering wheel and cried for the parents she'd lost forever and the sister she might just have lost too.

*

'Molly? Are you in there?'

Molly pulled the pillow over her head to drown out the sound of Ewan's voice. It was still dark and bloody freezing because the heating hadn't kicked in yet. So much for crocuses and daffodils, spring seemed to have made a U-turn and plunged her back into the depths of winter.

'Molly? Are you OK?'

'Of course I'm not OK,' she called back. 'It's the crack of dawn, it's minus fifty degrees and I'm not going out on that sodding tandem. So bugger off.'

She pulled the duvet back over her head, determined to ignore him. Her eyes were sore and gritty from crying and every time she thought of her row with Sarah, she had to squeeze her eyes shut to block out the barbs they'd flung at each other, that tore at her heart. She'd kicked Sarah when she was down. Even though she still thought she was right about Niall, it had been cruel to taunt Sarah.

The doorbell to the flat buzzed again.

She threw off the duvet and crept over to the window, shivering. Ewan was standing in the dying orange glow of a street light. Frost glittered on the grassy patch in front of the flats and dawn was streaking the azure sky with pink and red. On any other morning, it really would have been quite beautiful, yet everything she saw was tinged by guilt and regret.

Ewan caught sight of her. 'Molly!'

'Go away,' she mouthed.

He obviously couldn't hear and pointed to the tandem.

'Go away!' she shouted again.

Ewan put his hand behind his ear. Molly wasn't sure whether he really couldn't hear what she was saying, or was taking the piss. God, she didn't have the energy for this. That row had drained her.

'Bloody hell. Wait a minute,' she mouthed and dropped the curtain. She shrugged on a big fluffy dressing gown and pressed the entrance button on her intercom to open the main street door. The thump of his boots echoed in the stairwell and probably woke up everyone in the building who hadn't

194

already been woken by his shouts. Molly lingered by the door, and as soon as she heard him outside, opened it.

'Could you not have announced your presence a bit more loudly?' she asked him as he stepped into the hallway.

'If you'd been ready, I wouldn't have had to wake you up. We're behind schedule.'

'Stuff the schedule. I'm not coming.'

Ewan suddenly seemed to notice her pink furry dressing gown. 'Not coming? Are you ill?'

'No, but I'm not going out on that thing.'

'Oh.' His brow creased in confusion. 'Is everything all right?'

She already regretted letting him into the flat. 'Yes. I mean no. I'll be into work but I can't face training this morning.'

'I know it's tough and I don't want to sound like Pete, but if we don't stick to the training plan, we might not make it to the finish. I admit it's a bit chilly out there this morning but you'll feel better once you get going.' His tone softened.

'Ewan. I won't. Please shut up.'

Ewan peered at her. 'Are you sure you're not ill? Your eyes look puffy and red.'

'There's nothing wrong with me. I've had a big row about the bloody ...' Just in time Molly bit back the words she was going to say. She took a breath to try and calm down. 'Sarah and I had a massive bust-up about Niall last night, that's all, and I didn't get much sleep last night.'

'Oh. I see. I can see things must be very difficult for her, at the moment.'

She waited for him to offer to leave, already regretting saying as much as she had. She'd almost let slip about the Love Bug too, which made her come out in a cold sweat.

'I suppose it won't hurt to miss one session,' he said in a softer tone. 'You do look rough. Shall I make us a coffee?'

No, I want you to leave. I want to wallow in a pit of guilt and misery and work out how the hell I'm going to make things up with Sarah, my beloved sister who gave up her hopes and dreams to make sure I could have mine. And what did he mean "rough"? Molly caught sight of herself in the mirror on the hall table. Shit, her face was as lumpy and pink as her dressing gown but it wasn't Ewan's business to tell her.

'I ought to get dressed,' she said.

'Good idea. I'll put the kettle on.'

She dragged on her work uniform of jeans, sweater and sensible shoes and washed her face with cold water. Make-up would have to wait until her puffy eyes had calmed down. After a few calming breaths, she headed back to the sitting room where Ewan was waiting with two steaming mugs of coffee. The aroma revived her senses and she resolved to stay businesslike and get on with the day, while she tried to work out how to sort out the situation with Sarah.

Ewan, however, had other ideas. He wouldn't take his eyes off her as she sipped the coffee, like she was one of his study subjects. Molly squirmed in her seat.

'Bad row, was it?' he said.

Well, there was no point hiding it now, thought Molly. Damage limitation was the only option. 'Yeah. Look, I'm sorry about missing the training session.'

'You're close to her, aren't you?'

Molly's stomach flipped. Ewan wouldn't be deflected. 'Yes.'

'You're sisters. That's understandable.'

She sat down on the sofa, cradling her coffee. 'It's more than that. Sarah's the reason I'm here now.'

'Here?'

'I mean *here* here. In Cambridge. With you. At your lab.'

'Why?'

'As you know, our parents died in a car accident. I was almost fifteen and Sarah was eighteen. Our grandparents weren't young and the other set live in Australia. They'd have given us a home but we didn't want to have to move. Our auntie Carol would have had us too but she was going through a messy divorce and moved to a tiny flat. The authorities only let us stay together on our own because Sarah convinced them she could look after us both, with Carol's support. Sarah gave up any idea of going to uni to study jewellery design and took a job on a bank training scheme. She worked all the hours she could, making her way up the ladder while looking after me.'

Ewan groaned. 'God, I'm sorry. I knew you'd lost your parents in tragic circumstances but not the details. Even so, I *have* often thought about how terrible that must have been for you. I'm not a lump of granite but I've never discussed it with you because I've assumed you'd have mentioned it if you wanted to talk. And let's face it, I didn't know what to say about it. A few platitudes ... sympathy. What can you say about a tragedy like that? But maybe, I should pay more attention to the welfare of my team.'

Molly had to smile. Ewan's reaction was typical of many people's. There was nothing to say about what had happened. Only Sarah could ever understand how she really felt. Only Sarah who she had hurt and driven away. 'Don't beat yourself up over it. I can't cope with telling people to be honest. Their reaction ...' She smiled at Ewan to reassure him. That's what she and Sarah often did: comforted other people who knew their story, when perhaps they might have expected things to be the opposite way around. At least it gave her some measure of control.

'I can see why you're so close to Sarah, now,' Ewan said quietly.

'Sarah ... she was only a teenager herself really. She should have been out clubbing, getting drunk and sowing her wild oats. Instead she was trying to keep me on the straight and narrow. I wasn't that easy to look after. I wasn't doing drugs or anything but I was an awkward little cow at times. Morose ... geeky ... I drove her mad. Telling the teachers I knew more than they did. Telling Sarah I knew more than she did. Giving her a hard time.' She winced. 'God knows why she put up with me.'

'Maybe because she loved you.' Ewan smiled.

Her throat constricted. Ewan had hit the nail on the head with one simple statement. Sarah loved Molly. Molly adored Sarah. That was all either of them needed to know.

'And she didn't deserve me to throw it all back in her face. The things I said last night were so awful ...'

'Don't beat yourself up.'

'Sometimes we need to beat ourselves up. I do, this morning. I need to feel this bad to remind me of what she means to me and what I owe her.'

Ewan toyed with a stray coaster left on the table. It had a cartoon of Einstein on it. A jokey Christmas present from Sarah.

Ewan shifted in his seat, treating Molly to a great view of the muscles in his thighs. There was no hiding place in the Lycra, that was for sure. She felt guilty for lusting after him when she should have been feeling guilty but wasn't that natural? People were ultimately selfish; trying to survive and perpetuate their own genes. Ewan glanced at a photo on the mantelpiece.

'I won't say how sorry I am because that's obvious but it must have been terrible to lose them both at once,' Ewan went on. 'I can't even begin to understand what you went through ...'

'I still can't believe it's real. Sometimes I still wake up and think they're shouting at me to get out of bed and get ready for school.'

Ewan abandoned the coaster and reached across the table for her hand. His fingers, warmed by his mug, touched her cold ones. When she didn't pull them away, he closed his hand around them. 'I'm sorry for your loss, for the row with Sarah and for rocking up here at the crack of dawn like a bear with a sore head talking a load of crap about that fucking tandem when all you must want is to hide in a hole.'

His fingers applied just enough pressure to be comforting but not oppressive. His voice was like being rubbed with velvet. Now was the moment when, if it was ever going to happen, they would end up rolling around the bed and shagging each other's brains out. And yet ... that tingling feeling in her body wasn't lust, that scratchy tickle in her throat was something far more uncontrollable.

She thought of making for the bathroom but it was too late. The tears were already pouring down her cheeks, not gentle weeping but huge snotty sobs.

'It's OK ... It's OK ...' Ewan held her. Her shoulders heaved and she could have died of embarrassment. She dragged her hand over her face and cringed when she saw the wet and snotty patch on his top.

She let go of him. 'Oh God. Your cycle jersey. It's the new one, isn't it? I'll wash it. Take it off.'

'I can't. I don't have anything else to put on.'

Oh no, had she just asked her boss to take off his top in her flat? 'No ... um ... I was only trying to help. I don't know what came over me.'

'It's OK. I don't mind. You had a big row with Sarah and it reminded you about your parents. Life dealt you the shit-tiest hand anyone can get. You're allowed to have a meltdown every so often. We all are.'

Molly sprang further away from him and grabbed a tea towel drying on the radiator. 'Here, use this to clean your top while I get some loo paper.'

She rushed to the bathroom and washed her face again. Layers of snotty bawling had made her skin look like a new-born baby's: red and wrinkled. She wiped her nose and took the loo roll into the sitting room, where Ewan was looking at a photo on the window ledge.

'Are these your parents?' he asked. 'If it upsets you too much, please feel free to ignore the question.'

'Yes. That's me and Sarah on holiday with them in Naxos. I didn't want to go which is why I don't look that happy. Sarah was eighteen so she was allowed to go to a bar with some friends she met but I had to stay with Mum and Dad.'

He smiled. 'Bummer. How old were you? Thirteen? Fourteen?'

'Fourteen ... That was the last holiday we had before they died.'

He put the picture down. 'How did it happen, if you don't mind me asking?'

Molly sniffed but she knew she wouldn't cry again.

'Car accident. Our car versus a truck. We were on our way to our auntie's. She was going to look after us while Mum and Dad had a weekend away to celebrate their silver wedding anniversary.'

'You mean you were *in* the car when it happened?'

She nodded. She'd told the tale so often she now felt disassociated from it. She had the tale off pat, as if it was a story in a newspaper about something that had happened to somebody else. And the crying had been cathartic, either that or she had no more tears left. 'Sarah and I were in the rear seats. A van pulled out in front of us, although I can't remember seeing it. I only remember that Sarah and me, we were arguing in the back seat because we thought we were much too old to be babysat by Auntie Carol. We argued a lot but I loved Sarah to bits. We were only teenagers ... It seems a long time ago now. Most of the time.'

'My God, Molly. Were you hurt?'

'Sarah broke her leg, her right arm and cut her head. There's a scar under her hairline. The front of the car took the brunt of it. I was knocked unconscious or I blanked it all out. Dad was killed instantly and Mum died on the way to the hospital.'

Ewan appeared to swallow a lump in his throat.

'I got off lightly. Lots of cuts and bruises, and some glass from the windows was embedded in my arm but the doctors dug that out.'

'I've seen the scar in the summer but didn't think anything. Everyone has scars,' he said.

'I've seen yours.'

'My own fault. Climbing a tree, falling off some rocks on the beach when I was with my brother.' He rolled his eyes.

Her anger with him for turning up at the flat and seeing her cry had subsided. He was human, after all. There was hope; then she thought of the snot on his cycling jersey and cringed.

She threw him a smile. 'I hope your top survives.'

'It will.' He glanced down at his hands, awkward again. Perhaps there wasn't hope. He must regret getting so close to her, seeing her at a vulnerable, emotional moment. He was about to become the public Ewan again.

'I suppose we'd both better go to work,' she said, offering him a get-out, and stood up.

'I cried at work once, you know.'

She turned to find Ewan staring at his hands.

'What?' she said.

'When Anna left me. It was a month after I found out she'd been shagging the guy we worked with at a conference. I was conducting a meeting and without any warning – none whatsoever – wham, I burst into tears. It was possibly the worst moment of my life and I still want to die when I think about it.'

Finally, he met her eyes.

'What did you do?' she asked, still gobsmacked at him sharing such a personal moment. With her, too.

'The human resources manager was in the meeting and he led me out of the room and told me to go home. I've never been so ashamed in my life and even though everyone was kind afterwards or just pretended it had never happened, I never got over it. I left in the end.'

'Jesus.'

'Yeah.' Ewan stood up and wiped his hands on his tights. 'I'd better go home and get changed.'

'You don't have to ...'

Ewan swallowed hard. 'I think I do. I *have* to.' He spoke as if he was trying to convince himself as much as her. The moment between them had not simply gone, but vanished like dirty water down a drain. She felt freezing cold again.

'Please, don't worry about the top. I've had a lot worse. Will you be OK?' he added gruffly, already on his way to the front door.

'Course I will. Thanks for, um ...' Shit, she had no idea what to say. Everything had fallen apart, come together and fallen apart spectacularly again in the space of a few minutes. She went into professional mode. 'Well, thanks and you needn't worry. I'll be into work and I'll make the next training session.'

And he was gone, leaving her in the middle of the room, unable to move. In the space of a few hours, nothing had changed and yet everything had changed between her and Ewan, and between her and Sarah.

He'd shown a new and unexpected vulnerability to her. A caring side that she'd always suspected he had, but hadn't expected him to reveal. She thought back to Sarah's conversation with him in the church coffee shop all those weeks ago. Sarah had thought the sun shone out of his arse that day, after he'd helped her in the street.

He'd reminded her that blood was thicker than water and of how much Sarah loved her, and all the sacrifices she'd made for Molly to enjoy the life she had now.

'And she didn't deserve me to throw it all back in her face. The things I said last night were so awful ...' Molly groaned aloud, remembering her harsh words to her sister.

It was all very well, Ewan telling her not to beat herself up, but Molly *did* blame herself.

Sarah had made sacrifices to help Molly. It was time she showed Sarah how much she really cared about her. If that meant agreeing to use the Love Bug on Niall, then so be it.

Chapter Twenty

Molly called round to Sarah's house straight after work. She'd been terrified that her sister wouldn't let her in and had almost burst into tears of relief when the door opened before she'd even reached it.

'OK. I'll do it,' she said, the moment she got inside the sitting room.

Sarah slumped down onto the sofa. '*Really?* You don't have to do this out of some sense of pity. I'm not a basket case,' she said.

'It's not pity, but I *am* sorry for the shitty things I said yesterday. Nothing hurts me more than hurting you.'

'And I didn't mean what I said about Ewan. I can tell it's serious on your side and on his, I'm sure, deep down ... but my judgement on men isn't the greatest at the moment.'

The words "that's an understatement" almost slipped out but Molly stopped in time. 'I love you,' she said instead, hugging Sarah tightly.

'Let me and the bump breathe for a moment,' Sarah joked as Molly squeezed her hard. 'And I love you too, Mol, even though you drive me mad sometimes.'

'Are you making something for the bump?' Molly asked as they sat at the kitchen table with a drink. Sarah had obviously been knitting, judging by the balls of wool and needles on the table. 'Trying to. There was a link to a pattern for some cute little bootees on Mumsnet.'

Molly picked up the needles with their tiny pale-yellow woollen square. 'That is so sweet.'

'I hope so ... Mol, you're not doing this out of pity for me, are you?' Sarah asked.

'No. I'm not sure I agree with you wanting Niall back but it's your choice and I want you to be happy. If I can do anything to make you happy, then I will.'

'I can't tell you how much this means to me, Mol.'

Molly put the needles back down. 'I must be out of my mind and if anyone finds out or it goes wrong, I could be sacked, arrested and maybe even jailed ... It would be the end of my science career forever, possibly the end of any career.' She smiled, but inside she was physically ill at the prospect of what she'd offered to do. 'You have to swear you will never ever tell anyone. That's *if* I can manage to do it, and without Ewan or anyone at the lab finding out.'

'I swear.' Sarah crossed her heart but Molly wasn't reassured in any way. 'No one will find out. I swear that only you and I know about it and it won't go wrong. But I thought you said it was ready for clinical trials. Is it safe? What do we have to do? How does it work?'

'It depends what you mean by *safe*. It's definitely non-toxic and won't do him any physical harm but it's not exactly ethical, manipulating someone's hormones.'

'But it's not like actually *drugging* him, is it?'

'Erm,' Molly muttered. The Love Bug was a psychoactive substance that could change Niall's thoughts and behaviour. Molly felt slightly faint at the thought of it.

'I can't wait to see him come grovelling back.'

'Whoa ... Before you get too excited, it's not a miracle worker. It might not make a huge difference to Niall. The Love Bug is a hormone that facilitates ... um ... romantic bonding and only if it's very specifically tailored to the two people involved ... but I think I can deal with that part of things.'

'How do we give it to Niall without him noticing?'

'At the moment, we think a nasal spray is the best method of delivery.'

'So, you mean you could put it in an aftershave or perfume bottle or an atomiser?'

'An atomiser would work, yes ...'

'I've got an empty one upstairs,' she said excitedly. 'What do you need from me?'

'A DNA sample from you and from Niall. I can take yours now but we'll have to get Niall's too. A strand of hair would do, or an old toothbrush.'

Sarah's eyes gleamed. 'Oh, I'm sure I can find a hair. In fact, I can get one now.'

Molly waited, trying to suppress her rising sense of panic. Sarah was back in half a minute with a black plastic comb with some of the teeth missing.

'Here you go. Bit yukky but Ni left it in the bathroom when he called round last week. He's so bloody vain, far worse than most of the women I know.'

'OK. Thanks.' Molly popped the comb in a plastic bag, already worried about Sarah's blithe optimism. 'I can do a mouth swab on you. Cheek cells are brilliant. Shall we do it now?'

'OK, yes.' Sarah's eyes gleamed. What if Sarah was actually

207

suffering from a breakdown, not simply unable to let go of Niall? Molly could be making it worse but it was too late now – she'd resolved to do anything and risk anything to help her sister. Actually, she thought, as she pulled a pair of blue nitrile gloves from her bag, perhaps it was her who was having the breakdown, agreeing to do this.

Gritting her teeth anyway, she removed a 20ml tube and long cotton bud from the bag and placed it on the table.

'Open wide,' she said.

Sarah obeyed and Molly swabbed the inside of Sarah's mouth.

Molly put the swab in its tube.

'You can close your mouth now.'

'That's it?' said Sarah.

'Yup. That's it. The secret of life is in that tube.'

Sarah pulled a face. 'Wow. This all sounds like those old legends and spells. We did a poem at school called "St Agnes Eve". You have to do stuff like undressing in front of a mirror, or peeling an apple and the next man you see will fall in love with you.'

'But it's not a spell, it's science. You know I don't believe in any of that airy-fairy stuff.'

'No, but it is a *bit* like that,' said Sarah.

'No, it's not. That was a pile of crap in a poem.'

'OK, OK,' soothed Sarah 'I know that. Running a tiara workshop doesn't mean I believe Tinker Bell really exists.'

The atmosphere between them was starting to simmer again but Molly took a deep breath and resolved to stay calm. No way did she want another slanging match like last night. 'OK, sorry, I'm just a bit … antsy about this. Technically it's a medical product. I could and would get the sack if anyone finds out what I've done. It's unethical, immoral. In fact, I must be out of my mind.'

'Can you reverse the effects, if all goes wrong? Is there an antidote?'

'There are some drugs for other conditions, which are predicted to counteract it. We haven't done much work on those yet and there are only a few trials that have been done on fruit flies and the human volunteer trials of a similar hormone in the Netherlands and the US ... It will take a while to create the Bug you know. I'll have to transform a plasmid carrying the gene into permissive bacteria and then express it.'

Sarah's mouth was open. 'That sounds complicated ...'

'It'll be tricky but it is feasible. Of course, then I'd need to engineer the Bug to complement Niall's genetic coding.'

'Right ... of course ... um how long will that take?'

Molly waggled her hand and blew out a breath. 'A week or so under ideal conditions but remember I have to do this in secret alongside my normal work. I can't let anyone find out, especially not Ewan ... so maybe two to three weeks?'

Sarah's eyes shone with excitement. She hugged Molly. 'I'm so grateful.'

'You don't owe me anything. I owe you.'

'But I know you're taking a big risk doing this. You won't regret it, I promise.'

'Wait and see if it actually works before you thank me,' said Molly firmly.

'Oh, it will. You're a brilliant scientist.'

Molly smiled weakly and hugged Sarah back, thinking that she already *did* regret her offer. However, it if it gave Sarah comfort and helped her move on, then it would be worth the risk.

Chapter Twenty-One

A few days later, Niall stood in the doorway of the cottage. He'd come around to ask Sarah to sign some more papers relating to the sale which was now in progress. Judging by the extra room in his leathers, he'd lost more weight. Sarah wasn't entirely sure it suited him because he'd also lost the cheeky dimple she'd loved so much.

He took off his helmet while she closed the front door.

'You've had your hair cut,' she said.

Niall rubbed his hand over his head. 'Vanessa said I'd look better without the quiff.'

Sarah resisted the urge to ask if Niall did everything Vanessa told him. There was no point starting an argument now. 'She's right about one thing, then,' she said.

'Why didn't you tell me you didn't like it?'

'I didn't know I didn't, until now.'

Niall put his helmet on the hall table and followed Sarah into the sitting room while she tried to calm down. Ever since Molly had agreed to create the Love Bug, she'd been like a cat on a hot tin roof but now he was here, she felt strangely calm. Energised but definitely calm. She was determined to throw him off the scent by being on her best behaviour. Her strategy was to lull Niall into a false sense of security by making him think she was happy to sell the house.

They talked briefly about the house sale then Niall moved on to his family and work. Sarah marvelled at how easy it was pretending you weren't about to commit grievous bodily harm on your ex, for a short time at least. She was even enjoying herself, nodding in all the right places while Niall moaned about the change in his shift pattern and how knackered he was. Once or twice she thought she might even nod off, she felt so calm – must be her hormones – and suddenly Niall stopped talking about himself and looked closely at her.

'Are you OK, Sarah? You seem a bit out of it.'

'Just tired. I've had a lot of commissions and the house sale has been exhausting even though I've been able to stop the endless tidying now.'

'I know. I'd have helped out more but these shift changes have really buggered up my Circadian rhythms. Still, it looks really smart and I noticed you fixed the gate.'

'Oh, Liam did that.'

'Liam?'

'Liam Cipriani.'

'That bloke you almost killed with Toby? You mean he came back for the course?'

'He forgave me. He's been back a few times. He's making a tiara for his daughter's wedding and a bracelet and necklace.'

'Why did he fix the gate?' Niall sounded suspicious.

'He used to be a joiner but he runs a commercial property company now. I think he felt he wanted to help out.'

'So, he's definitely not gay?' said Niall.

'No.' Sarah shoved a packet of chocolate gingers at him. 'Have one of these. I'm addicted to them.'

'I shouldn't really … Vanessa would kill me if she knew I'd had trans fats.'

'She'll never know,' said Sarah wickedly, anticipating the moment that Vanessa found out Niall had transferred his affections back to her. If the plan worked of course. Molly kept warning her it might not have the desired effect but Sarah was confident. Molly was just being super cautious, as all scientists were.

'Don't bet on it. She can smell chocolate at fifty feet. Oh, feck it.' He picked a biscuit off the plate, bit into it and closed his eyes in ecstasy. 'God, I've missed crap food,' he mumbled.

'Have another one,' said Sarah soothingly.

After she'd been through the documents with him and added her signature, she expected Niall to leave but he seemed in no hurry to go back to Vanessa. He helped himself to two more biscuits and insisted on making more tea for them both. He told her about some of the patients he'd had to deal with and Sarah almost forgot that they'd ever split up. It was just like old times. She felt happier than she had done for weeks. The Love Bug could work; all Niall needed was a little nudge. She'd get to keep the cottage and the element of revenge would be sweet.

Should she tell him about the baby now? No, it was too big a risk.

Eventually, he said he was leaving and Sarah followed him to the door. 'You really do like my hair then?' he asked, glancing in the hall mirror. 'I wasn't sure at first …'

'Yes, I said I did. It really suits you.'

She waited for him to mention the comb, ready to deny having seen it, but he didn't.

Niall hovered by the door, looking sheepish. 'Sarah …'

'Yes, Niall?' She hung on tenterhooks. Was he going to say he regretted leaving her? There was a look in his eye: sadness, regret …

'Thanks for being so reasonable about this,' he said.

'What choice do I have?' she said.

He stepped forward as if to give her a hug, but Sarah moved away, unable to bear him touching her and worrying he'd feel her slight bump. 'It's for the best, you know. I think we'll both come to realise that … in the end.'

Chapter Twenty-Two

'You're working late again. I thought I was the one who kept Coco Pops and a sleeping bag in the lab.'

'Jesus Christ!'

'Were you expecting him?' asked Ewan from behind Molly who was up to her elbows in a biological safety cabinet. He slid onto a stool next her, keeping his hands well out of her way.

'I wasn't expecting *you*. I thought you were taking the day off to see your brother and his kids,' she said. Had he seen what she was doing? He must have seen the petri dish in the cabinet but he'd have no idea exactly what she was culturing. It could be anything and she had an answer prepared if he did ask.

'I've just come from the park. There's only so much harassment of birdlife you can do before you get reported to the council. Besides, the kids are knackered, not to mention Rob, so he's taken them back to mine for a nap and a wee dram. That's Rob not the kids. He says he doesn't know how Fiona copes with them and works as well. He's worried she might stay at this conference in Montreal.'

Molly smiled, beginning to relax. Ewan must have really enjoyed himself with his niece and nephews to make a joke about it.

'So, I need to do some work on my grant application in the lab for a few hours before I go back to Toddler Central.' He glanced across her workstation. 'So what are you doing here?'

'Oh, just double-checking a few things.'

'You seem to be here a lot, lately.' Molly's pulse spiked, dreading him probing for more details. It was always best to keep your lies as close to the truth as possible but she'd rather not have to tell a lie at all.

'You mean even longer than you?'

'Ha ... are you planning on being here much longer?' he asked.

'No, actually I'm almost finished.'

'You've been working long hours,' he said, surprising her with his concern. 'You should get some rest before the race next Sunday.'

'I was just about to go home.'

'Good,' he said gruffly. This is how he'd been since that morning at her flat. She deeply regretted her meltdown and guessed he regretted his even more. Maybe he was worried she'd gossip about him at work. He was paranoid about mixing his personal life with his professional one and now she knew exactly why.

'How are things with you and your sister?'

A pang of guilt stabbed her. 'Oh, much better. We had a heart to heart and made it up,' she said, realising she sounded overly cheery. 'Sarah joked about me and the tandem. Our parents would never have believed I'd get on one and take part in a race.' This was true. Sarah had said exactly that, and she and Molly had laughed about it.

'My brother doesn't believe it either.' Ewan smiled. 'He's

215

demanded video evidence. I'm glad you and Sarah were able to make things up so quickly. I'm sorry for what happened with her partner – Niall, isn't it? I know how she feels and I can understand why you think you owe her a lot, but I'm not sure even you can help her in this case. She sounds like she'd be well rid of him ... and you can't make people love you, can you?'

'Really?' said Molly lightly. 'Do you realise what you just said?'

'Yes, I do.'

'So, you don't think the Love Bug should be used to bring two people together?'

'Even if it was as effective on humans as it seems in theory, I can't imagine it being used beyond the applications we're working on already. I couldn't live with someone who'd been artificially manipulated to love me. What pleasure would there be in living a lie?'

'Not much ... some people would grab the chance of it. A rejected partner maybe ... who was desperate or out for revenge ...'

He cut her off. 'Then they'd need counselling, not the Love Bug.'

Molly felt slightly sick. Ewan was right, of course. No one should be forced or coerced to love another person and yet ... surely in some cases, it could be used to heal relationships that deserved another chance? Not that she thought Niall deserved one. Once again, she regretted even offering to help but it was too late now. Sarah had become fixated on it. Molly was more worried about her state of mind than ever.

'Hmm. I suppose so.'

He slid along the bench on his stool and switched on his

Mac. 'Do you think you're ready?' he asked, typing in his password.

'Ready for what?' she asked, still with her hands in the cabinet, effectively trapped.

Ewan frowned at her. 'For Sunday?'

'Oh, *that*.' Molly's shoulders sagged in relief that he'd moved on to the race. 'I don't think I'll ever be ready but I suppose I'll make it. I have a feeling it's going to be painful though.'

'Anything worth doing is painful sometimes.'

'I guess you're right. What's the plan for next week?' she asked, wondering how she was going to get the petri dish into the incubator while Ewan was in the room.

'I thought we'd have a light training session tomorrow, and on race day I could pick you up at the flat around eight and we can use the ride to the start as a warm-up.'

'Sounds like a plan.' She flashed him a smile. 'I'll probably get home now and get some rest. Put my feet up et cetera.'

But Ewan was already intent on his Mac.

She made a meal of turning off the safety cabinet and giving it a really good swab to clean it. In fact she used so much ethanol, she felt momentarily giddy. Fortunately, before she passed out on the fumes, Ewan left the lab to take a phone call. She hid the petri dish in the fridge behind one of her colleague's samples, ready to transfer it to the incubator when she had more time. The whole time her pulse hammered away in case he returned and asked her what she was doing. There was no danger of anyone recruiting her into MI5, that was for sure.

Finally, it was done. With a waved goodbye to Ewan, she cycled home and read some online papers, making notes on them so she had something boring and innocent to discuss during their ride, but it was hard to focus. Today's false alarm with Ewan had increased her misgivings even further. Was she raising false hopes in Sarah? Because no matter how much she tried to damp down Sarah's expectations of what the Love Bug could do, Sarah was obviously in no frame of mind to listen.

She'd tried to make Sarah think about the consequences again in the hope she'd decide against it and realise what a mad idea it was. What if the Love Bug didn't work? she'd told her. Sarah would be devastated all over again. And what if it *did*? Molly told Sarah she would spend the rest of her life feeling guilty and Sarah would be living a lie.

It was wrong on every front but she couldn't let Sarah down. Sarah was relying on her – and if she couldn't rely on her sister, then who could she rely on?

Chapter Twenty-Three

Sarah's heart sank when she found Liam at her door. Not that she wasn't pleased to see him – quite the opposite. She'd been trying to deny how much she'd missed him over the past couple of weeks and she was worried if she met him again, she might waver from her plan.

Molly's heart to heart had really made her think again about the plan to give Niall the Love Bug. What if it didn't work? How would she feel when he finally came crawling back to her? She wasn't stupid enough to think everything would be wonderful. Molly had said that making someone love you would be a cruel and hollow exercise and maybe that was right.

Now here was Liam at her door, confusing the issue even further. She *had* missed him, there was no denying that. She showed him into the sitting room.

'Do you mind me popping round?' he asked. Momentarily it was as if he'd picked up Sarah's own mood of uncertainty. She smiled at him. She still cared for him a lot, no matter what might happen in the future.

'No ... I was wondering how you were, actually,' she said, trying to sound as if life was carrying on as normal.

He hesitated before replying. 'I've been busy with work and

the wedding plans,' he said but Sarah had the strong impression that wasn't his real reason for keeping his distance from her. 'How are things with you? Not having heard from you for a little while, I didn't really know whether to call or not, but I do care about you, Sarah, so I thought you wouldn't mind.'

'Of course I don't mind. I like seeing you ... but it's just been a busy time, that' s all and ... Niall's popping over tomorrow evening. I have to sign some more papers to do with the sale.' Sarah kicked herself. Why had she told Liam that? Was she secretly longing to confess what she planned to do?

'So you *are* moving out of here?' Liam asked.

'Yes. I mean, probably, unless Niall changes his mind, of course,' she added hastily, digging an ever-deeper hole for herself.

'We both know that's not going to happen, don't we?' said Liam gently.

'It does seem unlikely.' Sarah felt horribly guilty. Liam was lovely, and she was deceiving him, deceiving Niall ... and herself.

'Sarah, the last thing I want to do is pressurise you ...' Liam began, as Sarah felt the ground shift beneath her. 'In fact, that's one reason I haven't called round or phoned for a while but I wondered if you'd made a decision about the business unit.'

'Oh, Liam, it's sweet of you to think of me but I don't think I could afford the rent,' she said, fearing her nose might shoot out, Pinocchio-style. Actually the rent was very reasonable and the way her business was expanding, she could probably cover it but she couldn't tell Liam why she was really turning his offer down.

He shook his head. '*Sweet*? I'm not being sweet.' Liam glanced down at his hands and Sarah thought he might be about to turn on his heel and leave but he ploughed on, brusquer than she'd heard him before. 'I was only trying to offer you a practical solution, not pressure you.'

'I didn't mean to be rude and you're right. I definitely need to do something about my situation but ...' She hated herself.

'Well, it's entirely up to you. The unit's not far from Molly's place if you still intend to share her flat in the short term. There's plenty of parking for your students – they wouldn't have to find spaces on the road like they do here, and the small business park where the unit's situated is on a bus and cycle route into town.'

'It was – it *is* perfect.' Sarah's stomach twisted with guilt. Everything Liam was saying made perfect sense. Everything she was doing was crazy and yet, a force within her told her to take the risky path. 'I don't mean to sound ungrateful but I don't think it's for me. To be honest, I haven't totally decided what I'm going to do – with the Kabin, that is.'

'OK. If you do change your mind, let me know.'

Sarah nodded.

'And please tell me if you don't want to see me again. I mean I want to carry on seeing you, as a friend, of course ...' His manner, so confident and businesslike, was now more hesitant, almost boyish. She should be drooling, just like her customers, yet she resented him for being so handsome, so sexy, so confident and so damn *nice*. The better he was as a person, the guiltier she felt and she didn't want to hurt him. If Niall did come back it could be very awkward for her to see Liam ever again.

'No, of course not.' Sarah's heart sank. She was half-desperate for him to leave and half-desperate that he *was* leaving. Their friendship – more than friendship – would have to end if – when – Niall was back in her life. She knew it and Liam sensed it although he didn't know why. But it was a sacrifice she'd have to make to get Niall back, wasn't it? Her baby – her and Niall's baby – would have a chance of having its own mother and father. This was a way they could all be together again. It was worth it, wasn't it?

Sarah's doubts were stronger than ever but if she didn't try, would she always be wondering what might have been?

'OK. I'll put the unit on the open rental market and see what happens. If you change your mind before we find a tenant, give me a call or drop me an email. I would never push you into anything you weren't ready for but remember, no matter what happens, I'll always be a friend, if you want me to be.'

He picked up his keys and brushed his lips over her cheek. 'Good luck with whatever you decide to do.'

Chapter Twenty-Four

With a pounding heart and clammy palms, Molly rang the doorbell of the cottage for a second time. There had been no answer to her first ring and she was about to phone Sarah to see where she was when the door creaked open and Sarah peered around the frame.

'Sorry I couldn't get to the phone. I was in the loo,' she whispered, glancing up and down the street over Molly's shoulder as if she was checking for surveillance police. 'You'd better come in.'

'Why are you whispering?' Molly whispered back.

Sarah pulled a face. 'You never know who's listening.'

'You mean, MI5?' Molly was joking but in truth she was all over the place herself. Then she told herself to calm down and reminded herself that *technically*, she wasn't actually doing anything wrong. OK, technically she was doing something very wrong. Her heart sank but she followed Sarah into the lounge and put her rucksack in the middle of the coffee table.

Sarah stared at the bag as if it had a bomb inside it. 'Oh my God. Is *it* in there?'

'Yes. Do you want to see it?'

Sarah nodded and Molly delved in her bag and pulled out a perfume atomiser.

'Here you go.' She held it out.

Sarah wrinkled her nose. 'Oh. It looks just like a normal perfume bottle.'

'Ah but that's the cunning disguise. I mixed the agent with some coloured water, glycerol and fragrance but believe me, you won't find *this* in Superdrug.'

Sarah took the bottle and held it up to the light like Indiana Jones. 'And one whiff of this and he'll fall at my feet?' she said in wonder.

'I wouldn't guarantee it. In fact, I doubt it.' Molly was desperately trying to dampen down Sarah's expectations. 'The effects may take a while to show, *if* they show at all. And like I told you before, the Love Bug only facilitates a predisposition to bonding. The truth is at this experimental stage, we don't know exactly what will happen or how long it will last.'

Sarah cradled the bottle in her hand. 'Are you sure it's not dangerous?'

'I'm sure it won't do Niall any bodily harm,' said Molly, more confidently than she felt.

'What if I change my mind?'

'If you're going to change your mind, change it *before* you try it on Niall. Are you having second thoughts?' said Molly hopefully.

'I don't know.'

'Then don't use it. You have to be really really sure about this, hon, for everyone's sake.'

Sarah stroked the bottle thoughtfully. 'I know.'

'And that you're not just doing this purely for revenge on Niall ...'

'No. I admit I *have* hated him as well as loved him, but even after what he's done, I wouldn't be that vindictive.'

'OK. I'll leave it with you. Sleep on it but promise me, if there's a shred of doubt in your mind then don't let Niall have it.' Molly felt almost light-headed with guilt. She wanted to give Sarah one last chance to see sense because her best chance of wriggling out of this situation was to persuade Sarah not to use the Bug in the first place.

'How long do I have to give it to him? Does it go off or something?'

'I can't say for sure. When *do* you plan on using it?' Molly asked.

Sarah pulled a face. 'Niall's supposed to visit at the weekend ... maybe then. I don't really know. But are you *sure* about me using it?' said Sarah, setting the bottle down on the table again. 'If you really don't want me to do it, if you're worried about getting into trouble ...'

'As long as no one finds out, we should be OK.'

'Why would they find out? I swear on my life that I won't tell anyone.'

'I know. I trust you but I can't help being nervous about this.'

Sarah hugged her. 'Me too, but I'm also so excited.'

Molly's stomach churned like a washing machine as she looked at Sarah's shining eyes. Her sister hadn't seemed so happy since the night of the New Year's Eve party, before the whole thing with Niall had kicked off.

Sarah smiled nervously. 'What's the matter? Do I have spinach in my teeth or something?'

'No, just the opposite. I hope this doesn't sound cheesy but you're glowing. Your skin and hair and eyes look brighter. You probably won't agree with me but pregnancy suits you.'

'Liam said that.' She lifted her tunic and the bump, though

small, was clearly visible on her slender figure. 'I don't feel sick anymore, thank God. Do you think Niall will notice my bump?'

'I don't know, but you will need to tell him *very* soon.'

'I know but I don't want to risk it until *after* he's had the Love Bug ... Molly ... have you ever thought of using this on Ewan?'

'No!' Her own vehemence surprised her. 'No, I couldn't.'

Sarah gave Molly a laser stare, the one she used to give her when Molly had kicked off again at school. 'Not even for a single second?' she asked.

'For a second and that's all. I've given up on him and I'll be glad when this race is over.' Molly meant it. 'And he *is* attracted to me, that isn't the problem, it's getting him to act on it. I wish he'd just come out and say if he wants us to shag each other or not, instead of fannying around all the time. Having to spend all that time inches from him, seeing him all sweaty in the Lycra leggings, my bum rammed into his nose. It's driving me mad.'

'Imagine how he feels, then,' Sarah said.

'That's just it, I don't know exactly *how* he feels and he doesn't seem to, either.'

'If he'd wanted to put you off, he'd never have suggested the tandem ride. No man would have suggested that if he didn't want to spend so much time with you.'

Molly sighed. 'No, I suppose not, but since I joked about the microbe/card thing, he's been worse than ever, as if he's scared of me. He hardly spoke to me on our last two training sessions but it's the race this weekend so I expect that will be the end of it.'

'Ewan seemed happy enough to be with you at the pub,'

Sarah offered. 'I thought he and Liam were getting on really well.'

'Ewan likes Liam, I could tell, but the bonhomie doesn't extend to me and when the race is over, I think that will be the end of our chances together, if there ever were any. I think Ewan's regretted asking me and he's relieved that the training and everything is almost over too. By the way, it was great of Liam to offer the van and the sponsorship.'

'He's a good man. Look, I'm sorry that I won't be able to come to cheer you on at the end of the tandem ride but I can wave you off.'

'It's fine. I didn't expect you to come out all that way to the finish. Waving us off will be great. I'll need all the support I can get!' Molly winced, thinking again that seventy-five miles was a hell of a long way. She dreaded to think what her nether regions would be like at the end of it.

'I'll miss Liam when Niall's back ...' Sarah said wistfully.

'You can't have it all ...' said Molly, hoping against hope that Sarah would see sense: that Niall wasn't worth having back and she was better off without him.

Sarah hugged her. 'I know, but you're willing to try – that's what matters – and let's face it, things can't get any worse, can they?'

Chapter Twenty-Five

Sarah stared at the crack in the ceiling. The same crack, surrounded by little puffs of peeling paint, that she'd been staring at for half the night. Since Liam and Molly had visited, she'd driven herself round the bend contemplating what she was about to do to Niall and to Molly. She must have dropped off at some point because somehow the birds were tweeting for all they were worth and a grey dawn had crept into the room through a gap in the curtains. Funny, but she couldn't remember hearing the birds singing before when she woke. Spring really was just around the corner.

She lay in bed for a little while, feeling the unmistakable fluttering in her stomach as the baby stirred too. A weak sun had replaced the gloomy dawn and shone a finger of light over her dressing table.

She hauled herself out of bed and made herself some toast and honey, and a cup of chamomile tea. Her appetite had vanished but she knew she needed to eat for the baby's sake. She was toying with a second slice when the doorbell rang. It was barely eight o'clock and she wasn't expecting anyone but the bell buzzed again like a swarm of angry bees before she had chance to answer the door. When she did, Niall was hopping about on the doorstep, red in the face.

'Sarah!' he cried, sounding relieved. 'Sorry, I know I'm early.'

'*Early*? I thought you weren't coming over until just before lunch?' she said, tugging her dressing gown tighter as the wind blew straight up her hem. 'I'm going out to see Molly off on her tandem race this morning.'

Niall frowned. 'Molly's on a tandem? What the feck for?'

'It's a charity ride. I promised I'd be at the start to see them off.'

Niall clapped his hands together. 'I won't stay long. Can I come in? I'm freezing my rocks off out here.'

Sarah let him in, wondering why he was in jeans and a hoodie not his bike leathers. Come to think of it, she hadn't noticed his bike outside the cottage, either. Surely, he hadn't walked from Vanessa's place? Maybe she'd given him a lift ... though Sarah couldn't imagine that Vanessa would come within a hundred yards of the cottage after New Year's Eve.

'I have to leave shortly,' she said, anxious that she might not have time to do what she needed and make it to the race. Niall's timing was rubbish. *Shit*. 'So, where's your bike?' she asked.

'I ... er ... I've sold it. It was costing me a packet to run.'

'I thought you said all it needed was a new silencer. You love that bike. Why have you got rid of it?'

'Vanessa thinks it's dangerous.'

Sarah had always thought Niall's riding the bike was dangerous but she'd also thought he was a grown-up so it was his decision.

He glanced around the room, seeming to take a great interest in the doors and ceiling.

'How did you get here, then?' Sarah asked.

'On my new bike.' With a sheepish grin Niall flipped a

thumb towards the window. Sarah looked out into the front garden and spotted a pushbike chained to the gatepost.

'A *mountain bike*?' she said.

'Vanessa thought it would be a good idea. I've been trying to get fit, you see ... maybe I should have done this charity race.'

Niall looked so embarrassed that Sarah resisted the urge to burst out laughing. 'I can see you've lost a lot of weight,' she said. He looked too thin, in Sarah's opinion and there were dark shadows under his eyes.

'Almost a stone.' He patted his flat stomach and it gurgled loudly. 'To tell you the truth I'm feckin' starving.'

His eyes twinkled and he threw her the cheeky smile that had attracted her in the first place. With the sharpened cheekbones and the short hair, he reminded her of a younger Niall, the one who'd left his stag night mates to chat her up at a club. She felt a sudden surge of love for him, followed by a sharp prickle of conscience. Oh God, he had no idea what she planned to do to him.

'Want a drink?' she said. 'Tea, coffee?'

He seemed surprised. Maybe he was expecting a Toby jug, she thought. 'I could murder a nice mug of tea, if it's no trouble.' His stomach rumbled again.

'I'll see what I can find to eat,' said Sarah.

'It has to be healthy ...' said Niall.

She smiled back at him. 'I'll do my very best.'

She went into the kitchen and took a few deep breaths. A strange calmness, almost a numbness descended on her. She'd finally made up her mind last night and once she'd decided, she'd known one hundred per cent that what she was about to do was the right thing.

Even so, she was dreading saying the words out loud. Dreading even more having to see the relief and happiness in his eyes when she told him.

'OK, I'd been hoping for a second chance but I've finally given that hope up. I accept it's all over between us and I have to move on.'

Her hands shook a little as she poured the hot water onto the teabag in the mug. She squashed the bag against the side of the mug, turning the tea a rusty orange, even though the smell and colour of it made her feel nauseous again.

When she'd woken up this morning, she felt as if a dense fog had lifted from her brain and her whole life. What had she been thinking, begging Molly to risk her career and liberty for such a crazy idea? She couldn't do this to Molly, or even to Liam or Niall – and definitely not to herself and the baby. She'd decided that she was going to take up Liam's offer of the craft unit. She'd never get another chance to rent such a perfect location at such a good price and even if she was taking advantage of Liam, she had to think of her future now. She'd decided that when Niall arrived, she would tell him about the baby and let go of the cottage – and him.

Giving Niall what he wanted didn't feel like victory for him and Vanessa anymore. It would hurt, it would hurt like hell, but it would also mean that she had won a small victory too: against the misery and madness of the past few months. Her prize would be hope and the chance to move on with her baby.

With a heart lighter than she'd had for many weeks, she took a deep breath, picked up the mug and headed into the lounge.

Chapter Twenty-Six

M olly couldn't believe that everything was going to plan – at least where the race was concerned. Ewan had called for her as arranged and the gentle few miles' pedal to the start of the event at one of the college sports fields had been the perfect warm-up. The sun shone down from a cloudless blue sky and she was worried she might be too hot in her cycling tights and new LC Holdings jersey.

The sight of scores of other tandems, their riders all buzzed and jokey and nervous, just like her, had sent her adrenaline and endorphins sky-high. The flags and banners of the charity were flapping cheerfully in the breeze and enthusiastic volunteers were bouncing around handing out free drink bottles, race numbers and power bars.

Liam had sent a driver who was following along in a van with spares for the bike and dry clothes in case of disaster, but Molly hoped they wouldn't need them. The start area had the air of a party atmosphere and she kept having to remind herself she was actually here to cycle seventy-five miles. With their sponsorship now totalling over a thousand pounds, there was no going back.

Some of their colleagues in the lab had held a bake sale to raise extra funds and their administrator and Ewan's fan, Mrs

Choudhry, had organised a quiz night and raffle, which had contributed two hundred pounds to the total. Sarah had also held a charity jewellery-making workshop too boost the funds. Added to the pledges from family, friends and colleagues in other departments, it was a massive amount but she and Ewan still had to complete the race or they'd be letting everyone and the charity down. The pressure made her stomach flip over and over. This was all too real ...

Over by the starting area, she spotted Pete with a clipboard going through what looked like a pre-race check with his co-rider. She'd seen Pete collecting his bike from the rack at work, on her way out of the lab when she'd smuggled out the Love Bug and taken it to Sarah's. If he ever found out what she'd done ... If anyone found out what she'd done ... Her nerves and worries about the race paled into insignificance compared to her worries about giving the Bug to Sarah.

Sarah. She should be here now. Maybe Molly could stop her from using the Bug on Niall. It might not be too late. Perhaps she'd even come to her senses and changed her mind.

Frantically Molly looked around for her, scanning every woman not in Lycra. None of them were her sister, but there were so many supporters milling around the competitors that perhaps it wasn't surprising.

Yet Sarah had promised to be there to see them off.

'Molly, can we go through the bike safety check one final time?'

Ewan was back from the Portaloos.

'Sure.'

She listened half-heartedly as he knelt by the bike and reeled off a list of components, although she was still searching the crowds for Sarah.

Oh shit. Pete walked towards them as Ewan was finishing his checks. Molly could see Pete's "stoker", a post-doc from the electronic engineering lab, holding their tandem by the start line.

Molly pasted on a devil-may-care smile.

'All set then?' he said cheerfully.

'I think so.' She sipped casually from her water bottle as if she was enjoying a cocktail.

Ewan straightened up and glared at Pete. 'We're good to go.'

'Not worried about losing another spoke?' Pete asked with a grin.

'No. The bike's had a complete service and is in tip-top condition,' said Ewan firmly.

Pete smirked. 'Never did get hold of that top-of-the-range model, then?'

'No,' said Ewan tightly. Molly wished for Pete to evaporate. With her worries about Sarah, the Love Bug and the race, she didn't want the added stress of fisticuffs breaking out between Ewan and Pete. Then again, it would mean they might be disqualified, which wouldn't be the worst thing in the world.

'Still, it's always nice to add a new level of challenge to these things, isn't it?' said Pete.

'We're fine. We've done the training and worked hard,' Ewan said calmly. Molly admired his restraint. She was a nanosecond away from squirting Pete with her water bottle. And where the bloody hell was Sarah?

'See you at the finish, then,' said Pete, obviously meaning he'd wait for them at the finish line.

'Grrr. I could thump him sometimes,' said Molly after Pete had sauntered back to his own bike.

'Don't let him get to you,' said Ewan.

'And you don't?' Molly shot back.

Ewan pulled a face but there was no time for a row because Barry, their support van driver, arrived. 'Shall I take your stuff to the van?' he asked.

'Yes, thanks,' said Ewan.

'Do you have everything you need?' he asked Molly.

This is it, she thought, as an even more massive lurch of last-minute nerves hit her. There's no going back for any of us. Sarah obviously wasn't going to see them before the start of the race. If she could see her, Molly might feel better. What if something had happened to her – or the baby?

'Um. I'd like to check my phone again. I can't see Sarah and I wondered if she'd texted me,' she said to Barry and Ewan.

'She's probably waiting at the start line. There are hundreds of people over there,' said Ewan.

Molly scanned the crowds of people around the start banner one last time but couldn't see Sarah. 'Maybe. I hope so,' she said.

Another announcement boomed over the tannoy, calling all the competitors to assemble at the start. Molly knew she'd have to check her phone at the end of the race. It was time to go.

Barry shouldered her backpack. 'You two had better go. I'll be in the support cortege and at the finish. There are feeding stations along the way when you need a top-up of your water bottles. If anything happens to the bike, I've got basic spares. I'm no expert but I used to have a tandem and I can fix most minor problems.'

'Thanks,' said Molly, twitching with adrenaline and anxiety.

'It's good of you to give up your Sunday,' said Ewan.

Barry grinned. 'No problem. Liam would have driven the van himself but he's got some important wedmin to deal with.' The tannoy blared again, ordering the competitors to the start. Molly's legs felt wobbly as hell and she hadn't even got on the bike.

'We have to go,' said Ewan, nerves adding brusqueness to his voice. He was clearly anxious about the race too, which wasn't encouraging. Shit.

'Oh God, what have I done?' she said, referring to the race and the Love Bug.

He smiled at her and squeezed her arm. 'We'll be fine. We probably won't beat Parasitic Pete but we'll make it and let's face it, he'd give anything to be your stoker.'

'What a horrible thought,' said Molly, knowing the moment of truth had come. 'Come on, let's get this over with.'

Chapter Twenty-Seven

Back in the cottage in Fenham, Sarah handed Niall his favourite mug and sat opposite him. Her stomach fluttered wildly as if a colony of big hairy moths were trying to escape.

Niall sniffed at the builder's strength tea as if it was nectar. It had made Sarah feel sick to make it but she wanted him in a good mood. 'Hmm. Lovely. You could strip paint with that. No one makes a cuppa like you, Sarah.'

'Not even Vanessa?' she asked.

'Vanessa doesn't drink tea or coffee, unless it's herbal.' He wrinkled his nose. 'Can't stand the stuff myself. Reminds me of cough medicine, but Vanessa says it's better for you and she is the health expert. She knows bloody everything about diet and nutrition. Unfortunately.' With a sigh, he sipped the tea and looked around him, peering closely at the decoration.

'The cottage looks smart. Have you repainted the door?'

'The frame was chipped when I threw Toby at you so Liam helped me fill it in and paint it and the rest of the woodwork.'

'I thought so.' In between sips of tea, Sarah could see him staring at the ceiling again. 'You've repaired those dodgy down-lighters too.'

'Yes. The transformer had packed it in.'

'Did Liam fix that too?'

'Liam can't do electrics. You have to be registered for that.'

'You'll have to send me the electrician's invoice then. I don't want you to have to pay for any work or have to ask strange men.'

'Liam's not a strange man. He's a ... a ... client and a friend.' Sarah hesitated on how to describe Liam. He *was* a friend, a very good friend who made her laugh and was always there with practical advice. He was honest, blunt even, and definitely pragmatic where business was concerned, but honesty was a good thing.

'Even so, Sare, I don't want you to rely on some guy you've only just met who's probably trying it on.'

'Liam's not trying it on,' Sarah replied patiently, sensing danger in Niall's tone. The last thing she wanted was a row to erupt when she'd tried so hard to stay calm before she told him she'd accepted their separation – forever. 'He only wants to help.'

'He's much too old for you. Don't be taken in just because you're desperate and lonely.' Niall gulped down his tea.

Anger bubbled up inside her. 'Niall, you can't tell me who I can and can't be friends with after what you did with Vanessa and while I might have felt very alone these past few months, I'm definitely not desperate.'

'I'm sorry. All I meant was that you deserve better than this Liam bloke.'

Sarah's good intentions were ebbing away. 'Better than what? He's sensitive and considerate, he's good-looking, he's got his own business, he drives a Range Rover ...'

'So it's his money you're interested in as well as his DIY skills?' Niall sneered.

'That's beneath you, Ni.'

'Yeah. Yeah ... but I still care about you, babe. I want you to be happy, no matter what's happened between us.'

'Well, we can't always have what we want, can we?' Sarah said curtly.

'No ... but ...' He sighed. 'Sometimes maybe we don't know what we really want until it's taken away from us.'

'What do you mean?'

'Oh, nothing. I suppose I was only thinking that the grass isn't always greener.'

'It's a bit late for that, isn't it?' Sarah said, thinking he was acting very oddly.

'I suppose so.' Niall let out a sigh. 'That was a great cup of tea. I've missed your cuppas. I've missed a lot of things.'

Sarah resisted the urge to say something sarcastic about Vanessa and gathered herself together with a huge effort. 'Do you want another one and a biscuit?' she said.

'I shouldn't. Vanessa says the tea's full of caffeine and that biscuits are full of crap ... Oh, go on then. One won't hurt.'

Sarah went into the kitchen, aware she was simply putting off the moment when they had to get down to business. Niall seemed very emotional, probably because he'd now realised that with the sale of the house, their relationship was well and truly over. Well, it served him right if he was feeling miserable and guilty at last. On the other hand, in his frame of mind, she wasn't quite sure how he'd react when she mentioned the baby, because no matter how badly he took the news, and how shocked he was, she would have to leave him in no uncertain terms that he was going to have to make a financial contribution towards its upbringing.

She hoped he wouldn't be too negative because she wasn't

sure she could keep her cool if he did. The kettle boiled and Sarah poured the water onto the fresh tea bag. While it brewed, she reached for a fresh packet of Hobnobs from the cupboard. A peace offering ... or something to butter him up.

'Is that a new rug in front of the fire?' Niall called through the open door.

'Sort of. A student was chucking it out so I got it.' It was true. Liam *was* a student.

'Looks expensive.'

'I doubt it.'

She poured milk into Niall's mug, added the hot water to a ginger teabag for herself, and leaned against the counter, waiting for the tea to brew. Niall kept talking, about the new rug and the decorating and how his cousin had been done for speeding again and his mum wanted to buy a campervan, at her age and ...

Sarah squashed the teabag, rolling her eyes at Niall's chatter. He just couldn't seem to shut up. It must be nerves or guilt or both making him rattle on and on about trivia. She decided to put the mugs and biscuits on a tray and walked into the sitting room.

Sarah froze, halfway through the doorway. Niall held the perfume atomiser in his hand.

Sarah's hands shook so much that tea slopped onto the surface. Oh God, no ...

'Who bought you this?' he asked.

Her throat dried. 'Molly ...'

He wrinkled his nose. 'Looks expensive to me. I thought Molly was always broke?'

'A boyfriend gave it to her. She doesn't like it so she gave it to me.'

'A boyfriend with a Range Rover, by any chance?'

Sweat broke out on the small of her back. 'Don't be silly. Anyone would think you're jealous of me and him.'

'Maybe I am ...' Niall said.

Tea sloshed onto the tray as she set it down on the coffee table.

'What do you mean, Niall?' she said, watching him pass the bottle from hand to hand, like a bomb. Sarah's heart was in her mouth. She needed to get the bottle away from him fast and he was acting so strangely.

'I don't know,' he said. 'I guess I just don't like the idea of another man buying you presents and doing jobs around the house. Our house.'

'It's a bit late for that,' Sarah said, her pulse leaping as Niall pulled off the gold cap.

Sarah stepped forward. 'Niall. Don't do that ...'

'Why? What's up?' He held up the atomiser. 'Why not? So it *is* from your new boyfriend after all?'

'If it is, it's none of your business. What do you care?' Sarah reached for the bottle but Niall pressed the aerosol cap. A fine spray with a pungent scent filled the air. Sarah's heart almost burst from her chest.

'Niall, stop it. That stuff's going all over the tea!'

She tried to snatch the bottle but Niall held it away and pressed it again. He sniffed at the scent and inhaled. 'Jesus. That's feckin' strong. Whatever bloke gave it to you, has shit taste or no sense of smell.'

'Molly gave it to me. I told you!'

'Come on, Sarah, we both know it was Saint Liam, your "handyman". I wasn't born yesterday.'

'So what if it was Liam,' said Sarah, grabbing the bottle.

'You don't give a toss, anyway? You've left me for bloody Vanessa. You're the one who's made me sell the cottage and ruined our lives. You're the one who's broken my heart. You're the git who's left me pregnant to bring up our baby on my own!'

Niall stood stock-still. His jaw dropped open. The air reeked of sickly fragrance. Sarah wanted to throw up.

'What did you say?'

'I'm having a baby. But what do you care? You don't want a family – you hate babies. You don't want to be burdened. You told me.'

'A baby? Like *my* baby?'

'Who the hell else's, Niall!'

'I thought ... well, him, Liam thing, the old guy.'

'No, not Liam's. Yours! Your baby, Niall. Get it?'

Niall collapsed onto the sofa, his mouth gaping. 'What? When? How long have you known?'

'Since New Year's Eve. Since before you went out on your shift. I didn't tell you because I didn't want to distract you when you had to go to work and I wanted to wait until we were together at home. Then when I got back you were shagging Vanessa ...'

'Oh Jesus ... but why didn't you tell me after that?'

'Would it have changed things? You said you didn't want a family.'

'I didn't. I thought I didn't but ...' He stared at Sarah. 'But now I know I'm going to be a dad. Now I know you're having my baby. Now I'm here with you ... everything's changed, Sarah.'

Sarah was light-headed with shock and horror. Her eyes switched from the atomiser to Niall's anguished face. There were tears actually glistening in his eyes. He'd seemed moody and jealous before he'd sniffed the Love Bug but now he was positively overflowing with emotion. Surely the Love Bug couldn't work that quickly? Molly had even hinted it might not work at all, but what if it *had* caused this turnaround in Niall?

She clenched her fist, horrified at the possibility. Molly had warned her enough about its effects ...

'But ... what about Vanessa?' she said croakily. 'I thought you and her were soul mates. You said she made you feel free. You can't have changed your mind ...'

'I've been so stupid and I know you might never forgive me,' Niall said, pleading with Sarah. 'We never had the connection that you and I have. In fact, I can now see everything more clearly than I've ever done. I love you, darlin', and I want to come back and from now on I'm going to do everything I can to put things right between us. *All* of us.'

Chapter Twenty-Eight

As they pedalled past the twenty-mile marker, Molly's euphoria had evaporated and the only tingling she was experiencing was the numbness in her bum. The clouds had come over as they'd been riding, first fluffy white ones, then dirty great grey ones that had unleashed a biblical deluge of rain on them. She thought about Sarah, hoping that she was dry and safe and that the baby was all right. What if something terrible had happened to the baby or with Niall?

Thirty-five miles in, she'd even lost the capacity to worry. She only had the energy to press down the pedals, one after the other, up, down, like a metronome. Despite her cycling jacket, she was literally soaked to the skin and the wind was cutting through her. They hadn't wanted to waste time changing their clothes so they'd just got on with things. The roads flowed with water, and she needed all her concentration to steer the bike and keep going on and on. Not only was it raining on them, and although the route was a quiet one, any passing car couldn't help but speed through the puddles and spray them with dirty, cold water. It shot up her nostrils and spattered her face.

She gritted her teeth, pushed harder on the pedals and

forced her aching thighs to climb up a gentle hill that led into one of the villages. It might have been Fenland and, although they had trained for some inclines, the rain, the cold and the fatigue had combined to turn her legs to lead.

And there were still over thirty-five miles to go – they were only just over halfway. She slowed almost to a stop and the bike wobbled.

'Come on, don't give up!' Ewan called from behind, obviously sensing her fatigue.

'I'm. Huff. Not. Puff. Going. Huff. To,' Molly croaked back, grinding the pedals round with all her might.

'I think I saw Pete up ahead,' Ewan shouted.

'Liar!' she called.

'Yes, but we have to get to the end. I'll buy you a massive roast dinner and a huge glass of wine when we do.'

Molly muttered something incomprehensible. She put her head down and tried to think of the steaming dinner, a hot shower, a great big slice of chocolate cake. And of Sarah. Sarah would be at the finish, surely, with Niall? Molly's stomach turned over. She had to get to the end to speak to her and find out how she'd got on and what had happened.

She didn't know how long it was before the rain stopped and the sun came out. Her sense of time, like her bum and legs, had gone completely numb, but she heard Ewan saying, 'There's the next drinks station coming up. I think we should stop and have a quick break.'

'OK.'

Molly pedalled on, grateful for the gentle downhill slope and the sun on her back, drying out her clothes a little bit. There were daffodils in the hedgerows and, over the hedges, the great flat fields glistened with water in the spring sun. It looked beautiful – but even more beautiful was the glimpse of the rest station a hundred yards down the road at the edge of the village. Only fifteen miles to go – she could do it, even though they'd never been this far before. Even though they were in no man's land ...

'Christ!'

She heard Ewan's warning shout and the next thing she knew, she and the bike were sailing sideways. She landed with a splash and for a second or so, her head was underwater. She spluttered and coughed, flailing, and then heard people running towards her.

'Molly!'

Molly heard Ewan's shout and was vaguely aware of him slithering down the bank and into the ditch. His face was black with sludge. He pulled her out of the ditch and onto the grassy verge. Molly winced and rubbed muddy water out of her eyes. She felt giddy.

'Whoa. Don't get up yet.'

Ewan kneeled next to her, his arm around her back. 'Jesus, are you OK?'

'I th-think so. What happened?'

'Black ice, I think. I think that downpour must have frozen on contact with the road.'

She started to shiver. 'How ... how's the bike?' she asked.

'I don't know. I'm more concerned about you.'

'You're all muddy ... You fell off too.' She didn't mind Ewan helping her to her feet.

'Don't worry about me – you kind of flew into the ditch.'

Two marshals in hi-vis vests ran up to them. 'Are you OK, love? We saw what happened from the feed station.'

'Have you got anyone who can check her over?' Ewan asked.

'I'm fine,' said Molly, feeling decidedly wobbly but with no intention of letting them know it.

'Let our first aiders take a look at you. To be on the safe side.'

'No. I'm fine.'

'Look at your elbow,' said Ewan gently.

Molly glanced down. Her elbow was bleeding and throbbing like hell. 'Now I can match you,' she joked.

Ewan put his arm around her and held her firmly. 'Come on.'

'I'm not giving up,' she declared. 'All those people are depending on us to finish. I can't let them down or we won't get the money we've raised.'

'I'm sure they'd pay up anyway.'

'No, I want to complete the race. For charity – and we can't let Pete beat us.'

He squeezed her shoulder. 'I want to finish it too but I'm not sure you should carry on, Molly. You could have concussion.'

'I don't!'

'Why don't you let the first aid guys check you out and then, if you really feel fit enough to carry on, we will ...' He smiled. 'But I'm afraid we might have to let Pete have this one.'

Twenty minutes later, Molly had a ridiculously large patch on her elbow and they both had dry clothes from the support van. While she was getting the once-over from the first aid team, Ewan and Barry had checked out the tandem, and while a little scuffed, it seemed safe to ride. The first aiders weren't happy about Molly carrying on but she'd been adamant. She'd thought of phoning Sarah while she was in the van but hadn't dared ask what she wanted to with the first aiders and Ewan around. Besides the signal varied between one bar and no bar. They'd been out in the middle of nowhere for hours so it wasn't surprising Sarah hadn't called, even if she'd wanted to.

'You don't have to do this, Molly,' Ewan said as he wheeled the bike back to her. 'You've had quite a knock.'

She folded her arms and winced. 'I'll finish this if it's the last thing I do.'

'That's what I'm worried about.'

'I'm touched.'

'Do you want me to pilot?'

'No way. If you do, we'll definitely never make it.'

She sounded sarcastic but it was all bravado. Her stomach was doing all sorts of funny things. She blamed it on the shock and not the rare experience of him being nice to her. His hair was damp and his face was blotched in mud and there was a graze down his cheek. He looked as sexy as hell. She would have shagged him if she ever had the energy again. Then she remembered Sarah and Niall and came to her senses. She couldn't think of anything like that until she knew what had happened. But there was still another fifteen miles to go. Her elbow throbbed at the thought of continuing but she ignored the pain.

Ewan climbed over the bike. 'Come on then, Victoria, let's go.'

'*Victoria?*'

'Pendleton.'

'Wow. A hot brunette ...' Molly teased as she lifted her leg over the frame.

Ewan either didn't hear or chose to ignore her allusion to the Valentine's card. 'Let's hope you can ride like her,' he said.

Was it possible to ride a bike while you were delirious? Molly wondered, as she pushed down on the pedals. She had no idea of how long it had been since the accident. Occasionally she registered a cheering group of volunteers or bemused locals shouting encouragement. Once or twice they stopped briefly and Ewan offered her a drink and told her there was only ten miles to go or five. Molly tried to shut her ears and wrap herself in a bubble. She ached inside and out but the pain in her elbow, strangely, had eased. That would be the endorphins, she reasoned, and woe betide her when the race was done.

Some of the support vehicles whooshed by them, the less considerate spattering them with water.

'Want to stop again?' Ewan shouted.

'No!'

She knew she would never get going again if she stopped.

'Not far now. A couple of miles tops,' Ewan called.

Molly bent her head down and willed her jelly like legs to work. The bike seemed to get heavier and she noticed they were climbing a long, shallow hill.

'Don't give up. Keep going. After this it's all downhill!'

She gritted her teeth and pushed her feet down. Her thighs burned as the hill grew steeper. East Anglia was supposed to be flat, damn it.

'You're doing really well, Molly. Not far now.'

She forced the pedals round; by now her legs felt as if they were welded to the tandem. Possibly they might have to be disconnected with a crowbar. She could hear cheering and clapping and whistling.

'Let's finish this in style,' Ewan called, and Molly felt him put in a final burst of power. The group of riders and supporters was coming up fast. She thought she heard Pete shouting and they sailed under the Finish line banner.

'Whoa!'

She braked a bit too sharply and they almost fell off the bike. People were cheering and volunteers ran up to take the bike and drape silver foil blankets around them. Someone handed her a plastic medal on a ribbon.

'Are you OK?' said Barry smacking her on the back. 'Well done! You did so well to finish after a tumble like that. I'll look after the bike now. You guys get some hydration and food.'

'Thanks.'

Dazed but elated, she looked around for Ewan.

Suddenly he was behind her, turning her around and pulling her into his arms. He hugged her so tightly, he almost stole breath away and then he kissed her. It was a big, wet, warm, muddy sweaty kiss that lifted her onto the toes of her cycle shoes. It went on and on and someone, possibly her, only stopped it when she couldn't breathe any longer.

He kept hold of her. 'You do know you're a completely barking mad, reckless nutter?'

Molly laughed, still gasping for breath. 'I love you too.'

He leaned back and looked at her intensely. She held her breath. 'Do you?' he said.

'Well done, mate!' Pete bounded over and slapped Ewan hard on the back before he could reply. He'd let go of her but Molly's head was still spinning. She didn't quite feel part of this earth. 'Molly. I heard what happened. You did well to carry on after that.'

'Thanks,' said Molly.

'You too, mate,' he told Ewan. 'Especially on that piece of crap.'

Ewan smiled. 'I'll take that as a compliment. How did you and Devi get on?'

'We came second. Not bad considering our training didn't go exactly to my schedule. I'm sure we can win next year.'

'Congratulations,' said Ewan, shaking Pete's hand while Molly sipped an energy drink, trying to calm down. Her elbow had started to pulse again and around them, marshals were scooping up empty cups and wrappers, and torn race numbers into black plastic sacks. Some of the tandem trailers had already started to pull out of the car park.

Pete spoke to her. 'I'll see you tomorrow, then. Good job you've got a driver to take you home, eh?'

Ewan muttered something then Pete jogged back to his partner. She and Ewan were left alone, with stray cups rolling around their feet in the wind. Ewan couldn't seem to take his eyes off her. The way he looked at her made her stomach swirl in a not-unpleasant way. It was probably the adrenaline and the shock because her legs were still wobbly.

Molly's phone buzzed. 'I have to get this! It might be Sarah.'

Ewan stood by as she checked the message. Please please let everything be fine.

Sorry can't make race. Hope all goes well. Don't worry about me.

Molly let out a huge sigh of relief then checked the time of the message. It had only just come through to her phone but had been sent a couple of hours before. The guilt of what she'd done came rushing back.

She texted back.

Are you *sure*? Are you OK? We made it!

Within thirty seconds, a reply pinged back.

Well done. J I'm fine. Enjoy yourself.

Fine? Was that all Sarah was going to say?

Ewan was watching her.

Molly held up her phone. 'Just making sure Sarah's OK. It's been a difficult time.'

He smiled and nodded.

A marshal handed her a plastic bag of something or other. Molly didn't care. She was shaky and shivery and didn't want to take her eyes off Ewan. He was muddy and sweaty and magnificent and strange. Like a different Ewan. Shit, maybe she really did have concussion ...

'Do you want someone to take a look at the arm?' she heard the marshal asking.

'No. It's fine,' she said.

'OK. If I were you, I'd get changed into some dry clothes, and have a sit-down. You look pale and you've had a hell of a shock,' said the marshal.

'I'll take care of her,' said Ewan.

'I don't need taking care of,' said Molly indignantly.

Ewan smiled and took her arm. 'I don't give a toss.'

Barry arrived. 'I've loaded the bike. Are you two ready to go back to Cambridge or do you want to get changed first?'

Ewan cut in. 'You can take the tandem, thanks, but Molly and I have other plans.'

Chapter Twenty-Nine

Molly followed Ewan into the reception area at The Feathers, a coaching inn situated on the cobbled town square. Even the inn sign creaked in the wind.

'But how will we get home tomorrow?' she asked as they waited at the reception desk after it became clear what his plans were. She could hardly believe what was happening. Ewan was booking a room – for them both – in the hotel.

'Train, bus, walk. I don't care. We'll worry about that tomorrow,' he said.

The only room left was a suite and Molly winced at the price but Ewan didn't bat an eyelid. He filled in the check-in card at the hotel.

'Do you have a car with you, sir?'

'Does it look like it?'

The receptionist tittered. 'Now you come to mention it. No. You've been doing the tandem challenge, have you?'

'Yes, and we won't need a space for the tandem. It's gone back to Cambridge.'

The receptionist smirked. 'Here's your key. Do you want your bags sent up?'

'No, we can manage, thanks, but we'd like some room service. You *do* do room service?' he added imperiously.

'I'm sure we can arrange something, sir.'

'Good. I'll call you when we're ready.'

'I have to let Sarah know we're staying over. She'll be worried.' Molly debated whether to call her, but seeing Ewan standing by their rucksacks decided her. Sarah would have called if she'd wanted to speak to her. Things must be going well with Niall – or perhaps he'd already left the house. Sarah must have decided not to give him the Love Bug and surely, she would forgive Molly taking this chance – possibly her only chance – with Ewan.

Molly texted.

Staying over with Ewan. In *one* room. o) Call me if you need me. Love you, sis. xx

She pressed send.

'Ready?' he asked, an edge of desperation creeping into his voice.

Ewan picked up his and Molly's rucksacks and headed for the oak staircase leading up to the guest rooms. 'Come on,' he said with a grin. 'Just one more climb to go.'

Those stairs ought to have been agony but with the prospect of getting naked with Ewan and room service afterwards, Molly found a new reserve of energy. Her memory of the moments after the race – in fact, everything after they'd ended up in a ditch – was hazy, but one thing kept coming back to her. Her words and Ewan's flashed on and off like a retro neon sign.

'I love you too.' ' Do you?' ' I love you too.' 'Do you?' 'I love you …' 'Do you?'

'Do you?'

Ewan dumped the rucksacks on the bed. 'What?'

'Nothing.'

He put his arms around her. Wow. Just the feel of his fingertips against her back, the lightest pressure on her sweater was making her giddy. Just the awkward, slightly shambolic presence of him.

He pulled her closer and kissed her. A little hesitant at first but growing stronger very quickly. She pressed against him. He pressed against her. He needed a shave, she needed a shower but, man, it was amazing. The smoky tang of his damp cycle top, the itchy scrape of his stubble, the hot strength of his tongue exploring her mouth. The peppery tingle that fizzed from her toes to her scalp, and lit up every nerve ending like a pinball table.

Was this what being in love was like? Could it really be this good yet this *weird*? So heart popping, yet so scary, like holding a giant rainbow-coloured bubble on your palm, afraid it would burst if you so much as breathed.

Ewan stopped kissing her but kept holding her.

Molly rested her head on his chest. 'Wow ...'

'Yes.' The word resonated against her cheek.

'We mustn't tell anyone about this at work.'

Ewan leaned back and looked down at her. 'Shouldn't it be me saying that?'

'No ... I just can't cope with the whole thing – the drama – played out in public. I know how you felt about your wife. This is private and personal for me too and I don't want people like Pete Garrick and the others teasing us and saying ... well, you know.'

'What kind of "you know"?'

'Stuff about us shagging.'

'We haven't shagged yet, Molly, and if they say anything, I'll thump them.'

'You can't, you're the boss. You have to be professional and we have rules and boundaries.'

'Absolutely. I agree.'

'Rule 1. No kissing, no sneaky looks at each other, no innuendos. No anything while we're in the lab.'

'Agreed.' He smiled. 'But we're not at work, now, are we, and we also haven't given them anything to talk about. I think we should put that right.'

'Hmm. I concur, Professor Baxter.' She squeezed his bum through the Lycra. Did he have any idea how long she'd wanted to do that?

He raised his eyebrows. 'So ... shall we have a shower before ...?'

'Or we could kill two birds with one stone.'

Moll's phone beeped. Ewan groaned then said, 'Go on, put us both out of our misery.'

One quick glance was all it took for Molly to heave a huge sigh of relief.

Wow. Go for it. Love you too.

'Permission to proceed?' asked Ewan.

'You bet,' said Molly.

The Feathers was old, all wonky floors and sloping ceilings but the bathroom, thank God, was pure twenty-first century. It had one of those double showers with the tiny shimmering mosaics and the acres of glass walls and the waterfall showerheads.

And her sore elbow *really* stung when Ewan soaped her back and the foam ran into the grazes.

'Sorry you were hurt,' he said and kissed her again, their bodies sliding together, tiny foam bubbles dusting the hairs on his chest.

'I am so sorry,' he said and crouched down in the shower to kiss her shins and thighs. 'This is how sorry I am.' He smacked a big soapy kiss in the middle of her arse.

She giggled at the intimacy of it. Not that she hadn't just been naked in the shower with him pressed against her back and stomach. 'No. You can't do that ...'

He looked up at her. 'Why not?'

'Because ...'

'Aw, shut up.'

He kissed her bum again just to show he could and then he got up and kissed her mouth. Molly slid open the shower screen door and they went into the bedroom, still damp, dripping wet footprints on the carpet. They stood by the bed and kissed again. After the kiss, Ewan sat on the bed and took Molly's hand. He lay down and she climbed onto the covers alongside him.

'Molly, forgive me for the past few months. I didn't know how to say how I felt – I didn't even know how I felt – but I do know I was an arse, blowing hot and cold with you. I'm sorry.'

Molly put her finger on his lips. 'Aw, just shut up and shag me.'

*

Molly pushed herself up the pillows. She heard Ewan thank the porter and lock the door behind him. Sleet pattered against the windowpanes behind the thick velvet curtains and a chink of street light filtered through. She felt completely chilled. Sarah must have chickened out and come to her senses, the bloody race was over and Ewan was standing in front of her, wearing one of the hotel's navy bathrobes.

He looked even more delicious than the tray of goodies that he was wheeling towards the table by the window. He lifted a silver dome from one of the plates.

'So, *Docteur* Havers,' he said in a French accent. 'Will it be ze steak frites or ze smoked salmon tagliatelle? Or a leetle of both?'

She burst out laughing. It was weird to see him in this mood. She wasn't sure she could cope with Ewan in happy silly mode. 'Is that meant to be French?'

'*Mais, bien sur, mon petit chou.*'

'It sounds like Dutch, or possibly Klingon.'

He pouted. '*Ma cherie*, I am wounded to ze core.'

She threw a pillow at him. 'Oh behave!'

'Hey!'

The pillow narrowly missed the plate and they both dissolved into laughter. Ignoring her bumps and bruises, she inched her way out of bed, shrugged on the spare robe and sat down at the table. Although they'd demolished the contents of the mini bar in between their sex sessions, there was only so long you could run on wasabi peanuts and Pringles.

She pulled the bottle of Prosecco from the ice bucket and filled their glasses. 'To the tandem.'

Ewan raised his wine. 'And to you for surviving.'

She smiled. 'I think we both deserve this.'

They tucked into the meals and ordered hot chocolate brownies and ice cream for afters. She was now sipping the last of the Prosecco in bed, with Ewan's arm around her. His robe had come loose, exposing one muscular hairy thigh. She walked her fingers up and down the muscle tantalisingly close to his groin, feeling desire twist low in her belly. Was this her fate from now on? To be permanently turned on? To spend every minute having sex with him, having just had sex or wanting it? It would kill her but what a way to go.

'I have a confession to make ...' said Ewan.

Molly rested her hand on his thigh. She couldn't see his face.

'Let me guess ... you sent the card and the EBV microbe.'

'It was the closest I could get to a Love Bug.'

She giggled and twisted around.

He looked puzzled. 'But I thought you sent me a card?'

'No, I didn't. I wouldn't dare.'

'Have I been that scary?'

'Ohhhh, yes.'

He blew out a breath. 'Well, someone did. It had a meerkat on it and a message written in capitals in pink gel pen inside.'

'Nope.' She suppressed a giggle. 'Was it from Mrs Choudhry? Or possibly chloroform man ...'

Ewan groaned. 'After everything I said about us not getting involved, I should have known that sending a card was cheesy and stupid and impulsive and ...'

'Funny and silly and human? Ewan, it's *fine*. More than fine. How long did it take you to think of the message?'

He closed his eyes. 'Too long.'

'Really? I thought you might have found it on the Internet or something.'

'God, no. I crafted it specially. Shit. That makes it sound even worse, doesn't it?'

'I did wonder for a nanosecond if you were behind it but then I realised you'd never send anything so silly and geeky and cheesy ...'

His face fell. Molly wanted to have sex with him again but

first, she was going to enjoy his agony for a little while longer. After all, he had made her suffer a lot over the past few months and possibly would do again. She hoped not but ...

'Oh shit.'

Molly bit her lip, desperately trying not to laugh at him then remembered his card to her. Her stomach did a little skip and a jump. 'So, I'm a hot brunette, am I?'

Ewan raked his fingers through his rumpled hair. 'You know you bloody well are but you also know that I shouldn't be saying that to you. I should never have sent the card or decided to do that bloody tandem ride.'

'You'll be saying next that you should never have employed me.'

'God, no. That was one of the best decisions I've made in my life, not that there have been many where women are concerned. I employed you because you were the best candidate. Brilliant and committed and I knew you'd fit into the lab.'

'And because you fancied me?'

'And *in spite* of me fancying you, I agonised over whether I would be able to work on the Love Bug with someone I was so attracted to, but then I realised that if I didn't hire you, purely on merit, I would never forgive myself and I didn't deserve to be in charge of any staff. I'd be a bastard if I didn't give you the job because I thought I might fall in love with you. That would be pathetic and cowardly. But this is incredibly unprofessional of me ...'

'*Incredibly* unprofessional. In that case, what was going on with the card and come to think of it, the whole tandem thing? If you wanted to go out with me, you only had to ask.' In the exuberance of the moment, Molly decided to conveniently ignore the fact that she'd gone way beyond unprofessional and risked her entire career to help Sarah.

'I wanted to but I couldn't. It's not only the thing with work, though I told Sarah that.'

'Is that why you said it? Because you knew it would get back to me and warn me off?'

'I didn't know what I wanted, or rather I *did* know what I wanted but I kept trying it to deny it and sabotage my chances. Then I'd be tempted again. Fuck, Molly, you have to know I haven't always been like this. The truth is that when Anna left me – when she went off with him – I thought I was OK, but I wasn't. I was bitter and twisted and I retreated even deeper into my work, even though she said that my work was one of the reasons she left in the first place. It's taken me this long to finally admit how I feel. I hope I've done the right thing.'

Wow. Wow, this was real and big. When he fell, he fell hard. Perhaps she should have known that, had always known it. Should she be daunted by going from zero to flashing neon signs so fast?

She asked herself and the answer was no.

'You know how it is when you've loved someone and you've been hurt,' he said idly stroking her leg, unable or unwilling to look at her. 'You're never the same afterwards no matter how much you want to be; but the past doesn't protect you, that's the shitty thing. You go on taking the risk, no matter how hard you fought against it. You understand?'

'Not really. This is the first time for me.'

He gasped, 'Christ. You don't mean *the* first time?'

'Of course not.' She giggled. 'Not the sex thing. But the other thing. The hurt and not being the same afterwards but still taking the risk.' She stopped short of saying the falling in love thing. She wasn't ready for that yet. '*That* part, this is my first time.'

Ewan shook his head in disbelief but the right kind of disbelief: the happy kind; the kind that was quietly and sweetly delighted to be first to make her feel like she wanted to take that risk.

*

Molly woke up expecting to see the light shining through the wonky blind that had bent when she'd thrown a copy of *Fifty Shades of Grey* at it. She expected to smell bacon frying from the flat below and hip-hop bouncing the floor. She expected to feel the soft brush of her tartan pyjamas against her skin.

Instead she woke to the scent of aftershave and a hot hairy leg against hers. On the pillow next to her, Ewan's dark hair poked over the top of the duvet. His eyes were closed and his thick lashes brushed his cheekbones. She wasn't at home; she was in a hotel with a man. With Ewan. Everything was wonderful in her world but despite the reassuring texts, she was still worried about Sarah. If she had decided not to use the Love Bug and Niall had left, Sarah was bound to be upset, even if she'd made the right decision. If Sarah had used it ... Molly pushed that prospect aside. She pushed her worries aside for a while longer; it might be selfish but she wanted to enjoy every private moment with Ewan while she could.

'Ohh. Owww.'

Her grazed elbow caught the sheets and that was when she realised that every bone ached, from her ankles to her hands where she'd gripped the handlebars. She'd never ached

so much or been so stiff but she'd also never been so happy.
Ewan let out a juddering breath and opened his deep brown
eyes, looking confused. Then they widened as they focused
on her.

'Molly?'

She smiled at his rough morning voice, far more like the
old Ewan. 'Yup.'

He rubbed his eyes. 'Oh God, was I drooling or snoring?'

'Why would you think that?'

'I know I snore sometimes. My brother told me when we
shared a tent on a stag weekend. Did I keep you awake?'

'Not after you meant to keep me awake.' He gave a rare
Ewan-ish grin, definitely laced with manly pride but Molly
forgave him. He propped himself up on one elbow and his
solid shin connected with hers.

Molly squashed down a gasp of pain.

'Sorry, are you OK?'

She grinned. 'Yeah, apart from feeling like I've been run
over by a truck.'

Gently, he rolled her on top of him. Her toes came midway
down his shins. Every movement hurt but she didn't give a
toss. His erection prodded her stomach. It was weird but
wonderful, his *thing*, the way it sulkily and imperiously
demanded her attention. Men, she'd decided overnight, were
a strange and faintly ridiculous species but at times like these,
pretty fucking magnificent – as long as they never found out.

'Can you stand the pain?' he asked.

'I don't know but I'm willing to give it a go.'

Chapter Thirty

Sarah opened her eyes in the bedroom of the cottage. As usual, the first thing she saw was the Lloyd Loom chair where Niall used to dump his uniform and keep his boots underneath. For the first couple of days after he'd left, she'd seen that empty chair and cried. Later the tears had dried to a tug of emptiness and resignation. This morning, the uniform and boots were back, like nothing had happened. Yet *everything* had happened.

She closed her eyes again.

Oh God, what had *she done?*

After Niall had begged her to take him back, and managed to stop blubbing, he'd made her lie on the sofa while he listed all the things he'd done wrong and all the ways he was going to make it up to her. Sarah had never heard him so contrite before, so overemotional or sentimental and it scared her. It had to be the effects of the Love Bug ... How could it be anything else? Hadn't Molly said it affected a person's hormones? Well, it had certainly affected Niall's.

The worry made her head throb and it wasn't until he'd finally gone to tell Vanessa he wouldn't be home that evening, that she'd realised she was too late to go to the race.

She wanted to talk to Molly more than anything in the

world, but she didn't want to ruin her moment with Ewan. She had to hang on until Molly got home before she told her what had happened.

And why should she disturb her sister? She'd got Niall, this was what she'd once wanted or thought she'd wanted right up until she'd woken up yesterday morning. Until she'd finally come to her senses and realised you couldn't turn the clock back, you couldn't make someone love you or it wasn't love at all. It was a false, horrible, sham and a nightmare.

But Molly could put things right, surely? She'd said the Bug wasn't *that* strong, that it only encouraged romantic bonding between the recipient and partner. It might wear off ... and if not, Molly had mentioned some kind of antidote.

Niall opened the door of the bedroom. He was carrying a tray, with a cup and saucer on it, a bottle and a vase with a daffodil in it. He was grinning from ear to ear.

'So, you're awake, babe?' Sarah forced a smile. 'Hmm.'

He put the tray on the chest of drawers. 'I've bought you a cup of ginger tea and your iron tablets. I've been reading up about nutrition for you and the baby. You need lots of healthy food. No crap. From now on, I'm going to treat you like a princess and our little prince or princess.' He gasped. 'I've just realised. Do we know whether it's a boy or girl yet?'

'*We?*' It was Niall's baby too, Sarah thought as she pushed herself up the pillows. She had to accept that, but his full-on model father act was a shock after she'd been managing on her own. 'Not until the next scan.'

Niall perched on the edge of the bed and took her hand in his. 'I have to come with you, babe. From now on, I swear I'll be with you every step of the way. I can't believe you coped with this on your own. I hardly slept last night, thinking of all those terrible things I said about not wanting kids. I didn't realise how I'd feel when it was my own.'

He hugged her then let go suddenly. 'Oh, I must be careful with you.'

'You don't have to wrap me in cotton wool, Ni. You know that, as you're a medic,' said Sarah, trying to keep things light.

'I know, but this is different, babe.' He stroked her arm as if she was a pet rabbit.

'Yes, but I've been managing the past few months on my own and I'm starting to feel a lot more like myself now.'

He shook his head. 'I don't know how you did it.'

Sarah gritted her teeth and tried to be patient with him. Despite his affair with Vanessa, she could no longer claim the moral high ground – and it was his baby. Their baby.

'No, come on and drink your tea and eat your breakfast.'

He put the tray in her lap. The smell of the pain au chocolat made her feel sick. 'OK. I'll leave you to have a lie-in while I tidy up downstairs and put the washing in. You must have been knackered from getting this place tip-top for all those viewings. Still, we don't have to worry about that now, do we?'

'No, we don't.'

The moment he was out of the room, Sarah shifted the tray and dived for her phone. Knowing she couldn't keep the bad news to herself any longer, no matter how much she ruined Molly's day with Ewan, she frantically texted her sister. The few minutes that followed stretched on and on. Molly would know what to do. She *had* to. If she replied. Having finally decided to ask for help, Sarah felt as if she would burst if Molly didn't reply immediately. She could hear Niall downstairs, whistling to himself, and the clashing of crockery as he unloaded the dishwasher. He'd never unloaded the dishwasher in his life, thought Sarah.

Her phone beeped and she opened the message.

It was from Liam. Sarah let out a groan.

Sarah, thanks for letting me know it's a definite no to the unit. I won't deny I'm disappointed you decided against it but I can understand why in the new circs. I wish you all the best and hope you'll be very happy. You deserve it. x Liam.

Sarah stared at the phone. What did Liam mean: "A no to the unit". She hadn't *definitely* said no yet and what did the "new circs" mean? What was all that about?

She dialled Liam's number. Sarah had a moment of panic when she thought she heard Niall coming upstairs but then she heard whistling from the kitchen.

Damn it. The call went straight to his answerphone.

'Liam,' she said in a hissed whisper. 'It's Sarah. I hope you're OK. If you don't want to speak to me, then that's fine, but I *really* would like to talk. It's important. Call me when you can. I mean no, *don't* call me. Text me or email me or I'll call you.'

Whistling on the stairs. Bugger. Niall was coming back.

Sarah shoved the phone under the duvet as Niall walked into the room.

'Were you talking to someone?' he asked.

'Only leaving a message for Molly. She's with Ewan and I didn't want to interrupt anything but now I'm a bit worried about her because I've not heard anything since last night.'

'Maybe her battery's low?' said Niall. 'Or if she's copped off with that Ewan bloke, they'll probably be shagging each other's brains out so I wouldn't hold your breath for a call.

Which is what I'd love to do now, if you weren't pregnant. I'll have to get some advice on that ...'

Niall tossed her a leery look.

Sarah flashed back a weak smile as her heart sank further. She thought back to all the nights she'd longed to be able to hold Niall, and touch him again. Last night, it had felt beyond wrong to have him in her bed under false pretences and the last thing she felt like right now was sex.

'I might WhatsApp or Facebook Mol in case her battery *is* dead,' she said, hoping to forestall any thoughts he had of sex.

'I'd leave her in peace with her randy boss.' Niall peered at her closely and nodded at the barely touched pastry. 'You haven't eaten much breakfast. Still feeling a bit icky?'

'I'm fine most of the time, but this morning I do feel a bit off,' Sarah said, which wasn't that far from the truth.

He clucked his tongue. 'Poor baby. Try and sip your tea. It'll keep you hydrated and settle your stomach.' Sitting on the edge of the bed again, he stroked her arm and watched her drink the tea. It tasted like vinegar and it was all Sarah could do not to a shudder. She'd no idea that having this fulsome attention under false pretences would have been so horrible, but she kept reminding herself that while Niall had been in the wrong initially, he wasn't responsible for his feelings now.

'Better?' asked Niall as she forced down more of the tea.

'Mmmm. In fact, I think I'd be a lot perkier if I got up and had a shower. I need to get up and do some work and then pop round to Molly's. Once she's home, of course.'

Niall gently but firmly pushed her back down against the bed. 'No, you mustn't go rushing off if you feel poorly. Molly

268

will understand that we need time together and she might not be back until tomorrow.' He winked.

'Tomorrow?' Sarah cried in horror. 'She won't stay away until then. They've got to get back for work.'

Niall frowned. 'Maybe they'll come in late. He is her boss, isn't he? Stop worrying about her, Sarah, and chill out. You're not her keeper anymore. You've done more than enough for her.'

Sarah forced herself to look happy. 'You're right but you know, I have to get up *some* time. I need my exercise,' she said, as sweetly as she could. 'The Bump needs its fresh air too.'

'Hmm. I suppose so.' Niall drummed his fingers on the bed. 'Oh, by the way, I thought you should know that Liam bloke turned up while you were asleep this morning.'

Sarah sat bolt upright and the remaining tea slopped onto the tray. 'What?'

'Careful.' Niall took the tray away.

'Why didn't you wake me up?' she demanded.

Niall curled his lip in disgust. 'Because it was only nine o'clock and you'd had a rough night so I left you in bed. I heard you get up a few times so I let you sleep in and anyway, there was no need to see him.' He lifted her hair off her face. 'It wasn't important so I don't know why the bloke bothered coming over when he could have emailed you. At that bloody time of the morning too! He mentioned something about you renting a craft unit across town but I told him we were back together and you were keeping the Kabin.'

Sarah's blood was up. Even though she'd half-guessed what had happened, she was still shocked that Niall was so blithely proud of speaking to Liam on her behalf.

'I told him his services were no longer required.' Niall's

voice hardened. 'He's very full of himself, isn't he? Probably imagines the laydeez think he's the strong and silent type with his Italian charm and his bloody flash car but if you ask me, he's an arrogant tosser.'

'I didn't ask you to do that, Ni.' She couldn't keep the anger out of her voice.

He held up his hands. 'OK, OK. I was only trying to help you. Hormones all over the place, are they, babe?'

'*My* hormones are *fine*,' said Sarah, in despair.

On the pretext of needing a wee, Sarah finally managed to get rid of Niall while she escaped into the bathroom and sat on the edge of the bath, trying to take some deep calming breaths. She did feel like crying but knew it wouldn't help one bit. What must Liam think of her? How hurt and confused he must have been when Niall practically chucked him out of the house. If she hadn't been so exhausted after her turbulent night, she wouldn't have slept in. But if she *had* been down when Liam called, what could she have said? She couldn't tell either Liam or Niall the truth because the truth was too awful.

One thing was certain: all of this conflict and rowing was bad for the baby. He or she kicked her with its little foot or fist – probably telling her to sort out her shit, and Sarah didn't blame him or her one little bit.

Chapter Thirty-One

M. Where RU? Sthing TERIBLE happened. S

Molly stared at the text message and caught her breath.

Ewan was in the shower, and she'd been quietly chuckling to herself as he did his best Hozier impression, which was very bad indeed. The smile had evaporated when she saw the text and she was about to press Sarah's number to see what had happened when another text buzzed through.

DON't call me. I will call u.

Oh God. *Why* couldn't she call Sarah? Was she in hospital? Was she losing the baby? She stared at the phone, unable to move as a dozen scenarios whirled through her brain. Her hands trembled and she could hardly breathe.

'Well, that's not a view I see every day.'

She looked up to find Ewan stood in the doorway of the en suite, rubbing his hair with a towel. Like her, he was stark naked and wreathed in pine-scented steam. Under any other circumstances, she would have used her last reserves of strength to shag him again but her only thought was to get to Sarah.

She shoved her phone back in her bag. 'I have to go.'

He raised an eyebrow. 'Like that? Do you want to get arrested?'

Avoiding his eye, Molly snatched her T-shirt off the chair. 'Sorry, but I *really* do have to go home.'

Ewan, understandably, sounded confused. 'Was it something I said? Or did?'

Molly tugged the duvet off the bed. 'No. It's Sarah – there's something wrong. Oh, where the hell are my bloody knickers?'

'Whoa. Slow down.' Ewan scooped up her pants from the rug and handed them to her. 'Here they are.'

'Thanks.'

He knotted the towel around his waist. 'What's happened? Is it the baby?' His tone was gentle and concerned.

Molly stepped into her knickers, almost tripping over in her haste to get them on. 'I don't know. She didn't say and she didn't want me to call her ...' Molly stopped speaking.

What if Niall had some sort of reaction to the Love Bug after all?

Or was it just Sarah having discovered that it hadn't worked on Niall at all?

Whatever way you looked at things, thought Molly, the party was over and the tough times were only just beginning. Sarah would blame her for the Love Bug not working, but Molly was ready for that and ready to support her through thick and thin. She could blame the batch, her own ineptitude, anything. Nothing mattered more than saving Sarah from Niall – and herself. But at least Sarah would think Molly had tried and failed and that she had to let go of Niall for good.

Ewan put his arms around her back and spoke soothingly. 'Can I do anything to help?'

'No, I mean, thanks but no.'

She slipped out of his arms and tugged her jeans up. What a selfish cow she'd been, shagging Ewan and enjoying every second, while Sarah suffered the agony of disappointment.

'Slow down. You can't help Sarah in this state of mind. Let me take you to see her.'

'No!'

Ewan held up his hands. 'OK,' he said in his super calm voice. 'I'll back off but for God's sake, take a few deep breaths before you leave here. Fasten your own life vest before helping others et cetera. You don't know the situation yet. It might not be as bad as you're obviously thinking. Better still let me come with you.'

Shame piled on guilt for Molly until she staggered under the weight. She'd let Sarah down, even if it was with the best of intentions and she'd deceived Ewan and was still lying to him now.

'No. That's good of you, but no thanks. Whatever's wrong, Sarah will be better with just me helping. I'll get the first train I can back to Cambridge but there's no need for you to rush back.'

'I don't want to hang around here,' said Ewan.

She grabbed her backpack and cycling jacket. 'I'd rather get off as fast I can. Do you mind packing and checking out? I'll settle up with you for the room later.'

'Forget it,' said Ewan. 'And if it'll help, I'll sort things out here while you go to her but can't you contact her ex if she's in trouble?'

'No. I mean, I don't know. I'll have to see what's happened first.'

'And she's given you no clue?'

'She just texted saying that something bad had happened

and that she'd call me, but I think I should head to the cottage and try and find out more. I'm sorry to run off like this, Ewan. It's been ... it's been good.'

'*Good?*' He walked over to her and held her. 'That's one word for it.'

'More than good,' she said, loving the feel of his arms around her but desperate to leave too. She broke away from him. 'I have to leave. I'm sorry.'

'Go on then, but please, promise you'll let me know how Sarah – and you – are? And, Molly, can we do this again?'

She nodded, barely able to speak past the terrible sickly lump in her throat and the panic scrambling her brain. 'Bye,' she muttered.

She leapt onto the train just as the guard was blowing his whistle. It seemed to call at every tiny village and town on the way to Cambridge but there was no way she could afford a seventy-five-mile taxi ride. She was in agony until she finally got a text from Sarah, saying that it had nothing to do with the baby and that she'd meet her at her flat. As Molly ran up towards the flat, Sarah was waiting outside in her car.

'What's happened?' she asked, the moment she was in the passenger seat.

'It's Niall!' Sarah's voice rose in pitch.

'Oh my God. Is he OK?'

'No, I mean, yes but ... Molly, please don't be angry with me after all the work you put in and the risks you've taken but I decided not to give it to him in the end.'

Molly let out a huge sigh of relief. 'I'm not angry, I'm relieved but, Sarah, there's something I have to tell you about—'

'Shh. Wait. Although I decided *not* to give it to him, I left the atomiser on the coffee table and Niall thought Liam had bought me some perfume and he got all arsey and started waving it around and ranting about Liam and then started spraying it ... and it was everywhere, stinking the room out ...'

'Are you saying that he accidentally inhaled the Love Bug?' Molly cut in.

'Yes! And he was crying and asking me to take him back. It happened that quickly, I had no idea how fast it would act ... He'd been behaving strangely before he sniffed it but that must have been a coincidence.'

'Sarah, wait ...'

'You don't realise what I've done. What *we've* done ... You see I've spent so many nights longing for him to come back to me and grovel, and for things to be like they were, but it didn't feel right and I realised I didn't want anyone to be forced to love me. Once I'd decided, everything seemed clear: I *don't* want him back like this – or like anything, in fact. Now I'm terrified it's too late. How can we stop the Love Bug? Is there an antidote? Are we completely ruined? Am I stuck with him forever? It's my own fault but, Molly ...'

'Sarah! Shut up and listen for a second!' Molly grabbed her hand. 'I don't know what's going on but it's not possible that the Love Bug has worked on Niall.'

'Why not?'

'Because ... the Bug I gave you was a placebo.'

Sarah gasped. 'What?'

'I'm sorry, I started prepping a real one but then I just couldn't go through with it. I left it at the lab and brought the placebo instead.'

'A placebo? You mean a *fake* Bug? I ... but ... are you saying you *lied* to me? Built me up and all along the thing could never work?'

'Yes. I know it was stupid but I wanted to help ... I really was going to help you but I also wanted to save you from hurting Niall, and more importantly yourself. I did prepare a real Bug. It was ready to go but then I came to my senses too. Sarah, you're my sister and I love you – and because I do love you, in the end I couldn't do what you were asking. It wouldn't be real.'

Sarah gripped the steering wheel and gave a huge sigh.

'Will you ever forgive me, hon?' Molly asked, hardly daring to hope that things might turn out to be OK after all.

'Yes ... yes, of course I will. I was out of my mind to even ask you. It was wrong but I've been in a dark place. I haven't known who I am or what I wanted. Last night, I lay awake and finally I felt something like me again. I decided I couldn't make Niall love me, that I didn't even want to. But ...' She held out her hands. 'If you gave me the placebo, *why* is he in my house, begging me to take him back?'

Molly held up her hands in despair. She had absolutely no answer, despite all her knowledge and training. 'I don't know. It must be a coincidence. What did you say to him before he sprayed the Bug?'

'Loads. We had a massive row and I ended up telling him I was pregnant.'

'And?'

'He was shocked. Horrified. Not that I'm having a baby, but that I didn't tell him and now he seems to be experiencing a massive guilt trip and he's begged me to take him back.'

Molly hugged Sarah. Niall's remorse must be genuine. So, he'd come back of his own accord. Molly wasn't happy about

276

that: it hadn't been part of the plan but if Sarah was happy and prepared to forgive him, she had to be too. Her days of interfering in Sarah's personal life were over. 'That's wonderful, isn't it? It's what you wanted. You got Niall back *without* having to use the Bug,' she said.

'Yes, I suppose so, but I feel as if I've been run over by a train and then I feel numb. Oh God, I really don't know *how* to feel.'

'That's probably the shock and trauma of the past few months. Is Niall definitely grovelling and sincere about coming back?'

'Oh yes. He's all emotional and ... well, to be honest I've never seen him so touchy-feely and plain weird. He can't bear to let me out of his sight. I had a job to get out of the cottage just to see you. He says he'll do anything to make it up to me.'

Sarah started the car and they drove the few minutes to the cottage and collapsed onto the sofas.

'What about Vanessa? Has Niall already broken up with her?' Molly asked.

'That's where he is now, or should have been. He's gone to tell her.'

'Jesus. I'd like to be a fly on the wall during that conversation. Do you think he'll go through with it? She had quite a grip on him.'

'I don't know. I'll find out when he gets home, won't I?' She hesitated. 'Are you *absolutely* sure you gave me the fake one and that it couldn't have had an effect on Niall? I find it hard to believe that he's changed his mind so fast.'

'Yes, I'm sure I did and it *couldn't* have worked. I'm not surprised he had a shock when you told him about the baby.'

'I keep wondering if I should have told him before but he was so adamant he didn't want any kids, and I was angry with him.'

'He's also had time to see Vanessa for what she really is – and had it occurred to you that he was jealous of Liam?'

'Yes but ...' Sarah groaned. 'Poor Liam. He's the innocent victim in all of this. I do like him. In other circumstances, I'd probably take things further but Niall told him I didn't want the craft unit because we were back together.'

'Oh dear ... but that's OK, isn't it?' Molly asked.

Sarah sighed. 'I'm not sure. I'm not happy that Niall took it on himself to interfere. I feel like everything in my life has been blown sky high and I haven't known which pieces to keep or which I wanted to ...' Sarah laid her head on the back of the sofa and closed her eyes.

Molly sat by her and held her hand. 'It's been very very tough but the future looks bright. You can start to rebuild things now with Niall.'

'I'm not sure I want to. He's so clingy ... Oh ...' She put her hand on her stomach.

'What?' Molly asked, worried.

'Feel that.'

Sarah took Molly's hand and placed it gently on her stomach. Molly felt awkward; it felt such an intimate thing to do, so weird ... and then, *wow*.

'You felt it?'

Molly did. The slightest ripple against her palm then a stronger movement, a small but unmistakeable kick. Tears pricked her eyes. Shit. She had to hold it together. She was emotional but Sarah was the one who was pregnant.

'That's amazing ...' Tears pricked her eyes.

'It's wonderful, isn't it?'

'Yes, and even though I know the theory inside out, the reality is weird and beautiful. Does it feel like *Alien*? Does it hurt?' Molly asked, sensing the gentlest ripple under her fingertips. Her own skin tingled strangely in response. This was her niece or nephew. Her flesh and blood too. Their parents' genes, their physical characteristics, elements of their personalities. Molly discovered and read about new genetic revelations every day in her work but never, until this moment, had she realised quite how amazing the creation and development of new life really was.

Sarah laughed. 'It doesn't hurt. It's more like a fluttering in your tummy. It's gentle at the moment and it is strange but lovely.'

Molly removed her hand from Sarah's stomach as a thought occurred to her. 'Did Niall give you any clue that he'd changed his mind about Vanessa before today?'

Sarah pursed her lips. 'Occasionally I thought he might be wavering. He sounded as if he had regrets on the phone a couple of times and yesterday before he took the Bug, he did keep going on about Vanessa making him eat healthily and sell his motorbike. I half wondered if he was having second thoughts about her.'

'He must have been,' Molly insisted. 'All those little comments of Niall's say a lot to me. He was having doubts and when you told him about the baby, it must have tipped him over the edge. I am so happy for you, Sarah, and you're not going to believe this, but I've got some pretty awesome news too. I think I'm in love ...'

*

As Molly cycled to the lab the next morning, she felt stiff and tired but almost dizzy with relief. The primroses seemed brighter than ever, the sky bluer and all those insane things you feel when life has handed you a second chance. She was in love and although, of course, love was only chemistry and messing with her hormones, she didn't care. She was pretty certain that Ewan was in love with her too. What's more Sarah had Niall back and Molly had stepped back from doing the most stupid thing she'd ever done in her life.

The journey flew by, her wheels had wings – or were on fire or something. She reached the lab and racked her bike. She was going to destroy the genuine Love Bug she'd created for Sarah and Niall, now while it was quiet and before Ewan got back from his symposium later that afternoon.

Thank goodness he'd never found out. No matter how good a man he was, how sensitive and how much he cared for her, he would never have understood or forgiven her for breaking every rule in the book.

It was as quiet as it ever got in the lab and she saw no one as she locked her bike up, swiped her card and went into her office. She unlocked the door to the lab, her fingers trembling a little as she fumbled with her bunch of keys. For a moment, she wondered what would happen if the petri dish with the real Bug was missing, if someone had broken in and stolen it like in a thriller or *Silent Witness* or something. The moment she saw the petri dish still at the back of the fridge, she laughed out loud at herself and in relief.

This wasn't a thriller, but it had almost been, if she'd been bonkers enough to actually provide Sarah with the Love Bug. She retrieved the petri dish and put it on the table.

One last look to remind her never to contemplate anything so stupid again and then she'd destroy it forever.

The dish stood on the table. Molly shivered in relief. Phew. How close was that? She picked it up again. And stopped. Squinted at the label. It was clearly labelled with her code for placebo.

She had to read the label again and spell out the letters in her head.

Her stomach swam and her legs were like cotton wool. She steadied herself with a hand on the table. No, this *couldn't* be possible. She must be tired and confused. Her mind was playing tricks on her after all the stress of the past few weeks or she was still exhausted from the bike ride and the sex, possibly dehydrated too. Because if the letters in front of her eyes were true and the label really did show the code for the *placebo – the fake Love Bug, that meant ...*

It meant that— She could hardly even let the thought into her whirling mind. It meant that Sarah must have the other one.

Her stomach clenched violently and she swayed a little. It was impossible. She'd been so careful. Her stomach squeezed harder and her hands shook as she picked up the plate. Her head throbbed. No. No. No ...

Niall had actually taken the real Love Bug.

How the hell had it happened? A fresh and horrible thought darted into her head. What if ... what if ... she'd labelled them wrongly? She'd been *so* careful. It should have been impossible to mix them up and yet judging by Niall's reaction, it was *possible* that she had but she couldn't be sure. Not one hundred per cent sure.

And what if Niall had taken the *real* Bug? If his change

of heart was a complete sham? Sarah would be devastated. She would never forgive Molly. Niall, for all that he was a worthless shit in Molly's opinion, didn't deserve this. And if anyone found out ... if Ewan found out – Molly's life would be ruined.

Chapter Thirty-Two

Sarah peered around the sitting room doorframe as Vanessa screamed abuse over Niall's shoulder. She was still in her uniform and must have come over the moment she could get off her shift. He'd tried to break it off with her in person, he'd claimed, but she'd been out so he'd left a message on her phone and then gone to work. Fortunately for him, Vanessa had been on a different shift. Unfortunately for Sarah, she'd come straight round to the cottage the moment she'd listened to the message. Her screeches would have woken the dead, and would definitely have the neighbours out before too long.

'You bitch!' she screeched. 'It's not Niall's baby, is it? It's that old bloke you're shacked up with. I fucking knew you were shagging him. I told Niall!'

Niall blocked the hallway, blocking Vanessa from flying at Sarah. 'I know you're pissed off with me, Nessa babe, but you'll just have to accept it. I've come to my senses and I'm back with Sarah.'

'Come to your senses? You never had any, you tosser! And how can it be your kid? He said you wouldn't shag him for months!' She poked a bony finger in Sarah's direction. 'You'd do anything to get him back, you cow.'

'I never said that. You're upset. I think you should go home and do some mindfulness.' He glanced at Sarah. 'This isn't good for the baby or you, Sarah. Go and sit down while I deal with it.'

'I'll complain about you to HR, you bastard. I'll say it was sexual harassment!' Vanessa screeched before Sarah could reply that she could fight her own battles. Sarah thought Vanessa would have trouble explaining away the tiara incident, but said nothing.

'Now, there's no need for that. Go home, Nessa. I'll talk to you when you've calmed down.' Niall tried to back Vanessa towards the door.

'No, I fuckin' won't.'

Niall ducked to avoid Vanessa's swinging fist. 'Calm down.'

'I will *not,* you cheating scumbag! You'll come crawling back to me but don't think I'll have you! And I'll sue you both.' She battered his chest with her fists.

'Ow! Stop it. There's no need for violence.'

'You think?'

Niall groaned as a blow landed in his stomach. For the sake of the baby, Sarah closed the door to the sitting room. The more soothing Niall became, the louder and shriller Vanessa grew. Once upon a time, she'd fantasised about a moment like this, even replayed just such a scene in her head. Now it was real, it wasn't funny at all.

Hearing Niall trying to calm down Vanessa and Vanessa's vindictive screeches was horrible. And had Niall really told Vanessa that Sarah had refused to have sex with him? Suddenly there was quiet. Sarah opened the door again and stepped into the hallway. A car door slammed, an engine roared and there was a screech of tyres. Sarah flew to the door just in time to see Vanessa roar off down the lane in her yellow Mini, a cloud of blue smoke billowing into the air.

Niall was patting Mrs Sugden on the arm, presumably trying to reassure her that no one had been murdered.

This is all my fault, thought Sarah. While she didn't have a choice in Niall's decision to have an affair, she did have a choice in how she reacted to the situation – just as she did now.

'That was even worse than I expected ...' Niall walked back into the room rubbing his jaw. His cheek was a livid red where Vanessa had landed a stinging slap. He sat down heavily on the sofa and put his head in his hands.

Sarah stood by the sofa, at a loss of what to do next.

He took a deep breath and reached for her hand. 'I'm sorry you had to see that but it'll get easier from now on.'

'It's going to be awkward at work ...'

'That's an understatement. Thank God I've been covering for sick leave or I'd have been on the same shift as Nessa today. I'll have to speak to my supervisor and get her to move me to another shift pattern so we can avoid each other. Come to think of it, I'm owed some leave so I should probably take it. You and I need some time to rediscover our relationship.' He squeezed Sarah's hand. 'Will you and the Bump be OK while I go to work? I'll have to set off soon if I want to catch my boss to talk this over.'

'I'm not a china cup. I won't break.' Sarah gritted her teeth and managed a smile.

'I don't want to take any more risks. Little Ni needs a calm environment.'

'*Little Ni?* It might be a girl ...'

'Little Sarah, then.' Niall knelt by her chair and laid his hand on her stomach. 'Feck, was that a kick?'

'Yes. Probably.'

'It's amazing.' He eyed her sternly. 'I hope you're keeping a movement diary.'

'I don't think there's any need for that.'

'I do. You can't be too careful.'

Sarah restrained herself from telling him – again – that she'd managed on her own over the past few months and didn't need his advice now. It was understandable he was concerned and wanted to help but she could cope. 'I promise I'll be straight onto the GP or midwife if I'm the least bit concerned but I'm sure everything will be fine,' she said. She gave him a peck on the cheek. 'Now, stop worrying and sort things out with your boss.'

'Yeah. Do you want a drink before I go out? You've had a stressful time today.'

'No. You go.'

After dithering a little while longer, he finally went upstairs to shower before dashing out to take Sarah's car to get to his shift.

The moment he'd gone, Sarah picked up her phone to call Molly but found two missed calls and a text that must have come through while World War Three had been breaking out with Vanessa. They were all from Molly and just said, "Call me asap". Sarah pressed Molly's number, hoping that her sister hadn't already split up with Ewan after less than two days together. She regretted her jibe about Molly lurching from one crush to another: Molly had seemed genuinely crazy about Ewan and now he'd finally decided to pull the poker out of his arse and return her feelings, she didn't want it all going pear-shaped for her.

No, it was probably Molly calling to say he'd proposed or wasn't he gorgeous or wonderful or something.

She heard Molly pick up. 'Molly. I'm so glad I've got you! You won't believe this but Vanessa turned up on the doorstep and nearly killed Niall.'

'*Sarah* …'

'You know it should have been funny and even though I can't stand Vanessa and it serves her right, I *almost* felt sorry for her …'

'Sarah!' Molly cut her off.

'What? What's the matter?'

'There's something I have to tell you.'

Molly's voice was full of doom. 'What? The Hot Prof's not messing you around, again is he?'

'No. It's not Ewan or me. It's about you and … and Niall.'

Sarah heard the break in Molly's voice. Goose bumps pricked on her arms.

'What do you mean, me and Niall?'

'Sarah … Oh God … I don't know how to tell you this. I'm so sorry, and I really don't know how it happened but you have to meet me …'

'What? Now? Where?'

'Not at the cottage. Somewhere … neutral.'

'Neutral? What do you mean?'

'I can't say over the phone. It's um … delicate.'

'*Delicate?* Molly, what the hell's going on and why do we have to meet somewhere else? Something awful's happened, hasn't it?'

There was a strangled sound that might have been a sob

or Molly choking, then a rush of words. 'Meet me on the Backs on the Orgasm Bridge. You know what I mean. I'll be there in an hour, and I'll wait for you.'

'An hour? I'm not sure I can get away.'

'It's absolutely vital. We've no choice.'

Sarah put the phone down. The baby squirmed inside her as if it had picked up on her agitation. Niall was going to want to know why she had to dash off at short notice but tough.

Swans glided serenely on the Cam as Sarah walked over the bridge that led from King's Parade onto the Backs. The guides were loading tourists into punts and the gaggles of tourists took selfies on the bridges. It was a fine day and though cold, the river was like the M6, packed with people laughing and shrieking as they floated along.

The state she was in couldn't be good for the baby. If Molly had been exaggerating about whatever-it-was, Sarah would go mad at her. Then again, she prayed that it was something trivial.

She'd know soon enough. Her heart almost leapt out of her chest when she caught sight of Molly cycling over the bridge towards her. Molly spotted her too and screeched to a halt a foot from Sarah. Her face was red and she was breathing heavily.

Molly was deathly pale under her cycling tan and there were dark smudges under her eyes. 'You'd better sit down,' she said, directing Sarah to a nearby bench. 'I'm-m s-sorry. I thought I'd been so *so* careful.' Molly sucked in a breath. 'But I think we've given Niall the real Love Bug.'

Sarah had been in the act of sitting down as Molly dropped the bombshell. The news caused her to collapse with an oof onto the seat. Around her, the meadows of the colleges were carpeted with spring flowers and the ancient gold stone walls glowed in the spring sunshine. Cambridge must be the most beautiful city in the world but she felt that it was mocking her with its tranquillity.

'Are you OK?' Molly asked, sitting beside her.

Sarah dragged her eyes from the idyllic scene around them and back to Molly's wild expression. 'OK? Of course I'm not. Please tell me that you're joking or I'm hallucinating? Did you really just tell me that that I gave Niall a *real* Love Bug?' said Sarah.

'I'm so sorry. I'm afraid it was active after all. I think it must have been ...'

'You *think* the one you gave me was the active one?'

Molly covered her mouth with her hand then mumbled, 'The thing is that the placebo is still in the lab and I've analysed it twice so I can only conclude ...'

Sarah put her head in her hands. 'Oh God.'

There was a pause. 'At least you have Niall back ...' Molly squeaked.

Sarah exploded. 'I don't want him back like this! I'd changed my mind – you know that. Mol, you *have* to do something! Provide an antidote. Tell me it will wear off. *Anything*.'

'Don't you think I'm trying? I've been working on an inhibitor ever since I found out. I've been in the lab half the night. Maybe it'll wear off.'

A man feeding ducks with his kids frowned at them.

Sarah managed to find the presence of mind to take a few deep breaths and lower her voice.

'You don't believe it will wear off, do you?' she asked Molly.

'I don't know, that's the problem. In one trial, hormone

levels were still elevated up to three years later ... The most likely outcome after this rapid peak is an – um – a slow decline.'

'Are you saying,' Sarah said very slowly, 'that the effects on Niall might last *three* years?'

'Three years for them to decline. There are no actual figures on how long it might take the whole lot to be erased from a human system. We just don't know yet.'

'What am I going to do?'

'What are *we* going to do? This is my fault too. My mess and I have to sort it out.' Molly hugged Sarah and when she pulled away, her cheeks were wet with tears. 'I can't tell you how sorry I am.'

Sarah put her arm around her, even though she felt like running away and hiding herself. 'This isn't your fault. I wasn't in my right mind when I asked you to do it and I made you think you owed me something because of what happened after Mum and Dad died. You don't. You never have. It's my responsibility but if you can do something, anything, to put it right, please do it and soon.'

Molly's cheek was wet when Sarah let her go. 'I wanted to help you. I thought I was ... Look, for now, can you try to humour Niall? Ewan's gone away to a conference in Switzerland until Friday so it'll give me time to try and find a way out of this without him being around the lab.'

'Is there a way out of this?' Sarah hardly dared ask the question.

Molly lifted her chin determinedly. 'There has to be and I swear on my life, I'll find a solution somehow.'

*

Over the next few days, Sarah tried desperately to distract herself by keeping busy with her commissions and workshops. The Bump was showing quite obviously now and she'd had to confess to her regulars. A few customers had noticed that Niall was back around the place and obviously thought things were hunky-dory again. Sarah knew that some of them also thought she was mad for taking him back.

Every moment with him was agony and she kept experiencing a terrible urge to confess, to blurt out what she'd done. Even if she had told him, what would it have achieved? He was so full of remorse and so determined to make things up to her that she doubted he'd believe her anyway. He might think that she and Molly had concocted the whole story just to get rid of him.

It was a welcome respite to have the excuse to get out of the house to pick up a missed delivery of beads from the sorting office. On the way home she'd driven past the craft units. There was no longer a sign up that advertised them as available to rent but she wasn't stupid enough to torment herself by driving into the complex and checking if the unit had a new occupier.

She tried to console herself that Liam's offer had come too soon for her. She hadn't been ready to move on then.

And now?

Now she had Niall back, but not in any real or meaningful way. It didn't matter that she'd stepped back from the brink and decided not to use the Love Bug. The end result had been the same. If only she'd never put the idea of the Love Bug into Molly's head, the mix-up would never have happened.

If only ...

She pulled up outside the cottage. She wasn't sure if Niall was home from work or not. He'd had to share a lift to work with a mate until he could buy a new motorbike. She unloaded the parcel from the boot of her car and carried it into the workshop, hoping Niall wouldn't want to help.

Then she let herself in through the back door. She heard a gentle thud and a soft curse behind the closed door of the sitting room.

'Sarah? I'm in here.'

Sarah walked into the sitting room.

Dressed in a tux, Niall was kneeling on the carpet – actually, on one knee on the hearthrug.

'Ni—'

She didn't even get the second syllable of his name out before he cut her off.

'Sarahwillyoumarryme?'

It came out in a massive gush, like from a dodgy tap. Sarah even leapt back as if she'd been sprayed with water.

'What?'

Niall took her hand. 'I said will you marry me, darlin'?'

Her stomach lurched and the baby kicked. 'Oh no, you can't ...'

Niall's smile faded. 'What's up?'

'Nothing. Nothing ... I'm just surprised.'

'Surprised in a good way, I hope?'

Sarah's throat was dry. 'It's so sudden, all the changes. I feel like I'm on a rollercoaster.'

He got up. 'You do want this? I often thought you did but you never said – but it's what women want, isn't it? I know I need to regain your trust and prove my commitment. The baby shouldn't make any difference but call me old-fashioned, I think we need to make this formal, to give you some security.'

His brow creased in total bewilderment. Sarah felt as if her world had imploded. This, possibly, could be worse than finding him in bed with Vanessa. While that had been raw and agonising, at least it had been real. She opened her mouth: the words on her lips. *The way you feel isn't true, Niall. We've drugged you, brainwashed you.*

'You don't know what you're saying …'

He snorted. 'What do you mean? Of course, I know what I'm doing! In fact I've never been more sure of how I feel. I'm asking you to marry me. It's what you always wanted, wasn't it, babe? You hinted often enough.'

'Hinted? I didn't!'

'Not in so many words but a man knows and I should have grown up and asked you.'

'*Grown up?* I'm not denying it would have been nice to be asked but I didn't spend my whole life waiting for you to pop the question and make an honest woman of me.' Instantly, she felt bad for snapping at him. 'I mean, I never expected you to propose,' she added soothingly.

He laid the box on the table in front of her. 'I'm confused.'

'You have to give me time to get used to … this new situation,' she said more gently. 'There's been so much going on in my life – in our lives – with the baby, and you leaving and now coming back. I need time before I agree to a big commitment like marriage.'

'Commitment?' Niall snorted. 'What bigger commitment is there than that?' He pointed at her rounded tummy. 'Why didn't you tell me before about the baby?'

'Would it have made a difference to you leaving?'

'Yes, of course it would.'

'No, it wouldn't,' Sarah replied quietly. 'You told me you couldn't think of anything worse than being tied down with a brood of kids like your relations.'

Niall groaned. 'Shit. I didn't actually mean *that*. I had no idea, then, that you were having *my* baby.'

'I felt as if you did mean it and even if you *didn't*, I was in no state to tell you. You had an affair. You left me for Vanessa. You were forcing me to sell the cottage and move the business. I thought that you leaving me on my own meant I owed you nothing and you wouldn't look after me and the baby.'

'I know. I'm sorry. I don't know how I can make it up to you other than prove it over the next fifty years but I swear I will.'

'Fifty years is a very long time ...'

'I know but I'll do it.' He drew a sign over his chest. 'Cross my heart. You're stuck with me forever now.'

Sarah closed her eyes and prayed for a miracle as Niall moved in for a long wet kiss.

The doorbell rang.

Niall twisted his head and rolled his eyes. 'Feck. Who's that?'

Sarah broke away from him. 'Don't worry. I'll go.'

Niall pulled her back into his arms. 'Leave it. I have other plans. We should celebrate this occasion properly.'

But I haven't said yes yet, thought Sarah.

The bell buzzed again. Sarah freed herself and hurried to the window. 'Oh! It's Liam.'

Niall groaned. 'Feckin' great timing. What does he want?'

'I don't know.' Her stomach fluttered. The last thing she wanted was Liam calling now but she didn't want to ignore him either. Maybe she could hint to him that she hadn't wanted Niall to refuse the craft unit on her behalf. But how?

Niall sat down on the sofa and patted the seat next to him. 'Leave it, babe. He'll go away.'

'I can't simply ignore the man and anyway, he's already seen me.'

'Shit.'

Ignoring Niall's moans, Sarah hurried down the hall and pulled open the door just as Liam exited the garden gate to the lane.

'Liam!' she shouted, dashing down the path after him. 'Please don't go!'

Liam kept his hand on the gate as she hurried towards him. 'I think I ought to leave, Sarah. To be honest, I don't know why I even thought it was a good idea to come over.'

'It is. You must come back. I need to explain,' Sarah was breathless with rushing and guilt. Liam was genuinely hurt, that much was obvious. He was a lovely guy but he'd reached the limits of his patience and she couldn't blame him.

'No, you don't,' he said. 'You're back with Niall. I'm happy that you got what you wanted.'

'Are you?' said Sarah.

He shook his head and blew out a breath of frustration. 'No, of course I'm not. Shit. Is that selfish of me to tell you? You know damn well how I feel about you.'

'Oh, Liam. Please try to understand. This is all so new and confusing for me ... Niall coming back so unexpectedly, I mean. I don't know how *I* feel about it yet. We're just testing the water for now,' she said, flailing hopelessly. She didn't want to tell any more lies but it was also impossible to tell him the truth.

'Sarah, babe. Are you coming in?' Niall stood squarely in the doorway, his arms folded across his chest.

Liam shook his head. His mouth was set in a grim line. 'I'd better go.' He turned away but Sarah grabbed his arm. 'No, *please* don't leave like this.'

Liam's eyes lit up with momentary pleasure then darkened in concern. 'Sarah, are you OK? What's going on with Niall? Because if he's upsetting you or hurting you, I'll ...'

Sarah took her fingers from his arm. The last thing she needed was another fight on her own doorstep. Mrs Sugden couldn't take any more drama, let alone Sarah. She had to let Liam go, no matter what he thought and how hurt he was. That was the price she would have to pay for the mess she'd got into. 'No, I'm fine. Niall's fine. I mean, he's a bit bewildered and up and down at the moment – we all are.'

Niall stepped onto the path. 'Are you coming in or not?' he demanded.

'Yes,' called Sarah. 'Go back in and put the kettle on, Ni.'

With a huff, Niall did as he was told, much to Sarah's relief.

Liam had waited patiently but was now stony-faced on the doorstep. She lowered her voice, her heart heavy. 'Thanks for coming to see how I was but you don't have to worry about me, I promise ...' A sudden idea struck her. 'Why don't you come inside and see for yourself that Niall's not holding me captive?'

She could see him struggling with his reply. 'If you're sure. I'll pop in for a *few* minutes but Niall probably won't like it.'

'He'll just have to put up with it.'

Seemingly encouraged by her decisiveness, Liam nodded. She showed him into the sitting room where Niall was manspreading on the sofa, his arm draped over the back, clearly occupying as much of his territory as he could. He glared at Liam and reminded Sarah of a small dog trying to look bigger than he really was. She half-expected him to start baring his teeth and growling.

'Please sit down,' said Sarah, hovering by the unoccupied armchair.

'Yeah, make yourself comfortable, mate, just like you have before.'

'Niall!' she snapped.

Liam ignored Niall's sarcasm. 'I won't sit down, thanks. I only called in to see how Sarah was as I was passing by.'

Niall barely concealed a snort of disbelief. 'Pass by this way a lot. Well, she's fine. Blooming, aren't you, babe?'

'Can I get you a coffee?' said Sarah.

'No, thanks.' Liam's voice was icy. 'I wanted you to know that we've found a tenant for the craft unit. They haven't signed yet but ...'

Niall cut him off. 'She doesn't need it, like I said.'

'I'm sorry,' Sarah said, seething inside. 'It would have been a wonderful idea. Thank you for finding it ...'

Liam's eyes clouded with puzzlement and hurt. Sarah was ready to burst with frustration. She wanted to tell the truth, anything would be better than this torment.

Niall jumped up from the sofa and put his arm around Sarah. 'Why don't you stay for something a bit stronger, mate?' he said, suddenly smooth.

Sarah glanced at him in disbelief. 'What?'

He grinned at Liam. 'In fact, we should break open a bottle of bubbly. Congratulations are in order. Sarah's going to need her own tiara. We're getting married.'

Chapter Thirty-Three

Molly stood up from the Mac and stretched her hands above her head. Her spine clicked as she straightened it and her eyes were gritty. Over the past week while Ewan had been at the conference, she'd scoured every online journal site for papers, tried out numerous tests in the lab and read every last word that was even vaguely related to the subject. She was still no nearer to the answer.

'Hello. Have you missed me?'

She almost jumped out of her skin as Ewan kissed the back of her neck. 'I've been bursting with frustration. I could take you right now in the lab,' he murmured into her ear.

Molly jumped up and grabbed him, snogging him hard. Anything to prevent him from seeing what she was looking at on the screen.

'Wow,' he said when she finally let him breathe. 'That was a welcome home. You've obviously missed me a lot.'

'Of course I have.' She beamed at him. 'I can honestly say the past week has felt like one of the longest of my life.'

While Ewan unloaded his laptop bag in his own office, she deleted her browsing history. Her time to find the solution had run out and she would now be left with a few snatched moments when Ewan was out of the lab. Which would be almost never. She swept biscuit crumbs off her keyboard and chucked a crisp wrapper in the bin. Her eyes already needed stalks to keep them up. How would she last until Ewan left?

He joined her in her office, holding up a giant Toblerone. 'Don't say I never get you anything.'

'Thanks,' she said, taking it from him. 'It's a big one.'

'What did you expect?' He winked and kissed her.

'You look good,' she replied, relieved to lose herself in his kiss and say something that wasn't a lie or half-truth.

He rubbed his chin. 'Really? I haven't had time to have a shave. I came straight here from the airport.'

He leaned down again. For a few seconds, she gave herself up to the warm pressure of his mouth and the rasp of stubble against her skin. It was hard to get used to this new Ewan; the smiley one who was in love with her. His tongue darted into her mouth before Molly realised she hadn't had time to brush her teeth that morning before rushing to the lab and that her breakfast had consisted of cheese and onion Hula Hoops.

She pulled away from him.

'What's the matter?' Ewan peered hard at her face. 'Are you OK? You look tired.'

'Oh, I've just been busy trying to get some better results for the new paper.'

'On the new paper? There's no rush yet. No need to spend all hours in the lab.'

'There was nothing else to do. The weather's been crap and I haven't wanted to hit the gym. My bum hasn't recovered from the race yet.'

'I could give you a gluteal massage. How's your elbow by the way?'

Molly rolled up her lab coat sleeve to show him the red scab. 'Healing. Very attractive as you can see.'

Ewan planted a kiss on her elbow.

'Ewan!'

'What's the matter?'

'People might see us.'

'So what?' He grinned wickedly. 'I don't give a toss.'

'I thought we were meant to keep things discreet.'

'No, *you* thought that. I've decided I don't care. While I've been in Switzerland I've decided that life's too short for lying and pretending you don't care about someone. I want this – us – out in the open.'

He kissed her again, long and hard. It ought to have been bliss, everything she ever wanted – Christmas, birthday and the Nobel Prize – all rolled into one. Instead, she wanted nothing more than for him to leave the lab as fast as possible and not come back until she'd sorted out the Jupiter-sized fuck-up of the century.

Eventually, her agony ended. Ewan let her go.

'Are you sure you're OK?' he said. 'I could order you to go home.'

'I won't be much longer then I'll go home.'

'I've heard that one so many times before. Don't turn into me, Molly. I'm sick of people thinking I'm an anal, obsessive, borderline personality disorder workaholic. I want to come out – as normal.'

'Then you'll stick out like a sore thumb in this lab.' She laughed, albeit hollowly.

'I don't care. I won't harass you tonight because I can see

you're shattered. Probably delayed reaction to the race and the accident. But I want to meet up tomorrow night and talk about telling people we're seeing each other.'

He put his finger on her lips. 'No arguments. It's an order.'

Chapter Thirty-Four

Sarah looked up to find Niall in the doorway to her workshop, carrying a tray of food. She put down the tiara she was making for a prom, and which had given her a few hours of welcome distraction. Her world had been normal once, she reminded herself. Hers and Molly's. Following the dark weeks and months after their parents had died, they'd somehow found their way to a new normal, built new lives ... Right now Sarah couldn't imagine ever growing used to spending the rest of her life with a man who'd been tricked into loving her.

He put the tea tray on the table. 'I thought I told you to put your feet up, future Mrs McCafferty?'

'I'm OK. I need to finish my commissions. I've had a rush order for a wedding,' she said with a smile.

'You shouldn't take on too much work, not with Little Ni on the way. Here, I bought your favourite biccies so you can build up your strength.'

'I thought you'd sworn off trans fats.'

'I've lapsed,' said Niall, taking a Hobnob from the plate with an arch of his shaved eyebrow. For a second, Sarah had a flashback from the pre-Vanessa days when life was simple and she didn't have to question her feelings for him.

'I'm not doing heavy work and I enjoy it. This middle trimester is fantastic compared to the first few months. I feel energised.'

'I'll never forgive myself for not being here and I'm going to make up for it. You look amazing, babe.' Niall plumped down next to her on the sofa and kissed her. 'And I want you stay feeling amazing.'

'If you let me get on with things, that would help. I'm not ill, only pregnant.'

Niall patted Sarah's bump very gently. 'But don't work too long because I've got a surprise planned.'

Sarah's skin prickled. 'A surprise? What?'

He tapped the side of his nose. 'You'll see.'

A couple of hours later, Niall stopped outside the window of the jewellers in the middle of the Grand Arcade.

'Here you are.'

Sarah stared at the window, dazzled by the sparkles and glitter of the diamond engagement rings nestling among a display of Easter nests, yellow chicks and fluffy bunnies. 'I ... don't know what to say.'

Niall put his arm around her waist. 'It doesn't have to be this shop, of course. This is just a start. If you want something less flashy or more arty, I've made a list of shops in town. There's three in here but we can head straight to one of the others.'

'I'm stunned.'

'I thought you would be.' He grinned happily. 'Want to go inside and try some on?'

'No. Not now.'

His face fell and Sarah took pity on him.

'Can we go and have lunch first and talk about it? I'm feeling a bit overwhelmed.'

Sarah found a space outside a café in King's Parade while Niall ordered. She'd suspected he was planning some romantic gesture or possibly wanted to buy a cot for the baby, but the engagement ring had completely thrown her. Tourists and shoppers buzzed past the roped-off café terrace, taking photos of the King's College chapel. A string of touts were trying to persuade people to hire a punt and the man was playing 'The Bare Necessities' from inside a black rubbish bin. It was all so normal – what she'd seen a hundred times – yet totally bizarre and surreal. If the baby hadn't wriggled she might have thought she'd been hallucinating for the past few months.

'Not too cold for you?' Niall squeezed into the chair opposite.

'No. It's a lovely day.' She forced a smile to her face.

'Aren't you glad you let me prise you away from the workshop?'

'It's a lovely gesture, Ni, but I ... um ... can't think about planning a wedding yet. I've so much going on at the moment, with work and the baby and all the changes in our lives.'

He looked crestfallen then took her hand. 'Maybe we can do it in a few weeks when you've had time to get used to the idea.'

Weeks? Sarah swallowed hard. 'Well, we'll see. Can we at least wait to plan anything until after I've had my next scan?'

His eyes lit up. 'Scan? You mean an ultrasound? That means I get to see Little Ni. I must come with you. When is it? If it's on my shift I'll take a day off. You do want me with you?'

She couldn't refuse. No matter what he'd done and what she'd done – did they cancel each other out? – she couldn't deny him being part of their baby's life. 'Of course I want you to be there,' she said.

The waiter brought their food and Niall tucked in, encouraging her to eat up her salad and jacket potato. Sarah had never seen him so happy. She knew she was putting food in her mouth, knew she was chewing and swallowing but she couldn't taste a thing. She saw a woman come past, tall and thin with inky poker-straight hair like Vanessa, but twenty years older. She felt something she never thought was possible: a sneaking sense of pity for Vanessa. And something else, something she'd known for a few days now, perhaps even weeks, but hadn't been able to admit or recognise until it was too late.

She didn't love Niall anymore. She would never love Niall again but having made *him* love her now, she had no choice but to stay.

Chapter Thirty-Five

Molly had missed Sarah's call while she'd been locked in the lab, so phoned her back.

'Molly. Something bad has happened.' Sarah sounded very down.

'Bad? You mean worse than what has happened already?'

'Yes. Niall's asked me to marry him.'

'What? Oh shit. What have you said?'

'He asked me a few days ago and I tried to put him off, hoping he wasn't serious, but today he wanted me to choose a ring. He's assumed I want to marry him.'

Molly squeaked in dismay.

'Have you had any luck with creating the inhibitor?' Sarah said desperately.

'I'm still working on it but Ewan's back in the lab after his conference.'

'He doesn't know what we've done, does he?' Sarah sounded very panicky.

'No ... Try not to worry too much, Sarah. It won't be good for the baby. I'll let you know the moment I have a solution.' Molly crossed her fingers then reminded herself that superstition was rooted in a tendency to generate weak associations. She crossed her fingers even harder.

That night, Molly lay on Ewan's bed after a mammoth sex session. Afterwards he borrowed her fleecy robe, seemed happy to look ridiculous, and went downstairs and made her a cup of tea. He brought the drinks up on a tray with a tulip in a jam jar together with a selection of biscuits arranged in size order on a rectangular platter.

'Here you are,' he said. The dressing gown came undone, exposing his glorious body. He was every woman's dream: the handsome, brilliant, difficult man who turns out to be passionate, tender and madly in love with you.

However, it was all Molly could do not to burst into tears.

His brow furrowed. 'What's the matter?'

'Nothing.' The words sounded strangled.

'You don't look very happy,' he said gently.

'Post orgasmic release,' Molly garbled. 'Nice arrangement of biscuits by the way.'

'I tried to tessellate them.' He beamed with pride.

'I can see that.' Molly selected a pink wafer even though she wasn't the slightest bit hungry.

Ewan picked up a chocolate bourbon but didn't eat it. 'Molly ...'

She nodded as the wafer melted in her mouth. It tasted sickly sweet.

'I've a horrible feeling that I may just possibly have fallen in love with you.'

'Wha ...?' The wafer smeared her lips with sugar.

'I think you heard.' He replaced the bourbon in its gap. 'Too much? Too soon? Is it because I want us to go public at the lab? Have I come on too strong? Shit. I'll never change. I'm a man – a human – of extremes but you know that by now.'

'Ewan, it's not you ...'

He groaned. 'Fuck.'

'No. Stop. It really is me. Please listen. Ewan, there's something I have to tell you.'

'What? You want to end it? Cool it?'

'No. No ... not at all. I'm happy. More than happy ... Ewan, it's not you, it's something else. It's Sarah ...'

He frowned. 'What have you and I got to do with Sarah?'

'Nothing but you see, she means such a lot to me and you know all the sacrifices she made for me ...'

'This is obviously leading somewhere,' he said lightly. 'Not hinting at some kind of ménage à trois, are you? I know it's supposed to be every guy's dream, but call me old-fashioned, I don't think I can handle both of you.' His eyes gleamed wickedly and Molly thought he'd never looked sexier with his rumpled hair and post-sex flushed chest. Which was why it was even harder for her to ask for his help.

'Ewan, shut up! This is hard enough for me to say as it is.'

He drew his finger over his lips and folded his arms. Molly would have, should have laughed but instead she felt like throwing up.

'There's something I need to get off my chest ...' She buried her face in her hands. 'Oh God, I can't do this.'

'For God's sake, spit it out.' His voice became serious. 'Whatever it is, I promise I won't judge you or be shocked. I'm a behavioural ecologist, remember? I've seen all that human nature can do. It can't be that terrible.'

Molly raised her head. Ewan smiled encouragingly. 'You know you can tell me anything.'

He laid his hand on her shoulder and spoke gently. 'If you're in trouble, share it with me. I'll do anything to help.'

'I may have – I think I have – given the Love Bug to someone.'

Ewan's hand was still on her shoulder. His eyes narrowed and he took his hand away while Molly felt like dying inside.

'Given the Love Bug to someone?' Then he pointed his finger at her and his face cracked with a huge grin. 'Ha ha. Very funny, Molly. You almost had me there.'

This was worse than him shouting. The fact he thought her confession so awful that it was a joke.

'It's true. I've given the Love Bug to Niall by mistake. I wanted to help Sarah get him back and so I made a placebo and he inhaled it but ...'

Suddenly, Ewan couldn't meet her eye. He stared out of the window, biting his lip.

'I'm sorry,' said Molly quietly. 'I never intended it to happen and I don't know how it did. It's just a horrible, awful mistake and I've tried to put it right but I don't know how.'

Ewan let out a long breath and met her gaze. He swallowed hard.

'You said to trust you, that I could tell you anything, that nothing could shock you ...'

'I know. I know ... But, Molly. *Molly*. Why the fuck did you think something so stupid would ever end well?'

'I didn't mean to. The samples must have been mixed up before I labelled them.'

He swung his legs out of bed and put his head in his hands. 'I can't believe this.'

Molly shivered. Blood didn't run cold but she knew why people described it like that. 'You see why I need an inhibitor.'

'No. What we need is a solicitor.'

'We can't tell anyone!'

'We might have to if we can't put this right! Molly, this is a serious assault.'

'I *know* that. But I never intended to do it. I realised it was a stupid idea and Sarah realised it was wrong and we both pulled back. I just wanted to make her happy, to pay her back for what she did for me, but I wasn't that stupid. I wanted her to realise that nothing could help her get him back and that she had to let him go. I was so careful!'

'Clearly, not careful enough,' he snapped.

Molly felt as if she'd been slapped. 'We all make mistakes.'

'I'm sorry,' said Ewan. 'I didn't mean to say that. I'm just ...'

'Shocked?'

'Disappointed. Taken aback.' He shoved his hands through his hair. 'Oh hell, I don't know.'

'I guess you need time to take it all in but please don't wait too long. I need your help to find an inhibitor.'

'Christ. This breaks all the rules in the book – theft, criminal damage, administering a noxious substance with intent to commit sexual assault.'

'Don't you think I thought of all those things? That's why I stepped back from the brink. I had no idea it would come to this.'

'No, but me helping you – even to sort it out – is aiding and abetting the administration of a controlled and experimental psychoactive substance. Technically it's a conspiracy to do all of the above.'

Molly felt more miserable than she'd ever done in her life. 'I'll resign, of course.'

'At the moment, I'm thinking that's the best-case scenario, Molly.'

She bit back the urge to burst into tears. Crying would

help no one and there was no way she was going to use emotional blackmail to get Ewan to help her.

'I understand that there's no going back, career-wise, from what I've done and I've put you in a difficult position.'

'You're wrong. I don't care about my position. I care about yours – your career, now and in the future. I care about the reputation of the lab and everyone who works in it, about the university and most of all our work. I care about you ending up in court if anyone found out.'

'No one but Sarah, you and I know what's happened, I swear. You can have my notice now, I won't wait to find another job but please, help me find a way to put things right.'

He was silent. Molly dug her nails in her palm, feeling the situation growing worse by the minute.

Ewan started to get dressed.

Molly hugged her knees as he zipped up his jeans. 'I can't tell you how sorry I am. Things were going so well.'

'Yeah, well, there you are. Things going too well. I might have known it would all turn to shit.'

'It's nothing to do with us ...'

'Isn't it? Doesn't this have at least something to do with me trusting you and you trusting me?'

'I didn't know you, like I do now, when I decided to create the Bug. You hardly spoke to me. You didn't trust me enough to tell me how you felt.'

'If I had, would you honestly have acted any differently? Would you still have made the Bug for Sarah?'

Molly hesitated. 'I don't know. Probably.'

'And would you have told me?'

'Probably not.'

He stared at her for a few seconds then reached for his

T-shirt. 'I need time to think about this,' he muttered. 'I'll call you. Don't email or text me or Sarah about it. Don't even hint. I don't want anything traceable back to any of us. No evidence.'

Later that evening, Molly had taken a bath that was too hot and eaten a dinner she didn't want. She replayed over and over the labelling of the Love Bug samples: the placebo and the real Bug. She went through their research again and scrolled through papers on the Internet, searching for any clue that would help her find an inhibitor.

Ewan called her as she was ready to give in.

'Meet me at the lab later and I'll see what I can do,' he said and rang off.

He was already in the lab when Molly got there.

'Where are the samples?' he asked.

'In our fridge in the outer office.'

'Right.'

'Ewan, thanks ...'

'I want to help you,' he said. 'I haven't changed what I said earlier but I think it's best if we don't carry on working together. I was offered a chair by a Swiss university while I was in Bern and I've decided to take it up.'

Molly was horrified. 'No, you can't leave Cambridge because of a situation I caused.'

'I think I should. One of us should leave and I don't want it to be you. Maybe this is the kick up the arse I needed to make a fresh start. It was a great offer, big salary, much higher research funding, a larger team. I knew I should take it for the sake of my research but I hesitated. Because I didn't want to leave you.'

'Are you punishing me, or yourself for daring to get involved in the first place?'

Ewan stared at her then said, coolly. 'This isn't about us. Let me see these samples. Maybe you've made a mistake. It's not uncommon that the bacteria didn't transform successfully. Both the placebo and the experimental sample might actually be empty of the plasmid so there's a chance that the sample you gave Niall isn't active.'

'It *is*. I've checked them both time and time again.'

'Let's start with the most obvious possibility, anyway. Let me see the samples and I'll do my own investigations.'

A few hours later, Molly's hopes that she'd somehow made a mistake were dashed.

'I'm right aren't I? The one I gave Niall is active and producing the Love Bug hormone, isn't it?' she said as Ewan examined the DNA results on his laptop.

He turned the screen towards her. 'I'm afraid so. I've checked it three times.'

'Shit.'

'Which means we definitely have to find an inhibitor.'

'That's what I've already been trying to do.'

He put the photos in his desk drawer and locked it. 'I'll have to do a Western blot to visualise the protein and that will take two days.'

'I've done that too,' said Molly miserably.

'I'll still carry one out while I work on the inhibitor. Now, tell me everything you've tried so far.'

Chapter Thirty-Six

'So, it's not a little Ni. I hope you're not disappointed,' said Sarah as they drove out of the clinic car park after her scan.

'No. I'm not. No way. Oh God. I know I've seen scans before but this is different; that was *our* daughter – our little girl.'

'I know.' Sarah was full to the brim of conflicting emotions: joy and sadness. When they'd watched their baby moving inside her, seen its tiny hands and feet, Sarah had shed a few tears. Niall's eyes were misty too and it hadn't mattered that he was with her under false pretences. The radiographer had asked if they wanted to know the sex and Sarah, against all her expectations, had said yes.

'I love you so much,' Niall had whispered in her ear.

Me too. The words she should have used and that he was probably hoping for stayed inside her. Sarah had been jolted out of the moment. It was all false. Perhaps not the love of Niall for his child, but his love for her. And hers for him.

She cared for him still and didn't want anything terrible to happen to him; and perhaps she could have forgiven him for the affair with Vanessa – *if* he'd come back of his own accord. But she didn't love him as she once had. She wasn't sure when it had happened; at some point when she was living on her own; at some point when in her darkest, most desperate moment she had become Sarah, not sarahandniall. Perhaps what he'd done was unforgivable. Maybe Liam had played a part in that. Maybe she'd simply learned to live on her own. Whatever it was, there was no going back; no inhibitor for that.

*

A few days later, Sarah was working on her knitting for the baby when she heard someone at the door. She was amazed to see Liam on the doorstep again, after all that happened, but the familiar rush of pleasure was instantly tinged with pain.

'Don't worry, I'm not staying,' he said, lingering on the step. 'Although I thought I'd risk life and limb and call round.'

Sarah had to smile. 'It's OK, Niall's at work.'

'It was your reaction I was more worried about,' he said.

'Relax. My jug-throwing days are over.' Liam made her smile again. He always had. 'You'd better come in.'

He hesitated. 'Are you sure? I don't want to make life more difficult for you.'

Sarah opened the door wide and stepped aside. 'You couldn't possibly do that, believe me.'

Ignoring his objections, Sarah took him into the kitchen. He smiled at the tiny half-finished outfit on the table and joked about learning to knit.

'How are the wedding plans going?' Sarah asked.

'How are yours?'

'That's a long way off,' she replied. 'Your daughter's big day is only a few months away.'

He blew out a breath. 'Tell me about it. I've project managed major developments that were less trouble! Seriously, I had no idea there was so much involved and the detail is mind-blowing – wine tasting, fonts on the place cards, flowers, and don't even get me started on the table settings.'

'Can Hayley help or is she still in Africa?'

'I've emailed as many of the details as I can to her and Kyle. It's their wedding after all. She comes home next weekend so we can sort some of the final details then but I've had to decide on other things for her, which is weird. Her fiancé is still on a tour in the Falklands but they're hoping to get married quarters after the wedding.'

'In fact, that's why I popped over. I wanted to give you this.' Liam pulled a card from his pocket.

Sarah put down her mug and took it.

'It's an invitation to the wedding, hot off the press. We haven't sent any out yet and I wanted you to have the first one. It's not for a while and I know it might be difficult for you to come but ...' He ended the sentence with a hopeful smile. Sarah was so touched, she almost burst into tears. After all the pain she'd caused him, he still wanted her at the big day.

'You didn't have to do that but thank you,' she said.

'I've not included Niall officially but you're both welcome, of course.

'I'd really love to come but it might be difficult.'

'It's OK. I know how Niall feels about me and I'm sure you don't want to do anything to jeopardise your relationship. Not now.'

'It's not what you think ...' Sarah blurted out.

Liam frowned. 'What do you mean?'

'Nothing ... I shouldn't have said it.'

'But you are happy that he's back? You're not in any kind of trouble, are you?'

'Trouble? No, no ... and if you're worried that Niall hasn't treated me well, or is hurting me, you couldn't be more wrong,' said Sarah miserably.

'OK. Well. Please keep the invite anyway if it won't annoy Niall – or hell, keep it even if it does. There's no point me hiding how I feel about you.'

'If things had been different.'

'If. Life's too short for ifs. I think we've both found that out. I have to go. I have a meeting.' He put down his mug, still half full of coffee.

Sarah laid her hand on his arm. 'Wait.'

He glanced from her hand on his arm to her face. His dark eyes held so many conflicting emotions: desire, disappointment, hurt and hope. 'What?'

Sarah was torn apart with agony. Should she tell him what had happened? Could she trust him? No, no one could possibly understand what she and Molly had done.

'I just wanted to say ...'

'Yes?' His voice was soft as butter. Hopeful ...

'I only wondered if the craft unit still available.'

His face fell. 'I'm sorry but no. The tenant we found signed. I had to let it go.'

'Oh, I see. I only wondered.'

'I hung on as long as I could but this guy really wanted it. He's a stained-glass artist.' He pulled a face.

'Oh, well. Good. I mean I'm happy you let it because I was bothered that you'd turned other people down while I was dithering.'

'It's fine. You got to keep the Kabin and that's what you wanted, wasn't it?'

'Yes. Yes, of course.'

He picked up his keys. 'In that case, I'll go. I'll just pop to the loo, if that's OK. It's quite a drive to the meeting.'

Sarah waited in the kitchen while Liam used the cloakroom. It was all she could do not to tell him that her reconciliation with Niall was all a sham and that she didn't love Niall anymore but she owed it to him to stay. She had never felt so low in her life – not even when Niall first left – and it was all her own doing. Liam was so kind and gorgeous, she felt worse than ever.

She heard the loo flush and walked into the hall to meet him. He twisted the catch on the front door.

'Oh, by the way,' he said with a grimace, 'I know this may sound a bit silly but you didn't find a comb of mine in your cloakroom, did you? It's only cheap but Hayley gave it to me one Christmas. It's silly and old but she bought it with her own pocket money and I've kept it ever since.'

'No, I don't think so ...'

'OK. No worries. I thought I'd used it to comb my hair the last time I was here. I had a meeting after I left, you see ...' He looked sheepish as if he was embarrassed about revealing a rare moment of personal vanity but Sarah felt a prickling sensation on the back of her neck. The baby kicked her hard and she let out a little "ooof" and clutched her bump.

Liam was instantly at her side. 'Are you all right?'

Sarah straightened up, slowly. 'Yes. Yes ... just the baby letting me know she's here ... Did you say the comb was blue?'

'What?' Liam looked puzzled that she was interested. 'Yes. Light blue and I think it had more than a few broken teeth.

Bit embarrassing really and I should have chucked it out years ago. Why?'

Goose bumps popped out over every inch of Sarah's skin. Her hands started to shake.

'Are you *sure* you feel OK? Because I'll cancel my meeting if I need to. I'm not leaving until I know you're all right.'

'Yes. I'm fine. I'm really fine.' She couldn't stop a grin spreading over her face. 'I think I may have thrown your comb away. I'm sorry ...'

'No problem. I can afford a new one. In fact, I already invested.' With a smile he drew a tortoiseshell comb from his pocket, the bog-standard type every man has one of somewhere.

'I'll be going then.' He brushed Sarah's cheek with his lips and her skin tingled. 'Have a good life, Sarah, you deserve it.'

Sarah's brief bubble of elation had burst. What if her theory was wrong? And if it was right, it meant she had to hurt someone badly.

She shut the door, her pulse skipping madly. The baby pummelled her and she looked down at her stomach. 'It can't be true, can it?' she said to her bump. 'It can't be possible? I daren't even hope that's the answer ...'

Trembling, she rushed into the sitting room and dug her phone from her bag.

Chapter Thirty-Seven

Molly peeled off her lab gloves and chucked them in the bin. Her back ached and her eyes were gritty and sore from lack of sleep. She'd just caught sight of the clock on the lab wall. How could it be eleven-thirty already?

Ewan was next to her, hunched over his microscope. 'I think we'll have to call it a day. Or night,' she said.

Without taking his eyes from the scope, Ewan waved a hand. 'Not yet. I think I might be onto something.'

'Really?' said Molly wearily, having heard Ewan – and herself – say that at least half a dozen times over the past week. All of their conversations had been confined to work or their attempts to find a solution to the "current situation" as Ewan had code-named her monumental cock-up. When it came to trying to find a solution, he'd have moved heaven and earth for her but outside of the lab, they might as well have been on different planets. She wasn't surprised he'd been angry and upset but she hadn't expected him to completely blank her. He seemed to have returned to previous frostiness and then some.

'I have to get something to eat and drink or I'll drop,' she said. 'I also need the loo. We've been in here for the past four hours. Do you want me to make you a coffee while I'm in the canteen?'

'No. Yes. I'll come and get a drink in a minute.'

'OK.'

Molly hung up her lab coat and walked past the canteen to get her Coke and a Mars bar from the machine. The doors were locked and all but one of the other labs and offices were in darkness. It was hard to imagine that night when she'd first danced with Ewan at the party. He'd blown her off then, now she'd scuppered her own chances but her own problems were nothing compared to Sarah's. All she knew was, having seen the man he could be, it was far harder to take the cold Ewan now.

She retrieved the can and trudged back to the lab. Food and drink weren't allowed but she couldn't care less. As she walked in Ewan was cursing.

'Sod you!' He aimed a kick at the dry ice chest.

Molly also smiled, then remembered why they were in the lab at nearly midnight.

'What's up?'

'Bloody thing's stopped working again and unbelievably, we've run out of gloves. Gloves! The one thing no lab can function without. It's ridiculous.'

Molly stood by, taking the rant like a tree in a storm.

'OK. One, the technicians will be in at eight and they'll take a look at the ice machine. Two, I think there's s secret stash of gloves in the store cupboard in our office and three, we're both totally knackered. Let's call it a night for now.'

Ewan stiffened, obviously embarrassed at letting his temper get the better of him. He pulled off his lab coat. 'I suppose I'm not functioning well and I don't want to make any more mistakes.'

Molly decided to overlook the dig, if it was one. They were both tired. 'Go home. I'll tidy up here and follow you out.'

'Are you sure you'll be OK?'

'Ewan. There are still a couple of people next door. And I've cycled home on my own hundreds of times.'

He rubbed his eyes. 'OK. I do need to go home.'

After Ewan had left, she cleared away some of the evidence of their tests and locked the door of her office. She picked up her bag and coat, and walked out of the office and straight into Pete.

He steadied her. Molly scooted back. 'God, Pete, you scared me. What are you doing here at this time of night?'

'I'm studying the DNA of a new species of South American deer tick. The sequencer was out of action earlier and I need the results for a paper I'm presenting on Friday.' He smirked. 'What about you? Rumour has it you and Ewan have been camped out in the lab together for the past week.'

'Um ... we're close to what could be a major breakthrough on our project,' said Molly.

Pete raised his eyebrows. 'Is it the mysterious super aphrodisiac that no one's supposed to know about?'

She winked. 'I could tell you, Pete, but then I'd have to kill you.'

He grinned. 'Well, I hope you haven't resorted to testing it on each other.'

'Of course not!'

'I bet Ewan's wife isn't too happy about him spending so much time here. That's what split them up in the first place.'

'What do you mean? His wife. They've been divorced for years.'

'She's back with him, apparently. Hasn't Ewan told you?'

Molly floundered. She was exhausted and frazzled and not thinking straight. 'Oh. He might have mentioned her but why would he? It's none of my business,' said Molly haughtily, telling herself not to take Pete's comment too seriously. He was probably only trying to stir things up.

'I only mentioned it because I thought you two had been an item and that you'd know all about it.'

'Then you thought wrong,' she snapped, then flashed him a smile, with murder in her heart. 'I have to go home. Hope your tests go well.' *And you can shove your ticks where the sun doesn't shine.*

Head held high, Molly marched on until she was sure Pete couldn't see her. Wearily, she collected her bike from the rack and cycled home, turning over Pete's revelation. *Was* Pete lying or embroidering rumours out of spite? Or was Anna really back with Ewan?

Maybe he'd decided to give his marriage another go since he'd found out about the Love Bug and ranted about Molly not trusting him. And yet, he hadn't mentioned Anna being back in his house. Even if she was at his house, did that mean she was back in his life?

Molly tossed her keys on the chest of drawers and flopped onto her bed, still in her clothes. Jesus, what a mess. What a monumental fuck-up ...

She woke up, still in her clothes. The clock showed four a.m. and her phone was beeping pathetically to tell her to recharge it.

Molly plugged it in and it let out a series of buzzes and beeps. Rubbing her eyes, she peered at the screen and saw the missed calls and a text from Sarah.

Its nOT Niall!!!!

323

She sat bolt upright, blinking at the text. What did she mean, it's not Niall? Not Niall's what?

A new text came through.

Think it was Liamshair on comb. HOPE so. Don't call. I call u.

Molly was still confused but light was beginning to dawn on her. She started to text Ewan then realised he would be at home with Anna. Then she started to text Molly then realised she'd be asleep with Niall. Shit. She sent an email instead.

Sarah – need items in question asap. Call me first thing.

Then she got out her phone and WhatsApped Ewan.

Ewan, re issues with latest project. Think may have found solution – poss rogue DNA. Need to confirm asap.

Would Ewan still be awake? Would he hear the message come through or would she have an agonising wait until morning? Molly stared at her phone, willing it to ping.

*

Molly woke at dawn. Ewan hadn't replied but Sarah had messaged her to say Niall had gone to work. Molly called her with instructions on how to collect the samples and shortly afterwards, she arrived at the flat, her face flushed with excitement.

'Have you got it?' Molly asked, hardly able to believe that the way out of this mess could be within touching distance. They'd had so many false dawns, she didn't want to get too excited but it was impossible to stop her heart from beating faster as Sarah pulled two plastic bags from her handbag.

'Yes. I picked a hair from his collar when he said goodbye

so unless it's someone else's, I'm pretty sure. I also brought this to double-check.' She handed over the sandwich bags. One contained a couple of hairs and the larger one held a mug.

'Thanks. These should do the trick. If I need a bigger sample, I'll let you know.'

Molly gave a huge sigh of relief. Normally only a police forensic lab would work with so little DNA but she was sure that she and Ewan could manage.

'I'm sorry for causing all this trouble,' Sarah said for the umpteenth time.

'Me too. Forget it now. I'll go into the lab and check it straightaway.'

'If it's right, if the DNA you used is Liam's, that means it couldn't possibly work on Niall?' Sarah said hopefully.

'Yes.'

'So his feelings *are* genuine after all?'

Molly nodded. 'There's no other explanation.'

'What about ... what about Liam?' said Sarah. 'Could he have been affected?'

'As long as he hasn't been near the atomiser, then any feelings he has for you are genuine too,' Molly said.

Sarah heaved a sigh. 'This is going to get complicated.'

Molly hugged her and smiled. 'Hon, I think it already is. Stay and have a cup of tea if you want, but I have to go to the office.'

As she cycled to the office, whizzing past two guys on racing bikes, Molly felt as if she had wings. They weren't out of trouble yet, but she was hopeful. The optimism was tinged with dread. If this avenue met a dead end, she didn't know what she would do next.

She arrived at the lab and went straight inside, hoping to see Ewan before her colleagues arrived. However, at the very moment when she was desperate to see him, he was late. Molly decided to test the samples herself and the minutes and hours ticked by and it was almost ten o'clock. People were heading to the canteen for coffee but Ewan still hadn't rocked up, which was unheard of unless he had an off-site meeting or conference.

Molly had sent him three messages, all unanswered, and she was beginning to worry that something terrible had happened to him. No one seemed to know where he was and Molly didn't want to ask too many people, too often, or they'd start to think she was paranoid or become suspicious of her motives.

Pete's comments about Anna being back haunted her, although her main focus was on sorting out the Love Bug issue. Surely her messages ought to have brought Ewan racing to the lab?

She paced the office, unable to settle to anything while the computer sequenced the tests on Liam's samples. She sat next to it, watching the robotic arm whirr back and forth.

The door opened and a familiar figure walked in. He looked like the living dead and obviously hadn't shaved.

'Ewan!'

'What's up?' he growled.

'Did you get my WhatsApp messages?'

'No, I haven't even looked at my phone yet.'

Squashing down her frustration, Molly almost danced around him. 'I think I know what's happened. Sarah thinks that she gave me Liam's hair, not Niall's. So that's why it didn't work.'

'You are joking?'

'No. I'm running checks on hair and saliva samples now to see if they're the ones I used for the Bug.'

'Oh God, I hope so,' he said gloomily.

'Aren't you pleased?' she asked.

'Yes. Of course. Let me know if you want me to cross-check.'

'I will. When I've got the results I'll have to go out and break the news to Sarah.'

'Yes, of course ...' Ewan seemed like a zombie. Molly suspected he'd had even less sleep than her. 'But that's a good thing, isn't it? Now she knows Niall's feelings are real. She'll be ecstatic, won't she?'

'Yes. Yes, I guess so ...'

'If it is true and I'm pretty sure that's what happened, something else is driving me insane. How did I mix the placebo and the real Bug up?'

Ewan sat down heavily in his office chair. 'I don't know ... you'll probably never know and it doesn't matter now.'

Chapter Thirty-Eight

Sarah paced up and down the riverbank by Jesus Green pool. They'd arranged to meet in Molly's lunch break so Molly could break the news in person. Sarah had found it nigh on impossible to concentrate on the beginners' workshop she'd been running, wondering what the results of Molly's tests would reveal.

Spring was bursting into life all over the city. Pots of primroses bloomed on the narrowboats moored by the river. A cat dozed on the roof in a pool of sunshine while moorhens pootled about by the banks. Sarah rested her hands on her stomach and felt the baby kick. In the summer she would wheel the buggy down here and show the little one the ducks, and when she was old enough, they would feed them together.

But would Niall be with them? Whatever news Molly had, he would have to be part of the baby's life. He was her dad, and it was important he played a role. Sarah would never deny him that, no matter what had passed between them.

She scanned the grassy open space next to the river, looking for Molly. She must have trodden the same short stretch of towpath at least six times already ... Her heart pounded as she spotted her sister cycling towards her.

The river path was busy with workers and students so

Molly had to dismount and wheel her bike through the crowds. In the last few seconds before Molly reached her, Sarah's stomach turned over. Was Molly smiling and happy? Sarah couldn't tell, as Molly wove in and out of the walkers.

Finally, Molly reached her. She had a smile on her face. Sarah almost passed out with the tension.

'Relax. It's definitely Liam's DNA,' she said.

Sarah let out a huge sigh. 'Oh My God. Are you *sure?*'

Molly undid her cycle helmet and hung it on the handle-bars. 'One hundred per cent. Ewan checked my results. The Bug couldn't possibly have worked on Niall.'

Sarah gasped. 'Ewan knows about this? Oh no!'

'I had no choice. I had to ask for his help to find an inhibitor, though in the end we didn't need one.'

Sarah let out a squeak of horror. 'So, you didn't need to tell him after all? You're in awful trouble with him and it *was* all my fault, giving you the wrong sample in the first place.'

Molly soothed her. 'Actually, I should have double-checked, not simply assumed it was Niall's DNA.'

Sarah was done in so Molly rested her bike by a bench and they sat down.

'What's Ewan said? Is he going to sack you or report us?' Sarah said.

'He isn't going to do anything. Technically, we haven't actually done anything wrong. Not now.'

'But he must be furious that we even thought of doing it and got into this situation?'

Molly nibbled her lower lip. 'He's not a happy bunny, I must admit.'

Sarah sighed. 'Oh, Mol, I hope this hasn't ruined things between you and Ewan.'

'It hasn't helped. He's hardly spoken to me since and we certainly haven't ... you know – but I don't think it's only this business with the Love Bug. I think his wife may be back in his life.'

'What?'

'One of the guys from the lab told me he'd heard Anna was staying with Ewan. He's acting weird again so I think there's something wrong that has nothing to do with the Love Bug. I haven't asked him while all this has been going on.'

Sarah hugged her. 'I'm so sorry, Molly. You two seemed made for each other.'

Molly sighed. 'I'm not sure anyone will ever be made for each other, even with the Love Bug's help. I'm not sure we should even try to do it ...'

'You don't mean that. But are you sure about his wife being back?'

'I don't know for certain. He looks like hell ... I suppose I should talk to him about Anna but to be honest I'm dreading what I might hear.'

'Oh, hon. You must be brave and talk to him. Look what happened after I spoke to Niall about the baby ...'

'That was different. I'm so happy everything's OK for you and Niall and the Bump.'

Sarah heaved a sigh. 'Yes ... I don't know what ... My God, is that who I think it is?'

Sarah tugged Molly's jacket. 'There over by the entrance to the open-air pool. It's Ewan.'

'What?'

'Is that her? His wife?' Sarah pointed at a petite woman with a ponytail standing by the pool a little way down the towpath. Ewan was holding her hand.

'I don't know. It must be. Quick, let's hide. I don't want him to see me.'

'Not easy to hide,' said Sarah looking at her bump but Molly pulled her under the fronds of a willow on the bank. They hung around in the leaves while Ewan and Anna walked past. They weren't holding hands anymore and were talking too far away for Sarah and Molly to hear what was being said.

'That's it, then,' said Molly gloomily after Ewan and Anna had disappeared by the side of the bridge towards town.

'You have to talk to him.'

'Right now, I don't want to.'

'Molly, you *have* to be brave. Confront him. We all have to be honest from now on, even if we hear stuff we don't want to. Talk to him. Right?'

Molly nodded. 'I'll do as you say but whatever happens to me, at least your life's back on course.'

It was dusk when Niall came home. They ate dinner and Sarah went to bed early, leaving him watching a Jason Statham film because he had the next day off. She tried to read a Parent and Baby magazine and practise her deep-breathing exercises but nothing helped.

She must have fallen asleep because when she came downstairs the next morning, Niall was crunching toast at the table over a copy of the *Sun*.

'Morning.' He kissed the top of her head and handed her a mug. 'Have you thought any more about getting an engagement ring?'

Sarah felt sick. 'Not yet.'

'I don't want to rush you but I think we should do it. We could go into town this morning, babe.'

'I don't know. I'm so busy with commissions. It's prime wedding season.'

'Busy? Too busy for choosing a ring and planning our wedding? Come on, Sarah, what's holding you back? If you feel you can't trust me, I swear on our baby's life that I will never let you down again. You do believe me, don't you?' He was pleading and Sarah told herself not to be such a coward.

'I believe ... I believe that *you* really believe that you won't let me down again.'

'What? What's that supposed to mean? I love you, and I can't think of a better way to prove it than to ask you to marry me.'

'Proving you love someone takes a lot more than putting a ring on their finger. It takes time.'

'Well, for feck's sake, I can't see into the future. I don't know what else I can do.'

'I think,' said Sarah slowly, 'I think that I need to spend some time on my own.' Even though every word was agony, Sarah knew she was doing the right thing. For her, her baby and ultimately, for Niall. She didn't love him in the way she had but she loved him enough to be honest with him.

Niall screwed up his face in disbelief. 'What?'

'I think I should be on my own for a while, with the baby.'

'What are you trying to say? That you want to leave me?'

'I want you to move out, Ni, and after the baby's born, I want to put the cottage back on the market.'

He jumped up, holding his head in his hands. 'You can't be serious? You were desperate for me to come back, you were feckin' devastated when I left. Don't try and hide it. I knew it. Vanessa knew it. You'd have done anything to get me back.'

'Not anything – and I couldn't care less what Vanessa

332

thought.' Niall stared at her. Her heart literally ached at the shock and misery on his face. She hated to hurt anyone that much; the responsibility of having that much power over any human being – the power to deal the cruellest blow to them – was horrible. He'd lost everything when he thought he had it all. She knew exactly how he felt.

'You can see the baby as much as you want. I want you to be part of her life,' she said gently.

'Well, thanks a lot!'

'Niall, I know it's hard but I've been thinking about this for a while and I'm really really sorry it hasn't worked out for us.'

'Jesus. Is it him? Is it that Liam? I knew he was a tosser, sniffing around, after you.'

'No, it's not Liam,' said Sarah, horrified at the way Niall was unravelling before her eyes.

'I don't believe it. I won't believe it. I'm going around to his bloody big office now to sort him out.'

He grabbed the car keys.

'It's nothing to do with Liam. Don't be stupid.'

Ignoring her, Niall rushed out of the kitchen and the front door slammed so hard, the walls shook.

Chapter Thirty-Nine

Molly wheeled her bike next to Sarah as they walked along the Backs causeway towards the city centre. Sarah was wearing a pretty tunic that showed off her growing bump. Her hair was thick and shining. Molly thought she had never looked more beautiful, despite the dark smudges under her eyes. Sarah hadn't been sleeping well since her split from Niall a few days before but despite the bump, there was also something lighter in the way she walked, as if a weight had been lifted from her shoulders.

They stopped on the bridge over the river. Punts glided beneath them and the brown water was scattered with blossom. Ducklings trailed behind their mums, making Molly think of her new niece or nephew. Perhaps, now, despite all the pain, they could look forward to the event with joy and pleasure.

For a while, they watched the boatloads of tourists and listened to the laughter and popping of corks from students who had finished their exams.

Sarah turned to her, regret in her eyes. 'Are you angry with me for causing so much trouble?'

'Why would I be angry?' Molly replied. 'You've done what you thought was right, what's in your heart. It must have been tough to tell Niall you wanted to split up.'

'It was one of the hardest things I've ever had to do. No matter what's happened between us, and although there have been times when I wanted him to hurt like I did when he left me ... in the end, I hated telling him. It cut me like a knife.'

'What happened at Liam's office?' she asked.

'Niall ranted for a while but he calmed down eventually. I was so worried he'd start a fight but Liam quietened him down.'

'Is Ni still staying at his mum's?'

'Yes. She's very upset too. She called me and said I was being a selfish cow not to stay with Niall for the sake of the baby. It was horrible.'

'I'll bet, but Niall's mum hasn't got to spend the rest of her life with him.'

Sarah gazed out over the river. 'Have I done the right thing, Mol? I wondered if I should have given it longer before I told him how I felt. I wondered if time might make a difference ...'

'Or it might just have prolonged his agony.'

'Yes. I suppose so. Living a lie would only have made things worse.'

'So you *are* moving out of the cottage?' said Molly.

Sarah nodded. 'Yes. After the baby's born. It's too much to try and move out now but after that we'll have to find somewhere else.'

'You're always welcome at mine.' Molly smiled and pointed at the bump. 'Both of you.'

'Thanks, hon, but won't Ewan have something to say about that?'

'I don't care. It's none of Ewan's business. We're still not sharing a bed at the moment.'

Sarah winced. 'Is his wife definitely back with him?'

'I don't know for certain but I think so, judging by the rumours and the fact he's hardly been in the lab. He's taken a few days off.'

'Why don't you ask him straight out?'

'I want to call him but not if Anna is there. I'm done with chasing a lost cause and it's up to him to tell me what's happening between us, not for me to go after him.' And Molly didn't *want* to face up to the truth.

'I don't blame you but do speak to him. Be brave, Mol, it's the only way.'

'I will. I promise.'

But Molly didn't. She went back to work and sat at her desk in the office, staring out of the window. Blossom had drifted from the trees and hedges onto the statue of Isaac Newton, giving him a very fetching pink and white hat. While she tried to focus on all the positive things about her life at the moment and remind herself how great it was to be alive, a pigeon landed on the statue's head and pooped all over his face.

She returned to her computer screen, thinking over Sarah's advice. Perhaps the near disaster with the Love Bug *had* helped Sarah realise that she could live without Niall. It had definitely tested her feelings for Ewan and his for her – but she still didn't know where she stood. Sarah was right. She knew she had to confront him, but she hated the idea of walking into some shitty embarrassing love triangle. And even if she had the wrong end of the stick about Ewan's wife, there was still the small question of him taking the job in Switzerland.

She returned to reading through some new papers on primate bonding while she waited for the results of her latest

test to be processed. She had to stop mooning about and get some work done. Ewan was right about one thing: relationships did distract you from your work.

'You must be Molly.'

Molly glanced up to find a woman smiling at her.

'I'm Anna Baxter, Ewan's wife.'

I know, thought Molly, her heart beating hard. Anna wasn't wearing a security lanyard. She wondered how she'd got into the lab.

'Actually, it's Dr Baxter,' said Anna, coming further into the office. 'You *are* Molly I presume?'

The hairs on the back of Molly's neck prickled and she looked around for Ewan but there was no sign of him.

'Yes, I am but ... where's Ewan?'

Anna shrugged. 'No idea. At home, I suppose.'

'You mean he doesn't know you're here.'

Anna sat in Ewan's desk chair. 'I don't really care. Mm. This is a nice cosy office you two have here.' She started to rifle through the papers on his desk.

Molly's skin prickled and she thought about calling security. Her fingers itched to pick up the phone right now. 'I don't really think you should be here, Anna, without a pass.'

Anna snorted. 'I don't care, *Molly*. I take it you're the girlfriend?'

'I'm not his anything. We're colleagues.' Molly's fingers crept towards the desk phone.

Anna laughed. 'Oh, come on. We're both adults. I know what's been going on.'

'Then you know more than me. Look, Anna, I think you should leave now. This isn't the right place or time to talk about personal and private stuff.'

'Oh, I think it's the perfect place since Ewan likes to take his work home and vice versa.' Anna picked up a mug that belonged to Ewan and rolled her eyes. 'Did you buy him this?'

Molly glanced at the mug, which was actually from the paper towel supplier.

'No.' She stood up and tried to sound assertive and in control even though her stomach was turning over and her palms were sweaty. 'I'd like you to leave my office, please.'

Anna shook her head and let out a sigh. 'I don't think I will until you tell me what it is about you that my husband finds so irresistible.'

Molly couldn't believe what she was hearing. 'Husband? Even if I had any idea what you're talking about, you're not married to Ewan. You're ...'

'Divorced? Actually, no.' Anna positioned the mug carefully in the centre of Ewan's desk.

'Anna? What are you doing here?'

Ewan ran into the office. His face was red and he was breathing heavily. Molly's shoulders sank in relief.

'Ewan ... I hope you don't mind me dropping into your office. I have to say I'm not impressed by what I've found.'

'That's enough.' Ewan glanced at Molly and back at Anna. He spoke softly. 'Come on, let's talk somewhere else.' He took Anna's arm.

She shook away his hand. 'Get off me,' she said. 'I've every right to be here.'

'This isn't the best idea, Anna.' Ewan let her go, but two of Molly's colleagues must have heard the noise and were standing in the doorway.

'Is everything OK in here, guys?' one of the technicians asked, looking very worried. 'Do you need us to call security?'

'No!' Ewan snapped then softened. 'Thanks, but I'll sort this out.'

Molly flashed her workmates a pleading look and they stayed outside the open door, watching. They were joined by one of the research associates from the adjoining office and a moment later, Molly heard Pete's voice asking what was going on. Molly cringed as the audience grew.

'Anna, you can't do this here. Come on home,' Ewan said gently.

She sneered. 'No way. I bet you'd like to see me dragged off by security, wouldn't you?'

'No. I'd hate it but that's what will happen if you don't leave right now.'

'What about you, then, Little Miss Angelic?' Anna pointed at Molly.

Molly felt sick to the stomach. 'I promise I wouldn't like to see you thrown out of anywhere. Ewan's right: go home and talk about this.'

Anna folded her arms. 'I'm not leaving.'

'But I am,' said Molly. 'I think it's better if I do.'

'Molly ...'

'Sorry, Ewan. You need to deal with this.'

Molly walked out of the office, feeling very shaky. Her colleagues stared at her and mouthed "wtf?" Ignoring them, she headed for the bathroom but behind her voices were raised even louder. Anna had changed tactics and was shouting, crying and begging Ewan to take her back. That thing in movies where the heroine is triumphant and delighted when the mad ex finally gets her comeuppance wasn't true. In real life, it was embarrassing, distressing and not funny at all.

Molly took a few deep breaths and splashed her face with water before walking back into the corridor. To her great relief, she spotted Ewan, with his arm around Anna, leading her out of the office and through a fire door into the garden. A security guard followed them out. What a bloody god-awful mess. Molly steadied herself with a hand on the wall. She hadn't thought Anna would hurt her for a moment but the scene that had been created would be the talk of the lab and Anna must be in terrible distress to barge in like that.

And Ewan was still married to her. Of course he was – but she'd assumed they were divorced ...

With her head held high, Molly forced herself to walk back into her office. A few of her colleagues asked her if she was OK but most were too polite and contented themselves with sympathetic glances.

'Molly?' Pete spoke to her. 'Anything I can do?'

'Not now, Pete,' she said haughtily, dying inside.

Despite the façade she knew that word would have spread round the department faster than an infectious disease. Everyone in the lab would soon be talking about the juicy love triangle involving Anna, Ewan and her.

She tried to do some work in the lab but she couldn't help replaying the scene from earlier, the desperation on Anna's face and voice. Here was Ewan hitting the roof because she'd told a white lie about the Love Bug – and yet he'd neglected to mention the fact that he was still married. She remembered how much in love he'd been with his wife once. So in love and so devastated when it had gone wrong, that he'd broken down in tears in a meeting. While Anna was clearly upset and vindictive, Molly couldn't help but wonder if she'd been the cause of putting the final nail in the coffin of a marriage that still had life in it. Did he still have strong feelings for Anna and was Molly only a distraction?

*

Molly was curled up in a chair trying to read a scientific paper on Neanderthal STDs, when Ewan buzzed the door of the flat. Unshaven and rumpled, he looked even worse than he had earlier in the lab. She braced herself for what she might hear: no matter how upsetting, she had to have things out with him.

'How's Anna?' she asked as he stood awkwardly in the middle of the room.

'Gone. Her sister came to fetch her. She's agreed to see her GP and get some help.'

'Oh no. I'm very sorry she's unwell. I wouldn't wish that on anyone.' Molly felt guilty.

'Me neither but we're going to support her through some treatment. You must have been wondering what the hell's been going on ...'

'I decided it was up to you to tell me.'

He shoved his hands through his tangled hair. 'She's been living with this guy in London. The one she left me for – but that's all gone tits up and he threw her out, the bastard. I don't really know why he did it but she's very down, understandably.'

'Poor Anna,' Molly said quietly and really meant it.

Ewan groaned. 'You know, at one time I would have been ecstatic for them to split up. I prayed for it, and I don't even believe in that stuff but now, well ... it was just horrific to see Anna in bits. No matter what happened between us, I hated seeing how that shot hurt her. I'm sorry you were dragged into this, Molly, with the business at the lab.'

'It's OK. I can stand a few whispers and snarky looks ... but is Anna right? You're still married to her?'

'Yes. People just assumed that we were divorced and I thought it was none of their business and why the fuck should I talk about it anyway? I know I said Anna was my ex and she is but I can understand I should have been more honest about the technicalities.'

Molly wasn't satisfied with that explanation. '*She* doesn't think she's ex anymore. And you're right, you *should* have been more honest.'

'I know but in every way that really matters she was – is – my ex. She moved out, she had an affair and I feel very sorry that things didn't work out for her and sorry for today. And I'm sorry for the way I freaked out over the Love Bug. I may have over-reacted.' He tried to take Molly's hand but she wasn't ready yet.

'When Anna turned up on my doorstep, I couldn't just throw her out but there's been nothing going on – like *that* – between us. Do you know how hard it has been to tell the woman I loved and who I still care for to leave my house forever? To walk away when she tried to get into my bed? I care about her.'

Molly stood firm. 'I understand that but, Ewan, you need to be sure that you're over her. When you've sorted out how you feel, when I've sorted out how I feel ... then maybe we could start again?'

His expression was agonised. She wondered if he was going to storm off out of the flat but then he declared, 'If that's what you want but I *promise* you I've never been surer of how I feel in my life.'

'And what is that, Ewan? I'm still in the dark.'

'I want you. I want us to be together. I don't want to go to Switzerland and I want to stop living a lie. I want us to be together and for everyone at the lab to know.'

'After what I've done?'

'That has nothing to do with the way I feel about you. With the fact that I love you. We've both done things we're not proud of. We've both hidden things from each other and kept secrets for the sake of people we love. Your reason for giving Niall the Love Bug was more excusable than mine for not telling the truth about Anna. It was cowardly. I'm grumpy and find it hard to show my feelings but please believe how much I want to be with you. Can you give me another chance?'

Molly hugged herself, still not ready to step into Ewan's arms. If she did, that would be it. She'd be on the path to forgiving him and ... Would that be so bad?

'I'm not perfect, either ...' he began.

Ewan smiled but made no attempt to touch her again.

'You know the worst of me too,' she said. 'That I'm sarcastic and outspoken and that my revenge will be terrible if you hurt me again.'

He smiled. 'I'm quaking.'

She stepped nearer, within touching distance. Ewan held out his hand. Molly took it and interlaced her fingers with his. She put her arms around him and looked up into his face. 'Two wrong people don't make a right one,' she said.

Ewan ran his finger down the side of her cheek and the ice chip in Molly's heart finally thought about melting. 'No, but we could have a bloody good time testing that theory.'

Chapter Forty

Sarah glanced nervously around Liam's office. She still wasn't sure she'd done the right thing in coming to see him. Was she adding fuel to the fire?

'Thanks for seeing me,' she said, as he gestured to the chair opposite his.

He smiled. 'I never mind seeing you. Why don't you sit down?'

Sarah didn't plan on staying but the baby was growing so much heavier and she'd rushed over to Liam's office in between workshops. She eased herself down into the seat and Liam sat behind his desk. Despite him saying he was pleased to see her, his expression was a little wary.

Sarah launched right in. Liam deserved straight talking. 'I'm sorry Niall stormed over here and kicked off. I'm afraid I'd just had to tell him some bad news.'

'Yeah, he made that clear. I'm sorry – genuinely – that things haven't worked out between you two.'

'They were never going to after he left the first time. I did try to stop him from muscling in on you at work. I told him there was nothing between us. That we're just friends.'

Liam frowned. 'Of course we are. We've nothing to feel guilty about.'

'Um. You might not have,' she murmured.

'What?' Liam said, looking hard at her.

Sarah regretted her comment, 'Nothing. I felt I had to come to apologise for him. I was so worried he might start a fight with you or you'd have to call the police.'

'Don't worry; I could see he was upset. He simmered down eventually but I was more concerned about you. I wasn't sure what had happened between the two of you at home. I almost phoned you but didn't want to make things worse.'

'Thanks, but I'm fine. Niall was very upset and confused but he's calmer now. He'll get over it.' Sarah toyed with a pen on the desk.

The shrill ring of the phone in the outer office and the laughter of other staff drifted into the room. Sarah twirled the pen between her fingers. He reached across the desk to her and his olive-skinned fingers were inches from hers. She knew that his touch would be warm and firm and that it would feel amazing.

'Sarah?' he said softly. 'You must do what you have to to be happy and make a new start for you and your baby. You must know how much I care about you – more than care – but my feelings don't come into it. I won't pressure you in any way.'

She found the courage to look at him, knowing how dangerous that was. Even looking at his serious, handsome face was lethal, listening to him speak in his calm voice, knowing he might smile at any moment.

'I really care about you, Liam, but the past few months have felt like a bomb has exploded in the middle of my life. I still haven't picked up all the pieces, let alone put them back together. What I need most right now is time. Lots and lots of time, with no deadline at the end of it.'

'I think I know – I *should* know how you feel. I've needed a lot of time in the past, way too much, but after that long, after waiting to find someone I want to be with – well, I can wait a while longer. As long as it takes.' He smiled. 'In fact, I won't even tell you I am going to wait. Think of me having a whale of a time, dating loads of women, clubbing in Cindies, getting drunk and thrown out of Vodka Revs.'

Sarah couldn't help but laugh. 'I haven't been chucked out of Vodka Revs for at least ten years.'

'They wouldn't even let you in at the moment.'

She patted her bump, definitely the perfect size for balancing a plate now. Her heart hurt. It was a good sign, wasn't it, that she felt real fear that she might lose Liam, a sharp pang almost of disappointment at him letting her go?

'Liam, I need to say something before I leave. It's probably a bad idea to tell you this and after I've said it, I want you to promise that you'll still let me walk away from this office and give me the space and time I need.'

Liam's eyes widened and then he said gently, 'No businessman or woman should agree to the terms of a deal they haven't even heard yet.'

'But those are my terms. I drive a hard bargain too.'

He drummed his fingers on the desk. 'For you, I promise.'

'It's this. I could so easily fall in love with you, *be* loved by you – come to rely on you – and that's exactly why I'm going to try very hard not to do any of those things. Not for a while anyway. Not until I'm one hundred per cent sure that it's you I want and that it – us – will be the right thing for my baby too.'

346

Sarah was amazed at how firm her voice was when every other part of her was shaking like a leaf.

Liam was lost for words for a few seconds and she liked him all the more for that.

'Wow,' he managed eventually. 'I'm not sure I feel better for hearing that or not. I – I guess I'm overwhelmed. But in a good way,' he added hastily. 'And I already love you as a friend and in every other way but I swear I'll wait until you're ready. *If* you're ready and until then, be happy to fix any damage to the house caused by you throwing items of crockery at whoever you decide deserves it.'

Sarah closed her eyes at the memory of her first meeting with him, but her heart was full of hope too. More hope than she'd felt since New Year's Eve. 'You'll never let me forget that, will you?'

'Nope.'

She eased herself out of the chair. She had to get out of the office before she changed her mind and ran to him right now. 'Thanks for not pressing charges against Niall and for not putting me under any pressure.'

He gave a crooked smile. 'It's a pleasure. Now, will you consider doing one thing for me?'

'That depends what it is.'

'Come to the wedding?'

Sarah hesitated. She wanted to go, very much. 'I don't know ... it's a family occasion and it might seem strange if I turned up. I'd love to see Hayley get married though. Can I have time to think about it?'

'Like I said, you can have all the time you need.'

'I will let you know. You'll need to let the caterers have the numbers.'

'Don't worry about that yet,' Liam said. 'I just wanted you to know that what you did for me – and Hayley – and I don't just mean the tiara; it meant a lot to me and Hayley. In fact, she's asked me to give you this card. I held back under the circumstances but it arrived with the last lot of post from her base.'

Sarah took the small envelope from him and opened the card inside. It was a thank you card with a teddy holding a flower. The message made her eyes fill with tears.

Thank you so much for helping Dad make my tiara. I absolutely adore it and I know how big a part you played in its creation. It would mean a lot to me if you came to the wedding, and you could see it in action!'

Hayley x

'Oh, Liam. That's beautiful. Thank Hayley for sending me such a lovely message. I – I – I'll be in touch.'

With tears in her eyes, Sarah said a hasty goodbye and walked out of the office. It had been on the tip of her tongue to rush to Liam and kiss him but she didn't dare. She owed it to him and herself to be absolutely sure of her feelings before she threw herself into another relationship and for once she was going to let her head rule her heart.

Chapter Forty-One

Molly locked up her bike in the rack outside her flat and trudged up the stairs. She was starving. Unable to face her spin class, she'd been for a swim in Jesus Green outdoor pool. The unheated water was a refreshing wake-up after the hot and dusty cycle ride from the lab to the pool. In the four weeks since Anna had turned up at the lab, summer had arrived with a vengeance. Molly thought of Sarah waddling around in the heat with the Bump. She'd be able to take her sister and niece swimming this time next year, though not to the unheated pool ...

She pushed open the door and saw the letter on the doormat. It was in a recycled envelope, not a padded one this time, but definitely a reused one. She opened it and pulled out a sheet of printer paper that was carefully folded into three, with sharp creases.

Department of Behavioural Ecology
Fenland University
Research Proposal

Objectives To determine the best way of persuading human female subject to move in with you.

Design Longitudinal cohort study.

Setting *House currently containing one lone male, some very dubious boxer shorts and a tandem with a wonky wheel.*

Subjects *Female – fit (extremely) and healthy, highly intelligent, talented and funny. Slightly barking mad at times but with a great arse. And breasts. And legs. And mouth. And earlobes. In fact, great everything. Observed almost daily over two years, ten months.*

Main outcome measures *Convince female subject to move into home with view to long-term commitment.*

Results *To be advised but hopeful despite past experience.*

Conclusions *A big smile on my face every morning and an even bigger one on hers. A better class of pants drying on my radiators.*

She smiled. A tear plopped onto the paper, smudging the printer ink. The doorbell buzzed and Molly hastily wiped her tears away. She dropped the letter on the coffee table and pressed the buzzer to let her visitor into the building.

She opened the front door and found Ewan standing there next to a large and overstuffed rucksack. He looked tanned but tired and Molly tried not to fancy him so much that it hurt.

'You're supposed to be in America at a conference,' she said.

'I was. I came straight here from the airport.'

'Have you been watching me?'

He shrugged. 'Might have.'

'That's stalking.'

'Sorry.'

'No, you're not,' she said.

'No, I'm not. Can I come in?'

'I suppose so.' She opened the door.

He saw the envelope on the coffee table. 'You've read the abstract, then?

She shook her head. 'You total nutter.'

He smiled proudly. 'I know.'

'And FYI, your pants aren't that bad ... but you really wouldn't like to have mine drying on your radiators.'

'It's a compromise I'm willing to make.'

Molly folded up the abstract carefully along its creases as Ewan watched anxiously.

'So what's your conclusion, Dr Havers?'

She popped the paper in the envelope. 'Your premise is good in theory, but I'm afraid that in practice it's not going to work.'

He gave her an intense look. 'Are you sure? I thought it was worth investigating myself but if you think that the time and effort involved wouldn't justify the outcomes ...'

'Oh, I do. I do ...' Molly couldn't keep up the pretence any longer. 'Ewan, I've just been offered the possibility of a new job.'

Ewan looked poleaxed. 'You don't have to leave the lab because of our relationship,' he said. 'I was an arse over the Love Bug and over Anna. I'm sorry.'

'You *were* an arse but I brought it on myself and I'm not leaving because of our relationship. I'm not even going because I almost did something so stupid, I can't think of it without cringing. I'm doing it because I've had a fantastic time here, I've learned a lot from you and it's time I moved on, started my own team.'

'I see,' he said quietly. 'You deserve it.'

'It's one of the London universities. They've only sounded

me out so far but the head of the lab says she's very keen and the job is mine if I want it. I'll have my own small team and a research grant. Not huge but enough to get me started. I've so many things I want to look at, so many ideas ...'

'That's great. I'm really pleased for you. I suppose there's no point me saying that I was going to encourage you to apply for a fellowship here ...'

'Were you?'

'Yes, but this sounds even better and I don't want to hold you back.'

'Thanks. My new employer may take up references,' she said.

'You know me. I'll be brutally honest,' he said sternly.

'Oh God, I hope not!'

'Maybe I can leave some things out.'

Ewan looked at her in a way that made her want to melt. With pride, with tenderness, with raw lust. He pulled her towards him and she didn't resist. 'London isn't that far. It's not the other side of the planet.'

He held her lightly as if he was afraid she would push him away if he put too much pressure on her.

'So you're not going to Bern?' she said.

'I decided my work here is too important and I don't like chocolate or cuckoo clocks – but it's too late, isn't it? If you're going to London ...'

'London isn't Switzerland.'

'No, it isn't. We could move somewhere in between. Lots of people commute.'

'They do,' said Molly, hardly able to speak, not making any sense.

'If you decide to move in. I know it's a big step but it would save rent. My place is closer to the station. There are a lot of practical reasons in favour of it. In fact, on balance, the move would be mutually beneficial for both of us. Even though you're moving to another lab, we'll still be working on papers together about the Love Bug and we're not far off a patent for it.'

'Don't call it the Love Bug, Professor Baxter.'

Ewan pulled her close. 'Oh, shut up, Dr Havers. Don't try to put me off. I want you to move in, most of all because it would be beneficial to me because I love you. I'm over Anna. I have been for a long time, longer than I wanted to admit. Because if I'd admitted it, I would have had no reason to be a coward and not tell you how I feel; how much I feel, which is scary.'

Molly felt she had to keep things light. If she really thought about what he was saying, she might burst into tears. 'I thought love was just a state of mutual co-dependency,' she said.

Ewan smiled. 'It is. Of course it is but it's also a zillion other things. Something we can't define, something different and unique to each of us. It may change. I can't guarantee it will last forever but I want it to.'

'What if we're deluding ourselves?'

'If I'm deluding myself, then so what? Fuck it, I like being deluded and not able to explain it.'

She'd never heard him sound so passionate about anything. Now she saw why and how he'd been hit so hard by Anna leaving him, why he'd lost it at work and since then; pulled down the shutters and kept his emotions locked away so tightly.

'As your boss I say congratulations on your job. I'm

sorry to lose a brilliant colleague and you deserve every success. As the bloke who loves you, I say: please move in with me.'

Whoa. Molly's throat dried. She cleared it before saying, 'It's something I need to think about ...'

'Why? Why not just do it?'

She laughed. '*Just do it*? Says Mr "test everything to destruction and then think about it" Baxter.'

'I've changed. Or rather I've realised that when you know you really really want something, there is absolutely no point in waiting and you should grab the opportunity by the balls.'

'Er. In case you haven't noticed, Mr world expert in primate sexuality, I don't have balls.'

'Really?' He sighed. 'If you're still not sure about moving in with me, I can recommend a way we can find a solution that's based on scientific research.'

She was half laughing, half crying. 'Oh, yeah, what would that be?'

'Well, it's well documented that bonobos have sex to resolve conflicts ...' He raised an eyebrow. It was funny and weird and touching to see him in this way: as if he'd shrugged a heavy pack from his shoulders and was almost jumping for joy. Molly wasn't quite sure of the man who was holding her in his arms but she was getting to know him. He'd never shown any emotion before because he felt too much, not too little.

And that she could understand, *that* she could love.

'I don't need a PhD to see where this is going,' she whispered.

Ewan cradled her face in his hands and dropped the gentlest

of kisses on her lips. His hands smelled vaguely of ethanol and she could hardly breathe but she didn't care. Nothing was perfect in this life and so many things were far from it, but she was certain that loving Ewan was the closest anything had ever been or ever would be.

Chapter Forty-Two

Sarah fanned herself discreetly with an order of service at the back of the church. There had been standing room only by the time she'd arrived but, embarrassingly, an elderly man had insisted on giving up his end of the pew to her. She was the size of a baby elephant and the early August heat was intense, making the crowded church feel stuffy. She knew that people might stare at her and wonder who she was and why she was there but she was desperate to see Hayley in her tiara and more importantly, she would never let Liam down.

She'd kept the wedding invitation on her mantelpiece ever since she'd received it, alongside Hayley's card. She thought about going for ages and hadn't been able to decide. Finally, a few weeks previously, she'd read the invitation and Hayley's card again as the Bump wriggled inside her. It was the afternoon of the RSVP deadline date and taking her courage in her hands, she'd replied that she'd be delighted to attend.

While she waited for the bride and Liam to arrive, she thought back to the previous evening and Niall's most recent visit. He was still struggling with their split but had stopped begging her to take him back. She knew exactly how he felt: the desperation, the pain, the disbelief, but it was early days for him and he was still raw. She'd said he could be at the birth and come along to one of her antenatal appointments with her.

She knew he hoped she'd change her mind. She knew she wouldn't. Living on her own wasn't all roses; even with Molly, her friends, her clients and the mums-to-be she'd made friends with at antenatal classes, she still felt the cottage was too big and too quiet for one. That would change, of course, soon enough and then she'd have new challenges to face as a single parent.

The other guests – none of whom she knew – glanced at her with sympathy and some curiosity but then the 'Bridal March' struck up and all eyes shifted to the aisle. Tears filled Sarah's eyes as Hayley walked past on Liam's arm. She looked stunning and the tiara was the perfect complement to her simple dress: not OTT but very pretty. There were sniffles all around and several of the men were suspiciously moist-eyed.

Sarah had seen quite a few brides wearing her or their own creations, but this was different; she'd never felt so close to the people involved. In his morning suit, Liam was so handsome and bursting with pride as he escorted Hayley to the altar, followed by two little bridesmaids and a pageboy.

Sarah wondered how Liam must feel today. He must be so happy to be walking his daughter down the aisle but missing his wife, Kerren, and wondering what might have been.

What was she doing here? Even though she was invited, she felt like an intruder. She was relieved when the vicar finished speaking and the baby next to her started wailing along to 'Morning Has Broken'.

The old lady on the other side of her said in a doom-laden tone. 'You've got this to come, you know, young lady.'

Sarah needn't have felt like an intruder. At the reception,

Liam had thanked her for coming as she'd made her way down the receiving line and Hayley had hugged her before he and the bride and groom had both been swept off by the whirl of the wedding. Sarah had been put on a table full of fun and interesting friends of the bride who all wanted to know about her job and she'd had her business card requested by a dozen guests. It had been a lovely, lively wedding with genuinely happy, friendly people and she was glad she'd plucked up the courage to attend. However, the room was stuffy and by the time the DJ had set up ready for the disco, her ankles had started to swell and the baby was obviously trying her new Olympic tumbling routine.

She waddled to the restroom and splashed her face with cold water. Her face was red and her back was aching from standing too long during the photographs. She didn't think she could cope much longer so she went back to collect her place card and service sheet when Liam appeared. He'd got rid of his jacket long before but still wore the dark blue cravat.

Seeing her holding her handbag and the service sheet, his face crumpled in disappointment.

'You're not leaving already, are you?' he asked.

'I was thinking about it. I get tired these days and the Bump is hinting.'

'It's selfish of me but can you stay a bit longer? I've hardly had time to speak you on my own.'

She laughed. 'It's your daughter's wedding. It's your job to talk to everyone.'

'I'd rather talk to you, to be honest.'

The DJ's voice boomed out, announcing that the bride and groom were about to take to the floor.

Liam winced. 'Ouch, the first dance. Hayley hates dancing.

Kerren tried to take her to ballet lessons but she threw her shoes at the instructor and stormed out and made us enrol her in the judo class instead.'

Sarah laughed. 'Are you sure she hates dancing?' she said, pointing to the dance floor.

Hayley and Kyle took to the floor. Sarah recognised the song: 'Never Tear Us Apart' by INXS. There were gasps and then applause as instead of the expected awkward shuffle, Hayley and Kyle waltzed off confidently.

'Bloody hell ...' said Liam.

People started to wolf whistle and cheer. Liam stood open-mouthed.

'Not bad for someone who hates dancing,' said Sarah. 'Great choice of song too.'

Liam's eyes glistened. 'I might have known she'd surprise me. She always has.'

After a few bars, Hayley and Kyle called for other people to join them and a few of the older couples started to waltz while younger ones laughed and fudged their way around the floor.

Liam blew out a breath.

'You must miss Kerren today,' said Sarah.

'Yes. I've had a few moments. It must have been scary for you too, turning up to a strange tribe's wedding on your own.'

'It was a bit weird at first but I've really enjoyed it. Your tribe are one of the better ones and Hayley looks amazing. Your tiara was perfect.'

'But don't give up the day job?'

She laughed. 'I don't think I could handle the competition.'

The formal waltz ended and the DJ started playing 'Thinking Out Loud'.

Sarah saw Hayley glance their way and mouth "Dad?" enquiringly.

'Would you like to dance – and not just because Hayley wants me to?' Liam asked with a wry smile. 'Unless you have any violent objections to Ed Sheeran?'

'None I can think of. But ... look at me.' Sarah grimaced.

'I am and I would say you looked gorgeous and sexy but that would probably be breaking the rules. Where did you get that dress?'

She glanced down at the vintage boho silk dress she'd rescued from the loft at the cottage. 'Thanks. It was my mum's. Eighties Monsoon but I still feel a bit like Dumbo.'

'You don't look like him. Now, will you dance with me? As long as we can shuffle because I definitely can't waltz.'

She laughed. 'Good, because neither can I.'

Liam took Sarah's hand and led her onto the dance floor. Hayley looked gleeful as she swept past and Kyle winked.

'People are staring at us,' Sarah murmured as Liam rested his hands on her waist.

'Of course they are.'

'You know what they're probably thinking?'

'That you and I met when you tried to kill me with a Toby jug? I don't care what they think. Do you?'

'Actually, no.'

Liam pulled her a little closer so that her bump touched his stomach. The muscles of his back were firm under the cotton of his shirt. Was it wrong for a pregnant women to be turned on by a guy who wasn't the father of her baby? Was someone somewhere wagging their finger? She didn't care. She rested her cheek against Liam's shoulder and closed her eyes, breathing in the scent of his aftershave, enjoying every shift in the muscles around his spine, and the gentle kicks of her baby. The music would have to end sometime and she'd still be going home alone but she also sensed that this was the start of a new beginning for her and Liam as much as it was for Hayley and Kyle.

'Oh!'

Sarah stopped dancing.

'What's the matter?'

'The baby, I think. Kicked me in the back. She's getting stronger.'

'Do you want to sit down?'

'Yes. I think I'd better, and then I should probably head home. It's so hot.'

Liam led her off the dance floor to a chair. 'Can I get you a glass of water?'

'Thanks.' Perspiration sheened her body and her dress stuck to her. The baby had stopped kicking. For now. A few people were looking at her, and she guessed putting two and two together and making ninety-five. She didn't care. She felt better, though a little hot. 'You crafty little madam. You knew what I was up to,' she murmured to the baby.

Liam came back with some iced water and Sarah took it gratefully. She sipped and started to feel cooler.

Liam took a chair next to her, looking concerned. Sarah felt embarrassed. 'Thanks, that's better. Owww!'

The glass slipped from her hand and onto the table. Water drenched the cloth, the floor and her dress.

'Sarah!' Sarah was doubled up in pain. Liam held her shoulders and she heard voices rushing towards her above the thump of the music. She wanted to wave them away but she felt faint and the pain in her back was agonising.

'Owww.'

'Take a deep breath, Sarah. That's it. Big deep breath.' Sarah was vaguely aware of a new voice. It sounded like Hayley's.

'Is she OK?'

Liam's voice filtered through to her as she took some deep breaths. The pain had started to subside a little but she was pouring with sweat and her dress was soaked.

'I'm sorry. So clumsy of me and I could die of embarrassment.'

Liam stood by anxiously. 'It's OK. I'll get one of the staff to clear up the water and get someone to drive you home. In fact, I'll come with you.'

'Hold on, Dad.' Hayley was kneeling beside her chair, the train of her dress spread out.

'Your dress will get wet,' Sarah said.

'It'll dry. How many weeks are you?' Hayley asked.

'Th-thirty-six,' said Sarah. 'And a couple of days. I'm so embarrassed at doing this at your wedding.'

'Don't be.'

'Oh God, there's water everywhere. It was only a glass.'

Hayley got up. 'Yes, but don't worry about it.'

'Arghhhh!' Sarah gripped the table and howled. Everyone was looking now but she didn't care anymore. She thumped the table as another crushing pain rolled over her.

As it gripped her and slowly began to subside, she heard Hayley speaking to Liam.

'Dad, can you phone for an ambulance please? I think Sarah's waters have broken.'

'What? Now? She can't be.'

Through a haze of crushing pain, Sarah heard Hayley speak. 'Dad. Trust me. She's having the baby.'

Chapter Forty-Three

Molly and Ewan had spent the Saturday having sex, picnicking by the river in the hot sunshine before heading back to bed again. Over the past weeks, they'd definitely made up for lost time and the novelty of being together hadn't worn off yet. In fact, they were more in love than ever and now, properly an item at work, much to Pete the Parasite's disgust. His face had been a picture when he'd found out they were seeing each other.

Molly smirked again at the memory of his horrified expression as she sashayed back from her kitchen for a chilled bottle of wine and two glasses. Twilight was falling outside as she carried a tray back to her bedroom, along with a bag of Kettle Chips.

Ewan sat up in bed while Molly handed him a glass of wine. He chinked her glass and took a sip while Molly had a large glug of hers.

'Cheers.' They touched glasses and Molly giggled.

'You know, I think I'm going to have to eat something,' said Ewan, putting his untouched glass on the bedside table and delving into the Kettle Chips. 'I know this isn't very romantic but I'm starving after all that action.'

They snuggled down as Ewan tucked into the crisps and

Molly topped up her glass. Ewan had just picked up his glass again when Molly's phone rang.

'Oh no. Don't answer it,' he said.

'I have to. Every time I don't answer my phone I miss something important. It might be Sarah.'

'I thought she was at a wedding?'

'She is. It's Liam's daughter's wedding. She was worried about going because she only knows Liam and she didn't want to look like a baby elephant. Actually, I told her she looked beautiful in Mum's silk dress. I hope she's had a good time.'

'I'm sure she has.' Ewan walked his fingers up her thigh and sighed. 'I suppose you'd better take the call in case it is Sarah.'

'Arghh.' Molly snatched the phone a second after it finished ringing. 'Oh, it's from Liam and he's left a message.' She frowned. 'How weird.'

Ewan collapsed back against the pillows while Molly listened to her message. Her heart rate took off.

'Oh my God!'

Ewan sat upright. 'What?'

Molly dropped the phone on the duvet. 'That was Liam. It's Sarah. They've rushed her to City Hospital. She's having the baby!'

Half an hour later, Molly hurtled through the main doors of the hospital maternity unit and skidded along the corridor towards the delivery suite. She'd already taken two wrong turns and ended up in the Ear, Nose and Throat department. She was almost dizzy with panic. Sarah had asked her to be her birth partner if Niall couldn't make it and she'd rather die than let her sister down.

It was a good job Ewan hadn't had more than a mouthful of fizz because he was able to drop her at Sarah's to collect her suitcase, which was packed and waiting in the spare room. She had to leave a message with Niall's controller and hoped he was already at the hospital, rather than on the other side of the county attending an incident.

The baby was coming faster than anyone had expected and almost four weeks early – would it be OK? Would Sarah be OK? Molly couldn't bear it if anything happened.

'Oh, Sarah. Why have you done this to us?' she muttered, then, dizzy with relief, saw the doors to the delivery suite ahead.

She ran into the waiting area to find Ewan pacing about in the empty room.

'Where have you been? I've found a parking spot and came straight here!'

'L-lost,' said Molly, hardly able to breathe. 'Any n-news?'

'I don't know. I'm not a relative so I haven't dared ask.'

Liam walked in. He was still in his morning suit and red in the face.

Molly grabbed his arm. 'Liam? What happened? How is she?'

'OK. It's all happening quite quickly but you can see her if you like.'

Molly's shoulders sagged in relief.

'What the feck's going on?' Niall, red-faced and out of breath, thumped into the waiting area and glared at Liam in disbelief. 'Why are the hell you here?'

'Sarah went into labour at Liam's daughter's wedding. Hayley's an army medic and she looked after her,' said Molly, still out of breath herself. 'And Ewan drove me here because I've had four glasses of wine and a packet of Kettle Chips.'

Niall looked at her like she was mad. 'Kettle Chips?'

'We were starving,' said Ewan indignantly.

'Right, you lot!' A midwife in blue scrubs stood with her hands on her hips in the doorway, glaring at Molly, Liam, Ewan and Niall. 'Would any of you fine people care to tell me which one of you is the partner?'

Chapter Forty-Four

Five months later

New Year's Eve

Sarah pulled up the blind and peered out of her window down into the street. The sky had been heavy all day and she thought she could see a few specks of snow drifting down in the glow of the street lights. In the distance, firework chrysanthemums exploded above the rooftops, all pinks and greens and blinding whites.

It was early in the evening for them – again – and she hoped no one would let off any in the street and wake up the baby Rowena. She'd begun to sleep through most nights and Sarah would love it if the baby kept to her new habit this evening.

She dropped the blind and went to the kitchen to get the glasses out of the cabinet, switched on the oven and started to unwrap some of the trays of Indian snacks. The combined live/work unit wasn't cut out for throwing wild parties but it was ideal for her and Rowena. It wasn't one of Liam's developments but it had been built by a design and build company who he'd recommended. The flat sat above a ground-floor workspace, and while it wasn't as rustic as Liam's unit, it was perfect for Sarah's growing business. There was even a nursery nearby where Rowena could be cared for a couple of mornings a week while Sarah went to offsite meetings.

The doorbell buzzed. Leaving the food, Sarah skipped downstairs, through the workspace and opened the door.

Molly hugged her enthusiastically. 'Happy New Year!'

Sarah held her sister tightly, thinking she'd never looked happier or more glowing. 'You too, little sister,' she said then noticed Ewan's absence. 'Where's Professor McDreamy?'

'Locking up the tandem.' Molly pointed to the bike racks in front of the unit.

Sarah followed Molly's gaze. Snowflakes had started to fall now and the road outside looked like it had been dusted with icing sugar. Ewan was securing the tandem to the metal rack.

'You haven't cycled here on that?' she said.

Molly laughed. 'We thought it was appropriate though we might be sleeping on your workroom floor if this snow gets any worse.'

'I don't mind. I've got a spare duvet.'

Ewan walked in carrying a backpack and kissed Sarah's cheek. 'There's a bottle of whisky and fizz in here,' he said, patting the bag.

'Oh, sounds good. Come on, let's get the party started.'

She took their coats and they congregated in the kitchen around the worktop.

'Can I do anything?' Ewan asked while Molly took the booze out of the backpack.

'That'd be great. You can heat up some of the Indian snacks. They're in the fridge – and make the salad if you want to.'

'No problem.' Ewan washed his hands and set to work. He

looked perfectly at home and happier than Sarah had ever seen him. Molly was positively popping with excitement.

'How's my little Rowena? Can I see her?' she asked while Ewan sliced up tomatoes.

'If you're very quiet. She's been a little minx today but I finally got her off half an hour ago. I hope she sleeps through our party.'

'I'll be quiet, I promise, you can trust Auntie Molly.'

Sarah opened the door of the nursery and they both tiptoed inside. Rowena lay on her back. Her downy blonde hair looked like a halo around her face and her tiny fingers curled above her on the mattress.

'Oh, the little angel. She is so cute,' Molly whispered.

'Sometimes,' murmured Sarah, recalling the screaming fit that Rowena had had just an hour before, and the state of the kitchen after she'd thrown her bowl of baby porridge on the tiles and the sleepless nights over the past few months and the days she hadn't even got out of her pyjamas or eaten anything that wasn't baby rice or Weetabix. Sarah thought she'd known what it was to love someone before Rowena was born, but now she knew she didn't. The sheer all-consuming love, the terror of losing it. Her mother had told her that no one knew real fear until they had a child. Now she knew why her parents had worried about her and Molly. She knew the dread they'd lived with, that they might lose either one of their daughters. She knew the deep and overwhelming love they had enjoyed for her and Molly.

Molly touched Rowena's blanket. 'Oh, she is so-ooo beautiful,' she whispered.

'She is now,' Sarah whispered back.

She stood by the cot, hardly daring to breathe as Molly

touched Rowena's hand very lightly. She still couldn't believe that Rowena was hers. Hers and Niall's. He was round at the flat several times a week and peace had finally broken out between him and Sarah. He was a good dad, she gave him that, and she was very happy that he was part of Rowena's life.

Sarah felt Molly reach for her hand and clasp it tightly, just as she had on her first day at school. They didn't have to say anything. They each knew the other's emotions instinctively.

They had cried after Rowena's birth once they were together without anyone around. Sarah had asked for Molly first. They'd wept buckets; knowing that their mum and dad would never know their granddaughter but that they would have been incredibly proud. Neither Ewan nor Liam could ever understand how that felt. Only she and Molly could share that special yet terrible bond or give each other consolation.

And after they'd cried, they'd wiped their tears away and resolved to look to the future. Molly, Sarah and Rowena. The three of them would manage very well, with or without a man by their sides.

But tonight Sarah sensed a change was coming. Tonight, she thought, for a little while perhaps, she was allowed to be Sarah again, not just a sister and a mummy.

Molly let go of Sarah's hand and they crept out of the room and back into the sitting room.

Ewan was filling a glass with fizz and smiled as they walked in. 'How is she?' he asked.

'Perfect!' said Molly.

Sarah showed her crossed fingers. 'Asleep. Angelic.'

Ewan laughed. 'Have a drink. You deserve it.' He handed Sarah a large glass. 'The first batch of food's in the oven.'

The doorbell buzzed again. Sarah's stomach fluttered, but this time there was no Rowena causing her butterflies.

She trotted downstairs and through the workspace to the front door. She was as nervous as a teenager on her first date.

Liam stood on the step wearing a Crombie coat and a dark purple scarf. Snowflakes were landing in his hair.

'Here you are,' he said, handing over a silver bottle bag.

'Are we celebrating?'

'I hope so.'

Sarah felt shaky as she took the bag. Liam shut the door behind him and walked into the workshop.

'You have snow in your hair,' she said, spotting the ice crystals melting.

He reached up and touched his head then looked at his wet fingers. 'Yes, it's getting worse. I might be stuck here all night if I'm very lucky.'

Her heart did a little flip. 'You might be.'

He took the bottle bag from her hands and put it on the work table. A wave of desire raced over her.

'Oh, Liam ...'

Her feelings were mirrored by the longing in his own eyes.

'I know it's not midnight yet but do you think,' he said softly, 'that it's too early for a New Year's kiss?'

Her own voice was husky with emotion. 'No. Not too early at all.'

They reached for each other at the same time and there was a clatter as boxes of beads tipped onto the tiles, knocked onto the floor in their eagerness to hold each other. Sarah heard hundreds of beads rolling to the four corners of the room while Liam kissed her.

Five months it had been. Five months of longing to see

him, of platonic walks along the Backs, and snatched coffees in buggy-friendly cafés, of emails and texts and calls – all at her request, all within her control while the damage of the past few months healed. Months of wondering if Liam would change his mind and not wait for her. He'd waited, of course. How had she ever doubted him?

She shook with the excitement of finally touching him. His coat was rough against her bare arms and his tongue teased its way into her mouth. She hadn't kissed another man for years, apart from Niall, and it was strange and different but completely wonderful.

At last the kiss ended and she didn't know who ended it or how but she was resting her cheek on the rough wool of his coat and he whispered, 'Happy New Year, Sarah.'

'Happy New Year, Liam.'

'So, can I finally stop waiting?' he asked.

She looked right into his eyes. 'I think so.'

A huge smile spread over his face. 'You *think*?'

'I'm only teasing you. I *know* I want you, I wanted you months ago but I had to be on my own, to see if I could do it. To be sure.'

'I was sure from the moment you threw that jug at me.' He kissed her again and they heard the sound of fireworks popping in the street. Beads crunched under her feet.

'Oh dear, what a mess,' said Sarah.

'Nothing that can't be cleared up.'

'Tomorrow.'

She took his hand and picked up the champagne. 'So, shall we tell Ewan and Molly?'

At the top of the staircase, two gleeful faces appeared, raising glasses of fizz.

Sarah laughed and Liam shook his head, his eyes shining with happiness and desire for her. 'I think they already know.'

Sarah thought of Rowena snuffling dreamily in her cot, and of the gorgeous, warm and sexy man leading her upstairs. What mattered was not a happy ending but a happy beginning and it couldn't possibly get any better than this.

THE END

Acknowledgements

There are two people I want to thank particularly, without whom I could not have written this book.

The first is my author friend, Jane Linfoot who, when I asked on Facebook if anyone had ridden a tandem, turned out to be an experienced rider. Jane made tandem cycling sound exciting, exhilarating and a bit dangerous! I shan't be having a go any time soon, even if Ewan were my stoker.

The second person is my daughter. Ever since I had the first mad idea for the *The Love Solution*, she has answered my questions, helped with my research and joined in the spirit of the book with enthusiasm.

She is an expert in her field (genetics), while I'd never set foot in a professional scientific laboratory until I started writing this book. Although the basis of the Love Bug lies in some degree of fact, the story is pure fiction. I'm not a scientist and I'm happy to admit that the only accurate aspects in the novel come from her. All the rest comes from me.

The other part of my research was a lot simpler. Thanks to this book I have learned how to make a passable bead necklace.

My thanks also go to my fantastic publishers, Avon Books,

whose patience in helping me get this novel to my readers has been epic.

Thank you, Katie Loughnane and Rachel Faulkner-Willcocks, Helena Newton and the team, for your faith in me and your editorial and marketing help. Thanks too to my agent, Broo Doherty, and my family for believing in me.

Finally, I want to thank my best buddy and bookseller friend, Janice Hume. This book is dedicated to Jan and her late sister, Alison. The thought of seeing their names on the dedication page has driven me on to finish it and see it published.

Hurrah. Finally, we did it.